STEALING WATERMELONS

Stealing
Watermelons

Fred Plocher

For Therese!
Thank you!
Hope you enjoy.

Plocher

NORTH STAR PRESS OF ST. CLOUD, INC.
St. Cloud, Minnesota

Published by
North Star Press of St. Cloud, Inc
PO Box 451
St. Cloud, MN 56302
www.northstarpress.com

To wounded military veterans.
We must not forget them.

Also dedicated to those who enter the arena of "making a living"
all by themselves.
When they start a business venture of their dreams
there are no corporate or governmental entity sofety nets to sofien a stumble or fall.
If they succeed it is not the result of decisions mqde
by a select committee sitting around a polished conference table.
That success comes from the individual's own decisions
and at the high price of risking his or her family's money and wellbeing.

Acknowledgements

Serendipity does happen. But don't kid yourseif, most of the time it needs a mighty push. This book would not have come about were it not for the push (not nag) from my wife, Mary Sue (MS), and neighbors Bob French and the late Pete Ogan, who all encouraged me to join the Highlands of Dove Mountain Writers' Group.

Mary Sue was the first reader of each chapter and from her I learned a few (but not all) things about the female take on things. The first few chapters were also read by Mary Stedrnan who reminded me that more words do not mean better writing or improve the entertainment factor.

Between laughs, the Highlands Writers Group led this rookie into the fascinating world of writing. I learned to let my mind and fingers wander around a keyboard in search of an entertaining story.

Thanks to that group's members: Trish Bradbury, Don Bueltmann, Norma Connor, Fran Crisman, Richy Feinberg, Bob French, Rich Melin, Sandi Nelson, Carl Pegels, Emmett (Semicolon) Smelser, and a special shout-out to Robin Verdon, who stuck with the chore for more chapters than anyone else.

The original edit was done by Harvey Stanbrough, an ex-marine who doubles as a hardheaded teacher of first time authors.

My research team included a high school classmate, Jim Johnson, who (as he says), "knows stuff." Also, Michael Tiffany, an Agent Orange survivor and Vietnam vet, helped with crucial parts. The rest of the team consisted of Mr. and Mrs. Google, who did a credible job. If there are any errors of fact in the following story, those miscues are the Googles' fault. For those of you who are familiar with the towns and highways near Lake Minnetonka and Carver County, Minnesota, you will see that I took many liberties with the facts. This is fiction, after all.

Thanks to the many friends who encouraged me as I worked to complete this manuscript. I used many of your names without permission so I ask your forgiveness, or if that's not needed, I'll accept your thanks for making your name maybe, possibly, even more semi-famous.

A special thanks to North Star Press of St. Cloud for taking a chance on this rookie. To Corinne and Curtis: I hope this gamble of yours was a wise one. You are risk-takers like I alluded to in the dedication.

Chapter 1

September 1954

BJORN

Well, that was hard.

New school—way bigger than my Victoria elementary. Couldn't even find the study hall in time. I'd promised Pa I'd make the best of the next two years.

New kids and older ones in there too, some townies from Waconia, but some small towners, what with the consolidation and all. Had to get to know some of 'em. I started with the guys sitting around me.

The kid in front of me had a farmer's tan. I tapped him on the shoulder. "Hi, I'm Bjorn. What's your name? Where y' from?"

He turned around and checked out my tow head and plaid shirt. He nodded. "Hey, there. Otto Schumacher . . . call me Shu. Farm near St. Boni. What's your last name? Where y' from?" His denim shirt had a yellow corn cob and *DeKalb* embroidered on its pocket.

"Olson. Victoria." I glanced at the teacher and lowered my voice. "Probably should keep it down."

"Don't worry about him hearing us. He looks to be two acres away. Besides, what are we s'posed to be studying? We don't have any books yet." His pale forehead was offset with ruddy cheeks. His hands were familiar with work. The kind of hands you gotta earn, like mine. They were leathery brown, probably from gripping the steering wheel of a tractor.

I caught the attention of the tall, skinny kid with broad shoulders to my right. He was squeezing a sponge ball in his left hand and had on a grey t-shirt with a Chicago Cubs logo. "Hi, I'm Bjorn," I said. "What's your name?"

"Ozzie Johnson, from Cologne. Nice t' meet ya." He waved a little and looked away.

I could tell the kid to my left was trying to ignore me. He was staring through his Coke-bottle glasses at the cracks in the plaster ceiling. He had a case of the zits and was a little pudgy. He was armed for classroom combat with four ballpoint pens and a yellow highlighter in his starched shirt pocket. A holster hung from his belt, not with a Roy Rogers six-shooter, but a slide rule. His hair looked like a young Einstein's and he had beads on a string in his right hand. I poked him on his shoulder. "Okay, how about you?"

"Oh . . . well, my name's David Grimm. I reside in New Germany. Also, I really do not believe we should be—"

"Hey, you four in the back—front and center, *now!*" The booming voice came from the front of the room, which was large enough to hold everyone from my grade school. Mr. Wagner sounded like an army drill sergeant I'd seen at the movies. The blackboard behind him framed his huge body.

My high school career wasn't getting off to a shining start.

As the four of us shuffled up the center aisle on the maple floor, thirty-seven pairs of eyes drilled into my backside. The giggling from the other students added to my bashful agony. I looked straight ahead, not daring to look at the gigglers or out the tall windows to my left, which provided a view over the football field to the three-thousand-acre Lake Waconia.

Being from a small town of three-hundred-fifteen souls hadn't prepared me for being in front of this crowd.

As I got closer to the teacher, I saw that his furry arms looked like Popeye's and his burly chest came close to popping his shirt buttons. He had that tough-guy look perfected by male teachers to keep restless students in line. He had a short, jock haircut with a high forehead. His glasses were perched up on his hairline.

He signaled with his thick finger. "Okay, heroes, follow me out to the hall."

We obediently followed. He closed the frosted glass door to the classroom and handed a clip-board to Shu. "If you girls know how to write, put down your names and home phone numbers."

Oh, no. Is he gonna call Pa?

After checking the names and matching them to each of us, he said, "Ladies, keep your traps shut in my study hall." Then his tough-guy voice and look magically were replaced by a friendly sales-guy voice and look.

"That's not the real reason I called you up front. I'm Coach Wagner and the school needs players for the freshman football team. None of you are signed up." He looked at Ozzie. "Johnson, you coming out for the team?"

"Oh . . . ah . . . I . . . my dad won't let me. He told me maybe I could go out for basketball and baseball, but not football."

Frowning, the coach said, "And why not?"

"He doesn't want me to hurt my throwing arm."

"You *that* Johnson from Cologne?"

"Yeah."

Coach Wagner had heard about Ozzie from the baseball coach. "Okay with you if I call your dad?"

Ozzie shrugged. "Well, yeah. Sure, you can talk to him, but I don't–"

"Schumacher, how about you? Got some meat on you–you've probably thrown a few hay bales around. You look like a player."

Shu looked down at his feet, like he was stalling for time to think of the right way to say things. "Sir, Pa needs all the help I can give 'im on the farm. Doubt he could spare me. Do you practice every day after school?"

"Varsity does. Freshman practice only two days a week plus a game day."

"I'll have to talk to Pa about it, sir. Fall's the worst time for me not to be around to help with the chores."

"Okay if I call your pa too?" Coach had heard all this before from many farm kids, but he had a way of convincing farmers to let their boys play for him.

We didn't live in the beautiful, touristy part of the country. We were from the beautiful *productive* part. We lived in the breadbasket of rolling fields of black loam intersected by wooded ravines, shimmering lakes, winding river valleys and semi-quaint small towns some thirty miles southwest of Minneapolis.

Instead of rolling surf on ocean beaches with bikini-clad girls and mountains with switchback roads and forever views, we had King Corn and Queen Bean along with alfalfa and grain: the Land of the Jolly Green Giant. No tour buses clogged up the roads here.

This is where Shu's old man drags his butt out of bed at 5:00 a.m. to milk the Holstein cows. That same smelly herd also needs his attention at 5:00 p.m.

"Olson, you gonna help me out?"

I could tell by his expression Coach was getting frustrated. He could see I was small for my age, but he needed all the bodies he could get. With fifty-five students in our freshman class and only twenty-four boys, he needed at least eighteen of us to make up a team. Probably only fifteen would be around at the end of the season as some wouldn't like the hard work and discipline. At small schools like ours, most players had to play both offense and defense.

"No, sir, ah . . . not interested. I can't. Dad's disabled and Ma can't make enough money by herself. She cleans some big houses on Lake Minnetonka, but I gotta make money too." The smell of the newly waxed hall floor distracted me for a bit. "Lumberyard manager said I could have all the hours I want. The way it looks, I'm outta here when I'm sixteen, so I won't be any help to you in the future anyway." I turned away so he wouldn't see my quivering chin.

"Sorry, kid. You gotta do what you gotta do, I guess. So Mr. Grimm, don't you let me down too."

I think the coach felt he had to also ask the kid with the Coke glasses and zits because he didn't want to make David feel bad.

"Well, sir, I have not been inclined to partake in athletic endeavors up to this point in my life. However, I feel I would like to be involved in all aspects of high school to help me become a well-rounded person. But I have heard football coaches and players tend to take the Lord's name in vain. I could not countenance that."

Holy cow. He talks like he's an English professor who has a dictionary stuck up his butt. At that point, I thought the coach would boot David squarely in the ass.

David continued. "And if there were any Sunday practices or games, I would have to be excused from those events. With those conditions, if you believe I could be of some value to the team, yes, I would be interested."

Then I knew how desperate the coach was. He turned slightly away from David and rubbed his lips with the back of his hand, and I could almost hear him thinking, *Jesus Christ, why do I have to kiss ass just to get enough bodies? Should'a been a basketball coach.* He was struggling to keep a straight face and his cool when the coach turned back to David. "Well, the State High School League doesn't allow Sunday practices or games, and I can assure you I frown on using the Lord's name in vain."

Ozzie whispered to me, "Shit, Grimm sounds like he's gonna be the dang pope someday." That did it. Our nickname for him became Pope. Small town social pressures dictated that almost everyone needed to attend church services whether or not they believed in a deity. David, I mean Pope, must have believed with all his being.

Coach said, "Okay, Grimm, let's give it a try. Stop at my desk after study hall to sign the forms for the team." He turned to us. "Johnson and Schumacher, I'll leave it up to you as far as telling your dads I'm gonna call 'em." He put his hand on my shoulder. "Olson, hang in there. And don't think just because it's legal to drop out at sixteen you should. Could be other answers to your family's problems. Now, ladies, get back to your seats and zip the lips."

Slinking back to our seats, we didn't so much as look at each other until the bell rang. I patted David on the back. "Good luck with the football team. Just to let you know, we've given you a nickname. We decided we'll call you Pope from now on."

David frowned and then smiled. "I never had a nickname before . . . at least to my face. Pope . . . Pope . . . that will take some getting used to." He went to sign the team papers with a smile on his zitted face.

Shu asked Ozzie, "What's the deal with your old man and your arm?"

"He thinks maybe I've got a shot at pro ball. He thought he had a chance, but never got drafted. Town team wants me to play for them next summer. Never had anybody my age on the team. I'm not sure I'm ready for that. Think your old man will let you play football?"

"Not a chance, and I'm not sure I wanna anyway. I just didn't want to turn Coach down cold."

Shu and Ozzie turned to look at me. Shu said, "What's with your dad?"

"He was working for Honeywell in the city as a master machinist working in the Norden bombsight area." I took a deep breath. "Some asshole on the next lathe let a piece of metal slip. It flew off the machine and hit dad in the forehead. He lost his left eye, has a long, red scar and has bad headaches sometimes. He still has buddies there. Honeywell paid off our mortgage and sends him a small check every month, and they have him in once in a while to train new guys."

Shu said, "Jeeze. Sorry about that. Must put a lot of pressure on you."

"Ya, well, it is what it is. What're you guys doing tonight?"

Shu said, "I've got chores 'til about eight, then I'm gonna crash."

"Probably play a little street ball," Ozzie said. "Then I'll turn on the new TV and watch some damn test patterns. The old man works for the railroad. Hope he's outta town."

Chapter 2

That same evening

Coach Wagner

Great supper, hon. I'd help clean up, but I've gotta make a couple of calls."

My wife rolled her eyes, smiled, and said, "Nice try, Bub. Grab a scrubber. Those pots and pans are your immediate future. The calls can wait. The burned-on grease can't. Who do you need to call?"

"I'm running short of time to get enough players for the freshman team. Talked to two kids today that said their dads don't want 'em to play. I'm going to call their dads. Gotta try to change their minds. Oh, yeah, I did get one recruit today. Had to promise him I won't swear. Can you freakin' believe that? He also talks like he's reading from a dictionary."

"Well, maybe you can replace the dictionary with a play-book. And I'm sure scrubbing the pots will give you time to come up with just the right spiel to convince those fathers."

She was right, as usual, and she looked great with her hair up like that. I could still smell her great pot roast.

Those two kids would look good in a Fighting Chiefs' uniform. I've got to figure out what to say to the dads while I scrape these damn pans. Got to get more of the kids from our small towns and farms. Most of the ones I've recruited are from here in Waconia. Twenty-five-hundred folks in town. They should supply most of the team. I handed her a pot. "Here you go, bright and shiny, am I excused now?"

"I guess so. Thanks for your help," she said as she patted me on my rear.

"Think I'll grab a beer, go to my trusty recliner and dazzle 'em with my logic on the phone."

"Go get 'em. Good luck."

My trusty recliner sagged in all the right places, unlike *my* misplaced sags. I dialed the first number. A man answered.

"Hello, Mr. Schumacher?"

"Ya."

"I'm Coach Wagner from over at the high school."

"Ya."

"I'd like to talk to you about letting your boy, Otto, play football for the freshman team this fall. He seems to be a good young man and just the type of boy we need. Our sports programs are important to the community. I know you want what's best for your Otto." I thought that well-thought-out logic would do the trick.

"Can I ask vat Otto said ven you talked to him about playing futball?"

"He said he was needed on the farm and if he was on the team he would have less time for working with you because of practices and games. You know, Mr. Schumacher, over the years I've had many other rural boys on the team with similar concerns. But they and their parents were able to work it out. The boys were happy to have been able to play and so were their parents."

"Mister Vagner, vat Otto said iss true. And I do vant vhat iss best for my boy. His future iss not futball. He has a gute head on his shoulders and vill do vell in his chosen vork. Please, sir, I vould appreciate it if you did not talk anymore to Otto about playing futball. That is for town kids. Goodbye." *Click.*

Another stubborn Kraut, just like me. All we've got around here are Scandahoovians and Krauts. I didn't understand Schumacher's crack about football being for town kids. Hell, the town folks depended on the farmers and the farmers depended on town folks. I guess a little bit of tension is inevitable though. Who wouldn't rather be the village feed mill manager instead of getting up at the ungodly hour of 5:00 a.m. to milk Bessie and her nineteen sisters? On the other hand, who wouldn't rather be his own boss on his own land instead of having to punch an unforgiving time clock six days a week to do the shitty jobs the boss would rather not do?

I got another Grain Belt before I called Johnson. *Well, at least this is easier than what I went through in Korea.* Gotta dial with my pinky—holes seem to be getting smaller.

"Hi, this is Ozzie."

"Hello, Ozzie. This is Coach Wagner. If your dad is there, could I talk to him?"

"Oh, ah . . . okay. I'll get him. He's, ah . . . I think he's out in the garage working on the car. I'll see if he'll come to the phone."

I sent Morse code with my fingers on the worn arm rest and wondered what took him so long.

"Hel-lo."

"Hello, Mr. Johnson. This is Coach—"

"I know, I know; the kid told me who it is. What do you . . . want?"

"Well, I was hoping to talk to you about Ozzie joining our freshman football team. I've heard he's quite the athlete, and I'm sure he'd find success in our football program."

"I think . . . you're more worried about your job and team . . . than about Ozzie."

Sounds like he's been drinking . . . gotta watch what I say. "Ozzie says you don't want him to play football because he might hurt his throwing arm. Injuries are not that freq—"

"Look, Coach, it's not just . . . his arm I'm worried about. I don't need him . . . blowing out a knee or shoulder either. If I would'a had better direction from my . . . freakin' coaches and dumb parents when I was young, I could've made it to the majors. A lot of people . . . thought I had what it would take."

"Well, I—"

"I'm not finished! I've got the kid on track to make it to the bigs. So far he listens to me, and I intend to keep it that way. I don't blame you for trying . . . to get him to play, but goddammit, leave his future to me. I'm his father , not you."

"Okay, okay. I hear you. I do hope you'll let him play basketball and baseball for us."

"If I agree with those coach's . . . systems, ya, I'll let 'im play."

"Well, Mr. Johnson, thanks for speaking with me. Have a good evening."

"Now, damn it, don't ferget. He's my son; not some kid . . . fer you to use to keep your fuckin' job." *Click.*

Holy Moses. With a father like that, a disaster could be waiting for the kid. I called to my wife. "Hey, babe."

"Yes?"

"Could you come in here and give me a little shoulder rub? Those calls didn't go so well."

"Sure, honey. Glad to do it. Beer wasn't enough to relax you, huh?"

"No. And I worry about some of these kids."

"You take your job too seriously."

"Today one of the kids said he'll have to drop out of school when he's sixteen so he can work at the Victoria lumberyard to help support his family. How am I supposed to respond to something like that?"

"Oh, I'm sure you handled it okay."

"One farm kid's old man just told me his kid can't join the team . . . too much work to do on the farm. The other dad I called sounded drunk and won't let his kid play . . . afraid he'll get hurt. Rub a little farther to the right. Ooh, that's the spot. Remember that Wartman kid from Victoria who graduated a few years back?"

"Sure, he was one of your favorites."

"Yup, I could joke around with him. He had a great attitude and was a good player. Used to give him crap about Victoria not having a water tower to name the town after because his old man was the well driller and wanted every house to have its own well."

"You've had a lot of good kids on your teams."

"I ran into his dad at a ball game this summer. Said his son graduated from Harvard with honors and is about to finish his residency at Johns Hopkins. He has two patents on medical stuff and is going to join Mayo on their orthopedic surgery team after the first of the year."

"Wow, quite the résumé already."

"Yup. And his dad said the kid always wants to know how the Fighting Chiefs are doing."

"I'm sure it's fun for you to hear about your former players."

"Yeah, and I guess they all had hopes and dreams. Probably some had dark secrets and a few couldn't wait to escape from home, but many settled here and found comfort in these parts."

"Am I on the right spot?"

"A little more to the left. Ooh, you're doing great. Some, like Wartman, did very good things, but others not so good. I sure as hell can't predict the outcomes of today's kid's lives."

Chapter 3

Late summer 1956, two years later

DAVID, A.K.A. POPE

Other than the episode with Coach Wagner in our first study hall, the four of us had little in common until last year when we were caught together stealing watermelons from farmer Thalaker's melon patch. Ozzie cased the patch near St. Boni prior to our bungled attempt at thievery. He assured us we would have no problem carrying out the heist.

How utterly unlike me to participate in such a juvenile sin. I am the intelligent one, with straight A's and the one who has kept the others out of trouble, except for that inexplicable lapse in my judgment. Peer pressure was my downfall. Never again. I must adhere to following my own moral compass.

Mr. Thalaker threw the switch on the spotlight, fired his 16-gauge shotgun in the air and yelled, "Hold it right there, boys, or I'll put a load of this here birdshot right up your tender teenaged asses."

I almost fainted.

Ozzie said, "Holy shit!"

Normally I do not like that sort of language, but I did not feel that was the time to condemn his choice of words.

The farmer said in a harsh voice, "Bring those melons up here to me. We'll have a little talk."

We trudged through the patch carrying the finest, largest melons we had found. The choice of taking the largest melons, guided by the moonlight, proved to be a significant error.

As we approached the farmer and his wife, I was reminded of that famous painting, *American Gothic*, of the farmer and his spinster daughter. However, this farmer was not holding a pitch fork—it was a double-barreled shotgun.

"Here's my plan," Thalaker said. "Instead of me calling the sheriff, you thieves will carry these here melons back to the high school in Waconia and put 'em on the front steps. I'll follow you in my pickup from time to time just to make sure you don't hitch a ride. When you git to the school, I'll bring you back to your jalopy. Oh, yeah . . . I'll have the jalopy keys now so you don't sneak back and take off."

I said, "But, sir, that is a long walk. It must be over six miles."

"Oh, really? Well then, if'n you don't agree to that, I'll call Sherriff Schalow."

"No, no, we'll carry them to school," we all said in unison.

"One more thing," he said. "My Matilda here is holding this here can of lard. Dip your pinkies in the lard and grease up them there melons. And you gotta deliver them melons to the school steps in A-1 condition. If you damage one, you have to walk back to the patch and git another one the same size." His face was shining with perverted glee as he talked.

While we greased the melons, Ozzie muttered, "Not what I have in mind when I think of rubbing melons." I was not sure what he meant.

Compounding my misery, about ten minutes into our little stroll I tripped and dropped my melon. When it hit the gravel road it split open and the tasty red innards splashed up on my shoes. I was devastated. Bjorn said, "That's okay, Pope. It could have happened to any of us. Let's stow our melons down in the ditch and walk back with you."

Ozzie and Shu grumbled a bit, but they went along with Bjorn's plan. I could have hugged him for taking the heat off me.

Thank the Lord, after we got the new melon and were about a fourth of the way to school, Bjorn came up with an ingenious way to arrange our shirts on two saplings he had broken off. Along with some help from our belts, two shirts hung from each pole and held two melons. We each shouldered one end of a pole and marched on.

Shortly after we had Bjorn's new system for carrying the melons in place, headlights came bouncing up behind us and farmer Thalaker's rusty pick-up braked to a halt five feet from me. A cloud of dust followed for us to inhale. He got out of the truck and slammed the door as he stomped toward us. "What sort'a contraption you got there?" He slowly circled around us and stroked the stubble on his chin. "Whose bright idea was this?"

Bjorn walked to Thalaker, got close to him and answered in a strong, firm voice, "Mine, sir. You said to carry the melons, and we're carrying the melons."

"Well, all right. Just be careful about coming up with any more fancy-dancy ideas."

We breathed a sigh of relief.

Walking six miles with heavy melons on our shoulders proved to be a lasting bonding experience for the four of us despite our differences. After the shotgun blast our mood was somber. We had serious discussions during the trek to school. Each of us spoke of threads of our lives that wove into the very fabric of our beings. We learned things about each other that we might never have known if it hadn't been for farmer Thalaker and his idea of melon patch justice.

We reached the main highway. Cars went past and some were occupied by fellow students who stopped to ask what we were doing. They drove away hooting and laughing and they spread the word all over Waconia. By the time we reached the school at about 10:30, dozens of students were on the lawn in front of the building. We didn't know whether they were going to cheer us or jeer us. They cheered.

A win-win situation unfolded. None of us were on the social "A" list at school. Bjorn and Shu could not participate in any extracurricular activities because of the work they had to do at home. Ozzie's sport activities allowed him to be wider known than the rest of us, but the chip on his shoulder diminished his social status. And I was... well, me.

After the night of the Melon Gang Walk, we went from anonymity to notoriety and began our tentative first steps up the rungs of the social ladder. Among future thieves, the afore-mentioned melon patch was now known to be too dangerous to raid, just as Mr. Thalaker probably planned when he made us do the melon walk.

That we gained acceptance and notoriety because we had committed a crime said something about the value system of our fellow students. As a comparison, my being the odds-on favorite to be valedictorian of my class was of no consequence in being accepted into the "A" crowd.

I went into the confessional the day after the heist. My faith never waivers, and the other three guys have stopped bugging me about being so pious. "Bless me, Father, for I have sinned. I went with three friends, and we robbed a farmer of some watermelons."

I did not think it was appropriate for Father Distel to chuckle in response to my confession before he told me to do three Hail Marys.

My acne was getting under control and my baby fat was melting away due to the football workouts. Even with those physical improvements, my uncontrollable hair and thick glasses made me less than a prize catch for my female classmates. But Ozzie, the cocky jock, chased skirts, blouses, sweaters and what they covered up with some success. He said during our melon walk, "Well, guys, guess what? I got to home plate last night with a gal over in Cologne."

I said, "Gee, I didn't know the Cologne ball park had lights for night games. Do you have girls on your team?"

That brought howls from the other three. I was embarrassed when Shu said, "Good grief, Pope. He means he felt bare boob and got in her pants." I firmly believe that sort of thing should be saved for one's wedding night.

Ozzie was the most stand-offish of the four of us, but from what he shared with us on the walk, I knew deep down he valued and needed our friendship. His home-life was miserable because of an angry, alcoholic father. Ozzie was a bit of a loose cannon with a hot temper, much like his father. His lantern jaw too often stuck out in defiance of something or someone.

Shu was the ever-loyal son and the only one of the four of us who had a steady girlfriend going into our junior year. Trudy was a cute, freckled neighbor of Shu's, and on our melon walk he admitted, "We are in love." This group's friendship was important to Shu, as he said, "I'm isolated out on the farm and not close to other guys."

His father bestowed upon him his stocky stature, all muscle due to the heavy work on the farm. He was nearly an equal partner with his dad concerning farm work and decisions they had to make about their operation.

I had always thought farming to be a noble calling. I read somewhere that after God rested on the seventh day he realized he needed someone to be the provider and caretaker of his creation. So on the eighth day he created farmers. Apparently God also needed someone to complain about his weather.

Bjorn was the nose-to-the-grindstone worker, helping to support his family. A growth spurt had left him taller than Shu and me, and his hair was even lighter than when we met. A square chin telegraphed his determination and hard work. His blue eyes were constantly taking in and analyzing his surroundings and devising ways to improve a situation. Leadership of our group came naturally to him.

***

ON THE HOT, HUMID THIRD SUNDAY in August, Shu picked up Bjorn and me in his very un-cool 1940 Ford, four-door sedan. It had a lowered rear end, but only because he had put a boulder in the trunk. It did not have a rumbling Hollywood muffler.

Shu had used his mother's vacuum cleaner blow-hole to spray paint the car a Farmall-tractor red. The finish turned out as rough as an orange peel. It had that "old car smell" of burnt oil and leaking gas, and only the Lord knows what had been spilled on the seats.

We headed off to Ozzie's town team baseball game. It was the St. Boni Saints against the Cologne Brewers. He struck out three times and got benched.

I looked around, then said, "Ozzie's dad is pacing behind the dugout. He appears angry and inebriated. That is a bad combination."

Shu said, "I'll bet Ozzie's gonna catch hell tonight."

Shu was right.

The next day, Ozzie told us what happened after the game. "My old man grabbed me by the back of my neck when I got home from the game; he pushed me through the living room and down on the kitchen floor. Ma was standing in the living room bawling and screaming at him not to hurt me. She had her hand to her mouth and blood was dripping down her chin on to her blouse. I got to my feet, but he grabbed me again and pushed me through the back screen door. I landed hard and got grass stains on my uniform." Ozzie was having a hard time looking at us as he told the story. His fists were clenched and he was shaking with anger. He looked down at his feet. "Last summer Bjorn helped me set up a net with a strike zone painted on it so I could practice my pitching. It's up against the side of the garage. My old man told me to get a bat and take a stance by the strike zone. I don't know how many beers he'd had at the game, but there was a half-empty fifth of Fleishman's vodka on the kitchen table.

"He told me, 'Goddammit, you're gonna learn how to hit a breaking ball if it's the last thing I do. I don't give a damn if your hands start bleeding from swinging too much. Don't just watch my hand when I release the ball. *See* my hand. Hell, see my fingers. See my fingernails and the dirt under 'em. Don't just watch the damn ball. See the seams and how they're goddamn rotating. An' don't back away like a chicken-shit when the ball's comin' fer your head— it's gonna break over the plate, and you better be ready to take a good cut at 'er.'"

I have to admit, I was mesmerized by the story, although I hated the obscenities. I could tell Shu was shaken by Ozzie's home-life. He put a hand on Ozzie's shoulder.

Bjorn just kept shaking his head.

Ozzie said, "His first pitch missed the net and crashed through the small window on the side of the garage. All that did was notch up his anger to a full-blown rage. The next three pitches almost hit me, but I was goddamned if I was gonna duck and be called a chicken-shit.

"Then he staggered to the house, leaned on the wall and barfed into the basement window well. I ran into the house to check on Ma. She had her blouse off to soak it in the kitchen sink. The water was pink. She was whimpering. We held each other awhile."

For the first time since I have known him, I saw Ozzie wipe a tear from his cheek.

"I'm through being the semi-obedient son. Screw it. I'm big enough now. If he ever comes after me or Ma again, I'm gonna kick his ass down the basement stairs and then go beat the shit outta him."

The three of us had left the game worried about Ozzie, and now we knew we had a good reason. Thank the Lord my parents are sober, God fearing people.

Chapter 4

The next weekend

SHU

We made it back to Bjorn's house at sunset on Saturday. The old man said I could take the afternoon off. We couldn't get in the fields because of the rain during the night, but he wanted me back in time to muck out the manure in the barn. Pope never had to work. His folks gave him a generous allowance, so he was available, and Bjorn's boss shut down the lumberyard for the afternoon because it was Labor Day weekend. The three of us had freedom staring us in the face.

Ozzie stayed home. He said he wanted to be there for the chance to confront his old man.

We spent the afternoon in Minneapolis cruising Hennepin Avenue in my tractor-red Ford and spent some time down at St. Anthony Falls on the Mississippi. The falls were thunderous 'cause the river was running high. Bjorn explained how the locks and dam worked.

Most guys cruise the streets to check out girls on the sidewalks or in other cars. I was looking but not touching 'cause I've got Trudy. Bjorn is so tied up in trying to make money, he never mentions girls, and Pope is . . . well, Pope, so I'm not sure why we were cruising Hennepin Avenue. Some of the girls did look really good, though. Pope said at one point, "Gee whiz, look at that lady over by the Golden Garter bar."

"That ain't no lady, Pope," Bjorn said. "If you've got some jingle in your jeans we'll call her over to give you a sex lesson in the back seat. If that doesn't light your fire, your wood is wet."

"Do not talk like that! I have control over my hormones. I am not like some animal. Sex is for marriage."

I didn't say anything.

The girls on the street probably took us for country bumpkins: uncool car, a guy with a farmer's tan, another with a plaid shirt, and the third with

Coke bottle glasses. I didn't think we were in danger of being mobbed by the city girls.

I used the necker's knob on the steering wheel to turn the Ford around and we headed for Victoria and Bjorn's place.

***

HIS HOUSE WAS SMALL, with white, weathered asbestos shingle siding, a green roof and green shutters. The single garage was detached and leaned just a bit to the south. The yard was well kept and the two window boxes were full of red geranium blooms, but the sidewalk and driveway were cracked and heaved up in spots, I guess some from frost and some from elm roots.

Bjorn started to get out of the rear door. I said, "See you at school next Tuesday."

Bjorn

As I WAS GETTING OUT of the car, I froze in the doorway and didn't answer for a minute. Then I said quietly, "I won't be there."

"Okay, then I'll see you there Wednesday," Shu said.

"Nope. Won't be there then either. Wilfie at the lumberyard said I could keep the full-time job I had over the summer. And I've got three homes where I keep up the yards and vegetable gardens. Shovel snow for 'em too. The family needs money."

Pope turned in the shotgun seat to look at me, angry disbelief written on his face.

"Plus, Dad and I are woking on some plans," I continued before Pope could speak. "He and Ma agreed I could always go back to school if things don't work out the way we hope. She'll be able to cut back on her house cleaning hours now that I'm going to keep working. It's hard for her to work and keep house too." I put my hand on Shu's shoulder. "But don't worry. I'll keep in touch with you guys."

Pope went ballistic. Still turned in his seat, he raised both his voice and his arms. "Do *not* do this! You *must* get a high school diploma. How will you ever get a decent job without an education? Mr. Utoft is really going to be upset. You are his star shop student. Have you consulted with him about this?" Pope shook his head and pointed at me. "Short-sighted is what this decision is. Your parents are letting you make a huge mistake."

I glared at Pope and quietly hissed, "Don't you *ever* say anything bad about my ma and dad. Just 'cause your folks have some bucks doesn't give you

17

the right to preach to me about working and schoolin'. You've got no idea what it's like to be poor. How about having to choose whether to spend your last buck on either food or heating oil? I've got a degree from the school of hard knocks already. Maybe now I'm going for one of those high falutin' master's degrees."

Shu kept his hands on the steering wheel and kept silent.

Pope wasn't finished. "And what is this *plan* all about? Sounds to me like you and your father are caught up in a huge pipe dream."

"Dammit, there you go again, talkin' shitty about my dad." I grabbed his shirt collar and jerked it.

"Look, Bjorn, I am sorry." Pope was calming down. "You are a good friend. I just want what is best for you. I am worried about you."

I didn't know what to expect when Pope got out of the car and came around to my side. He walked up to me and gave me a hug. I didn't hug him back. Jesus Christ, small town boys don't give each other hugs.

I turned and stomped up the cracked sidewalk to the house. Pope got back in the Ford.

SHU

I PUT THE CAR IN GEAR and gunned the motor to get the hell out of there.

Pope said, "So, why did you not try to change Bjorn's mind? You could have helped out, you know. You let me hang out on that limb all by myself."

"Well, you climbed out there by yourself. Besides, maybe I understand his situation better than you. You're book-learning smart, but where's your common sense? Your understanding of other people's lives falls short of the mark." I glanced over at him and gave him an easy punch to his shoulder. "Water over the dam. Don't worry about Bjorn, he'll be okay."

We drove a few miles in silence. Then I said, "Oh . . . my folks never hug me and don't you ever do it either."

Pope didn't say anything for quite a while. Guess I must have pissed him off. To break the ice I said, "You goin' out for football again? Practices started yet?"

"Yes, we began last week."

"Why do it? You never get in any games."

"I made a commitment to Coach Wagner and the team when I signed up two years ago. When I make a commitment I stick to it. Besides, I do contribute to the team."

"As what? Cannon fodder?"

"Hey, I contribute to the Fighting Chiefs in many ways."

"How so?"

"For instance, last winter I went to the Minneapolis library and did some research on body building and exercises. It seemed to me the coach needed to vary the exercises and calisthenics depending on the positions played. For example, why would an offensive guard need the same strengths as a wide receiver?"

I glanced at him, wondering where this was leading.

"Anyway, I drew up an exercise plan for each position and requested a meeting with Coach Wagner to discuss my ideas. He met with me after school one day." Pope took off his glasses to wipe off some dust.

"What did he do then? Kick your butt for being a smart-assed kid?"

"Hey, you know I do not like that sort of language. On the contrary, he thanked me for my input and even prepared handouts for the players with a suggested exercise program based on their position. He hoped they would work out on their own in the off season and he would incorporate those ideas when practice started."

"Holy cow," I said. "Gotta hand it to ya. Must've taken a lot of time. So how else are you contributing? Keeping the balls inflated?"

"If you are going to persist in making fun of my contributions to the team, let us change the subject."

"Okay, okay, I'm sorry. What else are ya doin'?"

"Well, on Mondays, following a Friday game, we review the game films. It occurred to me that a team probably would run certain plays in a given situation. Like on a second and six on their forty-five, what sort of play are they likely to call?"

I just shrugged.

"I asked Coach if I could take some of the game films home to study. He gave me three films. Sure enough, two of the teams had a fairly consistent pattern to their play calling . . . predictable at least seventy-five percent of the time."

"So what?"

"If we have a good idea of what sort of play the opposition is going to run we can defend against them accordingly. Now, Coach has to figure out how to obtain films of all the conference teams so I can chart their tendencies."

"You mean he bought into your theory?"

"Oh, yes," Pope said with pride. "He had heard something of this sort before, but never had time to do the research. It is only Coach and his assistant, Ben, who do all the work for the team. And frankly, Ben should probably concentrate on keeping the balls inflated."

"Pope, you're somethin' else. Sorry about the wisecracks."

As I pulled into the driveway of his sprawling, red-brick house, Pope turned, handed me some bills and said, "Here are a couple of bucks for gas."

"Thanks."

"How is it going with Trudy? She seems like a real peach," Pope said.

"Trudy and I are doin' fine, and yup, she is special. We've been neighbors all our lives and our thing kinda grew from playing tag in the hay mow to what we have now." I wasn't about to define "what we have now" for Pope.

"Great. Thanks for driving."

We said our good-byes and as I backed out of Pope's driveway my mind wandered off to be with Trudy, which was often the case.

I pictured us in our special place, under the pine trees in the windbreak behind her white, neatly kept farmhouse. The windbreak was put there to protect the house from the frigid north winds, but in other seasons we found another use.

The pines laid down a bed of soft needles every year and with a blanket on top of the needles, it made it a special place to lie, wind whispering through the boughs above with the moon and stars twinkling between the branches.

I'll never forget the first time we made love there. The moon was so bright I could see the freckles on her cute nose. We hoped it wasn't so bright that her folks could see us through the windows of the house. But we were in love and everything else was perfect. We didn't stop.

We took our time exploring each other's bodies. Even after a hot day, evenings cooled off, so there was a bit of a chill in the air. It's not as though that would have stopped us.

Depending on who was on top, either my broad naked ass or her fine shapely one was aimed at the moon. That was how we discovered our visitors: mosquitos.

Chapter 5

Two months later

DAVID, A.K.A. POPE

Homecoming was last Friday. The Monday before that, October 7th, 1956, will live in infamy for me.

That day a knock on the classroom door sounded while I was diagramming an algebraic equation on the blackboard. Mrs. Grover, the elderly substitute teacher, was more of a glorified baby-sitter than an algebra expert. I had been helping her teach the class, which met right after lunch.

She answered the door, stepped out for a moment and returned with a worried look on her face. "David, the principal and football coach want to speak with you in the hall."

Expecting bad news about my mother or father—like they had been in a car accident or something equally horrifying—I dropped the chalk and ran into the hallway.

Mr. Kraus, the principal, had a serious look on his face as he put his hand on my shoulder. "David, Ruthie Schneed doesn't have a date for the homecoming dance. She's the junior class attendant to the queen and as tradition dictates, a junior class football player must take her to the dance."

A sense of relief washed over me. I had no idea what Ruthie's problem had to do with me, but I suspected if there had been bad news about my parents Mr. Kraus would have mentioned that first.

Coach Wagner said emphatically, "*You* have to ask her to the dance. All the other guys already have dates."

He could have punched me in the stomach instead of saying that; the effect would have been the same. My knees almost buckled, and my head started to spin while my stomach churned. I could barely speak. "B-b-but I . . . I have n-never had a d-date! I . . . I c-cannot even dance." I took a step back. "N-no. I . . . I am sorry but I will not do it." I felt like I would faint.

Coach held his hands up, his palms facing me. "Enough of that," he said in a firmer tone than he usually spoke to me. "David, you don't understand. We're not *asking* you. We're *telling* you. Ask her *today*. You can't let the team down."

Coach and Mr. Kraus spun on their heels and left me leaning against a locker door for support. Team? What did the team have to do with this? My stomach was out of control, so it was fortunate the boy's restroom was across the hall.

I bolted into the bathroom and made it to the last stall. I knelt over the white, cool porcelain and threw-up my salmon loaf lunch. When under severe stress, I tend to upchuck. My glasses also fell into the toilet bowl.

I was rinsing off my glasses in a sink when the bell rang. I was panicked and desperate for help. I had to find Ozzie or Shu. Ozzie was always bragging about how many girls he went out with, and Shu had Trudy. They had experience I could count on. This was one of the few instances where Bjorn would be of no help even if he had been enrolled in school.

Shu saw me coming. "What the hell's wrong with you? You're white as a ghost!"

I pulled Shu into a corner and spilled the whole story. "You have *got* to help me. I do not know what to do. I have never had a date and I do not know how to dance. Ruthie will hate going with me, but will not have any choice. We will have an *awful* time. I feel like coming down with a case of leg amputation or—"

"Hey, hey, calm down!"

I could see him holding back a grin, but I believed he understood my dilemma.

"Let's think this through. Just relax. Let me think." Shu rubbed the back of his neck.

After a minute or two his face brightened, "Okay, first of all, with all the rain we've had and more in the forecast, that's gonna keep Dad and me from fall plowing, so Trudy and I will be going to the dance. We can double date. Oh, yeah, and I'll ask Trudy if she would be willing to give you a dance lesson or two this week. Shouldn't be that hard. Just slow dancing and the Lindy."

My panic was slow to recede, but Shu's comments helped. I knew I could count on him. "I-I do not know how to thank you. That would really be nice of Trudy and you. But, goodness, I still have to *ask* Ruthie. I am way too nervous for that."

"Christ, I hope you don't expect me to do *that* for you. Come on, suck it up, Ruthie is a nice girl. She won't bite. Get it over with before you have a conniption fit."

"Well, okay . . ." I wandered off feeling like I was headed for my execution. I had heard something about Ruthie being a little different from the other girls, but I thought she was cute and I was aware of her nice figure.

I ran into Ozzie on my way to find Ruthie and told him the Coach/Ruthie story.

Ozzie laughed and blurted out, "You mean you hafta take the Ice Queen to the dance?"

"What do you mean, Ice Queen? I thought she was just an attendant."

"Jeeezus, Pope, I mean, everyone else knows she's a cold fish—frigid—untouchable. She's a boy hater. If she ever has a kid it'll be history's second virgin birth."

"Then how did she get elected as attendant?"

"Most of the other girls voted for her. They felt sorry for her or some damn thing like that," Ozzie said. "Probably a few guys voted for her too. She does have great knockers."

"Oh, well, if she is a cold fish, as you say, that is okay with me. Are you going to the dance?"

"Hell no, I've got a date with a hot babe from Chaska. I'm gonna get me some back-seat tail. Borrowed some vodka from the old man's supply to grease the skids. I'm sure she'll respond to my persuasive powers."

I have always been troubled by Ozzie's attitude toward girls. However, that was not the time or place to lecture him about it.

***

RUTHIE WAS LEAVING the girl's gym class, headed for the locker room, when I approached her in the hall. She was wearing a sweaty, tight T-shirt and shorts, and she was still breathing hard from Mrs. Stenger's gym class. Her blond ponytail was almost undone, her forehead was damp and her cheeks flushed.

"Hi, Ruthie, c-could I speak with you for a moment?" I remember trying not to look at her chest, but not always being successful.

She looked at me like I was from outer space. "What'cha want?"

I know she noticed me peeking at her chest. She probably thought I was a jerk, just like all the other boys.

"Well, I would be honored if . . . if you would go . . . I mean, if you would allow me to escort you to the homecoming dance." I had practiced that line, but did not realize until later that I should have started out with some small talk first. I remember being so nervous perspiration was running down my sides from my arm pits and from my chest. It must have looked like I was lactating.

23

Ruthie rocked back on her heels, a look of shock on her face. I remember staring into her eyes, trying to get a hint of what her answer might be. I hoped she would turn me down. I would have done my duty for the coach and not have to go to the dance. She did not answer for some time. I assumed she must have needed time to assess her situation and my invitation.

Finally, hesitantly, but with an edge to her voice, she said, "Sure."

"Oh, that is wonderful," I said, but thinking the opposite. "I will ch-check with you later in the week to w-work out the details of when I am going to p-pick you up. By the way, we will be double dating with Trudy and Shu."

"Thank goodness," Ruthie said.

The next day I approached the coach during study hall. "Sir, I have asked Ruthie Schneed to the dance as you requested, and she has accepted."

"Thanks, David. I know that wasn't easy for you."

"Now I need a favor from you." I must say, I said that with some verve, after what I had done for him.

"What's that?"

"I need to be excused from football practice this afternoon. Someone has offered to give me dance lessons so I will be able to dance with Ruthie Friday night. After school today was the only time my instructor is available."

"Well, the first string is going to be practicing that new play you came up with. It would be fun for you to see it in action, but okay, go get your lesson instead."

***

SHU DROPPED ME OFF at Trudy's house on his way home to do his farm chores. I had my own chore to complete.

A sing-song voice answered my knock on the front door, "Come in, come in." I opened the door and an aproned, large-bosomed lady with a sweet round face came at me with arms outstretched. "You must be dat Pope guy! Velcome, velcome." She enveloped me in a bear hug. The rest of her body was in proportion to her bosom. She looked like pictures I had seen of the waitresses at the beer halls in Bavaria. "I'm Trudy's mama. Call me Gretta. Come vit me to da kitchen."

No fine restaurant's food could have smelled as good as the goulash she was preparing on the gas stove. Someone had moved the kitchen table to the side of the room to provide a large empty space on the linoleum floor. A record player was plugged in next to the sink.

Trudy came in. "Hi, Pope. I was upstairs changing clothes. Are you ready to get started?"

"Hi. Sure. Be patient with me. I have no idea what to do." She sure looked cute with her hair in pig-tails and wearing close fitting jeans.

"Don't worry, we'll start with a slow dance. Mama, wanna start with Johnny Mathis singing 'Chances Are'? Good. Here we go. Put your right hand in the small of my back. Move with the music."

"Okay." I said okay, but did not have a clue what "move with the music" meant.

"Don't keep looking at your feet."

Her hair smells good.

"Loosen your hips."

"Like this?"

"Yup. Let your shoulders move with the music."

"Okay." *She really is cute.*

"Hold me closer."

"Really?" I had never even held a girl's hand. Now she wanted me to hold her whole body closer. That sure felt good.

"Don't hold my arm straight out, bend your elbow."

That went on for a half hour or so and I thought I was doing okay. We stopped and leaned against the counter.

"Ya, Pope, you vill make a gute dancer with my Trudy's help, by golly. Von more lesson and you will be gute to go," Gretta said with a big smile. "Now sit here unt vee need to talk about other t'ings Pope must do on dis date."

I sat.

"Ven you pick her up, be sure to give her a corsage and pin it on her dress."

"Oh, my goodness, do I have to—I mean, do *I* have to pin it on? What if I stick her with the pin? What if—I mean—what about—what should I do if there is not much dress . . . where the flowers should go?"

"She vill guide you, don't vorry about dat. Now, either before you giff her the flowers or right after they are pinned on, giff her a compliment about how she looks. You know, maybe how nice her hair looks, or her dress, or just how cute she looks. Trudy, don't you t'ink dat's a gute idea?"

"Mama, you are right on the money. Pope, you listen to her."

I thought it might not be a good idea to compliment Ruthie on her fine figure.

Gretta shook a finger at me. "Pope, be courteous, I hear you are courteous by nature, so dis shouldn't be so hard. Open the car door for her.

Alvays let her go ahead of you in any line or tru any doorvay. Ask if dere is anything she needs, like a glass of punch. Unt, if her parents are dere ven you pick her up, introduce yourself to dem."

"Oh, no. I never thought of meeting her parents. I suppose Ruthie's dad will be glaring at me."

"Ya, probably. Didn't scare Shu away ven he took Trudy on dere first official date. My Herman just didn't haff a mean enough glare."

Chapter 6

Two days later

DAVID, A.K.A. POPE

Last Friday night, the night of the homecoming dance, was upon me far too quickly. I did not feel properly prepared.

Shu and Trudy were due any moment when I threw-up Mom's pumpkin pie. I started to dial Ruthie's telephone number to inform her I could not take her to the homecoming dance after all. Before I dialed the last number my conscience whispered that I needed to honor my commitment.

I had just finished brushing my teeth to rid my mouth of the vomit taste when Shu and Trudy pulled up. As I entered Shu's car I told them what I had just gone through.

Trudy said, "Pope, just remember what Mama and I taught you and use that noggin of yours. Shu and I will be close by, and we'll help you through this. Relax. You look very handsome in your blue blazer."

Shu turned and gave me a thumbs-up. That did not ease my anxiety because it was accompanied by a sly grin that told me he expected me to have an evening of problems.

On the way to Ruthie's I mentally rehearsed conversation starters to use, as Gretta had suggested. "Qvestions, dat iss vhat girls like, ask her qvestions about herself, her family, her life, vhat she vants to do after high school. Don't yust talk about yourself."

Sounding like a bus driver, Shu announced, "Get ready, her house is just around this corner." Sweat ran down my sides. My arm pits were gushing.

The bus driver added with a grin, "Okay, here we are. Go get 'er. And knock hard on the door, not like some wimp."

***

RUTHIE'S DOOR OPENED before I could knock. I was greeted by a grinning man and woman—Ruthie's folks.

I remembered Gretta's instructions. "Hello. My name is David Grimm, and I have come to escort Ruthie to the homecoming dance."

Her dad was holding a pipe in his left hand and wearing a dark-green cardigan. The pipe smoke smelled rather good. Her mother had Ruthie's figure, or vice versa, and was topped off with a bee-hive hair-do. My conscience told me I must not look at her female figure, especially one of my mother's age.

"How nice of you. I'm Ruthie's mother and this is her dad," she said this as her eyes swept up and down my entire body. After the sweep, during which her eyes paused a little too long at my glasses, she smiled and nodded.

I am not sure what that was all about.

They ushered me through the cozy entryway to the bottom of the open stairway. Ruthie's father patted me on the back and her mother guided me by my elbow. They seemed glad to see me.

Ruthie came down the stairs wearing a baby-blue, full-skirted dress. The dress color matched her eyes. She was not smiling, but she was not frowning either. She looked really good to me except for one thing. There was no easy place to pin a corsage.

"Hello, David."

"Hello Ruthie. You look really swell. Beautiful dress. Love your hair."

I fumbled removing the cover from the corsage box, one eye on the box and the other wandering over Ruthie's chest wondering where I was going to pin the corsage. I got the small white roses out, but dropped the box.

All four of us made awkward moves to pick up the box at the same time and came close to knocking our heads together. I was glad I had no more pumpkin pie in me as I was getting that feeling in my throat and stomach again. The feeling passed. We all recovered from the box retrieval, and Ruthie's mother took the corsage from me. Relief swept over my entire body.

"David, that's a nice corsage. Please let me do the honors and pin it on," she said as she took it and aimed for Ruthie's strapless dress. I could have hugged her mother for saving me from that seemingly impossible task.

After the goodbyes and some last minute, whispered private advice from mother to daughter, Ruthie and I walked out to the waiting tractor-red Ford. I reached for her arm, but she slowly withdrew it from my grasp. Shu and Trudy waved to us as we approached.

We reached the car and, per Gretta's instructions, I opened the rear door so Ruthie could enter. As she got in, I closed the door and bent down to see if she was settled. The top of her dress was now just above her belly button and staring back at me were two nipples. I thought I saw a scratch on top of her left breast with a bit of blood oozing from it. Frozen in time, my jaw dropped open as I tried to comprehend what had happened.

I had heard the term "wailing banshee" before, but did not know what a banshee was or what it sounded like. In that moment I knew what it sounded like. The cacophony of sounds coming from inside the Ford was unique.

The palm of Ruthie's right hand headed for my face but was stopped by the glass of the window. Her other forearm was busy covering her bare breasts. Her guttural screeching began. "Turn around! No, open the door! You blankety-blank, you shut the door on my dress! Blankety-blank you!" Even Ozzie would have been shocked at her language. Ozzie had said Ruthie was a boy hater. She now had more ammunition for her boy war.

At the same time Ruthie was screaming in the back seat, in the front seat, Shu was laughing hysterically and Trudy was yelling at him. "Don't you look! Stop laughing! It's not funny!"

Trudy then got out from the front seat, came up to me and pushed me away from the window. She opened the rear door to free the dress. Ruthie pulled up her strapless dress, tucked in her various body parts and got out of the car. She stood with her back to me and her forehead on Trudy's shoulder. Trudy had her arms around her, but Ruthie stood with her fists clenched at her sides. Ruthie's nice looking, bare shoulders were trembling.

"Blankety blank, blankety blank, blankety blank," Ruthie moaned.

I had thought things could not get worse, but then from behind me I heard Ruthie's mother running down the sidewalk, yelling, "What did he do to you? What did he do?"

Thankfully, Trudy came to my rescue. "Oh, it's okay. We just had a little accident."

"Well, there sure was a lot of yelling. Are you okay, honey?"

A long moment passed. Then Ruthie took a deep breath and said, "Yes, Mother, leave us be."

Praise the Lord.

Glancing at her mother's retreating bee-hive, I pleaded for forgiveness "Ruthie, I was so anxious to do the right thing . . . I am *so* sorry for my awkwardness. I certainly did not intend to catch your dress in the door. Please forgive me."

She turned toward me and shot daggers from her eyes, but said nothing. She got into the car, quickly pulling in the bottom of her dress. I went to the other side and slid into the rear seat with her. She was welded to the door on her side. The only way she could have gotten farther from me and still received a ride to school would be if she were standing outside on the running board.

Her only movements were to brush away tears and to bury anger in the clenching muscles of her jaw.

Shu was still chortling as we pulled away from Ruthie's house.

I saw the corsage, lying good side down, on the drive shaft hump on the floor. It probably came off the strapless dress and its pin must have scratched Ruthie during the partial disrobing. I did not know what to do. So I did nothing.

***

THE CAFETERIA SMELLED of the day's lunch of boiled ham and cabbage. Still, the place looked festive with the homecoming dance decorations. A mirrored ball with colored spotlights reflecting from it was suspended over the dance floor. The maroon and gold crepe paper streamers that hung from the ceiling helped the atmosphere.

A banner was taped to the wall over the table loaded with punch and cookies. It read, *FIGHTING CHIEFS! TOMAHAWK THE BADGERS!*

The Fighting Chiefs had prevailed in the afternoon game, 21 to 3. I did not get to play even one down.

Mr. and Mrs. Kraus and Coach Wagner and his wife were the chaperones for the event. I could tell Mrs. Kraus was not happy to be there as her face showed displeasure, and I overheard her say she was missing her quilting club meeting, and it was her turn to furnish the quilting wine.

Trudy said, "Let's grab that table in the corner." Thank goodness she took charge. She looked great in her non-strapless dress. if only I had been so fortunate. "We'll have a good view of the dance floor, and they're getting ready to put on the records."

Ruthie accepted my request for the first dance. It was "Put Your Head on My Shoulder" sung by Paul Anka. I guess she had no other choice but to do so. I was determined to not look at my feet or she would think I was observing her anatomy and new scratch. I said, "I like this song. Do you?"

She did not answer. She just nodded and looked past me to the banner.

"Do you like to dance? You are very good at it."

She did not answer. She just nodded, that time casting her eyes downward.

By the time I escorted her out for our fourth dance, I got the feeling Ruthie was dancing a little closer and seemed a bit more talkative. She actually said, "David, you dance very well." Maybe it was because she had time to cool down from the dress problem. She also had danced with some of her girlfriends in between our dances while I talked to Coach Wagner and his wife.

I wonder what she told her girlfriends about me.

I do not want to sound boastful. However, I believe my dancing ability, derived from Trudy's instruction, also impressed Ruthie and made her comfortable when on the dance floor with me.

After we left the dance, when we got in Shu's car, I was slow to close Ruthie's door.

I felt at ease on the way to her house and slid a little closer to her.

She slid slightly closer to her door.

The conversation between us on the way to her home was limited to one word responses on her part, but she did smile at one point.

Shu pulled the Ford up to Ruthie's house and waited. Trudy glanced at Ruthie and me until I finally got out. After an awkward pause, I walked her to the front door. Then came another awkward pause.

I handed her the corsage I had picked off the drive shaft hump, "I know this was not the perfect evening for you, Ruthie. Again, I apologize for the door incident."

After a pause, she looked up at me with those blue eyes and said, "David, thank you for the corsage . . . and thank you for taking me to the dance. All in all, I had a nice time. You're a very kind person. And David . . . I'm sorry for swearing at you. That was not like me, and I know swearing bothers you."

She then stood on her tip toes and kissed me on the right cheek, about an inch and a half from my ear and level with my ear lobe which actually put the kiss relatively close to the right side of my lips. She then turned to go inside.

I managed a feeble, "Good night."

That kiss was like a thunderbolt.

It told me I was not a complete jerk.

Chapter 7

Two years later, late winter 1958

BJORN

I felt uncomfortable being in the school building, being a drop-out and all. But I wanted to be with my buddies, and they wanted to be at the basketball game to support Ozzie. It was Friday night and the Fighting Chiefs were up by three points with a few minutes left in the fourth quarter.

"Sure hope he doesn't foul out again," Shu said. "He hardly ever makes it to the end of a game."

Pope said, "Yes, his dad says it is because he plays aggressively. I hate to say this, but I think he plays *dirty*. If Coach Dietrich was not also the baseball coach, I doubt he would put up with Ozzie's attitude."

Just then Ozzie leaped for and grabbed a rebound with both elbows churning. He crouched down to protect the ball and gave the Panther's number twelve an elbow shot to the balls.

The ref didn't see the blow.

"You son-of-a-bitch!" I could read number twelve's lips as he took a haymaker swing which Ozzie managed to duck.

The ref saw the attempted punch, blew his whistle and ejected number twelve, the Panther's leading scorer. Ozzie turned away from the ref, I suppose so the ref wouldn't see him laughing. The Fighting Chiefs won by seven points.

Our plan was that the four of us would meet at Schwalbe's Café after the game for a burger and a malt. Trudy was going to be there with her girlfriends. After eating, we would split up. Shu would take Trudy home, Pope had to get up early to go to an advanced solid geometry class at the U, and I had to get home to work on the plan with Dad. Ozzie figured he'd land a date after the burger.

Tommy Weber, the starting center, approached our booth after the game. "Ozzie said to tell you guys he can't make it tonight. Something about stuff going on at home."

Pope said, "All right, thanks, Tommy." After Tommy left, Pope looked at us. "The Lord only knows what that meant. Ozzie's home life has to be really tough on him. I pray for him. The rest of us are lucky."

I looked at Shu. "Speaking of stuff at home, turkey, how's the argument with your old man going?"

"Just cause I want to switch our farm from dairy to turkeys doesn't make *me* one," Shu said as he elbowed me in the side. "And I wouldn't exactly call it an argument . . . more like a discussion. Now the *discussion* has gotten hotter 'cause I think we should buy the Schultz farm next door."

"Jesus, kinda throwing a lot of stuff at your old man at one time, ain't ya?"

"Mr. Schultz's health isn't so good. I think they're ready to sell. Dad just shakes his head. In June, I'm done with school. If we don't get more land, I'll have to move off the farm and get a job in the city."

He sighed and went on. "Maybe workin' on an assembly line or carrying cement to a bricklayer is okay with you guys, but goddammit, I love farming. Being on the land, raising crops and turkeys, that's my idea of a good future."

Pope said, "Good luck with that. I envy you knowing what you want, but please watch your language."

Shu asked me, "And what do you and your old man have going tonight that's so damn important? Can't it wait 'til mornin'?"

I said, "Can't say."

Shu said, "Kinda tired of all your secret shit. Oops, sorry, Pope."

"Okay, Shu. We are all thinking the same thing," Pope said.

I knew I couldn't keep the plan secret from my buddies too much longer. "Hey, cool it. I'll explain the secret as soon as I can."

***

WHEN I GOT HOME that night, my pa and me worked on our plan 'til after midnight. We did it again for three hours on Saturday after I got home from work at the lumberyard and again most of Sunday. Ma helped on Sunday too. Over the past two and a half years we had spent hundreds of hours working on the plan. Tension was building. Everything had to be ready for our 10:00 a.m. meeting on Monday.

I wonder how I deserved my parents. Olga, my ma, and Karl, my dad, were salt of the earth folks and now treated me as a partner after raising me from a pup. I am an only child, but I don't think I'm spoiled. I did get my rear end pounded a few times, but that was always followed with a hug and an "I love you." I wondered why I didn't have brothers or sisters, but I never asked.

Even before Pa's injury, we never had much money. Ma cooked for the Lion's club meetings every second and fourth Wednesday in the winter, did the books for the oil co-op and cleaned some houses. She's a sturdy Swedish blond. Everybody depended on her and she didn't let anyone down.

Dad's work at Honeywell was kinda full time, but he was laid off quite a bit when there was no work even though he was their best machinist.

He was the player-manager (third baseman) of the town baseball team before the accident and was the go-to guy for every household in town for handyman repairs. He took me along whenever possible, be it as the bat-boy for the team or to hold his tools when fixing someone's kitchen sink. He's tall and lanky. kinda has a regal bearing—stands straight and holds his head high, even now when wearing the eye patch.

He rebuilt and maintains our old Plymouth, and it runs like new even though we have to baby the worn tires. I spent a lot of time under the hood with him. We also rebuilt that old power mower I use to mow other folks' lawns.

They have a quiet social life now pretty much like they did before dad's injury. Many times I've seen them sit side by side on the couch in the evening with her reading to him, all the while holding hands. Our family is not one of the church-going type. We probably hit the Lutheran pews (Pa prefers cushion ones) four or five times a year. That doesn't mean my folks aren't good people though.

***

"LET'S GO. WE CAN'T BE LATE," Pa said about 9:40 on Monday morning. Even though it was February, cold and windy with snow flurries, we walked the two blocks to the Community Bank of Victoria. Ma stayed home. Said she was too nervous to go along. Pa and I each carried a thick, blue, three-ring binder in our gloved hands.

Our overshoes made scrunching sounds in the snow. No one else was out and about except in cars. The green, hooded parka Ma found for me at the second-hand store did its job of keeping me warm. Wind still got to our faces though, and there was a drip of snot hanging from Pa's nose.

The bank was on Main Street in a two-story, red-brick building. An outside stairway, covered with what looked like a wood tunnel, led to four bachelor apartments on the second floor. Shorty and Belle's combination barber shop and beauty parlor was located in the right half of the first floor and the bank was on the left.

A bell tinkled as we opened the frosted glass door with gold lettering. The only teller, Shirley Schmuck, looked up from what appeared to be a romance novel. She was a well-kept fortyish lady with a friendly smile. Her metal teller's cage was painted forest green, but some rust spots showed through the chipped paint. A crack ran diagonally through the white marble counter.

"Hi, Shirley," Dad said. "We have a ten o'clock appointment with Harvey."

"Oh, hi, Karl, Bjorn. Ya, I know, but Mr. Cline called from the main office in Waconia a little while ago and said to tell you he'd be here as soon as he could. He might be a little late 'cause of the icy roads. Sorry. Magazines are over there. Would you like some coffee?" She tried not to stare at dad's eye patch and red forehead scar.

"Thanks, no cream or sugar," Dad said. We hung up our parkas on the hall-tree. We both were wearing plaid flannel shirts under the parkas.

Dad sipped his black coffee, but we were too nervous to look at the magazines. We reviewed our material, then looked around the room at the embossed metal ceiling and small, white octagonal tiles on the floor.

We also reminded each other what Dad's boss at Honeywell had told us about asking bankers for loans. "Just because they pass gas through pinstriped suits and you fart through denim doesn't make them better or smarter than you. You have a great plan to talk to them about; it's a good business opportunity for them. You need them, and they need you. Don't beg. Just present your case."

A slight smell of hair perm solution came from the beauty shop, and once in a while Shorty's cackling laughter filtered through the wall.

At ten after ten, Mr. Cline burst through the door, stamping snow off his rubbers. He was in his mid-forties and getting thick around the middle and thin in the hair department. "Hi, guys. Sorry I'm late. Looks like more snow's coming. Bjorn, don't forget my driveway and sidewalk."

Why did he feel he had to say that? I'd been doing his shoveling, mowing and weed pulling for four years. I'd never forgotten to do my job. I liked Mrs. Cline. She always gave me a nice tip and lemonade or hot chocolate. But Mr. Cline liked to play the big shot. He was the only guy in town who wore a coat and tie on weekdays.

"Come into my office and have a seat," Cline said as he nodded to Shirley and hung up his overcoat.

I had expected more of an office. A six-foot-high, gray safe stood behind his desk. It was flanked by green, four-drawer file cabinets. Cline's oak desk was plain, and some of the blond finish was worn off where his elbows rested. There were no windows, and with every move he made his wood swivel chair squeaked.

"Well, what's the occasion? Why did you ask for this meeting?" Cline asked, but he seemed rushed. I was surprised he didn't start with a little small talk before getting right to business.

"Ah . . . Harvey, we appreciate you takin' the time to see us," Dad said as he reached down to pick up the two binders.

"My son, my wife and me been workin' darn hard for a little over two years on this plan. You know us. You know our history."

"Yes, yes. Go on."

"In fifty-six, Bjorn drove me to Honeywell 'cause they called me in to train a couple'a guys. After the training session, the vice-president of the division, Jim Harms, called me into his office. After my accident and loss of my eye, my life hasn't been easy. After Harms talked to me, I thought my life was gonna be over, that I'd be useless to my family or anyone else."

"Why in the world would you think that?"

"'Cause he told me that in a year or two, they wouldn't be needing me to come in and train guys anymore. Even though I only did that a few times every other month, at least I felt I was still of some use. He said Honeywell had bought some land in St. Louis Park for a new plant. The company was gonna totally retool his division. All of the equipment I knew so well would be scrapped."

"So why couldn't you train guys on the new equipment?"

"They bought new high-precision machines from Switzerland, next-generation stuff. Even some automation. Out of my league. They've decided to go after aviation controls and government contracts for guidance systems, so they have to show they have the equipment to do the high-precision jobs." Dad threw up his hands to show his disappointment.

"Okay, but what's that got to do with this meeting?" Cline said, looking between Pa and me.

Dad cleared his throat. "We left that meeting, and I was a mess. Bjorn could tell I was as far down in the dumps as he had seen me since the accident. He drove us about five miles. All of a sudden he did a U-turn in the middle of four-lane Highway 12. I asked him what the hell he was doing. He pulled off the highway. He said he had somethin' to say."

Chapter 8

The same day, at the bank

BJORN

When Dad told Mr. Cline I had something to say after I made the U-turn in the middle of a four-lane highway, it reminded me how much my mind was spinning back then. As soon as Mr. Harms said they were gonna scrap the equipment, a light went on in my head. Maybe I'd be out of line to suggest the idea to Dad, but I also knew our family had to find a way out of our financial bind.

Dad continued our story with Mr. Cline, who used to be Dad's second baseman on the town team so Dad called him by his first name. "Harvey, since they were scrapping that equipment, Bjorn suggested we ask them to give it to us. Then we could start our own machine shop.

"Now I knew Bjorn was pretty dang smart, but you could'a knocked me over with a snowflake. I mean, why didn't I think of that?" Dad said with a broad smile. "Ever since then, we've been planning on starting our own machine shop."

Cline said, "But . . . but he's only a dropout kid, and you've only got one—"

Dad leaped to his feet and leaned toward Cline, his fists planted on the desk. "Kid? *Kid?* You know damned well Bjorn's been doing man's work for more'n three years. Ask Wilfie at the lumberyard if he thinks of Bjorn as just a kid. He'll tell you. Bjorn's reorganized the whole damn lumberyard to make it more efficient. And you know he's dang near the sole supporter of our family."

I pulled on Dad's flannel sleeve to try to get him to sit down and calm himself. It didn't do any good.

"What freakin' *man* in this town would have the *balls* to come up with this idea like Bjorn did?" Dad flipped up his eye patch. "And this eye socket might be empty, but the head behind it holds a brain with nineteen years of experience as the best machinist in the Upper Midwest. Now, would you like to hear the rest of our story? This town's dying and this bank's gonna die with it. The town, the bank, and we need to get this business going."

I thought Dad had overplayed our hand. We knew that bank was our only hope for a loan.

Mr. Cline leaned away from Dad's outburst, but he seemed to like the spunk Dad showed. "Look, I'm sorry. I should have said that in a different way, but you know other people are going to think the same thing." Cline was silent for a moment, then said, "Please continue."

"All right. Just to get that 'kid' thing out of your head, look at this letter in the Customers Ready to Go section of this binder," Dad said as he opened to the page with the letter from Mason Hoist and Derrick Company.

"What's this all about?" Cline asked.

Dad turned to me, "You tell 'im, Bjorn. And this is no time to be modest about what you accomplished."

I tried to speak in a firm voice, "Fred Mason, who signed that letter, is the best friend of Mr. Harms, Dad's boss and V.P. at Honeywell. We worked a lot with Mr. Harms to get the deal done with Honeywell. Anyway, Mr. Harms called Mr. Mason and asked if we could go up to Park Rapids and meet with him. Maybe he could steer some business our way."

Cline said, "I didn't think you were talking about making things as big as hoists and derricks."

I shook my head. "No, we're not. Mr. Mason's developing a new product: gas-powered snow sleds. He makes some now for the mining and paper companies to get around in the deep snow. So I went up there. Dad doesn't like to travel 'cause it starts his headaches."

"That has to be a round trip of over four-hundred miles. You went alone?"

"Ya, Ma packed food for me, and it was September when I went, so I slept in the car. Wasn't that expensive."

"Go on," Cline said as he snuck a peek at his watch.

"Well, I got there and Mr. Mason showed me what they were up to. They were designing the sled to be sold as a sporting thing, kinda like a motorcycle for the snow instead of a hauler like they built for those other companies. Gonna call the brand Polarcat.

"Mr. Mason was all excited about what he called 'snowmobiles.' He thought they could sell thousands of 'em. Had a few problems though. One of them was the design of the two front skis." I pointed to a picture of the prototype on the next page.

"The skis had to take a pounding, and because of that they made 'em of thick steel. They were very heavy, like the ones they used on the haulers. Plus, unlike the haulers, he wanted his new sport models to be real maneuverable. But the skis slid sideways too much when turning."

Cline said, "How much longer is this going to take? I'm s'posed to be back at the main office by noon." Then he noticed Dad getting upset again so he said, "This is all interesting. Maybe we need to schedule another meeting."

"Just let Bjorn finish this part," Dad said. "We'll leave you these binders, eighty-six pages of information. You study 'em and call us when you're done. Then we'll meet again, but it has to be soon."

"Sounds good. Go ahead, Bjorn," Cline said while drumming his fingers.

"Well, Mr. Mason showed me more, but he had another meetin' and said if I'd be around the next day I could look him up. I thought he was being nice because of his friend telling him about us. During the night I had some thoughts about the ski problem and did two sketches. I didn't sleep too good in the car."

I looked over at Dad, wanting some indication of how I was doing. He smiled and nodded.

"The next day I showed Mason my two drawings. I thought either one could help solve his ski problem."

Cline chuckled. "I'll bet he thought you were kind of a smart-assed kid to show him those drawings. After all, they'd been working on it for a while."

"Actually he said they'd test both ideas, pick the best one, and if we'd be close to competitive with our pricing he'd give us a contract to supply the skis for 'em. He gave us a chance to make other parts too. That's what that letter says."

"That's a hell of a long way to ship those parts. It'll cost a bundle," Cline said, still trying to shoot us down.

Dad's face was still beaming because of my story, but he said impatiently, "Harvey, turn to the next page. You think we didn't figure that out? You'll see a letter from Weathersmart Windows. They ship a truckload a week to the Twin Cities from Warroad, not too far from Park Rapids. Their trucks go back empty. That letter says they'd give us a low shipping rate just so they don't have to run all the way back full of nothin' but air."

"Well that's one thing you solved, but it's hard to build a business with just one customer. They could pull the order and leave you hanging," Cline said with an edge to his voice.

Pa said, "Look, Harvey, just study the rest of the pages in these binders, and you will see a very complete picture. Polarcat ain't the only company in the

Customers Ready to Go section. Oh, yeah . . . there's also a real important section titled Our Own Products Ready to Go. We're gonna make our own stuff too."

Cline looked up at us with raised eyebrows.

Pa continued, using Mr. Harms' ideas. "Now, here's what we need from our banker. It's outlined on the second to last page. In return for the loans we need, we'll give you mortgages on our house, car, all the business assets and equipment. You can even mortgage our underwear. And keep in mind the value of the stuff on the inventory list we're getting from Honeywell. That's on pages forty-seven through fifty-one. The replacement cost of that equipment alone is worth way more than what we're gonna ask in loans, and it's all ours."

"But it isn't new equipment. Honeywell's scrapping it."

"Granted, it's used, but it's well maintained and we also get bins full of spare parts. Honeywell would be using those machines for the next twenty years if they weren't upgrading to automated stuff." Dad looked at me. "Bjorn, why don't you explain the loans we need?"

That surprised the heck out of me. I thought Dad was going to do that. I gathered up my courage and started talking as firmly as I could. "We need a line of credit for one hundred thousand to remodel the building we'll operate from and to front-end payroll until cash flow starts. It'll also be used to buy a used truck, office equipment, and desks and other miscellaneous stuff outlined on page seventy-seven. And we'll need our banker to supply us with a letter of credit for fifty thousand for suppliers of raw material." I took a deep breath and hoped I didn't sound like I was begging. As Harms had said, "Act like the bank needs you."

"Karl, what's the deal with Honeywell? How did you guys talk them into giving you that equipment?"

"They're giving the stuff to their foundation, which in turn will give it to us. Tax reasons, I guess. If they order any work from us, we have to put everything else on hold to meet their schedule. If we sell anything we get from them, they get half the money. If we're still in business five years from now and are profitable, we have to start repaying them for paying off our mortgage on the house, but at no interest."

Cline said, "Well, understand, this is a stretch for us; to fund an unproven business, but you've got a thorough plan here. I'll study it and take it to the loan committee, which meets Friday in Waconia. I'll call you if we have any questions. Can't meet with you 'til next Monday. Same time." Then he added sarcastically, "Just looking through your plan, seems like the grammar and spelling could use some improvement."

Pa blew up. "Jeezus Christ, Harvey, we're tryin' to create a business and hire people for good jobs, not takin' a dang high-school English test."

***

THE NEXT MONDAY when we entered the bank, Shirley glanced up from her book and said, "Hi, guys. Mr. Cline and Mr. Maahs are waiting for you in the office. Go on in."

As we entered the office and shook hands, Cline said, "This is Jeff Maahs, the chairman of our loan committee. Please have a seat. We might as well get this over with."

Maahs said right off, "We didn't like your proposal. There were two major problems."

Pa's face went sheet white, and my heart leapt to my throat.

Maahs grinned. "One, the underwear mortgage is out of the question, and, two, you didn't ask for enough money."

Cline jumped in "Your plan is impressive. We don't want you to be undercapitalized—that's the death of a small business—so the amounts you asked for will be doubled."

When the news sank in, Dad bent over with his hands to his face, hiding his tears. My eyes got blurry when I saw his reaction. I put my arm around his trembling shoulders.

Cline yelled, "Shirley, bring in that champagne! And one Doctor Pepper."

Chapter 9

Spring 1958, two months later

BJORN

Wednesday, two nights before my buddies would graduate, Ma had invited them over for burgers. Shu, Ozzie, and I sat on our cracked front steps waiting for Pope.

He pulled into our driveway in his folks' aqua-and-ivory '55 Ford Fairlane hardtop convertible. It looked different from what we remembered.

"The Ford looks pretty spiffy. What'cha do to it?" Shu asked Pope.

"I washed and Turtle Waxed it. My folks took delivery on their new Edsel and gave this one to me as a graduation present, a reward for being valedictorian and getting the scholarship to the U." He patted the hood of the Ford."

He added, "They did not say it, but I know it was also because I decided not to attend the seminary."

Ozzie said, "Wow! Now you can go trolling for broads with your own wheels. Pretty damn nice present. Better get a necker's knob for the steering wheel so you don't run off the road while you're copping a feel."

Pope just shrugged. He hadn't had another date since he took Ruthie to the homecoming dance last year. He said, "Actually, I received another present last night at the year-end banquet for the football team. It means even more to me than the car." He reached into the back seat and pulled out a large, white cardboard box. He eased it onto the hood of the Ford and opened it. "Coach Wagner and the team captain presented this to me during the football team's banquet program." Pope pulled a maroon jacket with gold leather sleeves from the box—a letter jacket in Waconia High colors. "You know I did not play enough to earn a letter."

He unfolded the jacket and showed us the front with a large gold letter W on the left chest area and a football embroidered on the letter. Under it was bold stitched wording:

ASSISTANT COACH
CONFERENCE CO-CHAMPS 1956
CONFERENCE CHAMPS 1957

Ozzie jumped up and patted Pope on the back. "Proud'a you, Pope. You earned this letter just like the starters did."

Pope said, "I remember when you three were with me when I made my commitment to play for the freshman team. I am glad I stuck it out for four seasons. I did not get to play much, but I contributed in other ways."

"Congrats, Pope," I said. "Let's go out back. Burgers must be about ready."

Ma and Dad were sitting on card table chairs near the homemade grill in our back yard enjoying a cold Grain Belt. It was a warm day in late May so they were sitting in the shade of our sugar maple. Apple-wood smoke mixed with seared beef grease swirled out of the chimney on top of the grill. I figured that great aroma musta set off hunger pangs all over the neighborhood.

The guys went to shake hands with the folks and thank 'em for the invite.

I could read Ma's mind as they walked toward her. Many times she asked me what held our group together. Approaching her was Pope in his dress shirt and slacks, shiny penny loafers and thick glasses reflecting the sun. Ozzie wore his Washington Senators T-shirt, cut-off sweats, and high-cut tennis shoes. Shu had on his denim, short-sleeved shirt with the Farmall logo on the pocket, his forehead white as a baby's butt. I had my plaid shirt, jeans, and work shoes. We didn't look like a unified quartet. No wonder she didn't understand why we hung together.

Ma said to them with misty eyes, "I needed to do something to thank you three for keeping Bjorn in your buddy loop after he had to leave school." She always had trouble saying I dropped out. "It meant a lot to me and Karl, and I know it meant the world to Bjorn. A few burgers and potato salad is the least we could do." She stood up and gave each of them a hug and peck on the cheek.

Shu said, "Thank you, ma'am, but you didn't need to go to all this trouble."

"Bless you," Pope said.

As he elbowed Pope, Ozzie looked at me. "Well, putting up with you is finally paying off."

"Ya, I told her she should make you guys eat lutefisk and lefsa instead of burgers," Dad said with a grin. "There's some bottles of Squirt on ice over there in the wash tub. Help yourselves. I'd offer you guys a Grain Belt, but I *know* you don't drink it. Isn't that right, Shu?"

We all knew what was coming next. Pa just couldn't resist. He also couldn't keep the grin off his face. "I remember when Wilfie down at the lumberyard called one mornin' last summer. Said he was sending Bjorn home 'til noon. Seems he saw Bjorn hurl his breakfast behind a pile of two-by-eights. He thought it must be the teen-age bottle flu."

Hurling my breakfast that morning wasn't the only problem. I'd also had a headache from hell.

"When Bjorn got home—lookin' pretty pale I might add—I asked what the hell had gone on the night before and not to bullshit me. Shu, that's when he told me about your little keg party in your machine shed while your folks were up in Duluth. They ever find out about your little social event for your FFA buddies and these three dopes?"

Shu dug his toe into the ground. "Well, yeah. Took 'em about five minutes to know somethin' had happened. I didn't get all the plastic Hamm's glasses picked up. Dad found the tap ring for the keg, too. On the tractor seat of all places."

Dad had a good laugh about Shu's keg party being discovered.

Shu said, "He let me know he figured things out by stacking the Hamm's glasses and the tap ring on the kitchen counter. Never said a word about it, though."

Dad said, "Well, good for your old man. Enough of that. Ozzie, way to go for getting that minor league contract. But the Washington Senators for God's sake? Couldn't you get on with a closer team? Like the Cubs or White Sox?"

"For some reason, Mr. Griffith, the Senators' owner, wanted to sign some rookies from the Upper Midwest. My coach found out about it and contacted the team scouts." Ozzie broke out in a big grin. "So I leave for the minors in Charlotte next week. No guarantees. I just hope I can make the traveling roster."

"Well, good luck to ya," Dad said. "We'll be followin' your progress. Ain't gonna be easy in the minors. Lots'a ass time in busses between games. Bet your old man is proud'a you."

Ozzie looked up at the popcorn-shaped clouds for a long moment. "Ah, well, he was upset I didn't get drafted. I only got picked up after the draft. Said I should have worked harder in practices."

"I know deep down he's proud'a ya," Dad said. He suddenly looked a bit sad. "Guys, grab some grub. After you eat, we've got somethin' to show ya."

After we chowed down on juicy cheese burgers on homemade buns, potato salad that I always needed seconds of, and rhubarb pie, we felt like we'd never have to eat again. Ma's a great cook, and she kept shoveling food at us.

"Okay, enough eating'," Dad said. "Olga, you gonna come along? This is your show too, ya know."

"No, you guys go ahead. *The Honeymooners* are on soon, and then Steve Allen. Besides, it's kind of a guy thing."

I didn't know what the guys would think about showing them the secret we'd been working on for so long. For my folks and me, it was the most important thing in our lives, but the guys might just laugh about it. We walked the three blocks to the edge of town, turned a corner and saw the Quonset hut by the feed mill with our new sign:

OLSON & DAD, CO.
MACHINING & MANUFACTURING
(2M)

The guys turned to Dad and me with amazed and questioning looks on their mugs.

"It was Bjorn's idea," Dad said. "That's why it says 'and Dad' instead of 'and Son.' I insisted on that. The 2M thing is just a little fun jab at 3M. Let's go inside.

When we got to the door, Shu said, "What about this stuff on the door?"

The red lettering on the door read in large letters, SAFETY FIRST, with a painting of Dad's eye patch hanging off the T. Under that it read, FROM A HOUSE OF CARDS TO SOLID STEEL.

"Well, it was hard to put this together. The whole thing could have collapsed at any time." Then I told them the Honeywell story and more. "After we did the deal with Honeywell, the house of cards had to be built kinda in secret. Only a few people could know the whole story. We didn't want to be laughed at if we failed." And I didn't want to be further humiliated after having to drop out of school. "Sorry I couldn't tell you guys what was going on. I know it ticked you off when I wouldn't explain why I couldn't do some stuff with you.

"Anyway, we got an option on this building for a hundred bucks a year and the rest of the five-acre mill property if we want it. We showed 'em how much money we were gonna spend improving their property. They're moving out to the big new elevators near Waconia. Then we waded through a hundred other details." I figured I had accomplished a lot more by starting this business than I would have by graduating from high school, but I would never say that to anyone.

By then the guys looked dumbfounded by the story. Ozzie said, "Boy, I think you guys had some big balls to pull this off."

I said, "Of course, the bank was the big question mark, but so was getting some customers lined up. The whole thing took over two years."

Pope was patting me on the back when a car pulled up. Mr. Utoft, my shop teacher from high school, got out and Dad went over to greet him.

"Thanks for coming," Dad said to Utoft. "Bjorn wanted you to be here for this 'cause you were a big part of his short high school stay. He talked about how much he learned from you."

"What's this all about?" Utoft asked. He was in his mid-forties, short and wide with sparkling, inquisitive eyes.

Dad brought him up to speed with the story. Utoft said, "I'm flabbergasted. What a story!" He came over to me and gave me a long, firm handshake.

Then we took everyone inside. Just off the entry was a small office with three, gray metal used desks. "This is Olga's office, too," Dad said. "Here's something for you." We handed each of them a pair of eye protection goggles with their names engraved on the side. Then we gave each of them a little cabinet with their names on the top.

"Bjorn came up with this little cabinet with the handle on top to keep the nuts, bolts, washers and stuff for the home handyman to use. Look, the front of the drawers are clear plastic so you can see what the hell's inside. Olga said women would like it for their sewing stuff, too."

Ozzie said, "Pretty damn good idea there, Bjorn. Gotta hand it to ya."

Dad continued "Then your buddy here took the mock-up to Sears & Roebuck up in the Cities, and by God, they're gonna put 'em in their fall catalogue. And Coast to Coast hardware is also gonna put 'em on their standard inventory list for their stores. He's also got a bigger version on wheels for auto mechanics. Not bad for a dropout, eh?"

Uncomfortable with Dad's bragging about me, I said, "Mr. Utoft, we're gonna start with five full-time employees; best guys we can get, with better pay than the competition plus good benefits and profit sharing. To help make those guys more productive, we'll have part-time folks, farmers in the winter and teachers in the summer, to help the main guys with their work. We'd be honored if you would be our first part-time employee."

Utoft was speechless. Finally he put a hand on my shoulder. "Bjorn, you were the best shop student I had in eighteen years of teaching. I was really sorry you had to drop out. And thank you very much. I'll certainly consider the job offer and am honored you thought to invite me here today."

"You're more'n welcome. Now let's go into the shop area." I led them into the seventy-five-by-125-foot space with all the equipment and tools set up for production.

"Jeezus. I can't wait to show this to my old man. He'll crap his pants," Shu said.

After the tour of the shop, Dad said, "Mr. Utoft and I'll leave you guys alone now. Come back to the house in a while and you can each have *one* Grain Belt."

Chapter 10

Still at Olson & Dad, Co.

SHU

Bjorn, I wasn't kidding. My old man *will* crap his pants when I show him this place. I'm really proud of you and your folks. A little jealous, too." We were sitting in the Olson's & Dad's office after the tour of the production area.

I turned to Pope. "I guess we know what Bjorn and Ozzie'll be doing this summer. What about you?"

"Good timing with that question," Pope said. "Last night my new electrical engineering professor called. I met him when they had me down to the U to award the scholarship. Anyway, he said a friend of his called about an internship available at a fairly new company." Pope's face lit up. "He wondered if I would be interested."

"What company?" Ozzie asked. "What the hell's an internship? What's the pay?"

"Computing Data. It is in Bloomington," Pope answered quickly. "I would be a gofer for a Mr. Yetzer." He nodded toward Ozzie. "You do not get paid for being an intern. You are there to learn, not earn." Pope raised his arms to show his impatience with the pay question. "But the professor said the company would give me one share of stock for every day I interned. The shares are worth one dollar each. But I figure with Sputnik up there, science and computing are going to take off."

"Sounds like damned rip-off to me," Ozzie said.

"Ozzie, please. You know I do not like that language. And yes, I told Professor Sonnega I would be very interested in the position. I interview for it next Wednesday."

"Okay, Shu," Ozzie said. "What're you doin' this summer except pullin' teats?"

I was hoping I'd get a chance to tell my story to the guys. "Last Sunday after church, the neighbors, Mr. and Mr. Shultz, stopped over to see Pa." I stood up and slapped the desk. "Reason was, they wanted us to know they had to sell their farm because of his health, and they asked if we would be interested. Here I've been after the old man to ask 'em and now they walk in and ask us." I slapped the desk again. "Said they'd give us good terms if we had a certain down payment. Guess it paid for us to be good neighbors when they needed help."

"So did your old man say yes?" Bjorn asked.

"Well, you know him," I said, raising my hands to the heavens. "He and I almost came to blows. I told him this had to happen or I was outta there. We could borrow more on our farm to come up with the down stroke." Then I slapped the desk a third time. Guess the guys figured I was pretty cranked up about the story. "Guess what? Then my Uncle Helmut, who has the farm on the other side of us, gets into the act on Monday."

"Bet the s.o.b. tried to outbid you guys," Ozzie said.

"No. Turns out he's pissed 'cause he meant to ask Dad to buy *his* farm 'cause he's gonna move to Arizona due to his T.B. Now Schultz beat him to it. Okay, so Dad was about to do the deal with his brother instead of Schultz. Then I had an idea."

Pope said, "Oh, my goodness! Sounds like too much tension for me. What was your idea?"

"I'm thinkin', how can we get both farms? I mean, we can't afford to buy both, but my uncle needs money to buy a mobile home in a place called Apache Junction and after that some income. He's pretty sharp. Hates the idea of having to sell."

"Shit. Sounds like it's impossible. To get both farms, I mean," Ozzie said.

"Well, listen up," I said. "I carefully suggested to Dad that we should try something like this—borrow a little more on our farm so we could lend his brother money to buy the Arizona place. We manage Uncle Helmut's farm, run it like our own and split the profits with him. Then he pays us back for the Arizona loan over four years from the profits. Now he has the mobile home, income and still owns the dirt, and we have an option to buy it when he's good and ready to sell instead of being forced to sell."

"Damned brilliant!" Bjorn said. "What did you old man say to that? Kinda pushing him to the edge, weren't ya?"

"Dad said, 'Shu, you're crazy, ve vork too hard now.'" I smiled 'cause I liked imitating Dad's accent. "How do ve go from seventy tillable acres and add Schultz' hundert and ten and Helmut's ninety-five? Ve can't handle two hundert seventy-five acres of crop land. How could ve possible do dat'?"

"Sounds like your father was correct," Pope said.

I sat down and pointed to Pope. "I answered Dad by saying, by me working my ass off and us doin' some cropping with new methods and you getting rid of those damned cows and getting turkeys! Then we form a corporation so I can earn a share of it all.'"

"Holy shit, Shu! Did he belt ya?" Ozzie asked.

I shook my head and smiled. "No. Just walked away without saying a word. But then he turned around, pointed at me and said, 'Okay, I vill talk to Helmut, see vat he t'inks about your idea. You sure about dis? You got other t'ings to vorry about, you know.'"

"Wow, so did it all work out? Did your uncle buy the idea?" Pope asked.

I said, "Ya, now I've got my hands full, but I'm damned glad of it." My smile couldn't have been wider.

"Hey," Ozzie said. "Just a damn minute. What'd your old man mean by saying 'you got other t'ings to vorry about'?"

Oh, God, no, I thought. I got too carried away with the story. Shouldn't have told 'em what Dad said about "more t'ings to vorry about." Shit. Now what do I do? I paced around the small office, stalling for time, trying to think.

"Well?" Ozzie said.

"Just give me a minute," I said, rubbing my forehead. I'd been dreading telling the guys this ever since we'd found out.

"Oh, what's the big deal?" Ozzie asked.

I decided to just drop the bomb. "Well, I was wondering . . . late afternoon this coming Tuesday, would you guys be in my wedding?" I took a deep breath. "I wasn't gonna bring this up 'til after graduation. You have to promise to keep this a secret 'til after that or Trudy and I won't be able to graduate."

Dead silence. Mouths open. Other than saying "Yes," they were speechless. I'm sure their minds were spinning and they all spun out the same thought: *He has to get married.*

I wasn't going to say any more 'til somebody else talked. No one did for a long time. I thought of the day Trudy and I went to the Medical Arts building in Minneapolis after she missed her period. Up 'til then, she was as regular as the noon siren on the St. Boni creamery. When she came into the waiting room from the doctor's office, her look told me the whole story. I went to her, put my arms around her and said, "My darling Trudy, I love you. Please marry me."

Pope said, "We need to pray."

"You outta your friggin' mind?" Ozzie said with a hiss.

Pope pleaded, "We have to do this. Please. For me. For us. This has been an eventful day."

This was new territory for our group. We had put up with Pope's piety, but this seemed over the top, not something in our comfort zone.

Bjorn said, "Oh, what the hell, let 'im say one. Can't hurt. We all sure as shootin' need the big guy's help,"

"Jeezus, if ya insist, but I'm *not* holdin' hands with any guys," Ozzie said.

Pope knelt on the floor, his face tilted up to heaven and his hands folded by his chest. The rest of us stood, shifting from foot to foot, too uncomfortable for words. I peeked at the other two. Bjorn and Ozzie had their hands to their sides and their heads weren't bowed. I folded my hands and bowed my head. I guess I realized I needed all the help I could find.

Pope began in a sing-song, almost priestly voice:

"Dear Lord, hear our prayers, both spoken and silent.

"Bless the marriage of Shu and Trudy. Forgive them for their sins. May their baby be healthy. Let the sun and rain nourish their crops to ease the risks they have taken.

"Look over Ozzie as he faces life in new places with new people. Give him guidance. Help his folks find peace.

"Bless this factory and the people who will labor here. Protect Bjorn, Karl and Olga so the risks they have taken will be rewarded.

"Watch over me as I venture on to the university and internship.

"Thank you for our many blessings; forgive all of our sins.

"Oh, yes, and please watch over Coach Wagner.

"Amen."

After an awkward silence, Ozzie said, "Okay, Karl said we could have one. Let's go get a Grain Belt."

We shuffled out in a single file. If pressed, I'll bet the others would have admitted to adding a silent prayer of their own. Just like I did.

THE NEXT TUESDAY

ABOUT AN HOUR before the ceremony I was with my groomsmen in the machine shed leaning against the John Deere tractor. All but Pope were sharing a bottle of Thunderbird wine that Ozzie had brought. Pope looked more nervous than I felt. We all had on starched white shirts with maroon ties. That looked real good with our jeans, except Pope had on dress pants.

"Man, what'd your folks do when you told 'em you had'a get married?" Ozzie asked. "Ya dumb shit, didn't you ever hear of rubbers?"

I wasn't going to tell the guys why I didn't have a rubber handy. What happened with Trudy and me was our business. During the winter Trudy and I did it in the back seat of the Ford, where I had a supply of Trojans. But on an unusually warm April night, we headed for the windbreak for our first time this spring. I forgot the Trojans in the Ford.

"I'll admit I was scared. I asked 'em to sit down, said I had something to tell 'em. Pa expected another cow argument. I was stammering, so they knew I was shook up. Finally I told 'em they were gonna be grandparents. They didn't get it at first. Then Ma asked, 'You and Trudy'? and I said, 'Ya.' Well, then no one said anything for quite a while. Pa got up, shaking his head, and walked to the window overlooking the fields. He jammed his hands in his pockets. Ma looked at him with a fearful look. She walked over to him and they talked to each other, kinda in whispers. Then they nodded to each other and both of 'em walked over and gave me a hug. First one since I was a little kid. Ma said in my ear, 'Son, ve understand. And ve love Trudy too. I t'ink you never counted the months between our vedding anniversary and your birthday.'"

"Wow, what a relief that must have been!" said Bjorn. "How about Trudy? How'd it go with her folks?"

"Trudy's folks were just as good about it after her dad raised a little fuss. Her mom had Trudy go into more *details* about things though. Let's just say that one night later, Gretta hauled a blanket and my future father-in-law out to the same windbreak where their future grandkid was conceived." I had to grin.

Pope said, "We had better get out to the garden. You would not want to miss your own wedding."

When we got to the flower garden between the house and the windbreak, I could hear Trudy and her mom, who had Trudy in a big hug. "Ma, this looks so nice," Trudy said. "Thank you so much for doing all this on short notice."

Gretta was proud of her flower garden. "Baby, anyt'ing for my little darlin'. I can't get over how beautiful you look. Dat Shu is a lucky boy." She had repainted the white arched trellis and dressed it up with ivy and pink roses. My beautiful bride would walk through the trellis with her dad.

It would be a small audience. Close family and friends only. Twenty, rented white folding chairs were scattered in pairs throughout the garden on the grass paths. Pink bows were tied to the backs of the chairs. Appropriately, the seats faced the windbreak.

Chapter 11

Late fall 1959, a year and a half later

SHU

I got Bjorn on the phone. "Hey, Bjorn, could you stop out to the farm tomorrow night? Need to show you some stuff, and I've got a couple'a ideas I need to bounce off you." I was reluctant to make the call to him, but high debt and two seasons' of poor crop weather were taking their toll.

"Okay, but I gotta stop at the bank about four-thirty. I could be to your place about five-thirty or six. That work?" Bjorn asked.

"Ya, good. Come for supper."

The next night Bjorn, with his new Chevy pickup, pulled into the old Schultz place, where Trudy and I live. He must be doin' well.

The old frame house needed paint and some unsagging of the front porch, but I had my hands full with other work. Yeah, and the barn and machine shed used to be red. Now they were faded to lightish pink and weathered gray. The only bright and shiny thing visible was the Farmer's Co-op propane tank that lurked between the house and the granary. Put a propeller on one end and it would look like one of those dang midget submarines.

I opened the door for him, and he blurted out, "Mind if I say you look like hell? Haven't seen you since July. What the heck you been doing?"

As we shook hands, I said, "Ya, well, things are kinda tough. Losin' weight. Workin' almost 'round the clock."

Trudy came into the country kitchen carrying little Ellie, who was bawling. Dark circles around Trudy's eyes betrayed her forced smile. She shared my worries. Ellie didn't, but she cried anyway.

Bjorn's eyes lit up as he took Ellie out of Trudy's arms. "There's my little god-kid. Still as cute as ever. Good thing she takes after her mama and not her old man." Ellie stopped crying. "And here's a paycheck for Mama," he said as he handed Trudy a brown envelope.

"What's this?" Trudy said.

"Well, you came up with the idea of making an artist's cabinet like our nuts and bolts cabinet and by golly it's up and selling. We pay the idea people if we decide to produce their gadget."

Trudy opened the envelope and broke into tears. "Oh, Bjorn, you have no idea how much this means to us! Thank you, thank you!" She gave him a hug.

"You're welcome."

Wiping her tears, Trudy showed me the check and said, "You guys have a Grain Belt while I dish up supper."

We didn't have much to celebrate these days, but that check called for more than one Grain Belt.

Over fried chicken with potatoes and gravy, I leaned forward with my elbows on the chrome and blue Formica table. "We can't keep goin' the way we are. If our debt doesn't kill me, the old man will. He keeps reminding me it was my ideas that put us in this bind."

Bjorn said, "Well, next year's weather should be better."

"Ya, but that's only half the battle. We gotta reduce the debt, and I think I know how. Next spring the township's gonna blacktop the road out front. We'll get assessed for part of it, but over ten years."

"So how does that help? Trudy, this chicken's fantastic," Bjorn said as he helped himself to seconds.

"I checked with the county. Between this farm and our original one, we could plat out eight lots in the woods along the new blacktopped road. Bet we could pay off over half what we owe the Schultzes when we sell the lots, and we wouldn't lose any crop land. I wanna dam up the creek so each home-site would back up to a big pond. That's where I need your help."

Bjorn said, "Sounds like a great idea. How can I help?"

"I'd just make our driveway higher and wider to create the dam. But I need you to make a vertical extension to attach to the culvert under the driveway. Can't do that in the farm shop."

"Okay, heck, glad to do it. But you said you had a *couple* of ideas," Bjorn said, smiling as he saw my Trudy cutting the apple pie.

"This one gets a little complicated," I said, glancing at Trudy.

She nodded for me to continue.

"We can't keep plowing and planting the fields like we always have. There're too many acres. The work is killing us. There's new methods being done down south called minimum tillage. Been reading and studying about it. Farmers have been making their own equipment." I reached for an envelope of magazine articles and pictures and slid 'em to Bjorn. "With minimum tillage, plowin' and plantin' take one-fourth or less time, effort and cost, and it produces as good or better crops."

Bjorn looked at some of the pictures. "I'm trying to imagine what your old man's gonna think about these new ideas. You've already gotten him in deep doo-doo."

Pointing at Bjorn, I said, "*You're* gonna help convince him, *Partner*, 'cause together, we're gonna start a new division of your company to make the minimum tillage equipment."

"What?" Bjorn yelled as he pushed his chair away from the table.

I kept talking so he wouldn't say no. "I'll do the basic designs. You guys finalize it. I'll test the equipment and suggest improvements. When we've got prototypes, I'll hit the road in the winters to get dealers to carry the stuff and I'll promote the new tillage method wherever I can." I stopped to take a quick breath. "No salary. No commissions. Expenses only. I get to keep the prototypes. Trudy and I would get one-fourth of the profits. Okay? Deal?"

I could tell Bjorn's mind was spinning. "Whoa, hold on. Jeez, that's a lot to think about." After a little more discussion he said, "Well, I have to admit, it sounds interesting. But I gotta bounce it off the old man. Tell you what, let's meet at that supper club in Chanhassen Friday night at seven, company's treat. By then I'll have the old man's take on the deal." He looked down at has empty pie plate and mumbled, "Besides, I'd like you guys to meet someone."

Trudy said, teasing, "Really? Meet someone? Male or female?"

"Ah, well . . . ah, female. Name's Mary Katherine. Daughter of Mike O'Brian, one of our employees," Bjorn said, blushing.

"Holy Moses," I said. "Finally. I was beginning to wonder about you. Don't ever remember you even having a date. Been workin' all the time. What turned your crank about this one?"

"Oh, she brings lunch to her old man at the shop once in a while. kinda lights up the whole place when she walks in. Perky. Great smile. Redhead."

"Mary Katherine O'Brian, red head . . . Irish?" Trudy said.

"Yup. Dad and Ma like her too, even though she's Catholic. Can't wait for you guys to meet her."

***

IT HAD BEEN SEVEN MONTHS since we had a night out. Grandma Gretta was taking care of Ellie, and glad to do so. We were sitting in a red, fake leather corner booth waiting for Bjorn and his new friend. We were curious about her and nervous about what Bjorn's dad had to say.

"Shu, just remember, I love you no matter what. If his dad's answer is no, you'll figure something else out," Trudy said, squeezing my knee. "I have faith in you."

I said, "Don't know how you put up with what I've gotten us into. You're an angel. Oh, here they come." We stood and greeted them.

Bjorn did the introductions.

"A redhead," I said. "I'll never believe Bjorn again. He told us you were from India and had a jewel embedded in your forehead." That broke the ice.

"Well, I removed the jewel myself," Mary Katherine said. "I'm in nurse's training at St. Kate's, so I'm qualified to operate on my own head. Then I dyed my hair red." She was quick with the comeback and had a warm smile to go with it.

Trudy and Mary Katherine hit it off at once and did the lady thing about going to the powder room together. I sure could see why Mary Katherine got Bjorn's juices flowing.

"Let's order some Seven-Ups. Still not legal, but I've got a little flask of vodka in Mary Katherine's purse," Bjorn said.

After the ladies came back from the powder room and the drinks were served, it was question-and-answer time, so Trudy and I could learn more about Mary Katherine.

Mary Katherine said, "Bjorn's told me so much about you two that I feel like we're old friends. He told me a lot about Pope and Ozzie, too."

"Hope he only told you the good stuff," I said and then asked Bjorn, "By the way, you heard anything from those two lately?"

"I haven't talked to Pope, but a guy in a suit and with some government credentials came by asking questions about him. Somethin' about some kinda security clearance 'cause of his intern deal.

"Also, I got a call from Ozzie. He's still in Charlotte. Says he's got a roommate by the name of Angie. And, he wants me to hire his dad. He got fired from the railroad. Says that really sobered the old man up."

Trudy said, "Angie? Doesn't sound like a fellow ballplayer's name."

"Sure doesn't," Bjorn said and grinned. "I'm not sure what to do about his old man. Dad's leery of the idea, but he knows I'm on the hot seat."

I shook my head. "Oh, boy, if you do it, you'd better have your old man have a heart to heart with him. You know, Hank's a loose cannon."

"Ya, I know," Bjorn said. "But maybe he could work in the *new division.*"

Trudy and I didn't catch on right away, but after a bit our jaws dropped in tandem. We turned and wrapped our arms around each other.

Trudy got up and went over to give Bjorn a hug, "What great news! You're the best friend a person could have. Thanks for convincing your dad."

Bjorn was grinning from ear to ear as he reached over to shake my hand. "Dad's all for the idea, but he had some things to add. He was wondering what your monthly payment was to the Schultzes."

"Jeez, that's kinda private information."

Bjorn said, "We have to know 'cause he says you won't be any good to the company if you're under too much pressure. The company'll pay part of the Schultz monthly payment as an advance on your share of future profits. It's not a loan."

"Holy cow. That's more than generous of your dad," I said. "I'd resist that help, but I guess he's right. I gotta have my head working right to make this deal with you be a win-win for everyone. And it's not a gift but something we'll earn."

The waitress came for our order. The gals ordered walleye and Bjorn ordered loaded baked potatoes and big T-bones for us. For desert to share he ordered us a wedge of Lucy's famous carrot cake with cream cheese frosting. Said he wanted to fatten me up.

After polishing off the desert we all got up to leave. The goodbyes were more emotional than Bjorn and I would normally be comfortable with, but Trudy and I were very thankful for Bjorn's news and we were delighted to meet his gal.

On the way home, Trudy snuggled up to me just like when we were dating. "Quite the night, eh?" she said. "Help with building the dam so we can sell lots for more money, a new business venture to carry out your vision and meeting a new friend."

"Yup. How about we celebrate in the sack when we get home?"

Trudy gave me a shot to the ribs, but giggled and said, "Sounds good to me. And I sure liked Mary Katherine. How about you?"

"What's not to like? And I was happy to see Bjorn has something in his life other than work."

KARL

OZZIE'S DAD WAS over a half-hour late. I was walking through the rest of the mill property. If we're gonna make farm equipment we need more space. Some of the old mill buildings would work, but others would have to come down.

Hank Johnson caught up with me in the old bagging room. "Sorry I'm a little late. Dang wife fergot to wake me in time. Can't count on her fer nothin'." His thin face had a three-day stubble, and his eyes looked like they'd start bleeding any second.

"Well, okay," I said. "Let's sit here on these barrels. We need to have a talk about how we run things around here. Then we'll see if you still want the job and if we want to bring you on. I gotta meet with a supplier in fifteen minutes." I think my body language told him how pissed I was for him bein' so late.

"What's this dump gonna be?" Hank asked, brushing away a cobweb.

"We'll probably tear this part down and build an addition to the main building here. What was your job with the railroad?"

"Brakeman in route and switchman in the yards. Union helped keep the jobs separate most times . . . able to have more members that way."

"Well, here we cross-train so when one area is swamped, guys from another area can help out," I said.

"How about benefits? Union? Pay? Vacations? Stuff like that," Hank asked.

"Good benefits, competitive pay, Employee Council instead of a union, normal time off, and profit sharing," I was just glossing over stuff. I knew already I would vote not to hire him.

"Profit sharing?" Hank asked.

"Yup, ownership gets fifty percent after tax profit. Employees get forty percent."

"Karl, I hope you ain't doin' the books. Fifty and forty ain't a hundert."

"Ten percent is spent in the towns our employees are from. Employee Council figures out what it's spent on: ball teams, Scouts, church repair, food for the poor, stuff like that."

"Sounds t'me like the workin' stiff gets screwed here, too. I'm outta here," Hank said as he got up to leave.

I wanted to tell him to not let the door hit him in the ass, but I bit my lip. *Good riddance.*

Chapter 12

The next Tuesday morning

DAVID, A.K.A. POPE

Norma French, the Computing Data receptionist handed me a pink pen. "Hello. Sign the visitor register, please. With whom do you have an appointment?"

I chuckled and said, "Hello, Norma. Take a closer look."

She looked at me more closely and gasped, "Oh, my goodness, David! It's you! What the—where are your . . . ah, glasses?" She had almost said "Coke bottle glasses."

"I decided to get contact lenses. It is easier working in the lab with contacts instead of my glasses continually slipping down my nose."

She said, "Well, David, you look great. Mr. Yetzer wants to see you right away. I'll buzz you in."

I wondered why I had been summoned on such short notice. Usually I was not there on Tuesdays as that was my all-day lab with Professor Sonnega, my electrical engineering professor. I opened Mr. Yetzer's door with some trepidation. I was always awed by the view from his seventh-floor office. I usually looked forward to meeting with this tall, silver-haired mentor.

"Hi, David," Mr. Yetzer said. Then he pointed to the other person in the room. "Meet George Melchert, head of company security." Mr. Melchert stepped toward me and we shook hands. "Have a seat."

Mr. Melchert's lips were a grim, thin line. He made me a little uncomfortable. He never took his penetrating gaze off me.

Mr. Yetzer said, "David, I'll get right to the point, as we're a little short of time. You've been a great intern, but it's time for you to move on."

I thought, *What in the world did I do wrong?* I felt the color drain from my face and I got that old feeling in my stomach and throat. *I have done everything asked of me and more.* "I—I—well—why am I being fired?"

Mr. Yetzer and Mr. Melchert both laughed. "No, no. That's not what I meant," Mr. Yetzer said. "We have something else in mind for you. It involves some government work, and you'll need a security clearance if you agree to do what we have in mind."

Oh, boy. That old feeling started to leave my stomach, and I put my hand to my forehead, "Oh. What would I be doing?"

Mr. Melchert said, "Before we get into that, we have to discuss something personal. Army Intelligence has done a background check on you, and there's one area of concern."

"Background check?" What in the world could this be all about? "What area of concern?"

Mr. Melchert said, "It seems you're a young man who went all through high school with only one date with a girl, and that was arranged by your coach. You had no romantic relationship with the opposite sex. That raises a question." He shifted from foot to foot and seemed uncomfortable.

I said, "What question would that be?" The whole thing got pretty mysterious. I had no clue as to where this was all leading.

Mr. Melchert said, his eyes on me like dark on night, "We have to ask . . . are you homosexual?"

I was pretty sure I knew what homosexual meant, so my first reaction was surprise at the question. Maybe my answer took a second too long, but I had to recover from the shock of the inquiry. "No. I am not. But what in the world does that have to do with anything anyway? Just what exactly do you want me to do?" Maybe I should not have raised my voice and stood up at that point.

Mr. Melchert said, "Please, relax. We had to ask the question. It's a problem with security clearances. It could be a cause for blackmail."

While I was sitting back down, Mr. Yetzer said, "Sorry for the personal intrusion, David. We had to ask."

"Okay. I guess the answer to that question must be important to someone," I said, still confused about where this was all leading.

Mr. Yetzer said, "Thanks for your understanding. Do you realize you will be drafted into the military when you graduate? You have no deferment status."

"Draft? I never really thought about it. That is two years away."

Mr. Yetzer said, "What I'm going to propose will give you a deferment from the draft, but you would have to make a three-year commitment to another government agency away from Minnesota. That job would also be of great help to this company."

"I am having trouble following this. Could you please explain more?"

Mr. Melchert said, "Before we continue this conversation, I need to consult with the local Army Intelligence office regarding your security clearance. Can you be back here at two-thirty tomorrow afternoon to hear more?"

"Well, yes, if it is necessary." I looked at Mr. Yetzer and he nodded.

"We would appreciate it if you wouldn't talk to anyone about today's meeting," Melchert said.

***

I HAD TROUBLE SLEEPING that night, wondering what the rest of the story was going to be from the two men at Computing Data. I was anxious to hear the rest of what they had to say, and I left early for their office. Norma greeted me with the sign-in register again. This time she did not ask whom I wanted to see. She buzzed me right in to Mr. Yetzer's seventh-floor office.

"Hi, David. Right on time. Good man," Yetzer said.

Mr. Melchert mumbled something I did not catch. His lips and eyes still made me uneasy. "We can continue yesterday's conversation. Might as well get on with it. You have been granted a Top Secret clearance by the Army. The rest of this meeting is classified Top Secret. Please read this outline of what having that clearance means." He handed me a one-page, official-looking document, which I read and handed back to him. "Do you agree not to discuss this meeting with anyone? Do you understand what you just read?"

"Yes, of course."

Mr. Yetzer smiled. "We have just been awarded the largest government agency contract ever issued for data processing. We will be developing the software and building the mainframe." He paused and leaned forward with his palms on his desk. "We need three people from this company who would be willing to commit to three years working here for a while and then going with the equipment to spend the rest of the time at a military installation back east. You would be on retainer from Computing Data to that agency."

"But I have to graduate." I could not see how this would work for me.

"Professor Sonnega is a consultant on this project." He leaned back and folded his arms as if he'd solved my last hesitation. "He has the latitude to count your experience on this job as credit toward a degree. You'd also have to take some correspondent courses through him and a few courses at a college in Baltimore."

"This sounds interesting, but I am not qualified to work on something of this magnitude," I said, already knowing that he had all the answers. I was involved with some smart people here.

Mr. Yetzer got up and paced behind his desk, looked at the view of the Minnesota River Valley and spoke to me at the same time. "You would observe the process and the construction of the equipment. Your job would be on the user's site to trouble-shoot problems that crop up. You won't know what the computer is used for, but you will know how it works. You'd also have back-up engineers here to call if you need help. The mainframe will take up the better part of a large room."

I was getting excited. "Sounds like a great opportunity. I'd like to take advantage of it. Can you tell me more?"

Mr. Yetzer laid a map of the East Coast in front of me and pointed to a spot in Maryland. "You will be going to Fort Meade, just outside of Baltimore. That's the headquarters of the NSA—the National Security Agency. They collect electronic intelligence."

He looked at me for my reaction. I am sure he could tell he had me hooked. "There will also be times when one of the three of you will have to be in Frankfurt, Germany, at the I.G. Farben building, U.S. Army Europe Headquarters. The NSA will have one of our ancillary installations there, and another one in Berlin."

"I have never been outside of Minnesota. This sounds interesting and a little overwhelming. I probably would have to talk to my folks about this."

Mr. Melchert said, "Okay, but we'll supply you with a cover story that will explain why you're going out east. Remember, not even your folks can know the whole story."

"I cannot lie to my parents."

"You won't be lying. A cover story to protect national security is not a lie. This is important, and it's the real world. You're a man now. Your folks don't need to know everything you do.

"It won't be all fun and games. Your phone calls will be monitored from time to time and you might even be under surveillance. While based at Fort Meade, you'll also spend time in classes at Fort Hollabird, the Army Intelligence School in Baltimore." Mr. Melchert emphasized the sensitivity of the job. "Time-off will be limited, and you'll be on-call twenty-four hours a day, seven days a week."

Mr. Yetzer got up and came around the desk to put his hand on my shoulder. "Remember, David, this is important for this company *and* for you. In return for your three-year commitment, you'll have a great résumé, travel at Uncle Sam's expense, earn some money, graduate and be exempt from the draft."

I nodded and shook his hand. My unease about the whole thing was tempered by my faith in Mr. Yetzer. He would not steer me wrong.

OZZIE

I WANTED ANGIE at every home game. She knew I liked that, and she was good at doing things I liked.

From the time she caught my eye when I came out of the home team's locker room, we've been an item. Actually, it was her cleavage, which I could imagine getting lost in, and her great ass poured into short shorts that first caught my eye. And that's not to forget her long legs. When they were handing out bodies, she must have been in the front of the line.

Maybe she wasn't near the front of the line when they were handing out brains, but hell, neither was I.

I'd been told by one of the coaches to look out for broads like her. He said they wanted to find a ticket to a future with a guy who might have major league bucks. But what the hell, I need steady female skin next to mine. My eyes were wide open.

Unlike her ass, her face was a picture of innocence—the All-American-Girl look. Her auburn hair framed her cheeks and billowed like wild fire down her backside. Her southern drawl could charm the socks, or pants, off anyone. She was three years older than me.

Her boss at the Dixie Chicks Club let her set her own hours. She was the best dancer in his stable. Angie knew how to turn on the testosterone crowd. Nothing crude, but she moved that great body with a lot of class and teasing. Her stage name is Angelique.

When I was on the road I got an occasional piece of strange tail, and I knew Angie treated some of her customers to extra personal, intimate attention when I was gone. We were both okay with that. What the hell, it was not like we were married. But no chick I bedded-down on the road could match Angie in the sack. I think she invented sex.

My team had just finished the last game of my second season in the minors. Whether or not I'd make it to the majors was up in the air. I didn't get along with some of my asshole teammates, my pitching was a little spotty, and my temper got the better of me once in a while. But hell, sometimes I just overreacted. Like, once I caused a bench-clearing brawl when I brushed back a prick from Trenton, the Yankee farm club, with two pitches in a row. He called me a small-town hayseed. Twice.

But the brass must think I had enough potential and they knew I was a competitor. I wouldn't give up 'til they showed me the freakin' door.

Angie met me outside the locker room. "Baby, you were great," she said in that honey-dipped drawl. "Five strike-outs and six scoreless innings. Too bad the bull pen let you down again." She leaned her right boob against my pitching arm and gave me a kiss. She knew I'd be in a bad mood after we lost the game.

"I hope those losers will be outta here next year," I said. "Either that or I better be moved up. I'm tired of bustin' my butt only to have them blow the damn lead."

"Oh, Ozzie, let's go home. I'll give you one of my famous full-body massages, guaranteed to make you feel *much* better."

"Sounds great, babe. You do know how to please me."

We walked across the parking lot kinda slow 'cause we were groping each other on the way to my Buick. I wondered if we'd even make it home before we jumped each other's bones. "Oh, Ozzie, let's wait 'til we get to our luv bed. I wanna do you real good instead of a quickie in the back seat."

I backed off, but only 'cause she painted that real good picture of us in the sack. A couple of blocks toward our apartment, I remembered to tell her about December. "By the way, I got a call from Bjorn, a buddy back in Minnesota. One of our other friends, Pope, is gonna be gone for about three years. Bjorn thought we should have a little reunion in December before Pope leaves. He's arranging for some rooms at the Nicollet Hotel. I'd sure like you to come along so I could show you off to my buddies. Okay?"

I thought even Pope would get a woody on when he saw Angelique.

"Can I meet your folks too?" she purred.

"Maybe, but they'll probably be out of town." Be a cold day in hell when I'd let her meet my old man.

Chapter 13

December 1959, two months later

THE WHOLE CREW

O zzie teased Angie as they stepped out of the terminal to catch a cab. "Brace yourself. Snot's gonna freeze right in your nose. Minus twenty-one ain't nothing. I remember a few years ago it was thirty-nine below. Weren't anybody's car would start."

"Ozzie, why would anybody wanna live here? No wonder you like Charlotte. I hope Shu's wife remembers to bring me a winter coat," Angie said, shocked by the cold. "Think my eyeballs are gonna freeze? Get in the cab, quick."

Christmas decoration lights were the only thing that warmed the white tundra landscape on the way to the Nicollet Hotel in downtown Minneapolis.

Bjorn had arranged for two suites. Mary Katherine would spend the nights at St. Kate's even though she would have to get back for the eleven o'clock curfew; if the '54 Studebaker her aunt gave her would start. Pope thought he'd sleep back at his dorm to save a few bucks. That left one suite for Angie and Ozzie and one for Trudy and Shu. Bjorn figured he'd crash on a couch in one of the suites.

Everyone arrived at the hotel by five o'clock on Friday night. It would be a two-night, one-day affair. Angie and Ozzie were the first to arrive, so everyone gathered in their suite.

The two-room suite was the perfect size for the small reunion. However, everyone was disappointed in the threadbare, dirty carpet, which didn't invite one to go barefoot. The suite was located on the third floor, just even with the top of the neon sign outside the window that added a warm, red glow to the interior. The glow also made the pale, winterized Minnesotans' faces seem more tanned than their winter-white complexions.

Introductions were made for those who hadn't met. Mary Katherine said, "Just call me MK. My full name takes too much time to say, and you have a lot of talking to do." Bjorn was proud of her. Of course, he knew MK would light up the room.

"This is my roommate, Angie," Ozzie said. He had noticed the others checking her out. "We're really glad to be here, but Angie doesn't like your shitty weather." Ozzie knew she'd hike the guys' testosterone level, and he couldn't have been prouder.

Hands were shaken, backs patted and the reminiscing began.

"Man, the last time we were all together was at the wedding."

"Boy, that was a surprise. Way to go Shu, ya dumb shit."

"Remember Pope's prayer a few days before that? I gotta admit, I added my own silent one."

"Ya, and Karl giving us that beer. Only one though."

"Pope, how the heck can you see without your glasses?"

The boys' reminiscing went on and on, fully enjoying the moment, but they didn't ignore the gals.

Unfortunately, there was a chill among the gals. Trudy and MK hadn't been prepared for someone like Angie. She made them feel frumpy and unappealing in their practical Gopher sweat shirts and cold weather wool slacks. They couldn't help but notice how their guys kept glancing at Angie in her red slacks that were tighter than the skin on a Delicious apple. Her spike heels and a low-cut angora sweater, which accented her notable breasts, completed her outfit. A shiny necklace dangled in her cleavage to entice the male eyes.

Angie couldn't help herself. She loved flirting with the guys. When she talked to one of them she stood close, usually touching them in some way, and ran her ringed, polished fingers through her long auburn hair. Ozzie couldn't have been prouder.

In contrast, Trudy didn't even wear fingernail polish. Her haircut was designed for low maintenance—cute, but in a farm-gal sort of way. Gathering eggs, butchering chickens, canning vegetables from her garden, slopping hogs and tending to the old house and Ellie didn't leave time for what she considered being frilly.

MK lit up a room when she entered, but it was her face and personality that did it, not dangly, cleavage jewelry. Her nurse's training at St. Kate's demanded time and effort. Her clothing and make-up were determined by practicality and speed of application. Besides, she didn't want to upset the patrolling nuns with provocative make-up or clothes. She saved some of that for when she and Bjorn were alone.

"Well, let's get the party started," Bjorn said, wearing his standard plaid flannel shirt. "Angie's the only one here who's legal. Let's take up a collection and have her get us some adult beverages. I'll go with 'er to help carry the booze."

MK shook her head, indicating she wasn't thrilled with the last part of Bjorn's suggestion. To say she lit up a room did not mean she didn't light up a temper when needed. She bit her tongue.

Angie welcomed Bjorn's offer with a wink. Ozzie had told her about Bjorn's success in business. She thought he must do okay, moneywise. His blond hair turned her on too; there weren't that many blond guys in Charlotte. "Oh, Bjorn, you're such a sweetie for coming with me," Angie cooed on the way to the liquor store. "Let me take your arm so I don't slip on this nasty, icy sidewalk," she said as she pressed her breast against his side.

Bjorn couldn't get enough of her sweet southern drawl.

The liquor store clerk glanced at Bjorn as they entered. Suspecting Bjorn was underage, he started to ask for an ID. Angie interrupted with a question and wriggled out of her coat to expose her cleavage to the clerk. He forgot all about Bjorn.

When they returned to Ozzie's suite a bar was set up on the dresser and drinks were poured. Pope didn't know it, but Ozzie spiked Pope's cream soda with enough vodka to stun a Russian sailor. Rum and Coke was for the gals and Jim Beam and Seven-Up were the drinks of choice for Shu and Bjorn. Ozzie drank straight vodka.

MK said, "Pope, I really like your blazer. Oh, and I was wondering, why did you decide to go to school back East?"

The cover story was that Pope had been accepted into a special program at Whiting Institute of Electrical Engineering at the University of Maryland. His scholarship was also transferred there. "I just could not turn down this opportunity to go to the Whiting Institute in Baltimore," Pope said. "My professor here said that program is on the leading edge of technology." He was practicing embellishing his cover story.

Computing Data had not been able to find two other employees to accompany Pope out East. Professor Sonnega had put out the word to his contemporaries around the country and two others were recruited: Samuel from the Whiting Institute and Herb from Stanford in Palo Alto.

"How is your arrangement going with that snow sled company?" Pope asked Bjorn, trying to change the subject.

"Okay." Bjorn shrugged. "They like our quality, but they keep trying to get us to lower our prices. Company's doin' good. Sears is selling a lot of our handyman cabinets. We have a lot of custom machining work, too." He looked at Shu. "Got some other stuff in the pipeline too."

Pope said, "Glad to hear that. We are all proud of you and your family's business. Maybe we should go to dinner. I would suggest we go to the Nankin after these drinks. It is only a short walk." He didn't want them drinking any more on empty stomachs. He was on his second secretly spiked cream soda. *Here I am again, odd man out . . . the only one without a girlfriend.*

After polishing off their drinks they bundled up for the arctic expedition, a one-block trek to the Chinese restaurant.

Other than Angie and Ozzie, eating Oriental food was rare for the group. Most of the conversation at dinner was about the food and the décor of the restaurant.

Also, they tried to plan the events of the next day.

"There's a Lakers game tomorrow afternoon. It'd be fun to watch old Mikkelson and the rookie Baylor play together," Ozzie said. "Anybody else interested?"

"Depends. I'd like to go to the top of the Foshay Tower," Shu said while struggling with his chop sticks.

"Oh, I just need to be around somebody to keep me warm. This weather sure must be good for cuddling," Angie said as she leaned her shoulder into Bjorn.

MK was watching from across the table so he tried to ignore Angie, but she was also rubbing her thigh against his and he was blushing.

Ozzie knew what she was up to and was enjoying Bjorn's discomfort. He couldn't have been prouder.

MK felt she needed to counter Angie's slutty behavior and expose her lack of class. "I think we should go to the Art Institute. There's a showing of contemporary German artists. And, as a counterpoint, there'll be a string quartet playing classical pieces from German composers. It should be a lovely time."

Trudy picked up on MK's ploy. "After that we could go to the library. On the *Things to do Today* blackboard in the lobby it told about a book signing of the new cookbook, *Cook Together, Stay Together*."

"Well, it sounds like we have choices. For now let's get back to the room. I need to cure this thirst," Bjorn said.

Angie thought he was especially clever.

Back at the suite, Ozzie snuck vodka into Pope's cream soda and asked him, "You're the reason for this reunion, whaddya wanna do tomorrow?"

"Thank fou for asking," Pope said, wondering why his tongue didn't work at times. "We should go to the Saturday morning prayer pervice at the Basilica at eight-thirty."

"Oh, shit. Sorry I asked," Ozzie said.

"Well, I think it would be appropriate. After the prayer service we could go to brunch at the Normandy," Pope said. "Then we could catch the first half of the Laker's lame." Some of the others figured out why he was having tongue problems. "There are two plays running on Hennepin Avenue. The matinees start at three and there are tickets available. I would like to see *South Sacific*."

"I'm liking your ideas. I've never been to the Basilica or a professional live play," Trudy said, smiling about Pope's tongue problem.

"Thank you. After the play we can go to the top of the Foshay fower and then to dinner at the Polynesian Room downstairs."

There was general agreement with Pope's agenda for the next day, but Ozzie said, "Angie and I will skip the damn prayer service."

As the evening progressed the conversations became louder with everyone talking at once. At ten, Bjorn went with MK to see whether her Studebaker would start. It did, after they'd almost killed the battery grinding the starter.

She said, "Hope it's safe leaving you here with that *hussy* Ozzie brought. She's got so much paint on her face, her name should be Bimbo the Circus Clown."

"Oh, babe, you've got it all over her. I'm surprised you'd even think I'd wander from you." Bjorn gave her a long kiss as gentle snowflakes also kissed their cheeks. "Wish I was sleeping with you tonight."

"I know. Me too," MK said. "Sorry I'm all hung up about Ozzie's girlfriend. The one I should be pissed at is Ozzie for foisting her on us."

"Ya, he's kinda pushing the envelope more than normal this time. Please don't let it spoil your weekend."

When Bjorn got back to the room, he found Pope passed out on a chair. "Whoops, maybe we should call it a night. Gotta get up early for the prayer service, and it looks like we've all quenched our thirst." He nodded toward Pope. "Let's pour him onto the couch. Ozzie, you'll have to baby sit him tonight."

Bjorn and Shu carried Pope to the couch, undressed him and got him a pillow and blanket.

Ozzie staggered to the bedroom and swan-dived face-first onto the bed. He'd be sleeping with his clothes on.

ANGIE A.K.A. ANGELIQUE

IT WAS NUDGING MIDNIGHT. Couldn't sleep, and I had been tossing and twirling like a chick on a spit. The caffeine from the Coke kept me awake and the rum made me one horny bunny. Helping myself wasn't gonna satisfy my horny itch. I needed someone to scratch it. I had a plan. I slipped out of bed so I wouldn't wake the snoring Ozzie. In his condition, I don't think he coulda helped me anyway.

I put on my spiked heels and a white hotel robe. That's all. I slipped a room key into the pocket of the robe and went to the door. The red glow from the neon sign lit my way past Pope, who was passed-out. I carefully opened and shut the door so I wouldn't wake him.

I made sure no one was in the hall and tip-toed next door to Trudy and Shu's suite. I doubted she'd be awake, and besides, my target was Bjorn.

Here goes, I thought, and tapped on the door, knowing Bjorn was close by on the couch. No answer the first time, so I tapped again. Finally, Bjorn opened the door wearing only plaid jamma bottoms; his bare chest was muscular, like I had imagined. "Oh, Angie . . . hi. What do you want?"

"Can I come in?"

"Well, I s'pose." He yawned and stepped back to let me through the door.

I put my finger to my lips to shush him and closed the door behind me, real easy, so I wouldn't wake Shu and plain-Jane Trudy in the bedroom. The neon red glow flooded this room too. I untied the white robe and opened it so Bjorn could get an eyeful of my goodies. I leaned my bare breasts against his naked chest. "What I want is for you to keep me warm," I said as I slid my hand inside his jammas.

"Oh, man, Angie, wait. Just a minute," Bjorn whispered as he pulled away. "Wow, I must have given you the wrong signals." He put his hands on my shoulders and held me away at arm's length. "I'm flattered that a gorgeous woman like you would want me, but, I'm a one-woman guy and that's MK. Besides, I couldn't screw Ozzie's girl. Please understand. Don't be mad."

"Well, hey, actually that's kinda refreshing to hear. You're a cutie *and* a good guy, but I gotta say I'm sorry you feel that way. I was ready to show you a real good time." He may have turned down my whoopee time, but I noticed he still snuck a glance or two at my boobs. "Sure you won't change your mind?"

He groaned. "No, but you're sure a temptation. You look luscious." He shook his head, then opened the door and guided me through it with his hand on my back. Bet that stuck-up MK doesn't do him the way I would've.

I turned and gave him a peck on the cheek. "Any time, Bjorn. Just snap your fingers and I'm yours. Good night, honeybun."

Cripes, that whole deal made me even hornier.

Opening the door to our suite, I headed for the bedroom past Pope asleep on the couch. He looked as innocent as a pink baby in the red neon glow. Ozzie had told me all about Pope. Then I thought, *Hmmm . . . I haven't had a virgin since Billy Bob Conroy, and I did it in his grandma's attic when we were thirteen. I think it's time for Pope to be introduced to the joys of sex. No, maybe I better not . . . oh, what the hell . . . why not?*

I slipped Pope's blanket off to uncover my new target and knelt on the floor beside his couch. I took his little manhood in my hand. It didn't take long before it grew up, with the help of my fondling and stroking from my well-practiced hand, and it grew to a surprising size, I might add.

He moaned a little, but Ozzie's vodka kept him in la-la land. I mounted Pope like hopping on a Schwinn. Not much of a ride from him so I had to do the pedaling, real slow, I didn't want to wake him too soon. It worked for me real quick, maybe 'cause it was so different. I don't remember ever having a go with somebody who was asleep. I was having trouble keeping it slow. I really wanted to cut loose. I pulled my robe open, but left it on my shoulders and arms to keep out the Minnesota chill.

DAVID, A.K.A. POPE

WHY DID I HAVE a headache? My eyes were crusted shut. Something was happening, and it felt good. Oh, my goodness, was I having a wet dream?

I managed to get one eye partially open for a second and saw an angel with pinkish white wings. *Did I die and go to heaven? The dream feels so good . . . heaven.*

Then my body did an involuntary thrust and the angel cried out. I tried to sit up, but the angel pushed me back down and gave me a kiss with her tongue in my mouth.

Oh, my God! I was having sexual intercourse, but not with an angel. It was Angie!

My entire body and mind was in turmoil as I threw her off. She landed on the threadbare carpet with a loud thump and a louder expletive. But then she said, "Oh, Pope, that was great! But darn you, my left bun's gonna be black and blue."

I hoped her loud expletive would not wake Ozzie. If he poked his head out from the bedroom he would see Angie on the floor, spilling out of her open robe next to me, and me, standing like a confused statue, still in an aroused state.

"Your bun will be black and blue?" I exclaimed. "That is nothing! My *soul* has been ripped apart!"

I stumbled to the bathroom, knelt by the stool and did my normal thing when under severe stress. I threw up my egg roll, fried rice, sweet-and-sour pork, and cream sodas. I put my forehead on the cool Kohler rim. I did not remember much of the party. *Why does my mouth feel like a flannel shirt?* Then it dawned on me: someone must have put an alcoholic beverage in my cream sodas. I had promised the lord I would not introduce alcohol to my body. And God help me, I had committed to God and myself that my wife would be the first one. I had sinned. I needed to get to a priest for confession. A heavenly jury will find me guilty, but I remember the wonderful feel of her and how beautiful her breasts were. *At least now I know for sure I'm not homosexual.*

My next thought was about Ozzie. *Ozzie. He brought that she-devil into our midst . . . and I bet he is the one who got me inebriated. Ozzie . . . you . . . you bastard.*

Chapter 14

Two years later, September 1962

KARL

Dumb shit. Incompetent. Idiot. Over my head. Who knew what else they'd say about me. I knew what I'd be thinkin' if I were them, but I had no choice; I had to face 'em. So I called a meeting of the remaining employees for that Monday at nine. Dang it, they're all good folks; they were gettin' to feel like a big family. I've never had a worse weekend, worrying about that meeting on top of everything else.

The time for the meeting came at me like a freight train. Olga was standing by my side even though she had a hard time holding back tears. We were in the shop area. All the machines had been shut down. I tapped a wrench on the bed of a drill press to call the meeting to order. Everybody settled down, but there was tension in their faces. They probably saw the same in mine.

"I . . . I have bad news. There's no way to make this easy for you." I glanced at Olga, and she put her arm around my waist. "You all know we had to lay off seven of your fellow employees over the last few weeks. And now, we are very sorry to have to tell you, we have to close the doors. We've lost everything." I had a hard time looking 'em in the eye.

There was a stunned silence, then an uproar.

"What? How can that be? You're sayin' we ain't got jobs?"

"Jeezus, my wife's havin' a baby next week and now you're tellin' me I don't have work? You gotta be shittin' us!"

The younger workers were beside themselves with self-pity.

Mike, MK's dad, said, "Karl, how did this happen? What're you guys gonna do? Is there anything we can do to help?" His Irish mug was twisted with concern for us.

I said, "Please try to understand. There was a major screw-up and some things that were out of our control. Mike, thanks for worrying 'bout us. We'll survive. We're moving to Olga's sister's basement and Bjorn has taken an apartment above the barber shop. He's going back to work at the lumberyard."

"Where the hell is Bjorn?" a young welder yelled. "Whaddya mean, major screw-up and things outta your control?"

"I'll try to explain. Sears pulled their order for the handyman cabinets. Said an outfit from J.A. Pan & Company can make 'em for a lot less money."

A drill press operator hissed, "Screw the Japs. Let's nuke 'em again."

I ignored the comment. "Also, most of my contacts at Honeywell are gone, and we aren't getting much of that business. Polarcat's snowmobile orders are way down so they've cut back orders with us. Those things and a few other setbacks were out of our control."

"Okay, okay . . . so what was the big screw-up? Quit blaming other shit. You guys run—or should I say, tried to run—this joint."

That was the question I dreaded. "The big screw-up was we didn't apply for patents in time for the farm equipment. We've been served with a cease-and-desist order from the Court of Customs and Patent Appeals. Some bastards swiped our designs for the three-section field cultivator and got the order for us to stop production." I paused and put my hand to my mouth for a second to cover my quivering chin. "We aren't even allowed to sell what we have in inventory."

The younger employees were still murmuring about their disappointment in our management of the company.

"Right now Bjorn's in Chicago at the District Court trying to get the order lifted." I shook my head. "But it doesn't look good. We can't afford a patent attorney, and our case is so weak that no attorney would take it on condition of being paid if we won. There won't be a decision from the court 'til Thursday. But we feel we owe it to you to give as much notice as possible. We borrowed every dime we could for the farm equipment expansion. We have enough of that money left to pay your salaries for the rest of the week. Use that time to search for work." I couldn't talk anymore without breaking down.

Olga said, "The bank is calling our note due. They won't extend. Thank you for all your good work here. We are so sorry to bring you this news." She covered her eyes with her palms.

I added, "Ya, they're takin' everything but our underwear."

BJORN

THIS WASN'T THE FIRST TIME I was up against the big boys. I learned early on that if I had something to help the other side of the table, it didn't make any difference to them how young I was. But this meeting maybe was way out of my league, kinda like me going up against Floyd Paterson or Sonny Liston.

The conference room in the district court looked like a palace, all marble floors and alder-paneled walls. The drapes looked like they should be in a museum. A lot of trees had died just for the top of the conference table, and we weren't even meeting with a regular judge, just a mediator. I didn't need a mirror to check my hair; I just hadda look down at the table top.

"My task is to screen disputes and recommend those of merit to the court and make other bad claims disappear," Mr. Elfering, the distinguished looking but gruff mediator said from the far end of the table. "The court will sign off on my decisions."

My trip to the court in Chicago was going to be determined a success or a flop by Mr. Elfering, not a jury of my country-bumpkin peers.

"I've read the affidavit from the Land Master Equipment Corporation and can find no flaw in their claim," Elfering said. "Mr. Olson, I don't take kindly to someone trying to represent themselves. Your letter outlining your company's claim has no legal basis or case law cited."

Jesus, talk about coming right out with an opinion before I could even tell my story. That pissed me off. I had nothing to lose.

The three Land Master lawyers could hardly contain their glee. The elder lawyer had silver hair that set off his tanned face. The suit he was wearing probably cost more than my pickup. The other two were younger versions of the old guy and looked down their noses at my plaid flannel shirt.

There was a casually dressed fourth person on the Land Master side of the table, but nobody had introduced him. Also present was a bored court reporter. I guess she somehow did her job even though she looked half-asleep.

Elfering asked me, "Just how do you intend to counter the statements in the Land Master affidavit?"

"Well, how about I start with facts and the truth instead of a creative affidavit?" I said, glaring at Land Master's attorneys.

"Okay, keep this civil. And remember, you are under oath. You have ten minutes to rebut the Land Master case," Elfering said.

I slid a three-ring binder over to the silver-haired lawyer and one to Elfering. I was going to act confident even if I wasn't. "Our field tests of our nine-foot-wide field cultivator proved that the equipment worked great. Mr. Schumacher, our designer and tester, was surprised at how little power it took to pull the cultivator. Page three has a picture of our nine-footer."

"Did you apply for a patent on that piece?" Elfering asked.

"No. We felt it didn't have features unique enough to patent. Then Shu—I mean, Mr. Schumacher—watched an episode of *Victory at Sea* and got an idea from seeing the Navy planes with their wings folded on the carrier flight deck. He envisioned attaching nine-footers to each side of the original nine-footer, but with hydraulic lifters to fold them vertically for storage or transporting. Tractors like the IH 1206 could easily pull the twenty-seven footer, drastically cutting down field time. Pictures of the twenty-seven footer with wings up and down are on pages seven and eight."

Elfering asked, "When did you build your first twenty-seven foot piece?"

"Well, we had to contract with a hydraulic engineer to help with the design. We had our first prototype done around August last year."

"Did you apply for a patent then?"

I shook my head. "Not until the following February. We had to work out some kinks in the design. That application is on page twelve. That's when we found out that these bast—that Land Master beat us to the punch."

Elfering grinned. "Well, someone from Land Master must have watched *Victory at Sea* as well."

"No, sir. I think one of their dealers gave them the idea after Shu—Mr. Schumacher—told him about it. He was trying to get orders for future delivery. He shouldn't have done that before we had patent protection."

Elfering leaned his elbows on the polished table. "Your time is up. You have no way of proving that the Land Master Design Center didn't come up with this idea on their own as they claim with extensive back-up material. You didn't protect your idea by getting signed, notarized documents by third parties indicating they affirmed successful function and application of the prototype. I will make my ruling after lunch. We'll meet here again at one-thirty."

Elfering, the recorder and Land Master's three attorneys left the room. I remained seated with my head in my hands, knowing the trip had been a waste.

The guy who had not been introduced said, "Son, get ready for bad news. Elfering's going to put a fork in your claim, and it's going to explode like the *Hindenburg*."

I jumped to my feet, "Oh, yeah? Who are you anyway?"

"Name's Willard Fox. I'm president of Land Master."

I couldn't take any more of Fox's taunting and I was too worried about the ruling, so I stormed out of the room and wandered the marble halls of the courthouse instead of having lunch. Lotta people seemed interested in my plaid flannel shirt.

At one-thirty, the older Land Master attorney, Elfering, the recorder and I returned to the conference table. The old attorney had a smug look on his face. I would've given away my pickup to turn that smug look into a shocked frown.

Elfering stood and looked down at me. "Mr. Olson, I'm not here to judge ideas and creativity or to look out for the little guy. I have to go by the evidence provided. Your claim is denied. The cease-and-desist order remains in force. It is so ordered that Land Maser Equipment Company is awarded the patent. This meeting is adjourned."

Mr. Smug's face turned into a wide smile. I'm a poor loser. I didn't shake the asshole's hand when he offered it or give any reaction. So I froze my sadsack face like a Minnesota lake in January.

The others left the room. Beaten by the system, I stayed in my seat feeling like I had just attended my own funeral. My thoughts were racing. *We had a good run, but now it's over. Man, what coulda been. Gotta figure out how to keep Pa from ending it all. Ma's gotta get another job. Hope MK hangs with me after this mess. Like to kill that Land Master son of a bitch. Good workers, not their fault. Dammit, Shu, you really screwed up.*

Chapter 15

The same day and place

BJORN

Guess the family's goin' back to bein' poor. Gotta call the folks with the bad news. I'd rather cut off my arm. I wiped my flannel sleeve across my cheek and picked up my two binders. Then I left the scene of my defeat and shuffled off to the elevator.

Fox was waiting for me in the sitting area by the elevators. Behind him was a railing guarding the open atrium to the main floor, four stories down. It crossed my mind to jump over the dang thing. "Olson, I hear it didn't go so well for you in there." He nodded to a chair. "Have a seat, please. I'm very busy, but I'd like to talk to you."

I couldn't believe it. "Mr. Fox, you're the last person on earth I want to talk to. You've got a lot of nerve even showing your face." He wasn't a tall guy. The scar on his forehead didn't take away from his self-assured look. Neither did the odd shape of the back of his bald head that I had noticed in the conference room.

"It's your choice, of course. Sorry I rubbed it in back there; I wanted to prepare you for the worst. You don't know it, but choosing whether to talk to me or not could be the biggest decision of your life. Your family's future is on the line. I really think you should sit down. I have a proposal."

"A proposal? To what? Stick it to us again?" I waved the binders in the air.

Fox held his hands up. "Look, I don't blame you for being upset. We've been checking out you and your company. Good vibes. Honeywell and Polarcat think you guys run a great ship and are top-notch people. Please sit down. Maybe we can do some business."

"We don't have a business. Bank's shutting us down because of your company." I had a hard time being even semi-civil to the guy.

"Yes. You owe them three hundred twenty-seven thousand dollars. Our investment banker, Silverman Brothers, is prepared to buy the note from your bank and extend more credit at better terms if we can work out a deal."

"You know how much we owe? Do you hire spies?"

"Never mind. I told you, we've been checking you out. By the way, even though he has no choice in not renewing your note, your banker thinks you and your folks are salt of the earth. Now please sit down."

Begrudgingly I sat, but on the edge of the chair so I could take off quick if Fox pulled a rat instead of a rabbit out of his hat. "What's your proposal?"

"Within ten years, Land Master Equipment Corporation will be the largest name in farm and ranch machinery, turf-management equipment, and household lawn care in the country. Our equipment with the bulging bicep Land Master logo will be recognized everywhere."

"How could you possibly know that?"

"Because, Olson, great marketing, strong financial backing, a coming ag revolution and leading-edge quality equipment will get us there." He ticked off each point on his fingers. "But we can't make everything we sell. We need small manufacturers to make a lot of the equipment, paint it our ripe wheat color, slap on our logo and deliver quality products on time to our distribution centers. You can be part of all this if you wish."

"You sound awfully sure of yourself. I'd like to believe you, but why should I?"

Fox ignored that. "We're going to change farmers' and ranchers' perceptions of where to buy equipment by spending fortunes on advertising, huge dealerships, and sophisticated branding. Wall Street is betting on us. You and that Johnny Appleseed of yours couldn't do that even if you had gotten the patent."

I sensed a trap. "So first you steal our idea, then we become dependent on your company and next you squeeze us on pricing and threaten to move our production to another company. No thanks. I can only take the agony of going broke once."

"Your cynicism is misplaced. I'll ignore it for now because it doesn't jibe with your reputation. And just so you know, we didn't steal anything, which I'll prove to you if you give me a chance."

I studied my scuffed boots and shook my head. How could I believe this guy?

"Look, at least hear us out. Like I said, your family's future is at stake. Our corporate headquarters is only five blocks from here." He handed me his card and one other.

"John Philp is vice-president of our off-site manufacturing. He's going to keep tomorrow morning open to meet with you. Call him and set up an appointment. You owe it to your family. Oh, and he'll also take you to our R & D Center to show you products in the pipeline, and he'll prove to you that we didn't steal your buddy's idea. You should have taken us up on that offer two months ago. It would have saved me a hell of a lot of attorney fees and you a lot of agony."

I began to doubt our strategy on contesting the patent. Shu was sure we'd been screwed by the big guys, and I have to admit, so was I.

"We've checked out you and your company. I hate the thought of good folks like you going out of business. Now it's your turn to check us out. We're thinking this could be a long-term relationship, but if there isn't trust on both sides, it's no use starting to dance together."

***

I CLUTCHED THE PHONE at the Land Master office late in the afternoon of the next day. "Hello, Ma?"

"Ya, Bjorn? We've been so worried about you."

"I'm okay. Don't get off the phone, but is Pa there and can you get him on another extension?"

"Just a minute, he's out in the shop shutting things down."

As I waited I wished I could've been in the same room with the folks to give 'em the news.

"Okay, son, I'm here. You back in Minneapolis? We thought you'd be home by now."

"No, Pa, I'm still in Chicago. I won't be home 'til day after tomorrow or maybe even the next day. I'll let you know when I'll be back. I have to stay for more meetings."

"How'd it go at that court deal?" he asked, but he sounded like he didn't want to hear the answer.

"Never mind that. Too long a story to tell now, but Shirley from the bank will be over in a little while to give you back the keys to the house and plant. Everything's gonna be all right. You don't have to move to Ma's sister's."

Ma said, "Bjorn, I'm not sure I heard you right. What's Shirley gonna do?"

I said louder, "No moving. Shirley's gonna bring the keys back."

One of the phones dropped.

"I need you both near the phone tomorrow morning. We have some big decisions to make. I can't go into it right now. I have to meet with somebody and I'm already late."

Pa said, "I don't know what you did down there, but we sure as hell will be sittin' by the phone . . .ach, Olga, leave me be; you darn near knocked me over. Son, are we gonna be all right with the business?" His voice was breaking.

"Ya, Pa, I'm pretty sure. Looks like we'll be doing a lot of business with Land Master. I'm gonna call Wilfie at the lumber yard to tell 'im I'm not coming back to pile two-by-eights for 'im."

Chapter 16

November 1962, two months later

DAVID, A.K.A. POPE

I missed my buddies back home.

No one at NSA called me Pope; it was always David or Mr. Grimm. I had no close friends. The two other fellows I worked with, Sam and Herb, were somewhat like me—quite intelligent—but despite our similarities they were from different worlds, and those worlds did not mesh socially with mine. San Francisco and New York are a long way from New Germany, Minnesota. They did seem to get along with each other, so maybe it is just because I am who I am.

We lived together in a Fort Meade bachelor officer's quarters and worked on the same super computer, but we were seldom together as a threesome. Each of us was rotated separately every three months to Germany to live in a tiny, sparsely furnished NSA apartment in Frankfurt or a two-star hotel in Berlin. The trips were not by glamorous commercial air, but were on uncomfortable military or other government flights to Rhein-Main Air Force Base in Wiesbaden.

Whether in Germany or Fort Meade, the tight-lipped NSA people ignored the three of us except when a computer glitch needed fixing.

My lonely times in Germany were filled with work or going to pray at the Frankfurt Cathedral, which was a short streetcar ride from the apartment. The cathedral had been spared by U.S. and English air forces, as had the I.G. Farben building where the NSA office was located. Eisenhower wanted that building for his occupation force's headquarters. Farben was the chemical company that supplied the killer gas to concentration camps.

I still spent part of my cathedral time asking forgiveness for my sins at the reunion. Angie and Ozzie still haunted my thoughts. To me, nothing was more intimidating than my conscience.

I missed my family.

It was Thanksgiving Day in the States, and I went to the cathedral to give thanks. I struggled for a bit while formulating my thank-you list.

After choosing the pew four rows from the front and to the left of the main aisle, I knelt to pray. I chose that location for a reason. When finished with my prayers I got off the kneeler and slid back onto the pew.

One of my prayers was answered when I was tapped on the shoulder by the girl who always sat in the fifth-row pew on the left side of the aisle. I had noticed her off and on for over a year at the cathedral. I knew she also had noticed me as our eyes had met from time to time, but I did not know how to approach her.

The fifth-row girl spoke softly and in a surprising English accent, "Excuse my intrusion. I've seen you here often and you always look sad. You don't wear German clothes. Are you an American G.I.?"

I turned to face her. There were few people in the church, so we could have a quiet conversation. "Oh, hello. No need to excuse you. I am very glad you got my attention. I have wanted to meet you, but did not have the courage. Besides, I was finished with my prayers."

Her smile warmed my lonely heart. Her eyes showed sadness and she was wearing no make-up. She was wearing rimless glasses, had a turned-up nose and thin lips with no lipstick. Her scarf hid her hair, but I knew from seeing her in the past it was long and brown and she sometimes wore it in a bun. Her dark dress was covered by a long coat to keep out the November chill. Her shoes were sensible, no high heels. I had seen her here in warmer weather without a coat and could tell she had a nice figure, but she did not flaunt it.

"And, no, I am not a G.I., but am here every three months to do some work at the Farben building. I was born in the state of Minnesota in the U.S. I am surprised by your English accent. I assumed you were German."

"My mother is German, but my father is from London. They own a bakery a few blocks from here. I also work there."

I did not want to scare her off, but I was lonely and could sense she was also, so I took a chance. "Would you care to join me for a cup of coffee? I would enjoy some company."

"I'd like that," she said and held out her hand. "My name is Ursula. What's yours?"

"David, but I would like to ask you a favor. It might sound stupid or sacrilegious. My friends back home in Minnesota call me . . . Pope. It would make me very happy if you would do the same."

She pulled back a bit. I was afraid the Pope name shocked her. But, I guess my sincerity and her seeing me frequently at the Cathedral over-ruled her caution. "Okay, Pope, let's see if we can brighten each other's day with a little coffee and conversation. You can tell me about Minnesota. I'm sure I would love it there." She grinned. "And that name will take some explaining."

It was too raw to sit at the outside tables of the coffee shop so we went inside, which was overly warm because the sun was streaming in through the windows. Ursula turned to me. "Why don't we go to my parent's bakery? We could have coffee and a sweet there. I'm pretty sure it would be okay."

"It is very nice of you to invite me. Thank you." It seemed odd that she would say she was pretty sure it would be okay.

We entered her parent's *Zentrum Bakerie* and the woman behind the counter put her hand to her mouth and stared at me. She seemed shocked. "Ursula, who is this?"

"Hello, Mama. I would like you to meet Po—David. We've seen each other at the cathedral

Her mother seemed to recover. "Velcome, David. Glad to haff you here." She still looked gruff, but sounded friendly enough. "Let me get the coffee for you two . . . alzo zom cakes."

I said, "Thank you, and glad to meet you, Mrs . . . ah . . ." I realized I did not know their last name. "It was kind of Ursula to invite me."

The bakery had five small tables for customers and a long glass case full of wonderful looking baked goods. A pile of hard rolls was pyramided at the right end of the case, close to the cash register. Ursula said, "Those are our best sellers. I'll give you some to take home."

Fruit-topped cakes and pastries filled with custard, chocolate or fruit lined the rest of the case. I loved the smell of the place, and the sight of the baked goods made my mouth water.

Ursula's mother brought coffee and cake from the back room. She showed a faint smile. The rest of her face betrayed her tension. I soon understood why.

Ursula's father burst into the room from the back. His white baker's hat was askew and his right cheek was streaked with flour that accented his florid complexion. His nostrils were flared, his fists were clenched and his eyes drilled into me. Through clenched teeth, he said, "Ursula, who is this man? Why are you bringing strangers into our place? I thought you said you were going to that damn church, not to some bar to pick up a good-for-nothing looking for a hand-out."

"Papa, please. David is not a stranger. We have seen each other at the cathedral often, and that is where we met. He is a very nice man."

I was dumb-founded and speechless. What had I gotten myself into?

Ursula's father spun on his heel and stomped back to the ovens without saying another word. He did not have to say anything else. His message to me was loud and clear.

Ursula's mother put her hand on my shoulder. "Don't mind him. He is very protective of our little girl. You are the first boy she has brought home."

Well, that was easy for her to say, but it took me a while to get comfortable after the father's outburst. First boy? That was encouraging. Now I knew Ursula was not a tramp like Angie.

We drank strong coffee softened with cream and ate delectable cherry-covered Black Forest cake. Our chatter started in earnest, and we seemed to be getting along fine.

I said, "I will be leaving Germany in three days and will not be back until February. Could I call on you tomorrow?"

I thought I saw a flash of anger from her when I said I would be gone, but she collected herself and said, "Oh, by all means. The next day too?" She quickly put her hand to her mouth, probably because she realized she might be sounding too forward.

"Of course," I said. "I wish I did not have to go back to work now, so we could spend this day together also." I had one eye on the oven room door and was hoping her father did not hear us.

"I would have loved that, but I also have to work today. Father is counting on me," she said as she put her hand on my wrist.

Maybe I have found a companion.

OZZIE

A LETTER CAME from the Twins a month after our minor league season ended. I got kinda shook up when I saw it. Was it a notice to release me or . . . ?

My hands shook when I opened it.

It said I was invited to the major league spring training camp in Fort Meyers, Florida. *Holy shit!* I ran around my apartment, pumping my fists in the air like some lunatic.

I couldn't wait to tell Ma and the guys back home. Angie would be hot to trot after this news. I was getting a chance to make it to the majors. Then it hit me that my old man wasn't on the list of people I wanted to tell. Screw 'im. He'd deserted Ma.

The letter also said a team doctor would be in Charlotte in two days to give me and three other guys on the minor team roster a physical exam. Those guys were assholes. I hoped they'd flunk the exam.

My sphincter was puckered up for those two days of waiting for the physical. I showed up at the clinic where the letter said to be at two o'clock and asked the receptionist where the Twins' doctor was.

"Go down that hall and turn left at the end. Doctor Hoppe is in room seven," she said.

She was a cutie. "Not sure I know my left from my right. Maybe you could take me by the hand and show me where to go?"

She nodded knowingly. "Oh, one of those. Go now or I'll tell you where else you can go."

Bitch. I went down the hall and found room number seven.

The doc grinned. "Hello, Mr. Johnson. I'm Doc Hoppe with the Twins."

"Hi. I'm Ozzie. Nice to meet ya. What do we do first?" I asked, trying to be cool.

He said with a chuckle, "Well, let's get familiar right away. Get naked."

I said, "You sound like my girlfriend."

"Sounds like the right kind of gal." Guess he'd been doing this stuff a long time. Seemed like an okay guy.

Doc pressed, pulled, pinched and measured my various body parts. "Did you realize your throwing arm is an inch and a half longer than the other one?"

"Really? No, I didn't know." Then he worked his way down to my balls. Figured I'd haft'a cough next.

"Son, have you noticed a problem while urinating?"

"Well, ya . . . just yesterday. Maybe a little ache."

He felt around my privates. "Seems your testicles are a bit swollen. Do they hurt?"

"Once in a while. Only lately though." I was beginning to sweat. What the hell was he finding down there?

The doc pulled down on my love tool and greenish pus came out. "Umm . . . ah . . . son, I hate to tell you this, but it appears that you have Chlamydia, or maybe syphilis or both. You need to be more careful with whom you associate."

Jeezus, musta got that crap from that whore in Georgia. I'd better tell Angie to get checked out. She's really gonna be pissed.

"Oh, man. Can you give me somethin' to get rid of that stuff? You don't have to tell the Twins, do you?" I was shook up. God dammit, was that piece of tail in Atlanta gonna keep me out of the majors?

"Don't worry. I'll fix you up with the right prescriptions, but I'm going to have to put this information in your file. It won't affect whether you make the team or not. That'll be determined by the speed of your fast ball and how much your slider breaks. Also your control." He peered over his glasses, "But not your sex life."

Chapter 17

February 1963, three months later

DAVID, A.K.A. POPE

Herb, would you come with me tomorrow to pick up Sam at the base? He is coming in from Wiesbaden. Then you could bring him back here. I am going to stay and catch the next flight back to Germany."

"Oh, Pope, jeeze, it's my day off. I've got plans."

"Please? It is the only time the three of us will be together for a while, and I have an idea to bounce off you guys." I was excited. I felt I had an idea that would set up a bright future for us.

Adding to my excitement was the fact Ursula had written to say her mother agreed to allow her go to Berlin with me for a week if we had two separate hotel rooms. Her mother also had agreed not to tell Ursula's father about the trip until our departure day.

Herb said, "What the hell? Can't you tell me now? Waiting around the air base is about as appealing to me as getting jock itch. I spend too damn much time there as it is." He was a frequent traveler in and out of Andrews and not known for his patience.

"No, the two of you have to hear me out at the same time. You will see why. We need to leave here by noon."

"Okay, but this better be worth it or you'll owe me one big kosher meal from that Catholic billfold of yours."

***

WE DID NOT SAY MUCH on the way to the air base the next day as Herb nodded off shortly after we got in the car. I drove with a smile on my face, thinking of being alone with Ursula in Berlin.

Sam's flight was on time, and I led him back to the servicemen's lounge where Herb was waiting in a corner booth. Sam's black, curly hair was more tousled than normal, and he was suffering from jet lag. He looked like he had tried to sleep inside a clothes dryer.

Herb, with his cool Californian look, had Cokes ready for us. I sat opposite them in the booth.

After some small talk about our jobs, which were ending in a few months, and Herb grousing about having to come along because of my prodding, I pulled two thick manila folders from my canvas briefcase. "I am glad we could get together before my flight. My mind has been stirring around an idea I need to talk to you fellows about."

Herb shrugged his shoulders and Sam studied the ceiling for a moment, then said, "Okay, so what's the idea?"

"Well, it is about something we maybe could do for a career . . . a business to go into together. I do not have it all worked out. These folders just contain a lot of questions and loose ideas."

"We? *We?* A *business?* That's what this is about? You gotta be kidding!" Sam talked as much with his hands as his mouth, which was his custom.

Herb said, "Just great. You dragged me out here for some baloney like this?"

"Please hear me out." I leaned closer so no one else could hear me. "At Meade, you both know that it is not just NSA that uses the computer: the FBI, Army Intelligence, Naval Intelligence, and others use it also.

"In Frankfurt more than NSA uses the equipment too: the CIA, Army G2, and even the West German intelligence guys have used it."

"Okay, I'll bite. So what?" Sam asked.

"I know the Meade computer cost Uncle Sam more than one and a quarter-million dollars, and the Frankfurt equipment is probably in the eight-hundred-thousand-dollar range. At those costs, not a lot of civilian companies can afford to have equipment like that even though they would like to use powerful computers."

"Well, no kiddin'. So I say again, so what?" Sam said. I cautioned him to keep his voice and hands down.

I continued to the heart of my idea. "Computing Data has other powerful but less expensive models still too spendy for most companies to own. With our experience and connections—mine with Computing Data; Sam, you with your dad being an investment banker; and Herb, your mother being a V.P. with Wells Fargo—maybe we could form a company and get our hands on three of those computers from Computing Data."

They stared at me like students listening to a lecture way over their heads.

I kept talking, nodding first to Herb and then to Sam. "One for you in San Francisco, one for you in New York and one for me in Minneapolis."

"You've lost your mind," Herb said. "How the hell could we afford to buy them, and if we could, what the hell would we do with 'em?"

I said, "We are not going to buy them. We will try to lease them from Computing Data. Or, if they want, from a company your fathers might form. That same company could also lease Computing Data's computers to franchisees we set up in other major markets. Then we will go into the computer timesharing business just like NSA does."

"Selling time? I never heard of such a thing," Herb said.

I pointed at him. "Remember, those civilian companies want what these computers can do, but they cannot afford one. In effect, we give them what the computer can do but they only rent part of one. There are more details in these folders." I thought I had them hooked. I was not going to say any more until they reacted.

A pregnant silence followed. Sam and Herb stared at me with their mouths partly open. Then they leaned forward in tandem.

"You're *serious?*" Sam said. "Sounds like something young guys like us couldn't do. Besides, I've never heard of such a thing. You don't expect us to make a decision about this before you hop on the goddamned plane, do you?"

"Goodness no. I just want you to think seriously about it. I would like to know if it sounds at all interesting to you before I take off. I have a buddy back in Minnesota, the same age I am, who started a company a few years ago with his dad. Their company is doing great. Good ideas and brains are not exclusively the property of people older than us. Besides, the computer business is a young man's game. Back when I was interning at Computing Data the only middle-aged and older guys employed there were in administration."

"There're only about a hundred questions floating through my brain," Herb said. "What you're proposing is a complicated deal."

"Yes, that is true," I said. "As I mentioned, these folders will create more questions than answers. While I am in Germany and if you guys think this holds some interest for you, you need to do some research and come up with more answers. We need to develope a bullet-proof business plan to convince others this idea will work. Think about it, guys. Do you want to create your own destiny or work for someone else?"

"Hell, it's not as cut and dried as that," Herb said. "You gotta live in the real world and not in some pipe dream. I have to admit though, for a fly-over land guy you might have a hell of an idea to massage."

I said, "There is a world full of people out there who think the reason there is a sun is so it can create shadows. We have to believe the sun is there to grow things. And we have to find others who think the same way. And about us being young—what have we got to lose? We have nothing, so that is what we have to lose."

I was not going to beg for their participation. I had to get to the gate for my flight soon. If I had not convinced them at this point, maybe my idea was too much of a reach.

"I've got to go take a leak," Sam said. "Herb, why don't you come with me?"

So that was it. They needed to talk it over, just the two of them. The fate of my idea would be decided at a urinal.

I could not try to get my idea off the ground by myself. I needed the two of them and their connections, especially Sam's investment-banker father. I was about to give up on them returning from the restroom when they appeared.

"Here's the deal," Herb said. "We are forty-five percent sold on your idea. While you're in Germany we agree to work on the details of the business plan and talk to our folks about the possibilities. Oh, and thank you for thinking of including us in your plan." He patted me on the back.

Sam reached across to shake my hand. "Pope, you just might be a fly-over-land genius."

Chapter 18

One day later

DAVID, A.K.A. POPE

A milestone—finally, my last flight eastbound for NSA. After landing I had to get squared away with the Frankfurt office on some details, shape up the apartment and do some shopping before picking up Ursula the next day for our trip to Berlin.

I was anxious to see her. The bell tinkled like a sick telephone when I opened the bakery door. The smells again tried to seduce me, but Adam Zeller, Ursula's father, was ready for me, pressing down on the cash register counter with his fists. His eyes, more red than white, glared at me. "Mr. Grimm, or should I say *Pope*? Who the hell gave you that name anyway?"

"Oh, some friends back in—"

"I don't know why in the bloody hell my wife is letting Ursula to go to Berlin with you. It's like they plotted against me. They didn't even tell me 'til this morning. Just remember this, bub, when she returns I'll be able to tell if you laid a hand on her. She doesn't lie to me. If I sense something happened 'cause of your pecker, I'll pound your arse into the ground. You better be like the real Pope and keep your trouser mouse in your pants."

I stood my ground, as I had determined ahead of time not to be afraid of him. "Sir, I can assure you that I have only the most honorable intentions regarding your daughter. We have developed a fondness for each other through the mail after our first meeting at the cathedral. I will only be in this country three more months, and we want to spend quality, wholesome time together. Please trust me. Trust us."

"All right, but I'm warning you. No funny business or there will be hell to pay." He passed the edge of his open hand across his throat, I guess to indicate he would pass a baker's knife across mine if he believed Ursula and I had sexual intercourse. Of course, I would not do that unless we were married.

Ursula and her mother came down the stairs from the apartment. She was carrying a small cardboard suitcase and wearing sensible shoes. Her hair was not in a bun. Instead it caressed her shoulders. She took a quick glance toward her father and then smiled at me. My heart melted.

Of course we had not known each other long, especially with my going back to the States shortly after meeting her, but we had corresponded while I was gone, and I could tell from her letters we would get along wonderfully. I was anxious to have a female companion in my life, never having had a girlfriend before.

Her mother smiled at me also. It seemed she was happy to have her daughter accompany me to Berlin in spite of her husband's virulent disapproval. She did not look at her husband. I wondered why.

"Papa, don't worry. You know I'll be a good girl," Ursula said while looking at me, not her father. "And Mama, thank you for being so understanding," she said as she hugged her mother. Then she turned to me and took my arm. "David, let's go." She hurried me to the door as though she were escaping.

**

WE LEFT HER FATHER'S glare to catch the noon military-duty train from the mammoth Frankfurt station. From the station's mezzanine we looked down at the dozen or so idling train engines that exhaled steam and exhaust while inhaling people and baggage. The place seemed alive. Our combined sensations added to the electric excitement.

When we settled into our seats, Ursula said, "This is the first time I've spent more than one day away from my parents. I'm just tingling. This is thrilling."

I hoped it was not just being away from her parents that made her tingle. "For me, sitting here holding hands with you and going away for a whole week together is a dream come true." I tingled in my private place but kept that feeling at bay.

**

IT TOOK OVER AN HOUR before we came to the border. There were watch towers, fences topped with concertina wire and a no-man's land patrolled by rifle toting soldiers and their dogs.

The French, English and U.S. sectors of Berlin were an island surrounded by East Germany. The duty train was sealed; no one could get on or off during the trip though that Communist state.

After we crossed the border, Ursula could not stop talking about what she saw. "I can't believe this is Germany. It looks like a third-world country:

run-down buildings, horses instead of tractors, unrepaired war damage. And the people, dressed in drab clothes staring at us with blank, sad faces."

"I know. And hardly a car in sight," I said. "Here, everyone is equal, but they've been reduced to the lowest common denominator." Where there was snow, it was tinged with coal soot and looked like it needed vacuuming.

By five o'clock our train entered the U.S. sector of Berlin. It was a startling, different world from what we had just passed through, bustling with commerce, cars everywhere, neon signs and wonderful buildings surrounding well-dressed, seemingly happy people. West Berlin was a bright spot in a land that otherwise obliterated brightness.

The repair of architectural wounds of war there were well under way; many buildings bristled with construction equipment and had scaffolding clinging to their sides.

"Now, remember, Ursula, I warned you about the two-star hotel where they put me up, but it is clean. And we will not be spending much time there anyway because there is so much I want to show you. I do not have to spend much time at work—only eight to ten in the mornings and then call in frequently to see if I am needed."

She stomped her foot. "Well, I certainly hope your job won't interfere with my having a good experience here." I was certain her pouting was because she was tired from the long travel day.

The hotel was bare-bones basic. U.S. taxpayers would approve of my sparse lodging, but it was well located near museums, restaurants, government buildings, and where I worked. After we checked in, we agreed to meet in the lobby an hour later.

I have to admit, I did have thoughts of a sexual nature about Ursula during the train ride and as we were alone in the same hotel, even if we were in separate rooms. But for moral and religious reasons, I did not intend to act on those urges. I was not sure what Ursula's intentions were along those lines. We did not talk about such things.

At dinner that evening I shared some thoughts about Berlin. "You will notice the pace here is frenzied. People live for today, knowing that tomorrow they might be over-run by the Communists. Oh, and please do not be offended by some of the things you might see. Pornography is everywhere. In the evening, many women wear revealing clothing, and drinking alcohol as a way of life. The sex trade thrives, and I do not mean just boy/girl encounters." I shook my head.

"Pope, I've heard about that stuff, okay? I know how the world turns. Just show me around." She looked at some of the art work on the walls instead of me.

"Well . . . ah, yes. After dinner I will take you to Check Point Charlie and the building in which I work. I am glad you brought a heavy coat. It may get quite cold." I put my arm around her shoulders and squeezed her a little. She did not lean my way, but she did not pull away.

I asked, "Was your *schnitzel* tasty?"

"It was fine. Now, let's go." She did not ask how my *sauerbraten* was.

On the way to the check point we dodged a few inebriated people and aggressive prostitutes. We turned a corner, and the wall dividing East from West Berlin came into view. Ursula stopped and put a hand to her mouth. "Oh, no. It's higher and uglier than I pictured."

I let the view of the wall, the guards, the barbed wire, the spot lights and all the rest of the sorry scene sink into her memory. "Yes, and to our right is the building where I work—the one with all the scaffolding." I did not know it at the time, but that scaffolding was really an elaborate hoax. Its real function was to mask an antenna that intercepted electronic signals from the east.

The week roared by with me playing tour guide, and for the most part, Ursula seemed comfortable with our relationship. She hinted about how she would like to go back to the States with me.

Berlin's museums, parks and historical buildings kept us busy. On only two days did I have to go back to the office for short periods in the afternoon. Ursula accepted it easily the first time, but she seemed quite put-out the second. There were a few other flashes of impatience from her, but that was to be expected because of my amateur guide status.

On the last evening, I took her to my favorite Berlin restaurant to a table I had reserved overlooking Gendarmenmarkt Square and its imposing classical buildings. I wanted our last night in Berlin to be at a special place. This was my last trip to Germany for NSA and if I was going to go through with my plan, even though we had not known each other long, this was the time and place for it.

After dinner we walked out on the square. I nodded toward a bench. "Darling, let us sit over there for a moment and get organized."

"Organized? What the—I mean, what are you talking about?" She seemed upset about something. I would not pretend to understand the female mind as I had not spent much time around them. I guided her over to sit on a bench. Other people were nearby, which made me even more nervous, but I wanted to go ahead with my plan.

"I am not going to be your tour guide right now." I knelt down and took her hands in mine. I had memorized a little poem I had written for the occasion, but when the time came, it escaped me. "My darling Ursula, it has been wonderful spending a whole week with you. I believe we make a fine couple. I love you. I hope you love me. Will you be my bride?"

She looked pleased. After all, she had hinted how wonderful it would be to go back to the States with me. Still, it took a while for her to respond. Finally, she bent down to hug me. "Of course, David! Yes, I will."

I slid the engagement ring on her finger. She held it up to the light.

We suddenly felt conspicuous as the other people nearby cheered and applauded us.

"Ursula, I want to assure you that when I make a commitment, as I am now to you, I hold that as a sacred trust I must carry through. With that ring I commit myself completely to you."

She smiled and nodded.

We went to another restaurant complete with a polka band and dancers with traditional Bavarian dresses and *lederhosen* for a celebratory coffee before we returned to our hotel. We had decided over coffee we would get married in a month or two, as soon as we could make the arrangements and wade through the red tape, our parent's questions, and getting their approval. We agreed, especially because of her father, that if our parents' approval was not forthcoming, we were old enough to make our own decisions.

I walked Ursula to her room and kissed her goodnight. She seemed more responsive than in the past. "David, leave your door unlocked. I want to bring you a surprise."

A half-hour after the good night kiss, she opened the door to my sparsely furnished room. She was wearing her coat and the same sensible shoes.

"Here I am, Pope. Please go to the other end of the room. I want to show you some things."

I did as she asked, but in that small room I was not far from her.

She sounded different, almost like she had a smoker's voice. Her eyelids were at half-mast and she kept licking her lips. I felt uncertain and uncomfortable, wondering what she had brought me.

"Please stay there," she said as she slowly removed the coat from her naked body and draped it over the end of the single bed. Her eyes were cast down at the floor and she held out her hands, palms facing me, to indicate I should stay at the other end of the room.

Then she cupped her breasts and gently fondled those beautiful orbs. "These are for you after our wedding. I swear, no *boy* has ever touched them."

My eyes could not leave her and my mouth went dry. My inclination was to tell her to put her coat back on because I was afraid this would lead to the most intimate of acts. But I could not speak. I was aroused.

She reached her right hand down between her legs and stroked herself. She moaned and said, "This is for you after our marriage. I swear, no *boy* has ever entered me."

I stared at her and was indeed surprised and speechless by her bold display. Nothing, not even her unshaved legs, could detract from my desire for her.

She put her coat on in what seemed like slow motion, then turned toward the door, but as she left, she turned back to me and said, "Pope, I *do* know what men want."

I sat on the edge of the bed with my head in my hands. Guilt crushed me like a ten-ton boulder. I should not have watched her caress her body, and unlike her, I could not tell Ursula I had saved myself for her.

Chapter 19

Still February 1963

SHU

Dust and snow, kicked up by the smelly livestock truck, billowed like a storm cloud when the dirty red livestock truck rumbled out of Dad's farm yard.

Good riddance.

Dad was standing next to me as the truck carried away the last of his Holstein cows. Cows who had been his companions morning and night, days after weeks after months after years. Bessie and her sisters had been a huge part of his small world. He didn't seem ashamed of his tears. "Mein Gott, Shu, I'm getting too olt to argue anymore. No more veekly milk checks. You better know vhat you're doing."

The ladies, Ma, Trudy, and Gretta, had stayed in the farmhouse and pulled back the lace curtains to witness history being made. They knew emotions were raw between Dad and me; they chose to be distant spectators.

I put my arm around Dad's shoulder. He shrugged me off and stalked away. *How the hell could Dad become so attached to some dumb cows?*

Schumacher Farms, Inc., and Cargill had struck a deal. Now that we had our debt picture under control because of the sale of the new pond lots, Cargill felt comfortable financing the conversion of our farms to raising turkeys. We ended up with about the same amount of debt as before the lot sales, but the terms were below market rate, and they offered all the technical help we needed to get into the turkey business.

Pa went, or should I say I dragged him, to the last three of five meetings with the Cargill reps.

Cargill had opened a turkey processing plant in Mankato and needed a steady flow of birds from area farmers. They weren't just interested in supplying Thanksgiving dinners. Their R&D and marketing people had more than that in mind. I was sure it was a win-win proposition, plus we would no longer have to get up at 5:00 a.m. to pull teats.

Just as the livestock truck disappeared over the hill, Bjorn and MK pulled up. We had invited them for a tour of our new gobbler house and a symbolic turkey dinner. I thought this would also be a good time to clear the air with him about the Land Master patent fiasco and assure him we were okay with how the deal ended up.

Trudy came out of the folk's house to greet them and join the tour. "Hi, you two. Great t'see ya."

I said, "MK, I'm amazed you're still putting up with this tow head. Isn't he ever going to have the cojones to pop the question again?" They were a good lookin' couple, she with the best of the Irish genes and him with the hardy Swede look.

"Cut the b.s.," Bjorn said as he hugged Trudy and punched me in the shoulder. "Show us your new toys and road to riches. Then let's see if Trudy still has that magic touch in the kitchen. Last time I ate here started one hell of a ride. Her gourmet cooking weakened my good judgment."

I hoped Bjorn was joking about weakening his good judgment. The patent court deal in Chicago was a little over a year ago.

I could tell he wanted to steer away from marriage talk. MK had told Trudy on the phone she wanted to get her master's degree before getting married, plus she felt Bjorn needed to concentrate on getting his company back on track after the near shutdown. Evidently agreement was not mutual. Bjorn wasn't happy about it.

MK said, "It's so good to see you guys and to be out in the country. School and the big city are getting to me."

"Well, your choice," Bjorn said, without a smile.

"Okay, follow us over to our place and we'll show you gobbler city," I said. "Then we'll go see if I still have that magic bartender touch before we tackle Trudy's turkey dinner."

We pulled over to the old Schulz place and stopped where I had plowed a path. The walk would be easy. The ground was frozen but the sun was shining and the temp was a pleasant twenty-five or so.

We walked past the sagging, faded dairy barn and past our machine shed, now stocked with wheat colored equipment with the Land Master bulging bicep logos.

Bjorn and Trudy stopped in their tracks when they passed the machine shed and saw the shiny, red fifty-by-100-foot pole building. "Bjorn, remember when you showed us your company's first shop? Your dad had to explain why it said Olson and Dad, Inc."

"I remember. Now explain this sign," Bjorn said.

"Well, Schumacher Farms, Inc., means we are one of those bad-assed corporate farms the folks back east bitch about. We're still a family farm, but now big enough to give us more than a subsistence living. See where it says Poult Bldg #1? Well, we hope to have buildings numbered two, three, and four in the future. Poults are baby turkeys like we'll get from Swift and Company in Marshall next week. Five thousand broad-breasted whites."

"Dang. If you had four buildings that'd be twenty thousand birds. Sure you're not bitin' off too much turkey meat?"

"Nope," Trudy said. "The Cargill reps say it's possible with all the land we'll be cropping. My folks are selling us their farm. It was gonna be mine anyway, so they're giving us a great price and terms. Dad'll work for us for a few years and they can stay in the house free as long as they want."

Bjorn said, "Trudy, it sounds like you're all for this deal."

"Sure am. Shu and I are pulling the same wagon."

"Good. But Shu, how's your old man doing with all this?" Bjorn asked.

"Oh . . . well, things are kinda tense right now. You just missed the last of his pet cows leaving; they won't be sucking up our time anymore. He's probably having second thoughts after seeing 'em loaded into the truck." I nodded toward the machine shed. "With the new minimum-till equipment, we'll have time to tend to the gobblers, raise their food and still have some crops to sell for cash."

MK was wearing a frown during most of the conversation. Finally she said, "You mean you're going to have five thousand turkeys in this building? They're really going to be crowded. What an existence."

Trudy said, "We have to take good care of 'em. They're gonna be our bread and butter."

"When we get them they're tiny," I said. "You could hold three of 'em in one hand. I'd like to think they'll be cozy, not crowded. We'll keep 'em inside for eight weeks. After that they can graze free range from May 'til we ship the hens out next August and the toms in September. We'll hire Bjorn to come and figure out which ones are hens or toms."

"Oh, sure. You know I'd love to help, but I think I'm busy that day."

"When the next batch comes in we'll only get twenty-five hundred 'cause they have to spend all their time in the building 'cause of the winter weather," Trudy said. "But a benefit will be when Bjorn comes to figure out the boys from the girls, he won't have to chase 'em all over the grazing field."

MK smiled. "He'll probably be busy that day too. Thanks for explaining the numbers. It makes me feel better about how they'll be kept. I hope you have great luck with the gobblers."

Bjorn patted me on the back. "Enough talking turkey out here. Let's continue when closer to the bar,"

Back in our old farm house I served drinks while Trudy set out slices of sharp cheddar cheese with crackers and mixed nuts. Ellie was away entertaining Grandma Gretta.

"This kitchen with its slanted linoleum floor and old appliances won't stop my bride from turning out good grub," I said.

Bjorn said, "Floor might be slanted and the stove old, but at least you're livin' together." He was talking to me, but glanced at MK.

I didn't want to comment on that so I clinked Bjorn's glass with mine. "I hear Ozzie's been invited to the big league camp. Read it in the *Waconia Patriot*."

"Ya, he called me after he got the word. He was all upset about his old man leaving his ma high and dry. Wanted me to go check on her. I think she'll be fine. Hell, she's better off without that s.o.b. She's moving to Alaska to work for her CPA brother."

"Sounds good. Hear anything from Pope? I haven't."

"He called before he left for Germany again, his last trip, I guess," Bjorn said. "I told him about Ozzie going to the Twins' camp, and there was dead silence. I asked him if he heard me. Then he said he didn't want to talk about Ozzie. He was still pissed about Ozzie spikin' his soda pop at the reunion."

"I'll bet he didn't say 'pissed' though," Trudy said.

"No he didn't. But, then he said something else happened at the reunion that he blamed on Ozzie. He wouldn't tell me what it was though. I've never heard him so upset. I guess our quartet of buddies just got cut down to a trio."

"Oh, he'll cool off after some time goes by. Wonder what the other problem was? Speaking of buddies, Bjorn, I need to talk about the elephant in the middle of the room. I need to make sure we're all square in your mind. I don't want any hard feelings between us."

"Ya, Shu, I was thinking the same thing. I'm okay with our deal if you are. We gotta stay good friends."

"How's it working out with Land Master?" I asked.

Bjorn looked back at MK, and she nodded. Bjorn said, "Well, last week we hired fourteen more employees; t. That's after everyone came back from the layoff. We're gearing up and expanding some buildings. Land Master is sending us a lot of work. That's workin' out great and Polarcat's orders are growing."

"Great to hear that. Look, I think you did a hell of a job negotiating with Land Master. Trudy and I don't own a fourth of the division as we planned, but I'm also not bustin' my butt out on the road selling equipment."

"Shu, who knows, probably you letting the cat out of the bag too soon on the twenty-seven-foot design is going to end up to be a good thing. Better be, 'cause I reserve the right to kick your ass," Bjorn said as he laughed and patted me on the shoulder.

"I'll bend over and give you a good target if need be. You cut us a fair deal with Land Master. I can buy new equipment from them below cost. They finance it for us below market rate, and they'll slip me bonus money for any new ideas. How can I complain?"

"Okay, boys, let's have a group hug and get on with life," Trudy said. "Oh, ya, Shu has an announcement."

"Dinner's ready," I said.

"Not that, dummy. The other announcement," she said, shaking her finger at me.

There was a smile and a sparkle in her eye. Boy, am I lucky to have her by my side. We're gonna have our hands full.

I know I had a proud grin on my face when I raised my glass of Jim Beam and Seven-Up and said, "Oh, ya. We're getting us another shareholder. Gonna be a boy."

Chapter 20

Spring 1963, three months later

OZZIE

The home plate ump yelled, "Strike three!"

It was our last pre-season game in Fort Meyers. The Twins would be heading back to Minneapolis in a few days for the season opener against the Royals, and I had just gotten a save out of the bullpen against the Red Sox.

"Way t'go, kid," Earl Battey, our catcher, said after he ran out to the mound. "Hope that helps you make the team. We need a hard-throwing lefty in the pen." Then, like all good catchers do, he patted me on the butt.

"When will I know? The manager doesn't seem to know I exist, and Camillo told me he'd kick my ass if I ever screwed up when I relieve him."

"After you shower check the bulletin board. The roster should be posted by then."

I didn't really need a shower. I only pitched an inning and a third, but I figured I'd go nuts just waitin' for the roster posting so I lathered up in a hurry. I didn't want to b.s. with the other guys.

I hustled out of the shower, barely drying my butt before running out to the bulletin board outside Manager Mele's office. I was as nervous as a rookie sky diver. The major league roster was tacked to the bulletin board. The fourth line down read:

BULLPEN: *Dailey, Fornieles, Williams, Johnson.*

I damn near fainted. I wanted to let out one of them rebel yells, but I needed to keep my cool. I couldn't wait to tell Angie. I figured the guys back home would crap their pants when they heard the news.

Jeeezus, I'm on the same team as Killebrew and Oliva. Hey, Dad, stick that up your ass.

* * *

ANGIE HAD HER BARE FEET with painted toenails up on the dash of my new Buick Riviera hardtop, and the bottom of her skirt had slid all the way to her purple panties. Her auburn hair was waving in the wind from the open windows. I knew she loved the honks from the truckers as we passed 'em. She liked giving them a little show. She also had her blouse unbuttoned halfway and had forgotten to wear her bra again.

We were goin' north on Highway 61 along the Mississippi River, heading to our new apartment by Lake Calhoun. The home opener in was in two days. Life was good.

"Hey, Oz, think I can get me a dancin' job in the Twin Cities? We could still use the extra cash even though you're in the big time now."

"Hell, yes. You think guys aren't horny up there? Lots'a good clubs would want you up on their stage making the pole shiny."

Each river town we went through looked better than the last one. Even in early April the trees were leafing out and the river bluffs were different shades of green mixed with white and pink from the blooming apple orchards. Tug boats guided strings of barges riding low in the river with last fall's harvest. It looked pretty cool.

Angie said, "Sure looks better around here than when you took me to the reunion. I could learn to like this."

We had just pulled into the second intersection in Winona after the light turned green. Then it happened. We were T-boned on the driver's side.

I was crunched against the door, and Angie flew into my other side. I never saw the truck coming and was knocked out.

***

I CAME TO AT 8:25 THE NEXT MORNING.

"Good morning Mr. Johnson. I'm Mrs. Swanson, the head nurse for the trauma unit this shift. How are you feeling?"

Even through my fuzzy eyes she looked like all nurses should look; white starched uniform and hat, comforting smile and cute. Good bod too. She also looked like she would be able to handle whatever the hell was wrong with me.

I blinked my eyes and shook my head, tried to figure out what the hell had happened to me. "How am I? How am I feeling? *Where* am I? I feel like shit."

"Just relax, hon. You are in St. Mary's Hospital in Winona. The doctor will be in shortly. If your pain gets worse, ring for me, and I'll give you some joy juice to tone it down." She patted my right shoulder and bent down to look into my eyes.

"What happened to me? I hurt all over."

"You were in an accident on Highway 61. A five-thousand-gallon milk tanker from Land-O-Milk and Honey Dairy ran a red light, so it wasn't your fault."

"Oh, man. How bad am I hurt? How's Angie?"

"Doctor Bunker will talk to you about your injuries. Oh, and the lady who was in the car with you left this note." She reached in her pocket and removed a piece of yellow notebook paper.

I reached for the note but couldn't move my left arm, so grabbed it with my right hand instead. It took me a while to focus, and then I read it:

> Hi Ozzie,
> Hope you're feeling okay. I just got a few bruises, not too bad. Can you believe that darned truck? I didn't know when you'd wake up, but Doc said it wasn't a serious concussion so I decided to catch the train to Chicago. I'll figure out how to get back to Charlotte from there. We sure had a good time while it lasted, and I'll always have fond memories of you. Get well real quick.
> All the best, Angie

I was trying to figure out what she meant when the doc came in, so I put the note down. The doc had gray hair parted in the middle and a chin dimple deeper than Kirk Douglas's.

"Hello, Mr. Johnson. I'm Doctor Bunker. You had a close call, son, but don't worry. You should be just fine after some surgery and recovery time."

"Hi, Doc. What's wrong with me? I hurt bad all over."

"You've suffered a fairly mild concussion. You were lucky, as it could have been much worse. The concussion, a couple of broken ribs and a broken collar bone will heal themselves with care and time. We'll be operating on your left hip tomorrow to repair some damage. In three days, a specialist from Mayo will visit to repair your left elbow."

Panic like I'd never felt surged through me. "What's wrong with my elbow?"

"Well, some dislocation and crushed bone. We believe it can be successfully repaired."

"Crushed bone? Repaired? To let me do what, knit doilies?"

His face gave away the bad news that I knew was coming. "Look . . . okay, I realize you were on your way to the Twins's opener. The papers have been full of a local kid making the team. I'm sorry, but I really doubt you'll be pitching again. But other than that, you should have normal use of your arm after extensive physical therapy."

"Oh, Doc . . . I . . . no, please . . . y'gotta fix it like new. It's . . . I have no other life. Please, *help* me!" Damn it, I was crying for the first time since the fourth grade when the old man beat the crap outta me for pouring his vodka down the shitter.

Doc put his hand on my shoulder. "Son, I never get used to giving bad news. I'm sorry to tell you about your pitching career, but believe it or not, your injuries could have been much worse, even fatal. So keep things in perspective."

Perspective? *Perspective?* Yup, things started to get perspectivized in my thick head, including Angie. *That bitch! She thinks my ball career is over, so she left to find another ticket to the easy life.* I glared at the doctor. "Who's the bastard who hit us? What's his name? Is the idiot from around here? Soon as I get outta here, I'm gonna track his ass down and make him sorry he ever got behind a wheel!"

SHU

I LOOKED INTO OZZIE'S ROOM to see if he was awake. Bjorn was right behind me. It was two days after the accident, and Ozzie had had hip surgery that morning. Nurse Swanson told us it would be a good idea for us to be with Ozzie when he woke up from the anesthesia 'cause there was no one else around to wish him well.

"Looks like he's still in la-la land," I said. "I wonder if the hospital has any bandages left; he looks like one of those mummies."

Bjorn said, "Well, let's have a seat and wait for him to come around. This is gonna be tough on him. The nurse said no more pitching, and Angie walked out on 'im too." He shook his head. "What a bitch."

After forty-five minutes of us reading out-of-date *Collier Life* magazines, Ozzie groaned and moved his right leg. Soon after that, his eyes fluttered open. Bjorn and I moved to the side of his bed.

Bjorn tugged on Ozzie's exposed big toe. "Hey, buddy, how're y'gettin' along with the nurses?"

Ozzie was trying to focus on us. "Nurses are wonderful. Oh, God, I've got a bad headache. What're you guys doin' here?"

I said, "Hey, we were in the neighborhood. Thought we'd stop in."

"Ya, two hours from home and you just stopped in. Bullcrap. Thanks for being here," Ozzie said with trembling chin. "At least I can count on you guys. Pope here too?"

"Nah, he's back in Germany. Gonna be hitched to some Nazi fraulein. They'll be back in a week or so," I said. "Wedding's tomorrow in the Alps. His folks went over for the ceremony and to check out the Nazi."

"At least he's got himself a gal. Angie walked out on me. Dang it all—I've got nothing left—no woman, no job, no folks and half my body doesn't work. God, what am I gonna do?" He turned his bandaged head away from us.

Bjorn said, "Hey, dammit, don't go mental on us. We're here. What're we, spoiled *lutefisk*? Things'll work out. Don't worry right now about stuff you can't predict. We aren't going out of your life. And don't get all macho on us when we help you get back on your feet."

Ozzie took a few deep breaths. "I don't know how to thank you guys. The Twins are being great too. Even old man Griffith called me." Ozzie shook his head. "They're pressing the dairy to settle with me quick and even thinkin' about having an Ozzie Johnson night at the Met in July. They're givin' me a lifetime pass to home games. Imagine that. Doc says things could be worse. Guess I darn near got killed."

Nurse Swanson came in to check on Ozzie. "Could you fellas step out for a while? I have to make sure this guy is behaving, and I don't want any witnesses if I have to slap him around."

"Okay," Bjorn said. "But if you need somebody to hold him down while you work him over, let us know."

Out in the hall we both talked at the same time. I won out in the interruption contest. "Ozzie seems different, and I don't just mean his injuries . . . seems calmer."

Bjorn said, "Ya, I was thinking the same thing. The doctors must have shaved off some of his rough edges while they had 'im in the operating room.

"As far as Angie taking off, I say good riddance. I hope Ozzie realizes she was the entertaining kind, not the marryin' kind."

DAVID, A.K.A. POPE

I HAD FINAGLED with some Army brass to get the bridal suite at the Army Rest & Recuperation hotel in Bertchesgarten on a lake near the foot of the Alps. It was the night before our wedding, and Ursula's mother and my parents were with us in the dining room of the hotel for a formal meal that doubled as the traditional groom's dinner.

No one else would be attending our wedding.

My father, Eugene, stood up. "I would like to propose a toast to the soon-to-be bride and groom." Not being used to the strong German beer, his words were slightly slurred. I guess he looked like the stereotypical CPA—thick glasses and a good-sized paunch from sitting behind a desk too long. He had very little hair. However, he had perfected the art of the comb-over.

He raised his stein of Dunkelweizen. "David, I've always been proud of you. And now, I want to say I'm proud of your choice of a life mate." Turning to Ursula's mother, he continued, "And thank you, Mrs. Zeller, for raising such a wonderful daughter. *Prosit!*"

Birdie, my mother, a very prim and proper lady, raised her glass of lemonade to join the toast. I detected a skeptical look on her face that seemed out of place for the happy occasion. I wondered why.

***

THE WEDDING CHAPEL, the subject of many photographs, was postcard beautiful. Snow-capped peaks towered over the tiny building, which had a Bavarian bell tower and was surrounded by ancient pine trees.

The village priest spoke only German, so my parents did not understand a word he said. However, the cadence of the words was familiar as most Catholic services followed the same format. They interpreted the wedding service for themselves.

I successfully suppressed my urge to upchuck at that time of stress. However, during the ceremony, Ursula kept looking around at the interior of the chapel and never looked at the priest or me. She seemed uninterested in the ceremony and seemed to want it over quickly. I suspected it was just because she was as nervous as I was.

After the ceremony, Mother hugged me. "David, you look so handsome in your new suit. I wonder why Ursula doesn't have a new dress for the occasion." Until Mother brought it up, I hadn't noticed Ursula's outfit.

***

"LET ME CARRY YOU over the threshold, darling," I whispered in Ursula's ear as we opened the door to our bridal suite with corner windows overlooking the shimmering lake. The room's alder furniture was accented by print curtains and matching cloth lamp shades and duvet.

Ursula said sharply, "Don't be silly. Let's just go in and get this over with."

She went to our wedding bed and hurriedly took off all her clothes, dropping them to the floor where she stood. She did not seem to notice the flowers, chocolates, and fruit tray I had arranged to be delivered to the room along with the sparkling grape juice. She pulled down the duvet and sheets and lay naked on her back with her legs spread and her eyes closed. She had not said a word after, "Let's just go in and get this over with."

I was befuddled. I had pictured us slowly undressing and caressing each other, rubbing flower petals on each other's special places and feeding each other fruit and chocolates while having small talk and giggles. Then we might give each other a back rub, toast to our future and make slow, passionate love. This was not going at all the way I had imagined. I just stood there looking at her, not knowing what to do.

"Well, come on. Are you going to screw me or not?" She snapped without opening her eyes. "Let's get this over with."

Shocked by her language and attitude, I said, "I am not undressed yet. I did not picture our first time this way. I thought you wanted some romance and taking our time."

"Look, you're a man. I'm a woman. I know what men want to do to women. Don't play games. Let's get this over with. Then you can do it to me again in a few weeks."

Even though I was turned off by what she said and did, I had been waiting a long time for this and could feel myself getting hard. Maybe she was just playing a game and teasing me.

I undressed and lay against her side, snuggling up and kissing her neck, but she was still as a stone. She kept her eyes closed and said nothing more. Then I fondled her breasts. Still no response. I rubbed her stomach while working my way down between her legs and stroked her there. Still no response. Her game was starting to worry me, but I was past the point of stopping.

Kneeling over her, I gently entered her and felt the heat of her. Still no response.

Sudden guilt overtook me. Instead of giving Ursula my full attention I began thinking of Angie moving on top of me. Oh, dear, I wished I was more experienced in the ways of intercourse. She was not responding to my gentle thrusts in the same manner as Angie had. I thought I must not be doing it correctly.

Her non-response and my guilt coupled to soften my aroused state. I withdrew from her in turmoil and lay on the other side of the bed.

Ursula snapped, "Good grief, don't tell me you're finished already."

Chapter 21

June 1963, two months later

BJORN

I wheeled a pale Ozzie out of the Winona Rehabilitation Center. "Hey, this place ain't so bad. I don't know what you've been bitchin' about. The nurses look cute and seem to have done a good job rehabbin' your sorry butt." Shu and Pope had gone out to get Pope's hand-me-down Edsel to pull up to the curb.

Ozzie grinned. "They may look okay, but that's just to cover up their Brunhilda torture tactics. They were trained by the Gestapo. I'll bet Pope's Nazi wife was trained by them too. They kept saying, 'Your pain is our gain'" He had made good progress even though he had to use a wheelchair or crutches for a while and his left arm was still in a cast. The near-death experience had mellowed him.

"Hey," I said. "Don't let Pope hear you talk that way about Ursula. We'll figure out how to put up with her after a while." Pope pulled up to the curb and I maneuvered Ozzie's wheelchair up next to the Edsel. "Now, let's get you into the back seat. Shu, give us a hand here."

After we got settled in the back seat and were on our way back to my folk's house, Ozzie spoke with a humble, tamed attitude. "Bjorn, I can't believe your folks are going to let me stay with 'em. That's way above the call of duty. Hope someday I can make it up to them."

"Well, they've got my empty bedroom for you and they're hardly ever home. Both of 'em work too many hours seven days a week. They've got a housekeeper and cook too . . . old lady Schneider. She'll look in on you a couple times a day. Oh, and don't try any grab-ass with her or she'll belt you with a frying pan."

"Don't worry. I'll be on my good behavior," Ozzie said. "I could only grab her with one arm anyway. As soon as I find out what the insurance settlement will be, I can find an apartment and get out on my own."

I said, "How's the insurance stuff going? Anybody advising you?"

"The Twins are. They've been great. I should know something in a week or two. Sid Hartmann's broadcast and column about me helped put pressure on the insurance company. It brought a lot of nice cards and letters from folks too.

"Remember Barb Barsness from high school? I spent some quality time with her in your hay mow, Shu. Anyway, she visited me twice down here." Ozzie grimaced while helping move his left leg with his right hand. "She married right after high school to a guy who got killed in an ice storm while working for Northern States Power. Brought her six-year-old boy the second time. Seems like a great kid. By the way, Pope, how's your deal going with Computing Data?" Ozzie asked.

"Complicated. Mr. Pierson, Computing Data's founder, liked the concept so much he thought they should start a new division to offer the timeshare service themselves. We still could have our own company as we planned in our three cities. They would let us use all their legal, marketing and sales material free." Pope spoke with more than a little pride. "Also, I would get three percent of the new divisions' profits for them using my idea."

Shu said, "Wow. Think of that, Bjorn. Another new company division created by one of us country bumpkins."

Pope continued. "They will offer other metro area territories on a franchise basis if there are any takers or set up their own company stores if no franchise buyers surface. Mr. Pierson figures companies that grow while using Computing Data's timeshare system would buy Computing Data products when they get to be larger companies. It looks like Sam and Herb's folks could really do well with the business. They would be setting up the financing and leasing company. Sam and Herb will get a little taste of those profits."

"What does Ursula think about all this?" asked Shu.

"She does not like me to speculate about future events. The whole situation may take a year or more to put together, and she has trouble conceptualizing complicated matters. She gets angry when I bring up anything about what kind of future this could bring us." Pope shook his head, dropping the subject.

NINE DAYS LATER

MK SAID, "OZZIE'S BEEN with your folks for about a week now. How's it working out?" It was well past sunset, and we were sitting on the end of the dock at our company's log cabin on Man Trap Lake in northern Minnesota, a one-day, one-night stop on the way back from a visit to the Polarcat plant. Our full-time employees used the cabin as a benefit on a sign-up basis.

"Okay, I guess. I haven't heard any complaints from the patient or my folks, and Mrs. Schneider hasn't made Ozzie's concussion any worse." I pulled my bare feet out of the water and looked up at the sky. "Jeeze, I wonder how many gazillion stars are up there. They look close enough to reach up and touch." I listened for a moment. "And listen to those loons. Sounds like the male is putting a move on the lady loon now that the moon's reflecting on the water."

"It's beautiful. We should come up here more often. You really should take more time off. Do you realize how many hours you're either at the shop or on the road visiting your customers' plants? Almost all your waking hours."

I grinned. "You're the one who doesn't want to get married yet, so I don't think you have nagging rights. You know how hard it is to keep the company runnin'. There's not a lot of time for anything else. But you'll notice I do take time for you when your schedule allows." I snuggled my lips onto her ear lobe.

"How about you take time to put a move on me in front of the fireplace up at the cabin? Or are you too busy thinking about work?" She whispered in my ear. "We don't need a marriage license for that."

* * *

THE FIRE TOOK THE CHILL out of the air and our naked bodies. We sat on the floor softened by the couch cushions we had arranged for our love making. MK poured wine, even though I would have preferred a Hamm's. The surroundings added to our afterglow and a roaring fire lit the honey-colored log interior. Moonlight and the sound of whispering pines seeped in from outside.

The firelight found MK's face and body. That glow rivaled the moon's glow on the lake.

As good as it was, MK noticed I was quiet and kept staring at the flames, creating a long, awkward silence broken only by the crackle of burning logs.

After a while, she said, "What's with you? You seem far away, pensive."

After a long pause, I said, "Well, now, see, right there's a problem. I don't know what 'pensive' means. I don't know what a lot of words mean or how to spell 'em. I don't even have a high-school diploma, and you're going for your master's. I feel like I'm not smart enough for you." I turned away from her. "I don't have enough interests outside the business to have interesting conversations. I have to ask you to come along to visit customers when you have time. You keep the conversations going with them over dinner. You light up the room. They love you."

"Dammit, Bjorn. Stop that! You don't know it, but you're a genius. Why do you think those customers are so loyal? You solved problems for them that they didn't even know they had." She got up. The copper glow of the fire on her body made it hard for me to concentrate on what she was saying. "They hang on your every word when they escort you through their plants. You tell them how you can make things less expensive and better for them. You're smarter than all of them put together." She bent down and put her hands on my shoulders. "You're smarter than I am, too."

My view of her at that moment really distracted me.

"You come up with new products and how to improve existing ones as easy as those loons out there take to swimming. Your employees think you walk on water."

"That's a lot of b.s. I don't think you wanna marry a high school drop-out," I said, my eyes fixed on hers.

"Oh, for crying out loud. I told you, we need to delay marriage because you're tied up growing your business, and I'm up to my eye-balls working on my masters. There's no time right now for a good marriage. We can get married after I get my master's. I promise."

***

THE EMOTIONAL TEMPERATURE in my pick-up cab was less than warm on the ride back home from the cabin. When we arrived at the bank/barbershop building where my apartment was, MK jumped from my truck and stomped to her car. Before getting in she turned to me. "Just remember, I love you. I don't give a damn if you have a diploma, a degree or a coon skin hat hanging on your wall. That doesn't mean squat to me. You're the man I want to marry . . . but just not now." She got in her car, slammed the door and managed to lay some rubber with the Studebaker as she took off.

I was upset and anxious to get back to work so I didn't stop to take my overnight bag up to my room. I walked into the shop office and as soon as I saw the frown on Ma's face, I knew there was trouble. "Hi, Ma, what's up?"

"Hi, son. You'd better check the pile of mail on your desk. Especially the certified letter I put on top."

I walked to my desk and picked up the envelope. I looked at the return ad-dress. My hand shook before I opened it. I read it and sank into my chair. *Will MK wait? The folks can't handle the company by themselves. We'll be broke again.*

Pa came storming in from the shop. "Is that goddamned letter what I think it is?"

I figured Pa already knew what it was. I nodded.

Ma came over to give me a hug. Her cheeks were wet with tears. Even Evelyn, our stoic bookkeeper was sniffling.

Mike, MK's dad, came in from the shop with worry lines on his Irish mug. He asked softly, "Karl, was that Bjorn's draft notice?"

Chapter 22

July/August 1963, two months later

SHU

L ook, I know it's gonna be tough, but I'll help all I can while you're gone. Let's go down and talk to that V.P. Philp at Land Master before you leave for basic," I told a despondent Bjorn. "I might have a couple of ideas for equipment he may be interested in. They'll hang with Olson and Dad if we keep 'em up to date on how the company will operate while you're gone and if we slip them some new product ideas."

"Don't try to b.s. me. You've got your hands full with all those damn turkeys," Bjorn lifted his drink for emphasis. "Oh, ya, and a new baby."

"After October's harvest season I'll have some spare time to help your folks. It's the least I can do."

The two of us were sitting with Ozzie and Pope at Leo's Tavern. Bjorn had gotten there an hour before the rest of us after passing his army tests, and had also gotten a head start on drinking. The army had waived the requirement of a high school diploma after seeing his IQ scores. Bjorn's psych tests showed he had superior leadership qualities and the maturity of a thirty-eight-year-old. The aptitude portion indicated the army had many options for placing him in the right job. Uncle Sam wanted him.

Bjorn gulped down drinks as fast as Bubbles, the waitress, could keep him supplied. Pope kept an eye on Ozzie, remembering the reunion, to make sure no vodka got into his cream soda.

"I just know my folks are gonna end up broke again thanks to Uncle Sam's damned draft." He slammed his glass on the table and most of his Jim Beam and Seven-Up jumped over the rim. "Land Master and Silverman Brothers will pull the plug at the first sign of trouble."

Ozzie piped in. "Hell, I wanna help too. I don't know how, but maybe I could be your old man's driver when he has to visit customers. My rehab is almost over. Maybe my name would help him get in some new prospects' doors."

Pope said, "I have been thinking about how I could be of assistance. Your parents could benefit greatly from computer technology. When we get our office up and running I can have our programmer set up systems to help with your inventory, workman's comp, payroll, receivables, and so forth. It would take a great deal of stress off your folks, especially your mother."

With his hour's head start on us, Bjorn had way too much to drink and was staring glumly into his drink. "Well, Howdy Fuckin' Doody. You all must be feeling mighty guilty for staying home and sitting on your asses while I'm off saving the world."

Three of us exchanged worried glances. This was not the same Bjorn we were used to.

MK

Despite Bjorn's objections, I had organized a small gathering to wish him farewell on the night before he left for basic training. I knew he was concerned about how his folks and the business could survive while he was gone and was bitter about being drafted when he was needed to run the company. I hoped the party would cheer him up, and I knew what I personally had planned for him after the party would give him something to remember on the lonely nights to come.

We held the party in the small private event room of Leo's Tavern. A large banner was tacked to the wall paneling just under the water-stained ceiling tile. It was signed by all thirty-seven employees of Olson & Dad, Inc. Large red letters on the banner said GOOD LUCK BOSS WE LOOK FORWARD TO YOUR SAFE RETURN.

The Chaska VFW provided the food for the buffet table. They wanted to prepare Bjorn for basic training meals, so the menu consisted of chipped beef and floury white gravy on an over-baked biscuit, watery instant mashed potatoes, over-cooked pale green beans, mystery meat and doughy, under-baked bread. All of that was a tradition they had for farewell and welcome-home gatherings for the county's military guys.

Olson & Dad, Inc. provided the drinks, which were served from a folding table with a chipped wooden top. Olga and Karl were the bartenders. A few key employees had been invited to stop in for a drink and to officially say good-bye to Bjorn. The rest of the small group consisted of the guest of honor, Shu, Pope, Ozzie, and their ladies.

After the Olson & Dad employees had gone, the rest of the group good-naturedly ate the buffet food. Bjorn stared at his plate and never took a bite or said a word.

Olga and Karl kept the drinks flowing, and I noticed Bjorn was having much more than his share. Around nine-fifteen the party showed signs of breaking up.

Bjorn stood with one hand on the bar to steady himself. He spoke loudly, but with difficulty. "Hold up. Before anyone leavesh, I wanna make some toa-toashts." He was not smiling. He had everyone's attention.

"Firsht of all, to Pope." Bjorn raised his glass toward him. "He was able to get a cu-cushy job helping spies and traveling to fancy places, an' that kept him fr-from being dra-drafted." There were a few uncomfortable chuckles from the others.

"Then there's Ozshie. Played a boys' game, then got banged up, which lan-landed him seven years' worth of sh-shalary from an ins-insurance company for sittin' on his ass. Cou-couldn't pass an army phys—physical. No draft for him." Bjorn raised his glass to Ozzie. There were no more chuckles. Ozzie's face got red and his date, Barb Barsness, grabbed his arm and whispered something in his ear.

"Now, Shu . . . he did it the fun way. He knocked up Trudy and got—that magic marriage de-deferment." Bjorn raised his glass to Shu as Karl came around the bar and put his arm around him to stop the toasting. Bjorn pushed his dad aside. "I'm not f-finished."

I was wary of what was coming next. *What the heck has come over my Bjorn?*

"And here's to all the la-ladies preshent. You all got that damn magic female deferment." He raised his new bottle of beer to all the ladies, including the pregnant Trudy and the shocked Ursula.

"Lasht, but not leasht, here's to Ma-Mary Katherine—my everlovin' gal who re-refused to marry me, and is therefore directly reshponsible for me not getting a ma-marriage deferment." Bjorn glared at me but didn't raise his bottle in a toast.

"And here's to the fair-fairness of the Selective Shervice system." He turned toward the window and hurled his beer bottle through the neon tubes of the red Hamm's beer sign, shattering both the sign and the window.

Everyone stood in shocked silence, embarrassed for, but also angry at Bjorn.

He staggered toward the door, turned and yelled, "You can all g-go to hell!"

***

TEARS PULLED MASCARA down my cheeks. I felt miserable, but I stayed to help Olga and Karl clean up the mess.

Everyone else had left after thanking Karl and Olga. They didn't know what else to say. After all, what could they say?

Olga came over to me. "I'm so sorry for what Bjorn said about you. He's under a lot of stress and just has not been himself. I know he loves you very much. Please try to forgive him. He needs you in his life."

I spoke between sobs. "I won't see him for two months. How can we leave it like this? I've got to go see him, now."

"Yes, go to him," Olga said.

***

PULLING UP IN FRONT of the barbershop/bank building, I saw Bjorn's pickup with one headlight still on and the driver's side headlight and front fender crunched against a power pole. The driver's door was still open so I reached in to turn off the lights. I went up to his apartment and used my key to let myself in.

I found Bjorn lying on his bed, face down with his clothes on, passed out.

I went to the little kitchenette, filled a glass with cold water and took it back to the bedroom. Standing over his pathetic figure I slowly trickled water on his head until he jerked awake.

He reached to grope his wet head, "What the hell?" Then he saw me.

I looked down on the disheveled Bjorn with a mixture of love, disgust and pity. "Nice speech, soldier. That got you promoted from Private Feel-Sorry-For-Myself all the way to General Butthole. We need to talk."

His mind was probably pretty fuzzy, but I bet it was clear enough to know that I meant he would be the designated listener, not the talker.

"If you don't act fast, you'll have lost your three best friends, the respect of their ladies, and your folks thinking you can do no wrong. And, oh, yeah, I could be history too."

Bjorn sat up on the edge of the bed with his head in his hands, waiting for the verbal assault to continue, probably knowing he had it coming. But I waited for his response.

I could tell he was trying to come up with words to defend himself. I was ready to quash any such attempt. I out-waited him. In a situation like this, I'd learned that the first one to speak, loses.

He finally spoke. "Well, okay. Maybe I screwed up. Sorry. I really am sorry. What can I do now?" He reached for my hand, but I pulled away.

"No Bjorn, you didn't *maybe* screw up.

"For starters, you can't change being drafted, so face-up to it like a man. You lost the appeal to the Selective Service Board. Your number came up in the draft lottery, and guess what, it came up for thousands of other guys too. I strongly suggest you get on the phone right now and call all three of your friends to beg for their forgiveness for being such a rude ass. Also, talk to their ladies and apologize for your embarrassing behavior." I was standing over him with my arms folded, talking like an angry mother. "Early tomorrow morning you need to see you folks and apologize to them for your performance."

Bjorn mumbled, "You left out the most important person. You haven't said what I need to say to you."

My tone softened. "I figured you could come up with that on your own. And by the way, include an apology for making us wait two more months to play kissy face. That is, if I decide to stay in your life."

Chapter 23

October 1963, eight weeks later

BJORN

Staff Sergeant Hamerski spoke to me like a normal human being instead of in his drill-instructor voice. "Hey, Olson, the Company Commander wants to see you in his office right now. I'm going along." Basic training was over, and I had almost finished packing my duffle bag. Bad memories of the last eight weeks wandered through my skull.

During basic, I'd often wondered how my buddies back home would have reacted to whatever God-awful training activity we were doing at the time. Shu would do okay. Ozzie and the M.P.s would be familiar with each other quickly because of Ozzie's temper, which would have been aimed both at other troopers and at the drill instructors. Because swearing was elevated to an art form in basic, Pope would have set a modern-day record for saying, "You know I do not like that sort of language."

"Okay, Sarge. What's he wanna see me for?"

"You'll find out soon enough," he said with a rare grin.

Sarge and I entered Lieutenant Huber's sparse office in a *temporary* building, which had been thrown up during World War Two. It was still in use and had seen a lot of wear and tear. His office had a bare, unfinished wood floor and no curtains on the one small window. The interior walls consisted of a view of the two-by-fours holding the exterior siding. We each rendered a snappy salute and stood at attention. The lieutenant said, "At ease men. Have a seat."

The lieutenant was probably about the same age as me, maybe a year or two older, and was an ROTC grad from North Dakota. His spit-shined shoes did not have the gleam of a career military guy like Hamerski's and the creases in his uniform weren't as sharp. Unlike some other company commanders in our battalion, he was liked and respected by the men under him and openly depended on Sergeant Hamerski to help him wade through Army protocol and endless paper work. The sergeant had told me he had suffered through assisting other officers who didn't want to admit they needed help from a non-com.

"Private, I suppose you're glad basic is over, eh?" Huber said.

"Sir, don't know how to answer that. Either a yes or a no might not sound like the right answer."

"Okay, I'll withdraw the question. Let's get to the reason for this meeting." He tapped his finger on a file folder. "This file, which you will take to your next post, contains a Letter of Commendation. In this training cycle, the battalion had fifty-three squads in nine companies. As the squad leader of eleven seemingly difficult personalities, you led them to be the best squad in the entire battalion."

Sarge said, "Private, I picked you as a squad leader based on your qualification tests. For once, the army got the testing right. Your squad would have followed you over a cliff."

"Well, that'd be one way to get an early discharge," I said.

The lieutenant chuckled. "Of fourteen measurable training activities, out of fifty-three squads, yours was first in two activities, second in three of them, and third in three. Your squad never finished lower than eleventh in the rest. One of your squad's firsts, the timed live-fire obstacle course, tied a record going back eighteen years. Excuse my curiosity, but how the hell did you do it?"

"Well, sir, I didn't know we did that well. I don't really know how it happened, but I had some good guys in the squad." I shrugged. "You two were part of it too."

"It is obvious to Sarge and me—and by the way, also Major O'Connor— that you're a natural leader. We'd like to encourage you to apply for Officer Candidate School," Huber said while pointing a finger at me like one of those "Uncle Sam Wants You" posters.

I knew enough not to laugh in their faces. They had no idea how much I was needed back home, and I didn't want to disrespect their chosen army careers. "Geeze, thanks for your confidence in me, but OCS would mean I'd haft'a sign up for another year or two, and with all due respect, my ass can't wait to be a civilian."

***

I HEFTED MY HEAVY DUFFLE BAG over my shoulder and said goodbye to the few of my squad still in the old wooden barracks. I didn't want to tell the guys how I was going to travel from here. They were all going by Greyhound or charter buses. I hurried off to the base air strip. Land Master had sent their wheat-colored Cessna four-seater to Fort Leonard Wood to pick me up and deliver me to their Design Center in St. Louis where I was going to show them some new things Shu had come up with.

"Sorry I'm late," I said to the waiting pilot and shook his hand. "I'm Bjorn. I hope Mr. Philp can stay a little later. I've gotta catch the train for Minnesota first thing in the morning."

"No sweat. We'll still get there before dark. I'm Chuck. I'll radio ahead and tell him we've been delayed. Should I tell him why you're running late?"

"You know, it's the military. Hurry-up and wait."

The takeoff was smooth, which helped me relax. "This is my first time up in a small plane. I've been a little worried, but this is really cool." I noticed the pilot's prosthetic left hand, which made me a little uneasy.

"Sit back and enjoy. We won't be doing any aerobatics," the pilot chuckled. He must have seen me glance at his left hand. "Don't worry about my pretend hand, either. The controls on that side have been altered for me. Land Master likes to hire disabled vets. My Saber jet got hit in Korea. Glad to say the Mig that did it hit the ground real hard."

The trip was uneventful except that Chuck let me take the wheel for a while. It was noisy in the cockpit, but we had ear phones on so he could talk me through it. I was surprised how easy it was to control the plane.

Vice President Philp was waiting for us at the airport. "Hi, soldier. I thought we'd save time and talk in the car on the way to the Mayfair Hotel. That way we can skip going to the Design Center, and you can get on to other things."

"That's mighty kind of you. It helps my schedule, and I know you're busy too. Sorry I'm late." We shook hands as he patted me on the back. I said, "I can explain Mr. Schumacher's drawings on the way to the hotel. He has some thoughts about another future project too. We didn't feel right about doing this by mail and phone. I appreciate you taking the time."

Philp said, "No problem. I was in town anyway, and knowing you guys, I'm sure this will be a worthwhile meeting."

I gave Chuck an exaggerated salute, threw my duffle in the trunk and hopped in the back seat of the long black Caddy with Philp. He told the driver which hotel to head for. I didn't want to waste time with chit-chat 'cause I didn't know how long the ride would be, so I got right down to business.

"Shu—I mean, Mr. Schumacher—feels the current design for the chisel plow can be improved by adding cutter discs, mounted on the leading edge, to break up the prior year's crop remains. That would keep things from clogging up. Not much more power would be needed either. He's tried our prototype," I explained while pointing to the photos and drawings.

"Interesting idea," Philp responded.

"We've also got notarized drawings, photos, and statements from third parties," I said, memories of the patent debacle still haunting me.

Philp smiled. "Bjorn, don't worry, if our guys approve this—and I think that's likely—your company will build them."

"Sorry . . . I'm still kinda spooked about that meeting in Chicago."

"I understand. Do you think your company can handle more work while you're gone?"

That was the question I had been dreading. I answered with more bluff than conviction. "Heck, yeah. We've got good people and good systems in place."

Philp said, "You said you had two ideas to present . . . what's the other one?"

"This idea of Shu's is really about something that might happen a few years down the road. If anything ever happens with this, we hope you would call on us to make some of the components. No notarized documents on this."

"You guys keep up the good work and you won't have to worry about getting more work from us. You'll get all you can handle."

"Well, thanks. Think about the history of the tractor. The latest models are just bigger versions of the earlier ones. Two small wheels in front for steering and two large drive wheels in back." I reached for Shu's other sketch. "Pieces of equipment that tractors will be expected to pull are only going to get bigger, so they'll need more pulling power. This sketch shows a machine with four large drive wheels—four-wheel drive, just like a Jeep."

"Jeezus, maybe you guys should move to St. Louis and run the darn Design Center," Philp said and patted me on the shoulder. "Thanks for asking for this meeting. Your hotel's just ahead. No need for me to go in and prolong the meeting. I know you're in a hurry. I'll follow up on these ideas and get back to you or your dad about them. Good luck and I hope to see you again soon."

***

THE HOTEL'S FANCY LOBBY threw me off balance for a second. I'd been used to the old wooden barracks. I was glad I wore a plaid shirt and jeans instead of fatigues. I went up to the marble registration desk, and the cute blonde clerk asked for an ID before I signed in. "Oh, Mr. Olson, here's a message for you." She handed me a pink memo slip. I hoped she didn't mind when I checked her out. She was the first female I'd come in contact with in the last eight weeks.

I read the note and broke into a wide grin.

As the note instructed, I went into the dimly lit bar off the lobby. Seated in the corner with a book and a cup of coffee was MK.

***

AS THE MORNING TRAIN pulled out of the station bound for Minneapolis, MK sighed. "If you'd look in the dictionary for the word *horny*, you'd see a picture of yourself. I thought you'd never let me get to sleep last night."

"Well, in that same dictionary under that word, you'd see your own picture beside mine," I said as I squeezed her knee. "Two months without you kinda wound up my spring. In fact, I got this private compartment in case you decided to get all cooperative with me again. You know, to help me unwind my spring a little more."

"At ease, soldier. I'm still recovering from last night's maneuvers. By the way, what's your schedule for the next few days?"

"When we get in tonight, I'd better stay with the folks. Tomorrow I'll be at the plant most of the day, but I can stay with you at night, if I'm invited. Sunday it's Shu's kid's baptism, and Monday I've got to leave because I'm flying standby and I hafta report by Wednesday at noon."

"Oh, that doesn't leave a lot of alone time for us. On second thought, forget that at-ease order. Think your little soldier can come to attention?"

***

PA SAID, "SON, looks like army life agrees with you. Other than that buzz-cut, you look great," Ma had her arm around my waist.

"Well, there's not a lot of sittin' around and the food's only so-so. Lost some weight, I guess. Speaking of looks, you guys look tired. You workin' too much?" I asked, knowing the answer no matter what they said.

Pa said, "Oh, it ain't been so bad. Where they sending you next?"

"Virginia. Fort Bolivar for heavy-equipment school. Dozers, scrapers, draglines, that sort of stuff. It's better than some infantry outfit. I'll be there for six weeks, then probably go to Germany or Korea. The guys say Korea is the best kept secret as far as good duty is concerned."

"I hope they keep you in the States," Pa said. "That way you could get here to the shop once in a while. Everyone sure misses you."

"Well, believe me, I'd rather be here. Have the guys in the shop finished with that new entrenching tool I sent drawings for?" I asked. "I'd like to take one with me to Virginia."

"They're makin' two of 'em . . . should be done tomorrow. What's that all about, anyway?" Pa seemed put-out about the extra work to fit in the already busy schedule.

124

"The ones they use now are the heaviest dang thing a GI has to carry in his pack and the design is lousy. Plus, they must be expensive to make. Just off-setting the handle so you can get a full boot on the damned shovel is a big improvement, let alone the reduced weight. I wanna try to get an order for the army to test 'em."

THE WHOLE GANG

"I'M GONNA BE EMBARRASSED when all those people come over for dinner after church," Trudy said, holding baby Nick on the way to the baptism. "Putting up three rows of hay bales around our foundation hardly qualifies as a home improvement. Instead of building another new house for turkeys, maybe you should be thinkin' of a new one for your family. The kids'll have runny noses all winter from those darn cold floors."

Shu bit his lip; he thought this was not the time for an unfair scolding. "I thought the hay would help keep the house warmer. More turkeys will help pay for a better house in the future."

***

ON ANOTHER ROAD, Ursula was bending Pope's ear. "I still don't know why I had to come along. These are your friends, not mine. If Bjorn acts up again I'm going to slap him."

Pope had learned to walk on eggshells around his wife. "Dear, it would be hard to explain if you were not along. I was asked to be Nick's godfather, and I am proud to do so. Sorry about last night. Was I too gentle?"

***

NOT FAR BEHIND POPE were Ozzie, Barb, and her son, Danny. They were cruising along in Ozzie's Pontiac woody station wagon. They knew the way to the church. "You look great in that new peach dress," Ozzie said. "And, Danny, you're lookin' spiffy in that new blue blazer. What a guy."

Ever since Ozzie had taken Danny along to the pitcher's mound at Met Stadium during the Ozzie Night at the Met, Danny couldn't stay close enough to Ozzie and the feeling was mutual.

"Well, Oz, you're looking pretty sharp yourself. Must be a special day, huh?" Barb said with a bright smile. "Be good for you to see Bjorn again; good of everyone to get straight with him after that going-away party fiasco."

***

MK AND BJORN WERE running late. He drove her Studebaker faster than the speed limit to make up time. "Take it easy, soldier. I want to go to a baptism, not our own funeral," she said. "Hope I look better than I feel. You didn't let me get much sleep again last night," she said, but with a smile.

The cream-colored-brick Lake Parley Moravian Church sat high on a hill overlooking the lake. It was built before the turn of the century and was charming both inside and out. The members took pride in the denomination's motto: In Essentials Unity, In Non-essentials Liberty, And In All Things Love.

The Schumacher family had been generous supporters of the church for decades and liked the new pastor, Susan Hill. She had graduated from the Moravian Seminary in Bethlehem, Pennsylvania, five months ago. She was a rotund woman, and everyone loved her friendly demeanor.

Conversations and laughter filled the sanctuary as the entering folks were catching up on the prior week's happenings.

Ursula walked in slowly, wary of her surroundings because she didn't see a holy water font as she entered. She glanced from side to side, sizing the place up as she walked down the aisle. As she turned into a row of pews, she slammed on her personal brakes. The things she had seen, or not seen, since she had entered the sanctuary, sent ripples through the wrinkles of her brain. She hissed, "David! Get—me—out—of—here! This is a *heathen* place!"

"Dear, why? What is wrong?" Pope asked.

"Can't you see? There's no holy water basin! No crucifix! No kneelers! No stations of the cross! This is not a church! It's for *heathens!*"

"No, Dear. It is a Protes—"

"I said *get me out of here! Now!*" She glared at him with a rabid, determined look he was only too familiar with.

Pope knew from other episodes with her that he had no choice or things would loudly escalate. He took her by the arm and escorted her out of the church against the flow of people entering and took her back to the Edsel. "I have to go back in. I am going to be the godfather of this child. I am committed to do my duty. Did you take your pills this morning?"

"Heathens don't need godfathers! *We* will leave this instant!"

***

The baptism ceremony was a success despite the unexplained absence of the godfather and when baby Nick passed gas during the silent prayer. At the end of the service Pastor Hill asked the friends of the baptism parents to stay while the rest of the congregation was excused to go to the Fellowship Room for coffee.

As the rest of the congregation left the sanctuary, Pastor Hill said, "My friends, we have another short ceremony to witness."

She nodded to Barb and Ozzie, who rose from their pew and went forward to her with Danny between them.

Flashing a broad smile, Pastor Hill said, "Friends, it's time for a wedding."

Chapter 24

Six weeks later, December 1963

OZZIE

Don't we hafta save places for Pope and the Nazi?" I asked. I was with MK, Trudy, Barb, and Shu at the Crossroads Restaurant, and we were deciding where to plant our keesters. There were plenty of empty tables.

Shu glanced at Trudy and said, "Ah, no . . . they won't be coming. We'll talk about it later."

"Well, okay. I won't miss her, that's for dang sure," I said. "Great to see you all; first time we've all been together since Nick passed gas, and Barb and I got hitched." Barb gave me a friendly elbow shot to my ribs.

Once we decided on a table, a bored-looking waiter ambled over, took our drink orders and mumbled something about the nightly specials. It was early December, and the place was decorated with some tired, gaudy Christmas decorations.

"That was some surprise you two pulled on us," MK said. "What have you guys been up to since that big day?"

I squirmed a little, then met Barb's eyes, and she nodded. "Well, Barb and I've been going to business school." Funny how the other faces all of a sudden had their surprised masks on.

"What?" Shu said. "Why? To learn how to spend your insurance money?"

I looked around to make sure no one at other tables could hear me. "Barb's taking marketing and employee tax courses. I'm taking a course on writing a business plan and food and beverage laws. Next week we start different classes. This next part is on the Q.T. for now . . . we've got an option to buy *this* place."

Shu blurted out, "*This* dump? I wondered why you suggested eating here."

"Ya, this dump," I said proudly as I swung my arm, pointing out the place. "Price is right. Old lady Blanchar couldn't grab the pen fast enough. She wants out bad. But think about it. We'll have six acres of land across the road from and access to Lake Minnetonka. It's close to the western suburbs and to the main drag from the Cities to St. Boni and Hutchinson and at the intersection of Lakeside Road that heads up to resort country. Plenty of traffic, easy to find. Also, to top it off, Lake Minnetonka is underserved by good restaurants."

MK said, "Wow. Good luck. The restaurant business is tough. Sounds kinda risky to me."

"Well, I'm not gonna go into the details now, but Barb and I think we've got a great concept to turn this into a happenin' place." I pointed to the ceiling. "We'll live upstairs after we fix up the apartment. Also, we've got the insurance money to tide us over during the start-up. Karl introduced us to Cline at the bank, and he gave his preliminary okay, subject to their committee's approval of the final business plan."

Just then the bored young waiter arrived with the drinks. Most of them were what we'd ordered.

MK raised her glass in a toast "We all wish you success in your new venture. Here's to risk giving rewards and good ideas giving the satisfaction of authorship."

They all raised their glasses, each one probably thinking of their own risks, rewards, and failures. "Here, here! Good luck!"

After ordering our food, I asked Shu and Trudy, "So why aren't Pope and the Nazi here?"

Trudy lowered her voice. "Look, we wouldn't go into this, but Pope said it was okay to tell you. Ursula is in a psych hospital . . . been there a few weeks." Shu patted her on the shoulder. "Shock treatments, meds, the whole bit. Pope visits her every day and attends group therapy sessions with her. You know how he is when he makes a commitment. Pope's goin' through hell. He cried on the phone when he told us."

Shu said, "Seems she really freaked out after they got home from the baptism. She read the church bulletin Pope grabbed before he left the church. She saw our minister was a woman, and she started screaming and throwing stuff around. Pope had to hold her down so she wouldn't hurt herself or him."

"About the only thing they did together was go to mass," Trudy said. "Now she's very disappointed in the Catholic Church for not having women priests. She thinks it's more oppression of women. Ursula had been on some anti-depression meds, but she wasn't always taking them. She has depression, rage, and probably a few other screws loose."

I never liked the Nazi, but I and everyone else around the table were shocked about the problems she had. I felt sorry for poor Pope.

After the semi-wilted salads were served, Shu continued. "It gets worse. During the therapy sessions it came out that for years Ursula was sexually abused by her father. That may be some of the cause of her mental problems. Computing Data has been patient with Pope—he said he told them everything—but now they're insisting he find a local partner to help get his business set up. Seems like the two guys on the coasts have everything set to go, and Pope's having trouble getting going 'cause of his problems at home."

MK said, "Oh, man. Hey, guys, we all have to support Pope. Call him, send cards, go see him or invite him to lunch. It's tough to go through something like that alone." Everyone nodded, and the mood was more subdued.

Finally Shu asked, "MK, what'cha hear from the boyfriend . . . or is it fiancé?"

"Our engagement isn't official yet," MK said. "Bjorn's doing great. At least that's what he tells me when he calls a couple of times a week. He enjoyed the heavy equipment training and did real well. He also calls Karl or Olga every chance he gets. He's still worried sick about them and the business." She shook her head.

"Boy, I don't blame 'im," I said. "I drove Karl up to the army munitions plant in Arden Hills to see a colonel who's the uncle of one of Bjorn's instructors. Bjorn wanted Karl to show the colonel his new GI shovel." I pointed my fork for emphasis. "Karl slept all the way there and back; he looked like death warmed over."

"Yeah, my dad says the same thing," MK said. "At least Karl let Dad take over the hiring and firing, which should take some pressure off. And Bjorn called his old shop teacher, Mr. Utoft, and asked if he could spend more time at the shop and take a leave of absence from school. He agreed, and now he's managing the second shift scheduling and quality control."

I said, "So back to Bjorn . . . where's he goin' next?"

"He leaves Virginia the day after tomorrow for six weeks at the Army Language School in Monterey, California. I guess that'll give him some basic language training. He thinks he'll go to Korea from there to be an assistant instructor. Or it could be Germany, but Bjorn doesn't think the Krauts need training," MK said with a wink and a chuckle. "Shu, Bjorn said to tell you that." Then with a big smile she said, "I'm going to visit him out there in three weeks."

Trudy said, "Well, now it's time for a toast for MK. Go get 'im hooked. You two are meant for each other. Have a great trip to the west coast."

"Talk about hooking him, you've got the right bait, MK," Shu said while raising his glass.

"Sounds exciting for you, MK, but I've got some exciting news of my own," I said. "I figure I learned how *not* be a father from my old man, so I think I know how to be a good one. I've filed adoption papers for Danny."

The rest of the crew roared their approval, and MK gave another toast. "Here's to you, Ozzie. You'll make a great dad, with Barb's help, of course."

"By the way, Ozzie," Shu said. "This food sucks. It won't be too tough for you guys to improve this joint."

BJORN

I ENTERED THE HEADQUARTERS building at the Defense Language School and walked up to the WAC sergeant at the reception desk to show my orders. "Pfc. Olson reporting."

She took my orders and looked for my name in her assignment book. "Welcome, Olson. Here's a map to the mess hall and dorm. It's different than the barracks you've been used to. Two guys to a room. You're required to speak only the language you and your roommate are learning." She tried to act real official like, but she couldn't hold back a welcoming smile. "Three twelve is your room number. Good luck. Classes start tomorrow at zero eight hundred. Here's a map to your classroom building; the room is two eleven. Good luck, Olson."

When I finally found my room, my roommate wasn't there. At least the room was better than the barracks I'd grown used to, but it still had that Spartan military look. A bulletin posted behind the door said the school did not assign rooms by rank, and as far as activities in this room were concerned, no one was to pull rank. Someone had scrawled underneath, *No military chickenshit.* Under that were phrases in four different languages probably saying the same thing.

With no one to talk to, I decided to find the mess hall and my classroom so I would know my way around in the morning. The Asian Studies building was a typical military building, plain, with hallways painted light green and gray tiles on the floor. It smelled like it had just been cleaned with products designed to cover up other bad odors.

I found room two eleven. I thought the WAC must have made a mistake. The sign on the door said didn't say Korean, it said *Vietnamese.*

Chapter 25

February 1964, seven weeks later

DAVID, A.K.A. POPE

Oh, my goodness, please excuse me," I said when I nearly bumped a lady with my shopping cart as I turned the corner from the frozen food aisle. I had too much on my mind—trying to start the business, worrying about Ursula and looking at my grocery list crowded out concentrating on guiding my shopping cart at the Red Owl store.

"'S okay," the lady said as she hurried on to the checkout line. She was wearing a parka, a knit hat, boots, and sun glasses.

I watched her go, wondering why she had sunglasses on inside the store. I had a vague feeling I knew her. After a moment of reflection, it dawned on me. I called out, "Ruthie?"

She did not stop, so I said in a louder voice, "Ruthie Schneed?"

She stopped and turned toward me, probably trying to retrieve my voice from her memory bank.. "Yes? Do I know you?"

"David Grimm, class of '58." I should have thought of something more clever to say. "Oh, my god. I'm so sorry. I didn't recognize you. No glasses. Hi."

I approached her with a smile and held out my hand. She took my hand and glanced at the contents of my shopping cart: four Swanson's TV dinners, frozen pot pies, a head of iceberg lettuce and two cans of Chung King Chow Mein.

"Well, it has been six years, and I have contacts instead of the Coke bottle eye glasses, so you are forgiven for not recognizing me," I said. "It is good to see you. What brings you to Bloomington?"

"Tom—you may remember I married Tommy Webber—and I live a couple of blocks from here. How about you? Do you live here?"

"No, but I work close by at Computing Data. I just came from leasing some space around the corner for a new company and stopped here for some groceries."

"A new company?"

"Yes. It's a long story." I hesitated for a moment, not wanting to be too forward. "Do you have time for a cup of coffee? We could talk about that and old times."

"Sure, but I have to be home by six. Tom usually phones then, and he wants me home when he calls. He's a trucker for 3M. Has the Madison-Milwaukee-Chicago run every week."

We paid for our groceries and went next door to the Dew Drop In Café. It smelled like the evening special was pork and sauerkraut. The place was crowded with the Early Bird Special folks and giggly high schoolers, an interesting mix. The only booth available was next to the door of the noisy kitchen. Our waitress did not look happy when we ordered only coffee. Ruthie kept her sunglasses on.

We began reminiscing about our high school days and asked each other about classmates we had kept up with. Of course, I could tell her all about Ozzie, Barb, Shu, and Trudy. She barely remembered Bjorn as he had dropped out after his sophomore year.

"I'll never forget the time you took me to the homecoming dance," Ruthie said. "Sorry I was such a pill. That was back in my boy-hater days. You were so nice and such a gentleman."

"That was my only date in high school," I said. "I would not have known anything about dating if it were not for Trudy and her mother. I know I was not very cool."

"In my humble opinion, being a kind gentleman outranks being cool."

"Well, that is nice of you to say."

"And I'm still sorry I swore at you about closing the car door on my dress. It was silly to swear at you. I *know* my hem got caught in the car door when you closed it. My strapless dress stopped entering the car, but I didn't. It was pulled down below my you-know-whatsezz." She laughed and pointed to her whatsezz.

"Yes, I remember, and, oh, my goodness, I am so sorry." My face flushed.

She laughed so hard she took a napkin from the holder, took off her sunglasses and dabbed tears from her eyes. That was when I saw her black eye.

BJORN

"OH, MAN, HAVE I ever missed you," MK said as she threw her arms around me at the airport. I was on a ten-day leave between language school and being shipped out for Vietnam. She looked better than ever. I couldn't help but feel her familiar curves even though she was wearing heavy winter clothes.

"Likewise, I'm sure," I said and lifted her up for a quick twirl. "I'm glad you could pick me up. No problem getting off work?"

"No, babe. I've put in a bunch of overtime so I could name my days off when you got home. I'm yours for most of the next ten days. Patients at Waconia Hospital will just have to die without me. I can't wait to show you my new apartment."

"Well, let's stop in Victoria on the way. I gotta check in with the folks and see how things are going at the plant. Then I'll peek at your new apartment and at a lot more of you."

On the way to the parking ramp the winter air hit my lungs like a hammer, but it was great to be home with my gal, and I was anxious to see the folks, the plant, MK's apartment, and her beautiful body without her winter coat. I looked forward to seeing Pope, Shu, and Ozzie too.

On the way to Victoria, we passed the old Crossroads restaurant. "Big dumpster—looks like the remodeling's started. I hope Ozzie and Barb know what they're doing," I said. "It's a big, risky deal. Hope they survive."

***

LATER I STOPPED to see my folks. "Hi, Ma. Great to see you. The place looks the same," I said as Ma got up to give me her patented hug. But something was wrong. "What's up? You aren't your normal smiley self."

"Oh, Bjorn. It's so good you're here. Go say hi to your dad first—he's out in the shop with Mike—then we need to talk." She moved past me and pecked MK on the cheek and said, "Hi, my dear."

I didn't like the vibes as we walked out to the shop. Dad had just turned off a lathe. "Hey, Dad, still lettin' that lathe get the best of you?" I joked. I thought Pa looked thinner and paler than I'd ever seen him. His black eye patch was sweat stained.

"Mike, sounds like the army's turning their soldiers into smart asses," Pa said as he patted my shoulder. "Glad to see you, son. Looks like California agreed with you. Got some color."

"Ya, Pa, about as much as a tow-head can get. Hi, Mike. You takin' care of my old man?"

"Yup. I'm also pushing ropes and herding cats, all with the same success." A scowl crossed Mike's Irish mug, and then he smiled. "Mary Katherine was sure anxious for you to get back. 'Course, she wasn't the only one. I don't mean to rush your homecoming hellos, but we've all gotta have a talk. Utoft should be here any minute."

I'd been at the plant only a few minutes and already two different people had told me we had to have a talk. I doubted the talk involved good news.

The gravel crunched outside as Utoft drove up. He got out of his truck and joined us in the shop. "Hello, Bjorn. Sorry you had to come back to face the town problem," Utoft said with a handshake.

Pa said, "We haven't told him yet. Didn't wanna worry him before he got back."

"What do you mean by town problem?" I asked.

"Ah . . . well, tonight the town Planning Commission is holding a public hearing about a goddamned new ordinance," Pa said, shaking with anger. "A couple of 'em proposed that any manufacturing or industrial plant in town can't be in operation before 7:00 a.m. or after 7:00 p.m. Claims the noise is a problem for residents. We'd be screwed—oh, sorry, MK. We can hardly keep up with the work using two full shifts and plenty of overtime."

I tried to keep my cool. "Whose crazy idea was this? We're the only plant in town, aren't we?"

"Two assholes on the commission," Mike said, shaking his head. "Jorgenson, who we fired for drinking on the job, and Hartman, who we fired after seven of his co-workers asked us to. He was hard to get along with and bitched about everybody and everything. Now they're getting back at us."

Ma came in. "They need three votes to recommend the new ordinance to the council. And they've probably got 'em 'cause the two jerks usually intimidate the new gal on the council, and she votes with them."

"Jeeezus. Okay, I've got the picture. So what's the plan?" I said.

"I'm not goin' to the meeting," Pa said. "I'm so pissed I'd probably say something I shouldn't. Olga, Mike, and Utoft will speak for us. They have some facts to put on the table, like the fact that we pay thirty-seven percent of the property taxes this one-horse town gets."

"Plus, there's less than three hundred people in the whole dang town. That's about sixty-five houses. Of the thirty-eight people who work here, eighteen of 'em live here. In other words over twenty percent of Victoria's households are supported by this company. And, twelve of 'em work the night shift. They sure as hell don't wanna be laid off 'cause of some dumb-assed ordinance."

Utoft said, "They'll be at the meeting, too. We're giving them paid time off to attend."

Pa said, "Another point is that most of the night shift work is welding and painting, so there's not a lot of noise. And we've put up that six-foot-high solid fence and there's a lot of pine trees between the rest of the town and the plant. We hope you can be there, son."

I glanced at MK who was giving me "the look." "Sounds like you've got it covered and the Planning Commission deck is stacked against us anyway. Do the best you can, keep your cool, and let the employees do most of the speaking. I won't be there. I'll save my ammunition to talk to the City Council members individually. Is Wilfie from the lumberyard still mayor?"

***

AS EXPECTED, THE VOTE was three to two for recommending the ordinance to the council.

***

"HELLO, WILFIE," I SAID as I entered his lumberyard office.

"Well, Bjorn. Great to see you. Good of you to stop by," he said.

"This is not a social call, *Mr. Mayor*." His office hadn't changed since I had worked there ten years ago. The knotty pine walls were still in need of a new coat of varnish, and the floor tile design had been obliterated by dirt tracked in from the yard.

"Now, Bjorn, don't be that way. I s'pose you've got your underwear in a bunch about that ordinance the Planning Commission is proposing. I don't think the council will pass it."

"Well, I'm sorry but *thinking* it won't pass won't cut it with me. I have to know for sure the council won't approve it." I handed him a letter.

"What's this?"

"It's a letter from the Mayor of Waconia. He's also the chairman of their Industrial Park Commission. Read it."

Wilfie put on his glasses and started to read out loud:

"Dear Mr. Olson, It is my pleasure to offer the following terms for the relocation of your company to Waconia, specifically to occupy the city-owned plant formerly used by the bankrupt Viceroy Motorcycle Company. We appreciate your being available for negotiations while on leave. I'm sure you will find the following—"

"Mr. Mayor, you can finish reading it after I leave. It's kinda long and I'm in a hurry. I'm leaving for California this afternoon. Here are some more letters." I handed him several.

"You can't—I mean, what are you— ?"

"These are letters from every business in town, not that there are a lot of 'em. The bottom one is from the company who owns this lumberyard—your bosses. All of 'em ask the council to vote down the ordinance."

"Well, I don't appreciate—"

"I'm not here to be appreciated." I put a few more letters on his desk. "These are from both churches, the town baseball team manager, the little league coach, and the Boy and Girl Scout leaders, which are all supported by our employees and our company."

"You shouldn't resort to threaten—"

"I'm not threatening anything, Wilfie. I'm promising. Excuse me for being pissed. This whole thing screwed up my leave. I won't be back for over a year, and those two disgruntled assholes made Ma sit through insults about our company and our family. If you don't believe me, just read the minutes from the Planning Commission meeting. The council better vote down this crap, Wilfie. And while you're at it, you guys appointed Hartman and Jorgenson to the Planning Commission, so you can damn well un-appoint them."

"You can't tell us what to do."

"No, I can't. But I can strongly suggest what you *should* do. First, I *strongly suggest* you and at least one other council member visit Ma and personally apologize for the uncalled-for personal attacks she had to sit through at that public hearing. Second, I strongly suggest you vote down that ordinance *and* un-appoint those two assholes. But of course, as you said, it's your choice. Choose wrong and our company will move lock, stock, and barrel to Waconia. That, Mr. Mayor, I can guaran-goddamned-tee."

Chapter 26

April 1964, two months later

The olive drab Plymouth pulled into the Olson & Dad, Inc., parking lot at mid-morning. A grim faced major got out of the passenger seat carrying a canvas briefcase and headed for the office door. He was followed by his driver and associate, a staff sergeant. They appeared to be about the same age and their uniforms were crisp.

They went into the office, removed their hats, and approached Betty, the receptionist and payroll secretary, "Hello, I'm Major Dungey. We need to speak with Mr. or Mrs. Karl Olson. Are they here?"

She was not used to army brass standing by her desk and was impressed with their uniforms and military demeanor. It never dawned on her why two army men would be visiting.

"Hi. Ah, Karl—Mr. Olson—went with the trucker to Polarcat. He won't be back 'til day after tomorrow," Betty said. "Olga—Mrs. Olson—is out in the shop. I'll go find 'er. Can I tell her what this is about?"

"Just tell her we need to speak with her, please," Dungey said.

Betty got up and walked to the production area. Knowing the two army men would be watching her, she gave a little extra sway to her backside.

Olga

Betty came up to me in the shop and interrupted my conversation with Mike while he was repairing a drill press. "Olga, two army men are in the office and wanna talk to you. Sounds important. One of 'em's gotta lot of brass on him."

My heart almost stopped. "Oh, dear God . . . please no." I ran to the office. "I'm Olga Olson, what's wrong? Is it my boy?"

"Hello, ma'am. This is Sergeant Thortsensen and I'm Major Dungey. We're with the Army Quartermaster Procurement Office."

I put my hand on Betty's desk to steady myself. My heart started to beat again, and I felt the color return to my face. They didn't seem to realize what I was going through.

The major said, "We're here to conduct an unannounced inspection of your operation. We need to know if your firm can qualify to be added to the bidder's list for making a new army entrenching tool. Your application says your firm made the prototypes, but that doesn't mean anything when it comes to mass producing what we need."

"Well, welcome," I said. "But I didn't know we applied to be on any such list."

"Someone from here did or we wouldn't be here. Can we find a place to talk?" Dungey asked. He seemed to be in a hurry to get the visit over with. He probably was not excited to have drawn this assignment to a Podunk little town and small manufacturer.

I pointed the way to our small break room. "Ya, go through that door and have a seat. I'll put on a fresh pot of coffee. Then I'd like to have a couple of our guys join us. Is that okay?"

"Whatever you need to do," Dungey said impatiently.

After I poured their coffee and introduced Mike and Utoft, Major Dungey began to ask questions from an official looking checklist he took out of his briefcase. Mike was covered with grease and oil from helping repair the fork lift, but Utoft looked his usual well-kept self.

I was still a little shook up that the military was here and sorry there hadn't been a warning about them coming. I would have worn something better than my baggy house dress, and I certainly would have fixed my hair some way other than just in a bun.

"Okay, I need to confirm how many employees you have. I'm not sure the application information is correct."

"Well, it varies," I said. "Right now we have forty-one full time. Mike here thinks we need to add three more, and we have between twelve to fifteen part time, depending on the work load."

"That's all?"

"Ya."

"How many facilities do you have? It says on your application you only have one. How can that be?"

"Facilities? Ah, you mean—ah, oh no—I mean yes, just this one plant."

"Only one." He made a note on his list.

"I need to see your lost-time injury file."

"Don't have one," I said.

"What do you mean? Don't you keep a file on that?"

"I would if we ever had some bad injuries. You can check with Federated Insurance. We've never had one." I raised my chin a bit. His attitude was starting to tick me off.

"Unbelievable. Good." The major nodded as he looked at his list. "What union are your employees associated with?"

"None. Our people voted that down. Twice," Mike said.

"Oh, is that so? Hard to believe. All right. How many minorities do you have employed?"

"No one under twenty-one works in the plant," I said. "We do have some younger gals in the office."

Utoft leaned over and whispered in my ear. "He means other races, Olga, not how old people are."

Embarrassed, I tried to make a joke of it. "Well, Mike here, he's Irish. The only thing he ever did right was to sire my wonderful future daughter-in-law."

The major didn't smile.

"Our best welder is a Sioux Indian from Shakopee," Mike said. "We call 'im Chief. He's a real artist with a torch. Karl set him up in a corner of the shop so he could work on his metal sculptures in his off time."

"It's very disrespectful to call a Native American, 'Chief,'" Thorstensen said.

"Well, hell, that's what he wants to be called. He signs his art that way," Mike retorted. "You should see his wife. She's the most beautiful woman—other than my wife, daughter, and Olga, of course—that I've ever laid eyes on."

"Ya, we sponsored her in the Mrs. Minnesota pageant two years ago," I said. "She came in third. She's pretty shy. She has the stuff to strut, but she wouldn't do it like the fancy ladies she was up against. For the talent part, she displayed her Indian bead work on clothes she made."

"Enough of that." Dungey held up his hand. "Is he the only minority you employ?"

"Well, if you count part-timers, we have two Mexicans," Mike said.

"You mean Chicanos. Why are they only part-time?" Thorstensen asked with a scowl.

"Rita and Jose Sanchez—they call themselves Mexican, by the way—they're Shumacher Farms' hired hands," Mike said. "They live in Shu's uncle's house.

They work here three days a week in the winter and full time on the farm in the summer. They're a couple of our best part-timers. We have a lot of part time farmers here in the winter, and the same with teachers in the summer. What the hell's wrong with that?"

I put my hand on Mike's arm again. "You should see their oldest boy, Richy, play baseball," I said. "He stays overnight with us when he has Saturday practices and Sunday games. Karl gave 'im the nickname BP for Border Patrol . . . nothing gets by him. He's the best shortstop our town team ever had. Now he stitches BP on the side of all his caps."

Thorstensen rolled his eyes and muttered something that sounded like "racist." Then he said, "Don't you have any other races employed?"

"Other races?" Mike said. "Like which ones? The only people that live within twenty miles of here are Krauts and Towheads, 'cept me of course, the lone Mick, the Chief, and Shu's Mexicans. What do you expect us to do, import some Chinamen and guys from the Congo, or maybe some of them English sonsabithches or commie Ruskies?"

I put my hand on Mike's arm again.

The major tried to keep a business-like demeanor, but he also seemed anxious to get the meeting over with. He musta thought the meeting was a waste of time. He didn't continue down his checklist. "That about wraps it up. Thank you for your time." He stood, and Thorstensen followed his lead.

I glanced at Utoft and Mike. It was obvious we had failed their short test.

"Just a minute," Utoft said. "Anything on the list of yours about the percentage of women employed or female ownership?" His voice mirrored his disgust. "Aren't they what *you people* would call a minority?"

The two army gentlemen stopped and turned to look at Utoft.

"Olga here is one-third owner of this place. Counting part-timers, about thirty percent of her employees are women," Utoft said with a stern look. I guess army uniforms didn't intimidate him. The rest of us followed his lead.

I said, "I'm surprised you didn't want to see the production area. You could eat off the floor back there. You didn't ask to see any of the stuff we make and you didn't ask for our customers' phone numbers so you could ask them if they're satisfied with our work."

Mike said, "Why don't you talk to some of our employees, see how they like working here?"

I said, "Seems you guys are more interested in *what* people are instead of *who* they are. I don't know if we want or need your business. Our other customers don't feel the need to tell us how to run our own company. They judge us on the quality, value, and on-time delivery of our products," I took a deep breath to settle down. "We do things right or we lose their business. It's called competition. We're plenty busy anyway. Our son must have made the application to do business with the government without telling us. I'll let him know the whole thing was a waste of time."

The major rubbed his chin.

Mike asked, "Aren't you the guys who are buying those hundred-dollar hammers and those two-hundred-dollar toilet seats? I'll tell you what, this outfit wouldn't screw the taxpayers like that."

The major was shifting his weight from side to side, and his face got redder at every comment.

Utoft asked, "Sir, do you happen to know who designed the new entrenching tool?"

"No, I don't. Does it matter?"

Utoft nodded toward me. "Her son designed it. He's the founder and part owner of this company."

The major looked past us. "So why isn't he here?"

"Because he was drafted. He's in the army . . .Vietnam."

The major's face went slack. He looked at the floor for a moment, then motioned for Thorstensen to sit back down at the pinkish Formica table.

SHU

WE MADE IT A POINT to have lunch with Pope at least once a month. This time the group was made up of MK, Ozzie, Trudy, and me. We were at the Steak and Ale on I-494. Pope was there alone.

"Of course things could be better," Pope said, replying to MK's question about Ursula. "But, I think she is making progress. She is home most of the time now and the doctors believe they have configured the proper combination of drugs to keep her functional."

MK reached out and held Pope's arm. "You dear man, you have the patience of a saint. Describe 'functional.'"

"Well, if you observed her, you would be able to tell immediately that she is heavily drugged. She has large pupils and she is lethargic. She does not have the best hygiene nor care how she dresses, but her rages are under control. She agreed to go to mass with me the other day." Pope ran his hand through his hair. "Please, can we talk about something else? Ozzie, where's Barb?"

"She's a marketing maniac. Man, is she into it. Today she has appointments with feature writers for two different newspapers. She wants to convince 'em our concept and grand opening are worth a story. She'd have been here but the appointments were hard to get in the first place, and she was worried they might cancel if she tried to reschedule." He handed an envelope to Pope. "Here, she wanted me to give you this card for Ursula."

"Thank her for me. That was very thoughtful of her."

MK said, "Ozzie, you've got a great partner in her. Lucky you."

"Man, don't I know it," Ozzie said.

MK said, "Shu, I hear you guys are building another turkey building. Gonna corner the market pretty soon?"

"Ya, but Trudy convinced the rest of us this would be our last new turkey building," I said, patting Trudy on the shoulder. "She thinks, and we all agree, we shouldn't put all our eggs in one turkey basket. We're gonna go into raising high quality beef cattle in addition to turkeys."

"Tell 'em about your dad," Trudy said.

"Oh, yeah, Ma and him are in Arizona—Apache Junction—for a month with his brother. It's the first real vacation they've ever had. He told me before they left if it weren't for me pushing to quit that damn dairy business and go with minimum tillage they wouldn't have been able to go. Damned if he didn't give me a little hug. I don't remember ever gettin' one from him before." I felt kinda stupid when I had to wipe away a tear at the Steak and Ale. To change the subject I asked MK, "So what do you hear from your soldier boy?"

"He's enjoying his assignment as much as circumstances will allow. He likes the people he's instructing and says it's a beautiful country. While he's teaching them how to run the equipment, they're building a short air strip for small planes and short take-off cargo planes. It's near a little place called Chu Lai, which is near a town called DaNang. Some of the other advisors in his outfit are helping improve the port facilities in DaNang. It's just a little fishing village."

Trudy asked, "Are you gonna be able to see him before he gets out?"

"We've written back and forth about maybe meeting in Guam or the Philippines if he gets a leave," MK said. "Sure hope that works out."

Of course, she did not know about Mai Hue Quy.

Chapter 27

May 1964, one month later

OZZIE

B arb?" I mumbled. No answer. I was half-asleep during a toss-and-turn night. My feet were bound up in the sheet like a mummy's.

"Barb?" I reached over to nudge her, but she wasn't there.

She probably couldn't sleep, just like me. Gotta go find 'er. Okay, roll outta bed. Jeeze, what time is it anyway? What if nobody shows up?

The cold glow of the kitchen's fluorescent light seeped under the bedroom door of our apartment as I tried to wipe the sand out of my eyes. I tiptoed down the hall—didn't wanna wake Danny—and saw Barb slumped at our small kitchen table. She had our checkbook and expense ledger from the business in front of her. The clock on the wall above her head read 2:10. Each hair on her head was fighting for its own direction.

I laid my hand on her shoulder. "Couldn't sleep either, babe?" I whispered in her ear as I sat next to her.

"Oh—hope I didn't wake you," Barb said, reaching for my hand. "No, I can't sleep . . . can't keep my mind from spinning bad stuff. Darn personal guarantees on the loan spook the heck outta me. We never should have agreed to that."

"Well, Cline never woulda given us the loan without 'em. It'll be okay. We've got a good plan, and you've done a great marketing job."

"Well, let's hope so, but we signed Danny's future away when we assigned his dad's life insurance proceeds to the bank." Barb put her head in her hands. "That was gonna pay for his education."

"My insurance from the accident is on the line too, but we had no choice if we wanted to go ahead with our plans. Can't second guess ourselves now. We just gotta make this a success. We've practically worked around the clock for six months getting ready for this big opening night." I took her hand. "You're a great partner. Come on, we'd better try to get some sleep."

She looked at me, worry still lining her sleepy face. "But what if nobody shows up?"

***

TWO FIFTEEN-FOOT-TALL real palm trees flanked our double front doors, which were lined with split bamboo on both sides. We were scheduled to open at five o'clock sharp for our pre-grand opening party.

Our kitchen staff started food prep at mid-morning. Emmer, our head cook, seemed to have things under control and the smells coming from the stove tops and ovens gave me a much-needed confidence boost.

Barb had been working with the wait staff since noon, practicing every possible serving situation. I overheard part of her instructions. "You know, today is the opening of Ozzie's and my new business, but it's also the opening day of your own *personal* business. Don't treat this opportunity as just a job. Treat it like it's your own business. Your tip income depends on how you conduct yourselves. Frown or smile—which one helps *your* bottom line? Fast, accurate service or slow service—which one builds *your* bank account? Ozzie and I are depending on you, and you are depending on us, so it seems to me we're in this together. If we as owners do a good job, people will return and spread the word to their friends, which means you'll get even more tips. If you as wait staff do a good job, people will return and spread the word to their friends, and Ozzie and I will make money and be able to keep the place open so you can make more money." She was on a roll like Billy Graham.

I worked with the bartenders, both inside and at the Tiki bar outside by our large patio, to fine-tune an already efficient system even more. I also kept checking on the boat bar and crew. Six Twins players had agreed to buy a forty-five passenger cruise boat anchored across the road on Lake Minnetonka. It cost me taking them to dinner at Stillwater on the St. Croix River to show them the possibilities. Barb and I agreed to supply the food, the booze, the crew and the promotion and split the profits with the players.

The last glacier did a heck of a job of lake making. With over a hundred miles of shoreline among the bays and islands of Lake Minnetonka, the cruises would have varied routes. On the weekends we'd offer lunch and dinner cruises plus moonlight cruises. During the week we'd use the boat for private parties. Barb figured the sleek craft also doubled as a floating billboard for Danny's Island Escape for all the residents and other boaters on the lake to see.

We installed four huge aquariums in the restaurant: one behind each bar, one in the dividing wall between the main room and the Tiki patio and one in the middle of the main room. Each was stocked with tropical fish that flashed their colors like pole dancers.

The other tropical décor, murals of ocean-beach scenes, artificial palms to go with the real ones outside, sea shells scattered around, and fish nets suspended from the ceilings, were all in place—all very much *out* of place in Minnesota.

That was the point: *Escape to Danny's*. The food and décor were different, and the music wouldn't be rock and roll, but a variety to appeal to different tastes. We didn't just hang up an OPEN sign and hope for business, either. We planned events and activities, including fishing contests, snowmobile races—Bjorn got Polarcat to sponsor them—a palm planting festival, volleyball tournaments, classic car shows, a water ski show, great live music, and more.

Barb and I were especially looking forward to our Singles Nights when our wait staff would serve as the messengers for dance requests between customers. We thought our Hangover Sunday Brunch would be a favorite of customers too. It featured a Bloody Mary in a huge mug with a prawn draped over the rim, and the mug brimming with so much other stuff it was dang near a meal.

Danny's Island Escape was ready for our pre-grand opening party. We sent out invitations to a hundred and thirty people and their spouses, if they had 'em. We hadn't requested RSVPs, so the number of people who showed up would be a mystery 'til the party started. The invitations were sent to friends, but more important for future business, to influential members of the surrounding communities.

For ten bucks per head they got two drink tickets, a boat ride, unlimited appetizers and live music for dancing. It was one heck of a deal. The cost shortfall was part of our ad budget. We hoped someone would show up.

At quarter to five there was loud banging on the locked front door. Barb and I interrupted our last-minute panic to see who it was. We should have known: the gang came early. MK was standing in front of the rest of them and reading aloud from a parchment scroll: "Hear ye, hear ye, it is proclaimed by the undersigned friends of the proprietors that this establishment shall henceforth bring joy to its many future customers and profits to its founders. Barb and Ozzie, it is decreed that your creativity, hard labor, and risk will be amply rewarded."

After MK read the proclamation, the gang rushed forward to hug Barb and me, pat us on the back, and give us bouquets of flowers. Stupid me, I got kinda misty eyed.

Even Ursula was there, but she wasn't hugging anybody.

I looked past the palms to the parking lot; it was filling up.

BJORN

I WAS ASSIGNED to the Military Assistance Command Vietnam. Four other enlisted guys and I were sent from the MACV headquarters to Chu Lai to help train Republic of Vietnam (ARVN) soldiers in the use and maintenance of heavy earthmoving equipment.

Major Nguyen Tai—we Americans called him Major Guy, with his approval—was the ARVN officer in charge of the training facility, which would become an airstrip when the training and associated work was completed.

Major Guy took a liking to me. Once in a while he invited me to accompany my captain to the major's home for dinner. He liked to show off his relationship with Americans to his fellow townsfolk even though I was only an enlisted grunt. Besides, we always took a few cartons of cigarettes and bottles of booze as gifts for him. He was a good guy, probably in charge of this project 'cause it was near his home. He'd been wounded while fighting with the French against the commies. He'd lost one arm and walked with a cane

Major Guy's wife was a wonderful cook, and for these diner parties was helped by their daughter. The first time I attended one of those dinner parties, his daughter and I locked eyes—several times. At the next dinner I attended, I got up the courage to speak with her.

She was petite and strikingly beautiful. It was hard for me to take my eyes off her. It was hard to tell, but I guessed she was five or so years older than me.

"Hello, you speak wonderful English. Where did you learn it?" I asked, not quite sure how to break the ice, or even that I should. But then I thought why not? What's the harm?

"Thank you. I learn from French teacher. I interpret for French army. Teacher thought it good if learn English also."

"Wow, English with a French and Vietnamese accent. It's beautiful. I'm sorry, I should introduce myself. My name is Bjorn." I loved to hear her speak. *MK would understand. I've been away for a long time.*

"Born. That funny name. My name Mai Hue Quy. Call me May."

"No, not Born. It's Bjorn . . . oh, that's okay, Born is close enough." *This won't affect how I feel about MK.* "You don't have your father's name?" *MK might be dating too. Some doctor, probably.*

Her eyes teared up. Man, was she beautiful.

"Husband killed in war. He officer work with French army. Many killed in war. Sad time."

"I'm sorry about that. I shouldn't have asked about your name. Your family has a nice home here." *Who knows, MK might be writing me a Dear John letter right now.*

"Thank you. I live nearby so able to help if time. Also teach school."

It had been five months since I'd been in Minnesota. I was lonely and worried sick about my folks and the company. I'd forgotten how nice it was nice to talk to a woman. A week after the second dinner party, I asked Major Guy if it would be okay to ask May out for dinner. I guess the major had come to like me, so he approved. Several dates followed.

Ozzie had sent me an invitation to their pre-grand opening party. I was real happy for them, but at the time, I was also a little pissed. It reminded me again that I couldn't be home tending to my own business. I sent a note back telling him to hold on to my drink tickets until whenever the hell I could get back.

The day after Ozzie and Barb's party at Danny's Island Escape, May and I were on an ocean beach under our own palm trees and surrounded by sea shells.

Our plan was to have a picnic lunch she had prepared. But first, we comforted each other at our own island escape.

DAVID, A.K.A. POPE

"THIS IS A MOMENTOUS DAY. Our first good prospect will be here at one-thirty," I said to Ruthie. I had hired her to be my office manager even though her husband would let her work only three days a week. "Mr. Gestach is the president of a mid-sized bank in Chaska, and if our programmer is able to convince him how we could save him thousands of dollars a year, he should enter into a contract with us."

"Bring 'im on!" Ruthie said, pumping her fist in the air.

I liked her attitude. I knew customers would like her as well. It was nice to be around someone with some enthusiasm. Tom, her husband, forced her to resign her previous position at Northwest Airlines. She had become the department's office manager and put in too many hours, according to Tom.

Mr. Gestach was sold on our service early during the presentation. He said he would have to get his board's approval, but that was only a formality.

He stayed to work out the specifics of what he needed and made sure the programmer understood his bank's needs. He said, "If this works, I'll be happy to recommend Midwest Computer Timesharing to other bankers."

That was music to our ears.

At the end of the day, Ruthie came into my office to say good-bye for the day. "David, I'm so happy to work with you," she said as she approached my side. "You are such a gentleman. We make a good team." She then gave me a big hug, pushing her body close to mine. I believe I saw a bruise on her neck; it was partially covered by her turtle neck sweater until the hug.

I was not sure if it was appropriate behavior for her to put her arms around me.

"Yes, we do," I said, keeping my arms to my side.

SHU

SUNDAY, THE DAY AFTER the party at Danny's, Trudy and I sited and staked out our new house in the pasture overlooking the pond. We had worked on the floor plan together—well, I guess mostly Trudy did—so now was the time to locate where it would be built. We struggled to place the house in a spot so only two maple trees would have to come out if we put a curve in the driveway.

Evening fell as we finished the staking.

Trudy giggled. "Stop that! You'd think we were a coupla horny teenagers." She was playing hard-to-get, but I knew she hoped I wouldn't stop. She pretended to be shocked when I wanted to try some of the things she had read to me in an article called "Tips On How to Keep Your Marriage From Going Stale" in a woman's magazine.

We were in the pasture enjoying magazine-induced new sexual adventures on the exact spot where our bedroom would be next year. She had won the new-house debate and was feeling pretty frisky. She had read in the magazine that if you wanted to keep your man, you had to be creative and uninhibited in the bedroom. The author mentioned several suggestions, but she had no idea how much more creative and uninhibited her suggestions would seem to be if performed in a pasture under sugar maples.

Chapter 28

July 1964, three months later

SHU

Where did'ja go with your dad?" Trudy asked me as I came through the back door into the kitchen. She was standing by the stove frying chicken for supper. My stomach growled. She was using Gretta's recipe. It was better than Colonel Sander's. "I saw you guys pull out about two o'clock."

"Oh, well . . . we went to see the Kelzers. He called Dad about us maybe buying their farm. You know, it butts up to our south fence line."

"Oh, really? And what did you tell them?"

"That we'd hafta think about it 'cause it's a lot to consider. They'd carry most of the financing, but we'd have to borrow more on the folks' original farm to come up with the down payment."

"So that means you're considering it?" Trudy's voice rose an octave as she jabbed a chicken breast. "We've got the loan on the original farm, a contract for deed on this farm, one on my folks' place and two loans with Cargill on the turkey pole barns." Her voice was getting louder. She had been hitting the edge of the frying pan with the meat fork each time she ticked off a debt. "We just got a letter of credit for the auction house to buy the Angus cattle and next year we'll have a new house mortgage. Oh, and we owe Land Master for five equipment loans." She hit the edge of the frying pan seven more times.

I looked down to study my shoes. I was pretty sure this conversation was headed for the crapper. "Well, that does sound like a lot, but so far we've been able to make the payments." *Oh, boy, now she's really gonna get ticked, but I gotta tell her sooner or later.* "Actually . . . when we buy Kelzer's, we'll have to delay . . . I mean, we'll have to wait for a year or two to build the new house."

Trudy turned from the stove to face me. "*When* buy it? We'll delay *what?*" she was hollerin' at me and had a death grip on the meat fork. Her face was red and it wasn't from standing over a hot stove. "I thought you said *we* had to *think* about it. Sounds to me like *we* have made up *our* minds!" Ellie and Nick, who had been sitting at the kitchen table, looked up at their mother with wide eyes. They'd never seen or heard her raise her voice that loud.

"Now, honey, don't get all upset." I'm sure my farmer-tan face got paler as her anger grew. "We can always build a house, but that land won't come up for sale again for a long time. Dad agrees with me. He thinks we should do the deal."

Trudy shook with anger and pointed the meat fork at me. "Let me tell you something, mister. We've lived in this mouse-infested, drafty, leaky dump for eight years." She glanced at the petrified kids and tried to lower her voice, but the more she talked, the louder her voice got. "Your turkeys and machines get new digs, but your kids and wife don't. You *promised me* we'd start the new house next spring."

"I know, honey. I know. And I'm sorry, but this Kelzer thing came out of the blue. Please understand, putting their land together with ours would set us up great for the future."

"You talk like there are no risks, like draught, bad commodity prices, ruined crops from hail or too much rain. Dammit, you can't *do* this to me!" She was no longer concerned about what the kids heard or saw. "I work my butt off around here and I have an equal vote. You are addicted to land and machines. Damnit, take the cure and think of your family!" She held the meat fork high in the air.

"I *am* thinking about my family," I said quietly. "I'm thinking long range."

Trudy let the meat fork drop to the floor and threw off her apron. She stomped into our bedroom and seconds later came back with her purse. She grabbed the keys to the pick-up from the hook by the door to the front porch. "I quit. I'm going on strike."

"Honey, please underst—"

A chunk of wood fell off the jamb as she slammed the door. The kids started to bawl.

She ran out to the dust-covered pick-up, got in and tore out of the farmyard. The pick-up spit gravel and feathers flew as she ran over one of Ellie's chickens.

I was shocked by her leaving. I went to comfort the kids, who were still crying. Smoke billowed up from the burnt chicken and the potato water boiled over on the stovetop. Our green Maytag wringer washer was sloshing away in the corner of the kitchen. A familiar odor was emanating from Nick's diaper.

***

AFTER I READ the kids a bedtime story, tucked them in and told them their mommy would be back soon and feeling better, it was nine-fifteen and Trudy still wasn't home. I took the wet clothes out of the washer and ran them through the wringer. I wasn't sure what to do with them after that so I hung them on the clothes lines outside.

I soaked the cast iron frying pan with the burnt chicken remains and scrubbed the stovetop where the potato water eruption and flying grease from the chicken had created a glue-like concoction. *Women just don't understand the big picture. Maybe this house ain't so hot, but jeezus, we can't let that land go. Maybe she'd be okay if we brought in a house trailer for a year or two. I'll show her a spot on the Kelzer farm that's on Lake Mattson. We could build there instead of the pond. I wonder where she is. Maybe she's with Gretta.*

"Oh, hello, Gretta. It's Shu," I said into the phone. "I was just wondering, is Trudy there? I'm kinda worried about her."

"Ya, Shu, she's here. I vas gonna call you in a little bit. Taking a valk vit her dad now. He's trying to calm her down. I t'ink she vants to spend the night. She came in awful upset. Had her heart set on dat new house, ya know."

"I know. I'm sorry I upset her so bad. I have some ideas about how to make her feel better. Can I talk to her?"

"You are a gute man, Shu, and she knows dat, but I t'ink it vould be best if you didn't talk to her tonight. She's haffing a gute talk with her dad. Leaff her be. Kids okay?"

"Ya, they were upset, but they're okay now. Tell her I love her very much."

"Ya, I vill. Good night."

"Good night."

It was one of those tossing-and-turning nights for me. I spent most of the night fighting with my pillow. Sure, I was worried about my relationship with Trudy, of course, but I have to admit, she got me wondering about all of our debts, too. They were piling up.

At six-thirty the next morning I woke to the wonderful smell of frying bacon.

***

"WELL, HI. WELCOME BACK to Danny's," Barb said to us four days later. "Haven't seen you guys since the opening party."

"Hey, Barb, good to see you. Sorry we haven't been back. Been awful busy with the farms," Trudy said as she gave Barb a peck on the cheek. "We're here to celebrate a special occasion."

"Anniversary? Birthday?"

"No, we're celebrating not hitting each other over the head with frying pans. Our truce is now official," I said with a broad smile.

"Ozzie around?" Trudy asked.

"I'm not sure I understand that truce talk, but I'm glad I don't see any black-and-blue marks on either of you. Ozzie's out on the patio schmoozing with some customers and passing out free shots of Danny's Island Mimosas. We want the customers to be served by the owners so we can get some info from them."

"What info?" I said.

"Where they're from, where they work, can we put them on our mailing list? Stuff like that," Barb said. "All part of marketing. They like the free Mimosa shot. If we find out where they work, we suggest they swing their next office party to here or our boat. Have a seat. I'll go tell Ozzie you're here."

***

THE PEACE AGREEMENT was negotiated over a tense three days. Trudy had the outline in place shortly after I showed her the possible new home site by Lake Mattson and told her about the trailer house idea.

Trailer house, okay, but she insisted it had to be a double-wide. Trudy drew up the final agreement guaranteeing we would be in the new house in no more than two years. After that, we'd rent the trailer to another hired hand and family. Our pond lot would be sold immediately to pay for the trailer and to pay off the loan on the first turkey building.

I also had to agree I wouldn't order any new equipment unless it was approved by *all* shareholders of Schumacher Farms, Inc. The option to buy my uncle's farm, which we were now sharecropping, had to be extended three more years, which was fine with my uncle. Other than his farm, there would be no more land purchases unless *all* shareholders voted aye.

Trudy also wanted our Angus herd purchasing to be delayed at least two years until the other turkey building was paid off so we wouldn't draw down any money on the letter of credit. I reluctantly agreed, because she admitted that buying the Kelzer place was a good opportunity *if* we did the other debt saving things we incorporated into the agreement.

The signing of the peace treaty took place on the site where our new house would overlook Lake Mattson, exactly where the master bedroom would be. Making up was a wonderful thing, except the mosquitoes found the same old targets they had found under Gretta's windbreak a few years back.

***

I LOOKED AROUND just as Ozzie came in. "Hi, Ozzie. Got time to join us for a bit?" I said. "Looks pretty busy. How's it going?"

"Hi, yourself. It's going pretty good. Weeknights are slow, but picking up. Takes time to get the word out about a destination restaurant," Ozzie signaled for a waitress. "Let me buy your first round. What'll ya have?"

The waitress came over to take our order. She had on the garb all Danny's waitresses wore; a sailor's hat, a floral print tee shirt with one shoulder exposed (but no cleavage), and white denims with white deck shoes. Waiters and bar tenders wore same uniform except for the bare shoulder.

"Who's the band?" Trudy asked. "They're fantastic. Crowd seems to love 'em."

"Riverboat Ramblers from St. Paul. They do their banjo bit on one of the show boats on the Mississippi. We've got 'em under contract for Sunday nights for the rest of the year; another one of Barb's coups."

"Have you heard from MK or Pope?" Trudy asked.

"Not from MK, but Barb called to check on Pope. The Nazi is back in the hospital."

Chapter 29

August 1964, one month later

DAVID, A.K.A. POPE

Ruthie, I am very sorry to call you at home," I said slouching by the hospital pay phone. "I know Tom does not like me to call you there, but I have a scheduling dilemma."

"Oh, David, that's okay. He's not here. What's wrong?"

"Well, I have to meet with two doctors at eight-thirty this morning and do not know what time I will be able to get to the office." My elbow was at rest on the ledge of the pay phone counter and my forehead was resting on my hand. I had been up all night. "Remember, two officers from that large farmer's co-op are going to be at our office at nine-thirty to look over our operation. I was wondering if you could go in to open up, show them around and introduce them to the programmers. I realize it is your day off, but there is no one else I can depend on or trust as much as I do you."

"Oh, my. I just left a message on your home answering machine to say I won't be able to be in at all this week." Her voice sounded muffled. "David, what's the doctor's meeting about? Can't you change the time?"

"It is about—I—I am so glad I can talk to you about this—Ursula tried to kill herself last night." My voice broke. "Just as I was leaving the hospital last night she cut her wrists using a glass she broke."

"Oh, David, how terrible!"

"There was blood everywhere. She screamed at me to get out of the room and let her die. I have to meet the doctors when they are available, and that is at eight-thirty. I . . . I am running out of options for her care."

"I'm so sorry. Is she all right? I mean, I wish I could be with you to comfort you, David. You don't deserve to have to deal with something like this, you dear man."

"I am committed to see this through. She is my wife." I hesitated. "Why are you unable to come in this week?"

After a longer than normal pause, Ruthie said, "Now it's my turn to say I'm glad I have you to talk to about this."

"About what? Are you quitting?"

"Oh, no, I wouldn't leave you. I love working with you."

"Then why not come to work this week?"

"I'm not . . . presentable."

"Well, I happen to think otherwise."

"Ah . . . not today. Not unless you think Sonny Liston is presentable right after a fight. Tom got mad before he left for Madison . . . claimed I made the wrong breakfast for him. He hit me. Again. Son-of-a-bitch . . .oh, I'm sorry. I know you don't like swearing, but he hit me in the face this time. He usually hits me where it won't show. My lip is all swollen and bloody . . . I think my nose is broken."

I slapped my forehead, *I am such an idiot.* I remembered her black eye when we met in the grocery store and the bruise on her neck when she hugged me. It never dawned on me that Tom was a wife beater. "Oh, Ruthie, I had no idea. I am so sorry. What can I do? Have you called the police?"

"I don't dare. He'd kill me. And don't you get involved either."

"I *am* involved. I care for you."

"Oh, David . . . just hearing that helps," she said softly. "Tell you what. I'll find the phone number for the co-op and call 'em to ask for a change of the meeting day."

"Thank you. I know you will handle it well. We cannot lose a prospect. The bills are piling up and prospective clients are scarce."

"Yes, David, I understand. Good luck with the doctor's meeting. My thoughts are with you."

"And mine—and my prayers—are with you."

***

THAT NIGHT I HAD ONE of my frequent erotic dreams. For months, the dreams had been my only sexual release. Ursula and I had not been intimate for a long while. For some time my partner in my dreams had been neither Ursula nor Angie.

***

"BLESS ME FATHER for I have sinned. It has been some time since my last confession." The odor of incense permeated the air. I thought I knew which priest was in the dark confessional. The confessional experience was always awkward for me, especially if a friend was behind the screen.

"Our Lord is forgiving. Unburden yourself. God will comfort you," Father Distel said. "Please continue."

"Yes, Father. Ah . . . my wife tried to commit suicide. Her doctors asked if I had done anything to cause her actions. I do not think I did, but just the fact that they questioned makes me wonder whether I did something to contribute to her decision."

"Son, we can't control what is in another person's mind. I know you are a good Christian man. You mustn't take on that guilt. Let's instead forgive her for thinking she had the right to determine when she would die. That is up to God alone."

"Thank you for that, Father."

"Pray about it, son. You'll find comfort. Is there anything else you want to talk about?"

"Well . . . yes, I find myself having lustful thoughts about someone other than my wife. I-I know that is wrong. I try to stop, but I have not been able to do so."

"That is not unusual. Man is a sexual being. As long as you don't act on your lustful thoughts it's not a major problem, but 'Thou shalt not commit adultery' is one of the Commandments. It is not just a suggestion. Take it seriously."

"Of course. I know that."

I wondered whether Father Distel ever had lustful thoughts.

BJORN

CAPTAIN ABTS HAPPENED to be on site, so I hustled over to the command tent. I stepped in and rendered a quick, sweaty salute.

"Hey there, Olson . . . what's up?"

"Sir, we might have a problem. I just went with Barney, one of the mechanics, to look at a broken hydraulic line on one of the dozers."

"So what? Can't he fix it?"

"Sure, but that's not the problem. It looks to me like it wasn't worn out. Looks like a bullet tore through it. Clean cut and a big ding in the frame behind the hose."

"Oh, hell!" Abts said. "Let me get Major Guy, then take us over to see it."

I drove the two officers to the end of the future airstrip to check out the damage. The trip was kinda bouncy for 'em, but I didn't slow down.

"This didn't break by itself. It would be frayed instead of a clean cut," Abts said. "Major, we have a problem. I request you send out regular perimeter patrols to check for snipers or any other enemy activity."

"There has been no reported guerrilla activity in sector," Major Guy said. "Maybe this just stray shot from troops during target practice."

"We can't take that chance. We're here to train and advise, not to engage the enemy," Abts said.

"If insist, but think waste of manpower and time." Major Guy shrugged. "I will contact superior and ask to send down few troops to patrol area." I could tell he wasn't happy about the captain's insistence.

***

THE FIVE FULL-TIME U.S. personnel on site were a buck sergeant and three PFC mechanics, who trained eleven ARVN troops, plus me. I trained another nine to be heavy equipment operators. Captain Abts, our CO, dropped in weekly from DaNang. There were no on-site support people from MACV, so us G.I.s hired our own cook. We got a bump in our pay for having to buy our own food and hired help. I ate a few evening meals at May's each week, and a few breakfasts, too.

As long as I had to be in the dang army, I didn't mind my job and took pleasure in seeing the progress of the men I trained. Seven had never driven a motorized vehicle, not even a scooter, let alone heavy equipment. Two of them were sons of rice farmers. The only equipment they ever drove were water buffalo, and that was from the exhaust end. I praised their progress both individually and as a group. When I needed to correct or discipline one of the men, I did it quietly, out of sight of the others and with an arm around his shoulder.

If they pulled the wrong lever on the equipment, stepped on the wrong pedal, or steered too sharp or too little, it meant trouble. The hardest thing to teach them was to judge how deep the blades of the dozers or scrapers should cut into the dirt. The worst incident involved a trooper driving his dozer into the latrine pit while looking at and waving to a girl from the neighboring village.

The troops paid close attention to what I had to say. They were respectful and tried hard to please. They knew about, but didn't seem to resent, my relationship with the major's daughter.

Things were pretty casual and military dress was not enforced. This work was driving rough riding, smelly diesel equipment in hot, humid weather. The usual uniform of the day was a tee shirt, cut off fatigue pants and a native straw hat. A short time after the work day started even that garb would be sweat stained and dusty.

Because the other G.I.s on site had other jobs and didn't spend much time with me, I had no close friends among them. But I had May.

***

MACV WAS PART of a larger command, the US Military Assistance Advisor Group (MAAG) that had taken over from the French in training the ARVN.

Our airstrip work and training was proceeding ahead of schedule and the people at MAAG had been aware of our progress. They wanted to publicize some success stories, so General Akerberg, the honcho of MAAG, scheduled a trip to our site to inspect our work. He would also be bringing along some visiting press from the States. Captain Abts, Sarge, and I set up the plan for the general's visit.

When the general arrived, under the maintenance garage canvas, the mechanic instructors had a Cat engine torn down and were instructing the ARVN guys about putting it back together. At the north end of the project, ARVN troops were operating a scraper and a pusher dozer with no supervision. At the south end a crew of four ARVN and I set grade stakes, how much to cut or fill, and had a dozer and scraper running at idle as if ready to start moving dirt once the stakes were in place.

As the Jeep carrying the general, Major Guy and Captain Abts pulled up. I had my arm around the shoulder of one of my men who was looking through the transit scope. Unlike regular work days, we were all wearing regulation fatigues. Of course they were sweat stained pretty much all over because it was hotter than hell.

A MOMENT LATER

SUDDENLY A MORTAR ROUND exploded between the Jeep, which was slowing to a stop, and the transit tripod. Flying debris mangled the front grill of the Jeep, splintered the windshield and bloodied the driver with glass shards. The captain and general were thrown from the Jeep as it thudded into the shallow mortar shell crater. They were shaken, but unhurt. No one in the media jeep was injured.

Three of Bjorn's men, who were with him by the transit, were killed instantly. Most of Bjorn's unconscious body was catapulted through the air and slammed against the hot exhaust of the dozer. The landing broke his collar bone and several ribs, one of which punctured a lung, causing it to collapse. The hot exhaust pipe burned his neck and shoulder. His body, with blood spurting out, slid off the top of the dozer, but not before most of his right ear was cooked off.

Chapter 30

September 1964, three weeks later

SHU

Hello, Shu. This is Utoft over at Olson & Dads. Olga wanted me to call you."

"Yes, sir. Hi. What does she want?"

"I know you heard about Bjorn being wounded. Olga's too shook up to call you herself." His voice cracked. "We're all shook up."

"I understand. Any more information about 'im? We've been worried sick."

"Well, I can't sugar coat it. It's real bad. We don't know all the details yet, but we know he lost a leg, was severely burned, and has other injuries. They say he's not out of the woods yet."

"Oh, God." I had to sit down, quick. I could only guess what his folks and MK were going through.

"Anyway, he's being transferred to Fort Sam Houston in San Antonio. They've got a famous burn treatment center there at a place called Brook something or other."

"Jeeze, I didn't know he was in the States."

"He hasn't been for very long. He went from the hospital ship *Repose* to Guam. Then they flew him to San Diego two days ago, and next week they'll fly him to San Antonio. Guess he'll be there a while."

"Anything I can do?"

"As a matter of fact, there is. I contacted Mr. Philp at Land Master to tell him about Bjorn and him being transported to Fort Sam. He convinced the people at 3M to use one of their Convairs to fly Olga and Karl to San Antonio to be with Bjorn. He said they could invite others. Seems 3M sells a lot of stuff to Land Master and 3M also wants to do something for a wounded Minnesotan."

"Good for them. This mean I'm invited to go along?"

"Yes. The plane will leave Holman Field in St. Paul at two in the afternoon on Monday and return on Thursday morning. Can you go?"

"Nothing could stop me. Anything else I can do?"

"Yup. Could you call David Grimm and Ozzie, maybe see if they could go along? It would mean a lot to Karl and Olga, and I'm sure it would mean a lot to Bjorn."

"Of course. Consider it done."

"Mary Katherine is also going. She took a leave of absence from Waconia Hospital and got a job at Fort Sam over the phone. She'll stay there as long as Bjorn is there."

"That's great. I'm sure her being nearby will do Bjorn a world of good. She's the only gal for him."

DAVID, A.K.A. POPE

"DAVID, YOU CAN'T EXIST on frozen TV dinners. Let me fix you a nice pot roast," Ruthie said before leaving the office for the day.

"Thank you, but from time to time I also have things to eat at the hospital cafeteria."

"I won't take no for an answer. Tom will be in Madison tomorrow night. You can come over about seven after a short hospital visit."

"Having the boss over for dinner might be appropriate for a family or couple, but I do not believe it would be perceived as proper with just to two of us present."

"I happen to think it would be *very* proper," Ruthie said. "See ya tomorrow." She turned and left before I could say anything more.

***

EVEN THOUGH I was perspiring, I kept my suit and tie on as I drove to Ruthie's. Her home was a small stucco bungalow with a well-kept lawn and fragrant flower beds surrounding the porch. Low pansies were backed by snapdragons and taller hollyhocks. I do not know why I was nervous about being there, but I looked around to see whether anyone was watching as I approached her front door.

Ruthie answered the door wearing shorts and a snug, Twins-logoed tee shirt. Her attire reminded me of the time I asked her to the homecoming dance as she came out of the girl's physical education class.

"Welcome, David. I'm so glad you're here," Ruthie said. She smiled and reached for my arm to lead me inside.

"Hello, Ruthie, it certainly was nice of you to invite me, and I am glad to be here. Oh, my, your dinner smells wonderful. You must be a good cook."

"I just *loved* making it for *you*."

The interior of her home was neat and tidy and the décor gave off a warm and welcoming feeling. I tried not to look at the Twins logo on her tee shirt, but it was apparent to me she was not wearing a bra.

"Please make yourself comfortable," she said. "To start the evening, I've prepared my special spicy shrimp appetizer and opened a nice bottle of Matues."

"Oh, thank you, that sounds very nice, but I am sorry . . . I do not drink alcoholic beverages. I will just have water or lemonade with the shrimp."

"You poor dear . . . you need to relax. Loosen up. You're under so much stress. Please, let's share the Matues. Even priests drink wine." When she winked at me, I knew relaxing was out of the question.

Then again, the temptation was great, and I was aware Father Distel drank plenty of wine. "Well, all right. Maybe it is time for me to join the rest of mankind. The Bible says Jesus also drank wine . . . in moderation, of course."

"Yes, turned water into wine, didn't he? Here have a seat by me," she said as she patted the floral print sofa cushion beside her and poured our wine.

Ruthie clinked my glass with hers, and we both took a sip, then kept chatting. I felt a flush of warmth flow through my core. The shrimp dish was wonderful. I tried not to glance at the Twins logo during our chat.

"How was your hospital visit?"

"I did not have time to go. Herb called from our San Francisco office just as I was about to leave for the day."

"What did he want? He called yesterday when you were out and said he'd call back. I forgot to tell you he called."

"Well, you know, he and the New York office are subsidizing us. We are not carrying our share of the expenses. He wanted to talk about that, and talk he did, on an on."

"Oh, let's forget about business. Here, let me pour you another glass." She put her hand on my thigh as she leaned over to fill my glass. I guess I had started to relax as I did not object to the either placement of her hand or the refill.

"I forgot, I planned on proposing a toast," she purred. "Here's to the best boss ever. I'm so glad we found each other again. It's *so nice* to have a *gentleman* in my home." We clinked glasses again.

"That was very nice." I probably should have also proposed a toast at that moment but was a little tongue tied. My nerves were acting up again.

The phone rang and interrupted us.

"I'd better get that. It might be Tom checking up on me."

I stared at her posterior as she went to the phone.

"Hello. Oh . . . yes, he's here. David, it's for you." She handed me the phone with a questioning look.

"Hope you do not mind," I whispered to her. "I gave the nurses your number in case they need to reach me." I took the receiver. "Hello, this is David Grimm."

"I know who the hell this is!" Ursula yelled. "Who's the bitch who answered the phone? Why didn't you come to see me tonight? You were supposed to bring me some new magazines."

"Ah . . . we are having a staff meeting." It was the first time I had lied to her.

"Well, boss man, adjourn it now and get your butt over here. I want to—"

All of a sudden others were talking and yelling over the phone line. It sounded like there was some sort of struggle going on.

"I'm so sorry, Mr. Grimm. This is Nurse Ogan. Ursula saw the note you left with this number. We might have called you anyway. She's having a very bad time. She's refusing her meds. We might have to put her in restraints. Can you come right over?"

"I understand," I said. "Of course." The pot roast would have to wait.

Chapter 31

September 1964, a few days later

DAVID, A.K.A. POPE

Here's your wake-up coffee and a special treat," Ruthie said as she came into my office.

My eyes widened with surprise as I looked up from a periodical in which I was engrossed.

"I made you this special sticky bun this morning. It's still warm from my oven." She came to my side of the desk and leaned over my shoulder to place the treat and coffee in front of me. "I'm so sorry you had to leave early Tuesday night. We were having *such* a nice time."

"Thank you Ruthie." My senses were heightened as I got a whiff of her perfume. "About the other night . . . we need to talk. Please have a seat."

She sat on my desk, close to the sticky bun and me. She was wearing a short skirt.

"Ah . . . the programmer might see you. Please sit in the chair on the other side of the desk."

"But I like to be near you," she pouted.

"Please, the chair." I continued to stare at the sticky bun. *I must be going insane. The rounded, soft edges, the aroma and wet appearance of the caramel glaze seem sexual to me.*

I tried to not observe her legs as she slid off the desk. She walked around the desk, looking at me the whole way.

I said, "I need to discuss our relationship."

Her face brightened. "Oh, wonderful! Me too. There are so many things I want to say to you."

"First of all, it is obvious to me that our relationship has evolved from a business relationship to a personal one." I glanced at the sticky bun.

"Isn't that great? We need each other so much."

"Please, hear me out. You and I are vulnerable because of the circumstances of our marriages. The one constant in my life is my faith. I am a married man. I cannot lose my soul to pleasures of the flesh or your companionship."

"David . . . wait. What are you saying?"

"I have lustful thoughts of holding you, caressing and comforting you . . . of making love with you."

"Oh, me too, me too."

"But I cannot let that happen. I think God sent that phone call the other night to interrupt us before we . . . Ruthie, I have responsibilities, not only to my wife and business partners, but also to me maintaining my self-respect. I cannot allow any more complications in my life."

She looked stricken. "But, David—"

"Remember my good friend, Bjorn Olson? He might be dying, and I am not even able to take the time to say good-bye to him." I lowered my forehead to my hands.

"David, please . . . where are you going with this?" She reached for my hand.

I withdrew it. As firmly as I could muster, I said, "Ruthie, we must return to a strictly business relationship . . . either that, or you must resign." I could not look her in the eye. I returned my gaze to the bun.

She put her palms on her temples. "What? I mean . . . are you firing me?"

"We have a choice," I said, looking up from the bun. "Either to listen to our consciences or ignore them."

After a long painful pause, she dabbed tears from her cheeks and said, "Mr. Grimm, don't forget your ten o'clock appointment. I may be a little late tomorrow morning. I have to stop by the farmer's co-op office to pick up that contract."

She reached over my desk to take the untouched sticky bun and turned to leave.

"Thank you, Mrs. Webber."

I watched her well-defined posterior as she left.

***

"WAIT! HOLD IT! WAIT!" I yelled to the ground crew as I raced to the plane from the 3M hanger. "Let me board, just for a moment. Please."

Karl saw me as I ran toward the plane waving an envelope. He came to the door of the plane to tell the ground crew it was okay to let me on. I bounded up the stairs and stopped to catch my breath.

"Hello everyone. I am sorry to hold up your departure." I knelt on the Scotch plaid carpet next to Olga. She was sitting by the aisle in one of the twenty, first-class style seats just behind the polished maple conference table. Her face was lined with worry and sadness.

"Mrs. Olson, I hope you understand why I cannot go with you. I feel terrible about not going along," I said as I gripped her arm.

"Of course I do, Pope. Don't you worry about it."

"Please take this letter and read it to Bjorn."

She took the envelope and clutched it. "Pope, I know he will appreciate your thoughtfulness, as I do. Thank you. And God bless you for being there for your wife."

The co-pilot emerged from the flight deck wearing his uniform with a Scotch plaid tie. "Folks, we need to get going. Anyone not making the trip please deplane now. We just received word we'll be making a stop at the Quad Cities to pick someone up. It won't take much extra time as we'll be landing at Caterpillar's private strip."

"Who are we picking up?" Karl asked.

The co-pilot said, "Two guys from the Land Master Corporation."

KARL

THE HEAD NURSE of the burn and amputee unit, Nurse Amrhein said, "If you would all go into the family visitor room and have a seat, we can get started." She had a no-nonsense air about her, that's for sure. But, that was softened by a friendly, round, lined face and gray hair. She herded us into a room that looked more like a living room than a waiting room at a hospital.

All the stuffed chairs and couches faced in one direction, and the lighting was kinda soft. We sat down real quick. All of us wanted to get this started.

"First of all, I'd like to introduce Major Soltau. He will explain the incident that injured PFC Olson . . . at least as much as can be reconstructed," Nurse Amrhein said.

The major walked to the front of the room and looked us over. He turned to Nurse Amrhein and said in a low voice, but loud enough for me to hear, "These people don't all look like Olson's close relatives. We don't allow others to visit the critically injured, you should know that. The stocky guy with the farmer's tan looks Germanic, not Nordic. The red head looks more Irish than a shamrock and the skinny guy is a foot taller than our patient. And who the hell are the suits in the back row?"

The suits from Land Master talked to Olga and me after boarding the plane to explain why they wanted to speak with Bjorn. We were thankful they were taking the time to make the trip.

The nurse turned to us. "I'm sorry, we seem to have a problem. Only close relatives are allowed to visit the critically injured or to be present at injury status and incident briefings. It is obvious to us that all of you aren't close relatives of PFC Olson. Those of you who are not next of kin will have to leave the room."

I turned to look back at the others. They were looking at each other, trying to figure out what to do.

I got to my feet. "We've all come a long way to see our son and brother. We sure didn't expect this kind of treatment. Are you telling me that you discriminate against my adopted children? If that's the case, I demand to see someone farther up the chain of command."

"Well, no . . . of course we wouldn't discriminate against adopted members of the family. I'm sorry if we gave that impression. But who are the two gentlemen in the back? Certainly they're not adoptees."

Mr. Philp got to his feet and said in a loud voice, "Major, may we see you in the hall please?"

"Well, okay. Let's make it quick though."

Loud voices came from the hall, but soon quieted down. The major led the two men back into the room. I overheard him say, "Okay, but you'll have to have a psych doctor with you."

Major Soltau again went to the front of the room and put his hand on a small podium. "Let me first give my assurance to you all that PFC Olson—Bjorn—could not be in a better facility for his care, and I am very sorry he incurred such severe injuries.

"Families often want to know about the incident that caused the injuries. In this case we have eyewitness reports, one from a general and one from a captain, but the reports are very graphic. Perhaps some of you may want to wait in the hall instead of listening to this."

Olga and MK already had covered their eyes and lowered their heads. I'm sure they weren't anxious to hear the story, but they didn't leave. I and the rest of the guys stayed too. I felt I owed it to Bjorn to know what happened.

"As you know, PFC Olson was helping train ARVN soldiers to operate heavy earth moving equipment," Major Soltau said. "The project was going well and a general from the advisory headquarters wanted to visit the site with some media people to show off the progress. The site was not in a combat zone. Everyone in the compound knew of the general's visit a week ahead of time, so they could plan for it.

"Apparently, a Viet Cong sympathizer working in the ARVN mess area went AWOL and contacted local guerillas to tell them about the general's visit. He also knew where and when the general and media would be on the site. The Viet Cong evidently wanted to spoil the visit and show the media that no one was safe from their attacks. General Akerberg apparently was the target."

I put my arm around Olga's shoulder and held her. She was shaking and whimpering.

Soltau continued. "As the officers' Jeep was approaching Bjorn's position, the Viet Cong launched a mortar shell. It landed near Bjorn. As bad as Bjorn's injuries were, it was very fortunate that the general's helicopter was close by. Bjorn was put aboard and tended to by the captain and the general as the chopper took them to a hospital ship only thirty minutes away"

I jumped to my feet. "Hey, just a dang minute. Are you telling us that if that general wouldn't have come a'visitin' there wouldn't have been a mortar attack? And now you're making the brass out to be damn heroes for tending to my boy's injuries?"

Olga reached for my shirt sleeve and pulled me back down into my seat.

The red faced major, not used to being talked to like that, said, "Well, sir, I wouldn't—"

"Screw the rest of the story," I said. "We wanna hear how our boy is doing *now*."

The major slid out of the room without making eye contact, and Nurse Amrhein took over the presentation. "It has been my experience that it is best for family members to be presented with the medical facts as they are and not to sugar-coat them. In the long run it will help you cope. However, in the short run it may be hard for you to listen to the details. Please feel free to wait in the hall if you would rather not hear the details of Bjorn's injuries."

She waited to see if anyone would leave; no one did. I held Olga a little tighter.

"The mortar explosion propelled something that severed Bjorn's right leg just below the knee. Of course, this can be dealt with in the future by using prosthetics."

We already knew that. It still felt like a punch in the gut, though. Olga and MK were stifling sobs with their hands to their mouths.

"The blast also propelled shrapnel from the round itself and material from the ground—stones, debris and the like—into Bjorn's lower abdomen. This is a serious, ongoing concern because we are still fighting some of the infections more than three weeks after the blast. There have been six surgeries so far to remove as much foreign material as possible. And . . . I'm sorry to tell you . . . if Bjorn survives . . . ah . . . he will not father children."

MK put her head between her knees, I guess to keep from passing out. I was holding Olga with both arms. She was openly sobbing. Listening to this was harder than I had thought it would be. I asked her if she wanted to leave. She didn't.

"Perhaps we should take a break," the nurse said. She couldn't help but see the reactions to what she had to tell us. This part of her job had to be tough on her, too.

"Ma'am, please keep going," I said. "Let's get this over with . . . we need to know everything."

"The shock wave and gasses from this type of blast cause major damage to persons close by: PFC Olson is fortunate to have survived at all. Part of his body, especially his head, was screened from some of the blast by one of the trainees he was with. His eyes, although they will seem very red to you, should return to close to normal. The hearing in his right ear has been damaged by the blast, and you will notice an amplifier on his pillow by that ear. We don't know yet how the blast affected his left ear.

"There are secondary, but no less-serious, injuries from where and how Bjorn landed after being thrown by the blast. Some sort of diesel equipment was idling next to him and he was thrown on top of that and against the hot exhaust pipe." She took a deep breath and seemed hesitant to continue. "the . . . ah . . . the force of his . . . landing on the equipment and against the exhaust broke his collar bone and some ribs, one of which punctured his lung. Sadly, he also suffered severe burns to the side of his head, neck, and shoulder and . . . ah . . . most of his left ear was burned off."

Olga fainted in my arms.

Chapter 32

The next two days

OLGA

Please show Mr. and Mrs. Olson to room two-twelve," Nurse Amrhein said to the nurse in charge of the Intensive Care Unit.

"Yes, of course." She looked at us. "Hello, I'm Nurse Orsen. Please follow me." As she led us down the antiseptic-smelling hallway, she said, "Remember, you can stay with him for only fifteen minutes."

Our footsteps echoed off the barren walls.

"The trip from Guam and then San Diego was hard on him. He's on a lot of pain meds and heavily sedated, so please don't worry if he sleeps through your visit. Later this morning he should be more aware of his surroundings."

I was anxious to see him, but so afraid.

Dim light washed over Bjorn's room. Blinking monitors and tubes led from hanging plastic pouches, perched like vultures, to various parts of his body. They were mute testimony to the seriousness of his injuries. Karl had his protective arm around my shoulders as we approached Bjorn. The burned side of his neck and shoulder were under a plastic tent-like structure, so that side of him was not visible. We were glad to see the other side of his face looking normal, but thin. He looked peaceful.

I held a tissue close to my face, hoping I could keep my composure.

Karl took Bjorn's hand in his and directed his voice to the amplifier next to Bjorn's ear. "Son, it's your Ma and Pa." Then Karl looked at me and said very quietly, "His hand feels warm, but there's no reaction to my voice or touch." He squeezed a little harder and lifted Bjorn's hand. "Son, it's your Ma and Pa."

Still there was no reaction.

"Here, Olga, take this chair. Sit. Hold his hand. He's sleeping."

I sat and took my son's hand. Karl remained by my side with his hand on my shoulder. Both of us kept our eyes on Bjorn's face, willing him to get well. I avoided looking toward the partially vacant foot of the bed.

Our time went by too fast and Bjorn didn't wake up. Nurse Orsen came by and knocked gently on the door jamb to indicate our fifteen minutes had passed. We got up to leave. We'd have to give Pope's letter to Shu or Ozzie or read it to Bjorn.

We were almost to the door when a small voice came from Bjorn. "Ma . . . Dad . . . I'm sorry."

But his eyes were still closed.

***

MARY KATHERINE SPENT the morning visiting the area of the hospital where she would be working. As instructed by the nursing staff, she'd have to wait until the afternoon to see Bjorn. Shu, Ozzie and the others would have to wait until the next day. Shu and Ozzie spent that first day exploring the Alamo and other San Antonio highlights. The guys from Land Master spent part of the day at one of their suppliers and the rest of the time consulting with the hospital psychologists.

MK asked me to go with her to see Bjorn. She said she was afraid to be alone in the room in case she fainted. She was feeling sorry for Bjorn and probably for herself.

As we entered his room in the afternoon, she said, "Olga, hold my hand. My heart is in my throat. I'm trying to ready myself for the shock of seeing him."

I'm sure she wanted to throw herself on Bjorn to kiss, caress, and comfort him, but she knew enough to hold back. She held his hand and stroked his cheek. He didn't respond. Impulsively, she talked instead of staying quiet.

I stood behind her as she talked quietly. I wanted to be there for her but give them privacy at the same time.

"Hi, babe. It's your gal come to be with you," she said in a soft, sweet voice. "I'm going to stay here at Fort Sam as long as you're here. I'm gonna help get you well. Your folks will be back tonight and some other guys are here to surprise you. Oh, I love you so much. It's so good to—"

Bjorn whispered. "Love? . . . May? . . . May?"

"Sure you may. What would you like to do?"

"May?" He whispered again. He opened one crusted eye and saw MK. He looked confused. Wheels must have been turning in his mind, but they weren't getting any traction. He opened both of his red, crusted eyes and squinted. Finally, traction.

"MK? My God . . . that you?" he rasped in a whisper.

She smiled broadly. "Of course, silly! Who'd you think it was, Marilyn Monroe? Must have woken you from a dream."

His lips quivered and she wiped a tear from his cheek. "Where am I? Oh, it hurts . . ." He reached for her cheek, I guess to make sure he wasn't dreaming. "You're beautiful . . . it's been so long . . ." He winced from the pain and closed his eyes.

As the nurse told her the time was up, she kissed him on the lips. "I was thrilled by the feeling of your fingers on my cheek. I'll be back for more."

***

AFTER AN EVENING MEAL at a Mexican restaurant hosted by Land Master, Karl and I took another turn to visit Bjorn in hopes he would be awake. We sat with our drugged, sleeping boy for ten minutes before he opened one eye. The first thing he saw was me wiping tears from my eyes. "Ma . . . don't cry. Hi, Dad." He closed his eye again before we could answer him.

"Bjorn, my baby." I reached for his hand.

He swallowed hard and whispered, "I'm worried . . . about—"

"Mr. and Mrs. Olson, your fifteen minutes are up." It was Nurse Orsen.

BJORN

"GOOD MORNING, SOLDIER," Nurse Orsen said. I was kinda awake 'cause of the pain.

"Please . . . more pain meds . . . please," I whispered.

"Any more of that stuff and you'll be in la-la land."

"Good, that's where I wanna be." The next thing I remember was hearing a familiar voice. *Oh, shit . . . Can't people just leave me alone?*

"Hey, soldier, great to see you," Shu said.

"Hey, yourself," I whispered, only to be polite. I didn't wanna see him or to have him see me like this.

After a pregnant pause, there was another familiar voice. Ozzie said, "Woulda brought you a bouquet of flowers, but I didn't wanna look like a sissy carryin' 'em in."

"So big deal," I said. I wanted to be left alone.

They glanced at each other, probably hoping the other had something to say that would change my negative attitude. Another awkward pause followed.

"Oh, hey, I got a letter here from Pope to read'ya. He couldn't come along . . . got problems at home with the Nazi," Shu said.

"Thinks he's got problems?" I said, barely audible. "He doesn't know . . .

what the word means." I closed my eyes. *Please take the hint . . . leave me the hell alone.*

"Well, I'd like to read it," Shu said.

"Do whatever the hell you want . . . I don't give a crap," I whispered with my eyes closed.

"Okay, here goes." Shu cleared his throat.

> *Dear Bjorn,*
>
> *I wish I could be with you. I know this letter cannot make up for my absence, for which I am truly sorry.*
>
> *Remember the day you told us you were dropping out of school? At the time, I was sure you were going to be a failure in life. What you accomplished after that with your company was amazing. You are my hero.*
>
> *You could always do constructive things with your hands. I do not even know which end of a screwdriver to hold. You are my hero.*
>
> *Your choice of a life's mate in MK is perfect. You are my hero.*
>
> *Solving other's problems comes naturally to you, another reason you are my hero.*
>
> *You did not have to be wounded while in the army to be my hero.*
>
> *I want to share a prayer with you that I say every morning and evening ever since word came of your injuries:*
>
> *Dear Lord,*
>
> *Look after my friend, Bjorn. Guide his doctors and nurses as they comfort and heal him. Help MK, Olga and Karl through this time of worry. Give Bjorn a full, enjoyable and productive life. Amen*
>
> *Again, I am sorry I am not there, but I want you to know you are much on my mind.*
>
> *Your good friend,*
>
> *Pope*

"What a crock," I scoffed.

I'll bet Ozzie and Shu were glad the nurse entered and asked them to leave.

Two nurses and a doctor came into the room to change the dressings on my gut surgeries. The nurses tried some banter with me. I remained silent.

At noon, Nurse Orsen came in with lunch and sat by my bed to help feed me. I had no appetite and wished she'd leave. The nurse left with most of the mac and cheese and green Jell-O. Maybe if I didn't eat I would just fade away. I tried to sleep. Shortly afterwards, three men entered my room.

"Hello, Bjorn."

My right eye was open to just a slit. The dim light created three shadow-like figures. *Now what? Can't people just leave me alone and let me go? Who the hell are these guys? That voice sounds kinda familiar.*

The men musta seen the puzzled look on my face, probably some anger also. "Bjorn, hi again. It's John Philp from Land Master."

"Oh," I whispered. My throat was sore. I looked at him and eyed up the other two men.

Nodding to the man in the white doctor's smock, Philp said, "This is Doctor Van Riper, a psychologist with the hospital. He's not here to see you, he's here to keep an eye on me and Willard. We make him nervous," Philp said while pointing to the third man.

"Hello, Bjorn, I'm Willard Fox. We met a few years ago at the patent court in Chicago."

"Oh . . . ya. What're you guys doin' here?"

Fox, the CEO of Land Master, said, "Your buddies just told us you're doing an outstanding job of feeling sorry for yourself."

The nervous doctor raised his hand as a warning to Fox.

I tensed up and twisted my mouth. "Y'know, you can kiss—"

"We don't blame you for that. We've both been down that road, but we're not here as part of the pity party. We're here to welcome you to the Brotherhood."

What an asshole. I couldn't believe how cold-blooded Fox sounded. I stared at him in disbelief. "What the hell . . . are you talking about?"

The doctor stepped between us as if to stop a fist fight.

"The Brotherhood of Wounded Military Survivors," Philp said, ignoring the doctor.

"What the hell would . . . you guys know . . . about that? Some . . . smart-assed brother thing . . . you don't have a clue . . . what I'm going through," I said as loud as I could.

Philp sat down in the guest chair, bent over and pulled up his right pant leg. After a short time he hopped up and held his detached prosthetic lower leg high over my head. "Son, don't ever again tell me I don't have a clue."

Jeeezus! I stared at the leg. "Mr. Philp, I'm—"

"December ninth, 1950, Chosin Reservoir, Korea. I was shot through the calf of my leg, and my buddies tied on a tourniquet. I was in a foxhole with three other wounded guys for fifteen hours before the medics could finaly reach us. We tried to keep each other from freezing. Two of those guys died in my arms. I was lucky. Only my foot and wounded lower leg froze solid."

Before I could respond to Philp, Fox said. "Heartbreak Ridge, Korea. I was in a truck with seven other men with minor wounds. We were being hauled to the rear to get patched up and be sent back to the front. An artillery shell exploded behind me, right next to the truck. It flipped the truck over and sent it rolling down an embankment. The canvas top didn't provide much protection. Four men were killed in the rollover. I was lucky. They removed metal shell fragments from the back of my noggin and put in a steel plate. I still have some spare metal parts in my back. Bjorn, I also understand what you're going through. We both get it."

"Sorry . . . I didn't know . . ." I mumbled. "So why're you guys here?"

"Here's the way things progressed for the two of us," Fox continued. "We each came to a fork in the mental road of our recovery. If we had let our mind go one way, it would have led to a dark place of depression and dependence. If our mind took the other road, it could lead to pretty much a normal, fulfilling life. As members of the same Brotherhood, we're here to try to steer you down the correct fork in the road."

I squeezed my eyes shut to dam up tears. I listened, but I doubted my ability to take the road they wanted me take. All I really wanted to do was to leave this world.

"You know, in many ways you're damn lucky," Philp said. "You can look forward to life knowing you will never be this scared or hurt this much again." He reached over to take my hand. "Most people still have to face those things later in life."

I nodded. I tried to imagine how to have a positive take on my horrible condition and pain.

"The best way to be a good member of the Brotherhood is to help other members," Fox said. "At Land Master, over thirty percent of our non-factory employees are members of the Brotherhood, and about ten percent of the factory workers are also. Remember our pilot with the prosthetic hand who picked you up from basic training? Just think, Bjorn, you're in a position to build your company the same way we've done. I'm telling you, it's a damn good feeling and you can get there, but it's going to take courage and patience."

"None of our outside manufacturers are members of the Brotherhood," Philp said. "If you get yourself together, keep up your company's quality and value, we will feed Olson and Dad, Inc., all the work you can gear up for. Think about your old man. Did he let losing an eye stop him from being one of the keys to your company's success?"

It looked like Dr. Van Riper started to relax.

I didn't relax. I thought about the fork in the hard road ahead of me . . . I didn't know if I even wanted to get to the fork.

Chapter 33

Two weeks later, Octover 1964

OZZIE

I know its dang late, and I know you're tired and you wanna go home," I said as I opened the meeting with all twenty-two of Danny's employees. "Thanks for staying." It was just after closing, and we were all in the main bar room, which smelled of smoke, spilled beer, and fried food. The kitchen crew looked cooked, and the wait staff had wiped off their tip-getting smiles.

Most of the staff were too tired to notice the unsmiling, fiftyish-year-old couple lingering by the front door.

Business had been good, but not great. Despite our working twelve- to fourteen-hour days, Barb and I were barely able to pay mortgage payments, payroll, food and beverage costs, or living expenses. According to our accountant, with the current level of business we should have had more black ink on the bottom line.

There was a knock on the main door by the palm trees. One of the strangers opened the door and Officers McKinney and Noterman entered, wearing their deputy sheriff uniforms and side arms. They looked grim. I nodded to 'em and they nodded back. Sheriff deputies knew they could always count on a free cup of coffee at Danny's, and I cultivated that relationship 'cause you never know when it would come in handy for them to look the other way or for other special favors. I had arranged this visit by them and it wasn't for a free cup of coffee.

I moved behind the bar and stood next to Howie who was washing drink glasses. Barb sat across the bar from us. Howie was the dashing lead bartender who loved to show off to the ladies by flipping booze bottles in the air and fancy pouring of the spirits.

"You all work hard, which Barb and I appreciate. We especially like the way you feel free to give us suggestions on how to improve things around here,"

I said kinda hesitantly to start the meeting. But I wanted something in my tone of voice to make a few of the employees uncomfortable. "We hope you're happy with the tips and pay. Of course, we know that not *all* of you are satisfied with the money your job pays."

I reached into my back pocket and pulled out an envelope, laid it on the bar and removed a stack of nine photos. "I'd like to introduce the two folks standing with the deputies; Mr. Jimmy Schmidt and Mrs. Glenda Schmieg. They work for Calhoon and Associates, private detectives. They've visited us, together or separately, seven times over the past few weeks. Maybe you recognize them now. They take great pictures with a very small camera."

I grabbed Howie's shoulder, spun him around, bent him backwards over the bar and held him there with one forearm. Clean drink glasses shattered on the floor.

Our gathered employees watched in horror, getting the object lesson that I intended. My old temper was taking hold. With my face twisted with anger, I held up a photo with my free hand. "Here's a picture of Howie's car trunk loaded with bottles of booze with Danny's inventory labels on them." Grabbing more photos to hold up, I said, "And here are pictures of this bastard pocketing customer's money that never made it into the cash register."

Howie struggled to get off the bar. "Goddammit, let me go!"

"Deputies, did you see this damned thief slip, fall and land backwards on the bar?" I asked.

"Yup, must'a been a loose ice cube or somethin'," McKinney said.

I pulled Howie off the bar, but still held on to his collar. Barb threw a wet, dirty bar towel in his face. "Howie, how *dare* you steal from us? We work our butts off around here and try to treat our employees right. And this is how you treat us?" She pointed at the pictures.

Howie looked around at his fellow employees who had their eyes cast down rather than look at him. They were getting the message loud and clear. "I'm sorry," he mumbled through the wet towel.

I said, "We won't press charges, but here's the deal." I turned him toward me so he couldn't help but to look me in the eye. "You'll let the deputies into your apartment tonight to recover any of our booze you have there. Also, it seems your car is not running. You will have to leave it here until you pay us five hundred bucks, which is probably only part of what you've stolen from us."

His expression turned from embarrassment to anger. "What'd y'do to my car?"

"The tires, battery, and a few engine parts have been removed for washing and buffing. It seems they were a bit dusty. The cleaning will be finished when you hand over five big ones. Just a little security for the debt." I glanced at the officers. They nodded in agreement.

"That's blackmail! You can't do that! I need my car!"

"Just watch me. The deputies will offer you taxi service tonight so you don't need your car to get home. And by the way, don't bother trying to get another bartending job in this state. I've already spread the word about your sticky fingers."

Barb turned toward the other employees. "Any questions?" she asked with a smile. Few of them met her eye, and there were no questions or comments. "Okay, then. Meeting's adjourned. Good night and thanks again for staying late."

As Barb and I were turning off the lights and shutting things down, I said, "Message sent."

She said, "And received, I'll bet."

POPE

"MR. GRIMM, I WAS wondering, would it be possible to increase my work days to five a week? I can't make it on just three days of pay and there's plenty for me to do around here," Ruthie said.

"Well, Mrs. Weber, I will have to ponder that. As you know, we are not covering our overhead as it is."

"Yes, I know. I do the books. But it's very possible we could bring in more business if I spend more time on the job."

"Maybe, but why the need for a change? You never mentioned a financial concern on the home front before. Tom still has the same job, does he not?"

"That's personal."

"I understand, but the more I know, the more likely I could go along with the idea."

She studied her fingernails. She seemed to be stalling for time. Finally, tears in her eyes, she said, "I've moved out. I'm living in a woman's shelter where he can't find me. I . . . I guess you need to know anyway 'cause he's under a court order to stay away from me."

"Oh, Ruthie . . ." I cleared my throat. "I mean Mrs. Weber, I am so sorry. I do not understand why he treats you so badly. You certainly do not deserve that. If I were your hus—I mean, anyway . . . yes, of course, beginning on

Monday you may plan on working five days a week. And I believe you are correct. Together we will find more customers."

I hoped I could control myself. Being around her three days a week was already difficult. It was a good thing my conscience had such a strong grip on my urges.

Chapter 34

The same day

BJORN

MK entered my hospital room with her usual light-up-the-room flair. I saw her through the slit of my better eye. She had my favorite candy bar, a Snickers, and a Coke for me. She always remembered my favorites. When she was with me the night before, I had told her about having a dermabrasion treatment on my second-degree burn areas scheduled for this morning. It still hurt like hell, and to make it worse, a skin graft on some of my third degree burn areas was scheduled for the next day.

I guess she saw my right index finger keeping time with the music from the overhead speaker so she knew I was awake. I was dreading this. She said, "Hey, babe, candy girl is here with a Coke and a kiss."

I opened my eyes and greeted her with a brief smile, which I quickly turned into a serious look. "Hi. You always know what to bring me. Thanks. But please sit down. We need to talk."

"Okay, what's tonight's subject?"

"The elephant in the middle of the room," I whispered.

"Really? Sounds serious."

"Ya, we've never had a more serious talk. I've been trying to figure out how to say this to you for over a week. There's no easy way . . . I just have to say it as plain as I can."

She frowned. "Well, good grief, spit it out, you know we can tell each other anything. That's our deal. That's the kind of relationship we have."

"Ya, I know. Hmm . . . ah, I don't want to be a burden to anyone." She opened her mouth, but I shook my head to stop her from speaking. "Let me finish. It's not fair to you to stay. I'll be here for over a month and then to Walter Reed for the fake leg. Ah . . . you have to get on with your life and . . . and I have to concentrate on healing."

She took my hand. "What are you saying?"

"We've had a great ride. You're a wonderful woman, but we have to call it quits. You know in your heart I'm right."

"Bjorn, you don't know—"

"I'm not whole anymore. I'm . . . I'm not the same guy you started out with."

"Bjorn Olson, shut your mouth! You're my guy and I love you. Thick and thin, good times and bad, we're together." The expression on her freckled face was changing from cute to panic.

"No . . . I'm not your guy. You deserve better. I lost more than my leg in 'Nam. I don't just mean other physical things either . . . I did . . . something . . . hard to get the inside of my head straight."

"Oh, shush. You'll feel different about this tomorrow."

"Dammit, *listen* to me! I'm *serious*!" I said as loud as I could, but still not loud enough for the effect I wanted. I tried to sit up, but couldn't. I pointed to my crotch. "It's not just that my little soldier down here may never salute again. I'm not the same guy you knew before. How damn plain do I have to say it? I need and want out. I have to concentrate on recovery and not you. I will not be a burden to you or anyone else. I need to rebuild myself in more ways than one."

"Selfish . . . that's what you're being . . . just selfish. Don't you love me anymore?"

"Love has nothing to do with it." I shook my head and took a deep breath. "You know you've had the same thoughts yourself. Don't kid me. You've got a wonderful life ahead of you without me—do it—take off with my good wishes." *Oh, God, I'm gonna miss her.*

"How can you be so cold after all we've been through?"

"Cold? How about realistic? How about let's face the music? I know you won't admit it, but you've wondered about this yourself." *This is hard . . . God, don't waiver.*

"Okay, yes I have, but I came to a different conclusion. We could still have a wonderful life together like we always planned."

"Oh, sure. Maybe a nine percent chance of that. Take the ninety-one percent chance and find someone else. You'll have choices. Other guys will be knocking your door down. And for God's sake, don't pity me. I'm gonna fight my way through this and come out okay. Just not okay enough to think I should hold you back from a better life. I love you too much to do that."

"Let's talk more about this tomorrow night." She held her hand to my cheek. "This is not like you. This can't be happening."

I pushed her hand from my cheek. "There won't be any more tomorrow nights for us. I've told the nurses . . . ah . . . to not allow you to visit me after tonight. For both of our sakes, we have to end it now. It's over. Please, no more talking. Just leave and go back to Minnesota."

She looked at me in shock and some anger. I guess I caught her off guard. "Bjorn, you have no right to—"

"Please. No more talking. I can't take this anymore." I reached for the nurse's call button. MK started in again but I held up my hand to silence her.

The Nurse Orsen came in. "PFC Olson, is something the matter?"

"Yes. Please escort this lady from my room.

Chapter 35

June 1965, eight months later

SHU

I pleaded with Cline while I leaned on the banker's blond oak desk. "Whaddya mean you can't help me? What am I s'posed to do?"

Cline shrugged. "Look, who knows how long this drought will last? We can't take a chance on another loan for you. There might not be a crop this year. I've had to say the same thing to many other guys who are long-term good clients and friends. You'll just have to cut back on some things."

"Cut back? We've already got seed and fertilizer in the fields. What do you expect me to do, pick 'em out of the ground and send 'em back to the dang farm store?" I asked with my arms outstretched.

"How about Wilson? Can you cancel your turkey order with them?"

"Jesus, that's why I need a loan now. I took delivery on five thousand birds last week."

"Well, you've got crop insurance, don't you?"

"Ya, but I can't collect 'til next fall. They gotta know there was no crop first. Then we'll only get about half of what the crops are worth."

"Okay, there's only one other thing I can think of. I hate to say it, knowing Trudy and all, but you'll have to put off building the new house."

It was a good thing I had a farmer's tan 'cause all the rest of the color drained from my face. Trouble was, I knew he was right. My peace agreement with Trudy was about to be flushed down the crapper.

***

"'NOTHER GREAT MEAL, Trudes," I said after wolfing down her version of Gretta's goulash and cole slaw. "Wanna take an evening stroll down to the lake? We can take the kids up to the folks' place."

"Okay, sure. What's with you? It's not like you to want to take a walk after working all day."

I shrugged. "It's a nice June night . . . bugs aren't too bad yet and we'll take the fly rod along. Sunnies are spawning and biting like crazy. We'll catch a mess of 'em and have the folks over for a fish fry tomorrow night."

We headed for Lake Mattson by a short-cut through the fields. As our every step kicked up a puff of dust Trudy asked, "Think the corn will be knee high next month?" The soil was shrunk from the lack of moisture, cracked and looking like a jig-saw puzzle. It was dead-mouse gray instead of black.

"Hell, we'll be lucky if it'll be up at all . . . and those that do germinate won't be *ankle* high by the Fourth of July."

"Shu, do you think I'm a city slicker? I was just joshing; I know darn well the crops are gonna be bad this year."

We held hands and walked in silence for a long while, each of us stealing glances at the other, afraid to talk about how the drought might impact our finances.

"Look, here are the stakes for the new house," Trudy said as we got to the woods overlooking the lake.

"Ya. Let's go down to the shore and catch some sunnies." No way did I want us to be where the new house was already staked out.

"Shu, hold up, just a minute. Look, I know it's gonna be a tough year 'cause of the drought." Her jaw was set and she stared off down to the lake. "I think we should hold off on starting the house."

I couldn't believe my ears. "What a woman! I'm so lucky to have you!" I picked her up and swung her around. "I met with Cline this afternoon. I was going to have to tell you tonight that he won't give us a mortgage for the new house 'cause of the drought. God, I didn't wanna disappoint you."

"Shu, I'm sorry you worried about that. I love you."

We didn't try for sunnies. Instead we stripped off our clothes, walked through the spawning beds and lily pads into the cool water and went for a skinny dip. Good thing Ellie and Nick weren't with us.

POPE

HERB YELLED AT ME through the phone. "Pull your head out of your ass and get some damned customers! You're dragging us down the shitter with you!"

"You know I do not appreciate that sort of language," I said.

"Shit, you haven't heard anything yet. If you don't straighten things out there in fly-over land I'll teach you a whole bunch of new words."

"I have an appointment tomorrow with a very good prospect. Things will get better. My wife is home from the hospital, so I am able to concentrate more on—just one minute, Herb." Mrs. Weber had stepped into my office and waved her arms to get my attention. "Yes, Mrs. Weber?"

"There's a policeman here. He needs to talk to you. Says it's urgent."

"Herb, I have to go. I will call you back shortly." I hung up, then got up and went to the reception area and wondered what this was about. I was certain my car was parked legally.

"Yes, officer, what can I do for you?" I said.

"You're Mr. David Grimm?"

"Yes."

The officer put his hand on my shoulder. "I'm afraid I have bad news. Your wife apparently jumped from the balcony of your apartment this morning. She did not survive the five-story fall. I'm very sorry."

A blackness came over me, and I staggered backwards and fell over a chair. Mrs. Weber and the officer rushed to help me up.

***

After the funeral, Trudy and Barb flanked me in a corner booth at Danny's. Both had a consoling arm around me. Trudy said, "Pope, y'gotta stop blaming yourself. There was no way to know this was gonna happen. The doctors released her from the hospital and you relied on their judgment. What else could you have done?"

"That is easy to say, but in the end, God will judge me as wanting because she died in my care, and for that I am ultimately responsible. My God and my conscience speak clearly to me. They always have." I was not tearful anymore. I was drained of emotion.

Bjorn slid in to the booth next to Trudy. "Pope, your conscience has'ta understand that no one is responsible for somebody else's actions. Christ, if that weren't the case we'd all be in the guilt prison."

Bjorn's long tow-head hair covered his partially reconstructed ear and scarred neck, but he still turned that side of his head away from the person to whom he was speaking. He had been released from Walter Reed hospital last month and was almost used to walking on his new prosthetic leg. He was living in the room at the plant that he had instructed his folks to build. He had even sent them the plans and specifications while he was in the hospital.

Ozzie said, "Hey, I never had anybody close to me die, so I have no words of wisdom about that. All I know is that life has'ta go on." He motioned to the waiter to bring another round while he stubbed out his Pall Mall.

"Ya, that's right," Shu chimed in. "Pope, just remember that your buddies are here for ya."

"Enough about me. I do not wish to dwell on my emotional sate any longer." I said. "Please, Bjorn, how are you doing and what is new at Olson and Dad?"

"I'm okay, but things are kinda tense at work right now. Dad and I aren't speaking."

"What the heck happened?" Shu asked. "You've always had a great relationship with him."

"Well, I . . . ah, canceled a new contract with the army to build more entrenching tools. I didn't talk to him or Ma before I did. Really upset him bad."

Ozzie asked, "Why the hell would you do something like that? A contract like that is money in the bank."

"I don't wanna profit from that military stuff anymore. Sure as hell, before long we'll be sending combat troops to 'Nam. Kennedy probably would've just to prove to the world how tough we are after the Bay of Pigs fiasco, and now with him dead, good ol' boy LBJ for sure wants'ta pull the trigger. I'm dead set against it," Bjorn said as he slapped the table with his palm.

"Shee-it, man. We gotta stop those commies somewhere," Ozzie said, his face growing red with rising anger. "Might as well be there. What the hell, you turn into a pinko?"

Bjorn clenched his fists. "It's a damn civil war, Ozzie. It's none of our goddamned business, and I'm no damned pinko!"

"All right, you two," I said, holding up my hands. "Calm down, please. Everyone is entitled to their own opinion. Relax. We are among friends here, you know."

"Yeah, quiet down you guys," Barb said. "Other customers are wondering what all the fuss is about."

"Okay, okay, but I'll make you all a deal, 'specially *you*, Ozzie," Bjorn pointed a finger at him. "I go to the VA hospital at Fort Snelling twice a month for more rehab and a check-up. Then I stay the rest of the day just to talk to the guys recuperating from injuries they got in 'Nam. I wasn't the only so-called *advisor* who got wounded over there. You come along and spend a day with me making the rounds, and then we'll have this little chat again."

Ozzie looked down at his lap, "Look, sorry about the pinko deal. But, goddamn it, I still think we gotta stop the bastards somewhere. It might as well be there."

Shu interrupted the debate. "Anything else new at work, Bjorn?"

"Ya. I've been working on two new product lines for quite a while. I can't talk about 'em yet. I've had a lot of time to think and observe my surroundings in different hospitals and rehab joints."

OLGA

I WAS RELAXING in the break room with coffee and a powdered sugar doughnut for dunking while I paged through the *Waconia Patriot* when I came to the announcement section. A picture of MK with a man caught my eye. Under the picture it read

> Mr. and Mrs. Michael O'Brian are proud to announce the wedding of their daughter, Mary Katherine O'Brian, a nurse at Waconia Hospital. The groom is Dr. Conner Prescott Smyth, III, of Edina, Minnesota. He is an internist with the Lakeshore Clinic in Waconia and is the son of Dr. and Mrs. Conner Prescott Smyth, II.
>
> The newlyweds will be residing at a new home now under construction on Sunset Point on Lake Waconia after returning from a two-week European honeymoon.

My heart sank. My hands shook. Mike never told us. Karl and I didn't get invited to the wedding. Can't say I blame him or MK. *Oh, Bjorn, what could have been.*

Chapter 36

June 1966, one year later

Mrs. Weber, a.k.a. Ruthie

Backseat groping wasn't the only by-product of Single's Night a Danny's Island Escape. In the two years of the twice-monthly event's existence, Barb and Ozzie knew of five weddings, four engagements, and a few more cohabitations that got their start at those special nights.

Reservations were required and accepted for only twenty-six men and the same number of women. Barb told me there was always a waiting list. An Island Buffet and a glass of champagne were included in the price, as was the small band made up of piano, bass, and sax players. Dim lighting and slow music set the mood.

Ladies received a flower to tuck behind their ear—left side for "looking for a long term relationship," and right side for "just out for fun." I didn't know where to put my flower, and I dressed very conservatively so I wouldn't give some jerk the wrong idea of my intentions.

Tables had large numbers on them so a customer, male or female, could ask one of the waiters or waitresses to deliver a dance request to, for instance, "the gal in the red sweater at table seven from the guy in the gray sweater at table four." Turn-downs were less painful that way. Instead of saying no, you just ignored the request.

I had not been friends with Barb or Ozzie in high school so I was surprised at their pressing me to come to this Single's Night. They countered every excuse I could come up with. I dreaded getting into a relationship with someone I didn't know well. I fantasized about stabbing and castrating the next guy who tried to hurt and abuse me.

Pope was the guy I wanted, but a girl could only drop so many gentle hints. Ursula's death and my divorce certainly opened the door to that possibility, but Pope had not responded or shown any interest, so I thought maybe I should venture out into the dating world. I told Barb I would show up for the Single's Night. There I was, uncomfortable and wishing I were home sitting on my couch with a glass of wine and a romance novel.

The rotund gal I was seated with wasn't getting any dance requests and her messages had been ignored. I felt bad for her. She seemed nice, and I think she was anxious to show a guy a good time in his car's back seat. I kept getting requests but hadn't worked up the courage to accept any. I'd removed the flower from my ear and ordered my third glass of some kind of white wine that was priced as the house special.

Ozzie stopped by and said, "The guy at table six has sent you several dance requests. Maybe you should turn around and see if he looks okay."

I suppressed a sigh, but turned to see a bit of a geek with a silly grin on his face. My heart did a flip-flop and I raced across the dance floor to him as he hurried toward me. After darn near knocking each other over, our embrace was long, and in my case, close in all the right places. I buried my head in his chest and sobbed with joy. Pope held me really tight. It was as nice and comfortable as I had imagined.

"My dear Ruthie . . . it is so wonderful to finally hold you," he whispered in my ear. "I felt I had to wait one year after Ursula's death to tell you of my feelings and to hold you in my arms. To do so sooner would not have been appropriate."

"Oh, David, I've been waiting for this day. Don't ever let me go. Every day at work was both torture and joy. You were untouchable but still close by."

BJORN

MY CORNER BOOTH at Michael's Steak House, around the block from the Mayo Clinic, was perfect: dim lighting and away from other diners, just as I had requested. I had been in a meeting earlier in the day with some of my advisors for our new hospital and rehab equipment division, which would soon be ready for production in Waconia.

This time we had met in Rochester 'cause the two Mayo docs on the advisory board were on call. It was a good, productive meeting, and I was glad to have Nurse Amrhein on board. She had moved to Des Moines after retiring from Fort Sam. Interior designer, Mary Stedman, had some great sketches for the equipment and color samples for the mock-up rehab room. It looked inviting instead of scary, just what I had asked for. I just hoped the evening would go as well as the meeting had gone.

I was making equipment sketches on a napkin and nursing a Manhattan when a woman cleared her throat to get my attention. I looked up to see a very presentable, but not over the top, fortyish brunette lady dressed in a navy blue blazer, a white blouse buttoned to the top, a gray knee-length skirt and shoes with modest heels. She was carrying a classy, large shoulder bag.

The doorman came through, I thought. *She looks just like I requested.*

She said, "Mr. Jones, I presume?"

"Yes, hello." I rose from the booth and offered my hand.

She took hold of my hand. "Mr. Delaney, the Kahler Hotel doorman, said I would find you here. Plaid shirt and long blond hair. My name is Vivian."

"Nice to meet you, Vivian. Please have a seat. Call me Ben." I couldn't help but notice her deep-blue eyes and full lips. Her glasses only added to the classy look. "Let me order you a drink. What would you like?"

"A martini on the rocks would be nice. I won't have more than one of those, but it's a good starter. You picked a nice place to begin our evening." She gracefully sat down across from me.

"Thanks, it has a good reputation."

She said, "Hmm . . . before we continue, I have found it helpful to get the awkward *business* of the evening over with quickly. That way it clears the air for more entertaining things."

"Oh . . . oh sure. Of course." I felt kinda stupid 'cause I didn't get what she meant right away. I reached for an envelope in my back jean pocket and slid it over to her.

She opened it and glanced at the contents. "There's more here than Mr. Delaney told you to provide. Here, take some back, you must have miscounted." She slid the envelope toward me.

"No. It's yours. In my other life I like to pay employees more than expected. In most cases I get what I pay for." I kept my damaged ear turned slightly away from her even though I was pretty sure my hair was covering it.

Her martini arrived and she held her glass up to clink mine. "Well, you're very generous. I hope I don't disappoint you. You said you pay employees? You seem awful young to be doing that. Oh, and I'm not your employee. You're only renting me."

The only other time I had paid to have a woman was in Chicago after a meeting at Land Master. It was a disaster. She came to my hotel room already high on something and reeking of alcohol and sweat. She was a stripper at a club down the street and had just got off work. She wanted to get it over with so she could go meet her boyfriend. I paid her right away and told her to leave without having touched her.

This time I had been very specific with the doorman, and I had paid him well. *So far the extra cash seems to be paying off in spades.*

"Mr. Delaney said you have a suite at the Kahler. Are you in town just for tonight?"

"Yeah. I had to have a suite for a small meeting. Sure is a nice hotel." *Sure nicer than my room at the plant.*

"Well, you know, they cater to royalty from all over the world. Movie stars, too. Yes the rooms are very nice."

"You've seen some?"

"Ah . . . yeah," she raised her eyebrows slightly. "May I suggest we order an appetizer and a salad now? If we are still hungry later we could order more from room service." She locked eyes with me and smiled.

I liked the way she took charge. "Sure, and you order for us. I'm not fussy."

She motioned for the waiter, then ordered crab cakes, a chopped salad for two and two glasses of white wine. She didn't look at the menu. We kept up the chit-chat about nothing in particular until the food arrived. As we ate, she moved the conversation to what I expected of her up in my suite.

"Mr. Delaney said you had some specific requirements of me during our get together. May I ask what they are?"

"Ah . . . this is not easy for me . . . to talk about."

"Ben, just say whatever you need. I've heard it all, and I understand men's needs."

"Okay. Well, I was . . . injured. I have not been . . . ah, intimate with a woman for over two years." I was unable to look her in the eye. "I don't know if I can . . . you know. I'm not sure how things will go. I asked Mr. Delaney for someone with a medical background, mature and classy. He got the mature and classy part right. How about the medical part? I think I'm going to need . . . a lot of help. I'm afraid to even ask a woman out for fear of my failure to . . . perform." I looked up.

The corners of her mouth turned up. "Ben, I'm a psych nurse. My husband is also. We have very expensive habits and tastes. This little side line provides us with the money we need for the lifestyle we want. My husband and I provide intimate services to some patients here, but mostly to spouses who stay while the other is undergoing lengthy treatment and recuperation at Mayo. Mr. Delaney, the doorman, is very choosy about who he matches us up with."

The bill came, and after I paid it, Vivian said, "Let's head up to your suite. Have the front desk send up some wine. I prefer a full-bodied red after I've had something to eat."

We continued talking while walking around the block to the Kahler's front entrance. Mr. Delaney opened the door and tipped his red hat. Behind Vivian's back I gave him a thumbs-up and a shy smile.

After entering the suite, she said, "Ben, excuse me while I make myself more presentable." She took her shoulder bag into the large, marble bathroom.

"Oh, sure. Okay. I'll open the wine when it comes."

Room service arrived with the two bottles of wine already uncorked. I had to go through the tasting routine, then slipped the man a nice tip and waited for Vivian to reenter the room.

She did, but not wearing a blazer and a skirt. Her tasteful negligee was not quite transparent, but the clinging fabric left little to the imagination. It was white and trimmed with blue satin that matched her eyes. She had taken off her glasses. I also got a whiff of sensual perfume. My heart was beating faster than before she'd gone to change clothes.

"You look beautiful . . . and very desirable," I said as I handed her a glass of wine.

"Thank you, and not just for the wine."

"Could we just sit and relax for a while?" I said. "Maybe sip a little wine? I'm new at this sort of thing, and I'm kinda nervous." *Maybe I should ask her to leave and not put myself through this.*

"No rush. You have me for the night. I enjoy your company, so don't sit across the room. Join me here on the love seat." She patted the soft leather cushion next to her.

After more conversation and another glass of wine, I started to feel at ease. "Guess you must think I'm a little strange. Bet most guys just wanna get on with it."

"Most of them do, but everyone's different. But forget that, this is only about us. Now why don't you get more comfortable? I'd like to watch you undress. It looks like you've got a great body." She smiled and gave me a kiss on my cheek.

"Oh, well . . . ah, let me turn down the lights. Okay?"

"Whatever you wish."

After dimming the lights I went to the far side of the bed and took off my plaid shirt. But then I hesitated and stopped undressing, leaving my t-shirt and pants on. "I have scars. Maybe it would be best if I turned the lights all the way off."

"Hon, we all have scars, some inside, some outside. I'll turn the lights down a little more, but I want to be able to see you. Don't you want to be able to see me?"

"Yeah, sure." I slowly took off my t-shirt, afraid to look at Vivian, afraid to see her reaction to the scars on my neck and shoulder. I was sure May or MK would have been repulsed.

She came to me and kissed my scarred neck and shoulder. "Wow, nice abs, chest, and biceps. Now your pants."

"I . . . maybe . . . let's just stop here and have some more wine. You've already earned your money. It's just been wonderful to have the company of a beautiful woman like you."

"Nonsense. What's bothering you?"

"I've got—hmm . . . I've got more wrong with me. My—ah, part of my . . . ah, leg is missing. I'm walking on a fake leg. And I've got a lot of scars around my . . . you know . . . my lower stomach and ah . . . my privates. Sorry. I'll understand if you want to leave."

"Ben, the best lover I was ever with had only one arm. He treated me with respect, like you. He was gentle, like you. He didn't talk down to me, like you. Men think of women in physical terms first, then emotional. It's the opposite with women. Here, let me help you unbuckle those jeans. Then remove the fake leg. Women like skin on skin. Plastic, not so much."

After undressing, I took off my prosthetic leg and reached up to Vivian and gently pulled her down on the bed with me. It was good to lie side by side with a woman again, and this was some woman. She seemed to be honestly unfazed by my scars and short leg.

I removed her clinging negligee with a little help from her and gazed at her perfect body: no scars and all the parts were the right size and in the right place. That should have been enough to get my juices flowing, but I guessed it would take a little more than just having a look.

We took our time. We kissed, gently at first, playing with each other's tongues and exploring the other's bodies with our free hands. God it felt good, but the important thing was not happening.

I buried my face between her breasts. She purred. She turned me so I was on my back and she was straddling me, with her breasts brushing my lips. By now I was starting to panic, getting such a bad feeling that not even her nipples on my lips could shake my disappointment. Nothing was going on down below.

"Vivian, I'm sorry. It's sure not your fault, but my worst fears are—"

"Hon, just relax. Let me help you with my lips."

Even after her best efforts, my little soldier refused to come to attention.

"Ben, I think we should take a break. You've put way too much pressure on yourself, and we should have taken more time. Let's put those hotel robes on, order up some sirloin tips in mushroom sauce and sip a little more wine. I'm not going anywhere until you have to check out of this room in the morning."

"You're very understanding. Yeah, maybe a break would help my noggin and other organs. Just having you along side of me all night sounds dang good. You know, I am kinda hungry. How about some onion rings too?"

She brought the robes out of the closet while I made the room service call. We sat on the love seat, curled up in the terrycloth robes and sipped the full-bodied red.

"With how many women have you made love?"

"Well, jeeze, that seems like a strange question."

"I think you need to talk about that. It might lead to something."

"Well, okay. Two. I asked the first one to marry me. She said she wanted to be my wife, but only after we both got further along with our lives."

"Did you love her? Did you go together a long time?"

"Of course I did. Ya, a few years."

"Then why was there a second lover?"

This questioning made me uncomfortable. "Geeze, that's pretty blunt and really none of your damn business."

"Whoa, Ben, I sounds to me it would be good for you to talk that through with somebody. Shrinks are pretty expensive. Try me instead. And while we're at it, here are three more questions. Did you still love the first gal when you made love to the second? And, did you love the second at the same time as the first, or was that just a fling?"

"You're getting awful personal, and I don't appreciate it one bit. Maybe you should just leave."

"Sorry for the intrusion, Ben. I really think talking about this would help your . . . situation. Many times, sexual performance problems are as much of a mental problem as physical."

"All right, dammit, I loved 'em both at the same time. I still do."

"I take it they are no longer in your life?"

"You can say that again."

"Do they know about each other?"

"God, no."

Room service knocked on the door and Vivian got up to let him in with the order. "I'm sorry," she said to him. "We should have ordered another bottle of wine. Please bring us another one when you can. Set the food over here. Thank you very much." She handed him a ten as he left.

I ate pretty much without saying anything, still a little pissed at her. But I guess she meant well.

After the next bottle of wine came, we shed our robes and propped ourselves up on the bed pillows to sip some more of the grape. She didn't probe me with any more personal questions.

"Let's just relax now and fall asleep close to each other," she said while rubbing the back of her hand on my cheek. "Anytime during the night or in the morning, if you feel the urge, just give me a nudge and we'll make it happen."

It was a great feeling to have her, or I guess for that matter, any woman I might care for, in bed with me.

I woke up several times during the night.

My little soldier remained at ease.

Chapter 37

September 1966, three months later

OZZIE

I slid my hand under her nightgown. Barb's right boob was my intermediate goal.

"Oh, no. Not tonight. I'm tired."

It was 3:00 a.m. I'd woken up when she came to bed.

Disappointed, I said, "That's nothing new. You're always tired."

"And how many times have I caught you cat napping at all hours of the day?" she said. "It takes two to play. You've been zonked out when I wanted to do more than just chat. Right now I wanna sleep," she yawned. "It was two-thirty when I finally could get to bed after closing up. Beer truck's gonna be at the back door at nine and I have to check the delivery."

"Ah, shee-it. Maybe I gotta make an appointment with you to play hubby and wife."

"Maybe," she said as she moved my hand away from her silky thigh.

***

JUST BEFORE NOON the next day I was pushing a cart full of food over to the dock so the boat crew could get the buffet set up on board. The maples on the lake shore were in their fall color blaze, torching a clear blue sky. Danny's popular "Fall Color Lunch Cruise" would be at capacity that Saturday afternoon. As I rolled the cart out on the dock, Barb stepped off the boat with a mop and pail. Her hair was hanging in her eyes and she looked beat.

"Sorry about last night," she whispered, pushing strands of hair from her face. "We've got to talk. It's not only our sex lives that need fixing. The only thing we have time to talk to each other about is the business, and that's while we happen to be working close to each other. Thank god Danny is a good kid. We need to spend more time with him too. Something has to change soon."

"Well, at least we're making money now," I said as we walked back to the kitchen. I draped my arm over her shoulder.

"At what cost? If we were being paid by the hour our boss would be arrested for slavery. My God, between the two of us we must put in two hundred hours a week," Barb said. "I'm worried about what this is doing to Danny, too."

"Okay, okay, I get it. Maybe we can figure out how to get some time off."

"Maybe? *Maybe?* No, not maybe. We darned sure *will* figure out how to get outta here for a while. We're burning ourselves out."

"Funny thing; I've been thinking about something that'd help," I said.

"Like what?"

"I wonder if Ma would move back from Alaska to help us out. She's working for her CPA brother, so she must understand numbers. With her handling the cash and bookkeeping, the rest of the crew could get along without us for a week or so. I know she'd like to spend time with Danny."

"Not a bad idea for a dumb jock," Barb said as she gave me a light punch to my shoulder. "See, all I had to do was cut you off to get your *other* head n gear."

"Hardy-har-har. If it works out with Ma, where would you like to go to rediscover my inner, intellectual self?"

"Well, jeeze, haven't thought about that, my head's too deep into running this place to have thought about fun stuff."

"Let's think about it. I'll call Ma tonight and see what she thinks about moving here. Then we should start planning a vacation. You know, maybe Trudy and Shu would like to go along with us."

"What? I can see I'm gonna have to keep you cut off for your mind to work better. We need time by ourselves."

"Promises, promises. Hey, how about a bus-man's holiday. We could take a driving trip and stop at interesting restaurants along the way to pick up ideas . . . in between makin' whoopee, of course. Hell, we could even write off the vacation."

"Hmm. Maybe you're only a semi-dumb jock. Now you're thinking with the right head."

***

"GREAT NEWS, BARB, Ma loves the idea," I said after calling Alaska that night. "She'll be here in about a month. Gotta sublet her apartment and give her brother time to hire somebody else. Now, how semi-dumb am I?"

"Come here, genius. Gimme a squeeze," Barb said with a sly smile.

I went to her and held both of her buns in my open hands, pulling her to me. That was all though, we were passing each other in the kitchen where two cooks and a waitress were witnessing the action.

I laughed. "Start researching our vacation route. You're in charge of that. I'm not smart enough."

"Okay. Hey, I haven't seen Bjorn in here for a while. What gives?"

"Probably too busy going to the damn peacenik rallies. Besides work, the anti-war stuff and seeing the old gang once in a blue moon, he just hibernates."

"Well, hey, go easy on him. He's been through a lot."

"Ain't we all."

BJORN

MA SAID, "YOU KNOW, your dad wants to be at the meeting, too. Do you think you could be civil to him? Put the war stuff aside for a while, okay?"

"I won't start anything if he doesn't, but I'm not gonna take any crap from him," I said.

The meeting with the two Silverman Brothers' investment bankers, Benjamin Dauwalter and Jacob Ploen, had been scheduled for three weeks. During that time several phone conversations had taken place between us in Victoria and the Silverman people in New York. Also, they'd had a CPA and an attorney at our place for the last two weeks doing what they called "due diligence" work.

Dauwalter had rented a suite at the Radisson Hotel in downtown Minneapolis for the gathering. Ma told me before the meeting she wouldn't be nervous. Her self-confidence had never been a problem for her even when she was a cleaning lady. She knew her business-like appearance mixed with her solid Nordic features would help her hold her own as the only woman at the meeting.

The contrast between the fancy New York suits and Pa's and my plaid shirts was kinda obvious. But I figured they wanted what we had to offer and we wanted what they had to offer, so the hell with buying a suit just for this meeting. We didn't need to impress them with clothes. The small talk portion of the meeting didn't last long, I suppose 'cause of the tension between Pa and me.

After Ploen got soft drinks or coffee for everyone he got down to business. All of us were sitting around a small, highly polished conference table. "There are just some minor details to work through," Ploen said as he passed around an outline titled *Preliminary Memorandum of Agreement*. "We want this to be a win-win situation. I believe we've all agreed upon the basics in prior conversations.

"To summarize, Silverman Brothers will forgive your outstanding debt with us and issue you a certified check in the negotiated amount in exchange for a one-third ownership in your company. We will also contribute the other agreed upon amount to help with the start-up costs at the new Waconia plant. Am I correct so far?"

Pa glanced at me while I looked at the ceiling and nodded. Ma said, "Ya, so far so good."

Dauwalter said, "We all agree that your hospital and rehab equipment division will be expanded to include the manufacture of exercise equipment. We will help recruit well-known college coaches and professional athletes, among others, to serve on an advisory board and to endorse the exercise products. This will be expedited by the director of Marketing we encouraged you to hire.

"We will help organize franchised exercise operations around the country to feature your equipment. Our target markets include sports teams of all levels, the franchises I just mentioned, community fitness centers, and even home use. And again, Bjorn, thank you for this idea."

Ma reached over and patted my shoulder. Pa gave me an approving look.

"In the past your company made products for other companies to sell to the end users," Ploen said. "Now, with the new division you enter the world of selling directly to the end users, which is a whole new ballgame for you of inventory control, sales and marketing, spare part inventory and so forth. If done correctly it can be profitable for all of us."

"We know how to design and make things," I said. "And we know we have to hire good people to help with the other stuff."

"I know you are aware of the challenges and I am confident of your—or should I say, our—success," Dauwalter said. "We will have our legal department draw up the items in this memorandum in legal form. You should also have your attorney check over the contracts," Ploen said. "These are large sums of money for you. I hope you will also have a financial advisor review the numbers. Maybe there are better ways to structure the transaction for your purposes."

"Ya, that's a good idea," Ma said. I think the amount of money was beyond belief to her.

"We still run the show, right?" Pa asked.

"Of course," Dauwalter said. "You folks have created a great company. We don't want to change it. Your quality products, reputation, community involvement, employee relations, and innovation are enviable." Then he said with a shrug and a chuckle, "Besides, you have two votes to our one."

Ploen said, "But, remember, as part of this agreement, we will take the company public in three to five years." Nodding to Ma and Pa, he continued. "At that time you probably will be ready to retire anyway. With a public company, the operation will be overseen by a board of directors.

"Surely they will want Bjorn to continue in an important role. Keep in mind, this is part of your exit strategy. It will also be the time when you folks will be more handsomely rewarded for what you've created. And frankly, it's when Silverman Brothers will be rewarded also."

"Any other questions before we all sign the memorandum?" Dauwalter looked at each of us. There were none, so he continued. "There are a couple of items not on the memorandum we need to discuss."

Pa turned to me with that oh-oh look.

Ploen looked at the folks. "First of all, it is our understanding that you two have not taken any time off since the company started over ten years ago. You've been working six and a half to seven days a week. As a bonus to you, Silverman Brothers would like to send you on an all-expenses paid, two-week tour of the Scandinavian countries."

Ma's hand flew to her mouth. She let out a squeal of surprised delight.

Pa shook his head in disbelief. "Well, we did go to the company cabin a coupla times. Really, we can't be gone from the plant that long. Besides, the trip's not necessary. You've been very generous with—"

Ma interrupted. "Shush, Karl." She had tears in her eyes and her Nordic stoicism was ripped away by a smile across her face. She leaned over the table and grabbed Ploen's hands. "Oh, thank you so much. That's been a dream of ours for many years."

"You're very welcome. You deserve a vacation, and we know you will enjoy the trip," Dauwalter said. "And there is one other thing we need to discuss."

I'm sure Ma couldn't imagine it getting any better. I noticed she moved forward in her seat to hear about the next goodie.

"In preparation for taking the company public, it is important that present management not attract any negative publicity," Dauwalter said.

Ploen looked at me. "Bjorn, in order for this deal to proceed, you must . . . ah, curtail your anti-war activities."

My heart pounded as my jaw dropped in disbelief.

Pa glared at me.

My gut churned, but my mind was clear. I got up, went to the door, opened it, turned and said, "Sorry, gents, my soul is not for sale."

Chapter 38

Two weeks later, October 1966

Bjorn

"Pope, wanna go with me to an anti-war pre-march rally Saturday morning?" I asked him over the phone. "I know it's only a week before you're gettin' hitched, but I'd like some company. Plus, I got something I wanna talk to you about."

"What time? I would need to be back by six-thirty or so. Ruthie and I are going to her parents for dinner. Are you going to the march also? I am not sure I am cut out for that."

"I'd pick you up about eight in the morning. We'd be back in plenty of time for you to chow down with your future in-laws. I can't join the march, I gotta stay behind the scenes."

"Why is that?"

"We're going to sell part of the company. The buyer insisted on me cooling the anti-war bit. I balked. Long story. Folks were really upset. So, Ma negotiated a compromise on it. I agreed not to do marches, public statements or letters to editors. I can't have my picture taken with any anti-war activity, I can only do personal financial contributions to the cause and work with vets to recruit them to join. After I agreed to those things the buyer stayed on board."

"Wow, selling the company is a surprise, even if it is only part of it. But why go to the pre-march rally if you are not going to participate in the actual event? It sounds to me like you would be violating your mother's negotiated promise by attending the rally."

"Ya, I know. Just this once I'd like to sneak in 'cause I gave the organizers a big check three weeks ago. I'd like to see what they intend to do with the money."

"Who received the check?"

"A philosophy professor from the U is one of the organizers . . . name's Redman. There's also a professor from one of those St. Paul colleges . . . Hamline, I think. He's a political science prof . . . name's DeBower. I got their names and addresses from a friend."

"It would be an interesting life-experience for me to go with you. I will be ready at eight. Oh, yes, what was it you wanted to talk to me about"

"It can wait 'til Saturday morning. See you then. Goodbye."

***

SATURDAY DAWNED A CRISP, blue-sky day, perfect for the Gopher football game against the Badgers—or an anti-war march.

"Where is the pre-march rally?" Pope asked as he slid into my pickup.

"Here's the address." I handed him a slip of paper. "It's in an abandoned warehouse on Washington Avenue. Down by the slums, bums, and strip joints, but close enough to downtown for the march. Remember, I gotta get outta there right after I talk to those guys."

I was wearing my typical plaid shirt and jeans. Pope had on his typical dark suit with a white shirt and an askew tie. We drove downtown in my red GMC.

"Bjorn, you said there was something else you wanted to talk to me about."

"Oh. Ya . . . hmm . . . I'm afraid this isn't good news. Well, I guess it doesn't really qualify as news, it's only my opinion."

"Your opinion about what?"

"Buggy whips," I said quietly.

"Buggy whips?"

"Ya. Companies that use'ta make 'em aren't doing so hot these days."

"You are being too obscure for me to understand. What is your point?"

"Well, you know, I talk to a lot of people in the business world, especially at Land Master and Polarcat." I glanced over at him. I wanted to lay this on him kinda easy, but I didn't know how I could soft pedal it.

"The general feeling of the big boys is that computers will be getting smaller, more powerful and less expensive in a few years. If they're right, and I think they are, computer timesharing is gonna go the way of the buggy whip companies. I don't want to see you get hurt in that trend."

"What?" He seemed almost angry. "I am sure Computing Data would have warned me about that by now if it were true. I am not worried."

"Sorry, but word on the street is they are also ignoring the trend. They're staying with the big stuff while others are concentrating on computers so small that every company could have one. Heck, people might even have 'em in their homes someday."

"Oh, shit! No—no, sorry. I did not mean for that to come out. Goodness, I never swear. If what you say is true, have you thought about what could I possibly do about it?" His face had grown a little more pale.

"Sell your branch to your partners as soon as you can. Then come to work for us. You can be our V.P. of getting us up to speed with the new technologies."

"But . . . but I would be obligated to tell them why I want to sell."

"Let the buyers beware. Here's Washington. I think we need to take a right." I pointed my finger at him. "Pope, they're big boys; they should have their ears to the ground themselves."

He shook his head. "I could not do that to them."

"Remember two things, Pope: first, those guys would hang you out to dry in a heartbeat. Second, maybe I'm wrong and you would be making a big mistake by selling now, but I doubt that."

Pope looked worried. "I appreciate your concern about my business. You seem to have given the problem considerable thought." He stared out the passenger window. "I will need to do some research and pray about this."

"Hey, Pope, we must be getting close."

"Oh, yes, here is the address. You can park over there," Pope said, pointing to a space next to a bent-up chain-link fence laced with a gardener's nightmare of tall weeds.

The faded white letters on the abandoned red-brick warehouse were barely readable. I thought they said something about a wooden barrel company. Most of the windows in the building would let in light, but also bugs, birds, rain, and snow. The blacktop parking lot looked like it had been the target of a bombing raid, and weeds and seedling trees were reclaiming the prairie, even if it was in the middle of the city.

We parked, then headed toward the space where the door used to be. Organizers of the event had set up Coleman camp lanterns in the dim interior 'cause there wasn't any electricity to the building. A loud five-piece band was warming up in a far corner. A few student types were helping set things up and the sweet smell of marijuana was already in the air. Some of my 'Nam buddies would feel right at home.

I walked up to a thirty-five-ish-looking guy wearing a corduroy jacket. "I'm looking for Redman."

The guy pointed to his right. "He's over there. I'm DeBower, something I can do for you?" He looked Pope up and down, suspicious of the suit, tie, bare cheeks and chin.

I shook his hand. "Hi. I'm Bjorn Olson. I sent you guys the money to fund this rally. This is a friend of mine . . . David. I just wanted to stop by and see what you guys were doing with my money."

"Great. Thanks for the funds. We're going to put on a hell of a show with it."

"I figured a couple of professors oughta know how to pull off something big so I wouldn't be wasting my money or the opportunity."

"Here comes Redman now." DeBower nodded toward a tall man headed our way. "We'll be happy to explain how we're gonna get the media's attention." He turned to Redman. "This is Bjorn Olson and his friend, David. Bjorn funded this shindig. He wants to see how we spent his money."

Redman was at least six-foot-five. He was stacked loosely in a skinny body that looked like it might tip over from the weight of long, black snarly hair protruding from every surface of his head. "Thanks for the money. It's for a good cause," Redman said as he shook our hands. "Very nice to meet you both. We have a lot to do, so the tour will have to be brief."

"That's fine by me. I can't stay too long," I said.

"To start with, we used more than a few bucks just to rent this dump. The size, location, and bad condition are pluses. No way we can damage this place more than it already is," he smirked. "I know you smell the weed smoke; it covers up the urine smell from the bums." DeBower said as he waved his arm and pointed to the interior. "Over here is the T-shirt concession. We had these printed up and we'll sell 'em, but at less than what you paid for 'em. Why don't you take one?"

There were five styles to choose from: *HO, HO, HO CHI MINH; ONWARD CHE; GO GO MAO; GI=BABY KILLER* and *REMEMBER KENT STATE KILLINGS*. The first three carried the likeness of Ho Chi Minh, Che Guevara, and Mao Tse Tung, respectively, and the other two had graphics meant to anger.

"I'm not sure I like glorifying dictators who killed millions of their own people," I said. "What's that stuff in the next booth . . . and what's that smell?"

"You've got to understand, we have to rile these kids up. We have to work the media, too," Redman said.

We moved to the next booth. "You bought fifteen of these fatigue jackets," DeBower said. "Then we printed *GI=BABY KILLER* in white on the front and back along with red blood drops. The smell is from the fuel oil in those water pistols. See that stack of dolls over there? You bought them too. We put the word out for marchers to bring more dolls."

"What's all this about?" I asked.

Redman said, "We're going to have everybody on the march carry dolls and make a pile of them in the middle of the intersection of Eighth and Nicollet, over by Dayton's Department Store. Then we're going to light a fire under the dolls and fifteen students in those fatigue jackets will squirt fuel oil on the fire. You know, baby killers."

What he was selling, I regretted buying.

Redman and DeBower just didn't get it. "For cryin' out loud! You're making the enemies into heroes and the troops into the bad guys instead of the assholes in Washington!" I yelled.

"Media'll eat this up," Redman said condescendingly. "We have our cameraman friends from WCCO and KSTP-TV clued in. We told them where to be to get the best shots, second floor windows facing the intersection. Hell, I bet we even make the national news. We think we'll have over two-hundred marchers."

DeBower was getting exited. "Man, can you even imagine the stink and black smoke from an eight- to ten-foot-high pyramid of burning plastic dolls and fuel oil? It's going to be great! Then the marchers will block access for fire trucks from all four directions. It's going to be a hell of a show."

The two professors had proud grins on their faces.

"The police will probably stop you," Pope said.

"Nah. They think this is going to be a pep rally for the football game this afternoon. The pigs will look pretty silly." DeBower smirked.

Pope leaned toward me and whispered, "I do not like the looks of this. You have to stop them."

"I know, buddy," I said.

Redman continued the tour. "This next booth is where we'll be selling shots of tequila for a quarter. Loud music, a little weed and booze will get the boys and girls riled up and ready to raise hell on the march."

"Bjorn, you must put a stop to this, now!" Pope hissed, waving his hands at the tequila. The professors heard him that time.

I looked at them. "Guys, what the hell are you doing? I trusted you to do the right things 'cause you're professors. You're giving protests a bad name, and frankly I'm ashamed I trusted you with my support. We're all gonna regret this whole damn circus."

Redman retorted, "You don't understand. In order to get the media's attention, we have to be outlandish. Without the media going nuts, the whole thing would be a waste of time and your money."

I shook my head. "Sorry, but I won't be part of making the troops look bad. Baby killers, my ass. Go after the fat-assed, short-sighted politicians instead."

DeBower snickered as he jabbed his finger into my chest. "Too late, my friend, your check has been cashed."

OLGA

As SOON AS I WALKED in the door I pulled Mrs. Schneider's pot roast from the fridge and put it in the oven. I turned on the five-thirty national news, kicked off my shoes, sat down and closed my eyes for a short eye rest while I listened. It had been another long day at the plant, but we had gotten the payroll done on time.

I heard the announcer say, "And here is the CBS Evening News with Walter Cronkite."

Mr. Cronkite began: "Good evening ladies and gentlemen.

"Another sad ending to an anti-war protest took place today, this time in Minneapolis. Three University of Minnesota students and a Macalester College student were burned to death during a war protest in downtown Minneapolis. The students were part of a group spraying fuel oil on burning plastic dolls when their clothing caught fire. Their fatigue jackets were printed with the words 'GI equals Baby Killer.' Names are being withheld pending family notification.

"Several more protesters were severely injured when they attempted to keep fire trucks from reaching the blaze. As you can see by the video taken by our Twin City affiliate, WCCO, it was a large and intense fire.

"The inferno was started in the middle of a major downtown intersection on top of a utility manhole. There was severe smoke damage to Dayton's, the largest department store in the Upper Midwest. The burning fuel oil and melting, burning plastic from the dolls seeped through the manhole into a utility tunnel. Plastic and rubber wire coverings and plastic pipes in the tunnel caught fire and smoke was drawn into Dayton's mechanical room and then spread throughout the store by the air-exchange system. All soft merchandise in the store has smoke damage. Other downtown Minneapolis buildings suffered a similar fate; but nothing compared to the loss of four young college students.

"Minneapolis Mayor, Charles Stenvig, himself an ex-police chief, said, quote, 'This was an organized protest and by god we are going to find those responsible.'

"In other war news . . ."

***

I THOUGHT, *Oh, my, those poor kids. It's a good thing Karl isn't home from work yet. All these doggone protests really upset him. I thought maybe I should call Bjorn to see if he wanted to come over for pot roast. It's one of his favorite things to eat.*

Chapter 39

That same day, October 1966

BJORN

Pope, we gotta do this," I said as we crossed the entrance plaza of the imposing Federal Building just a few blocks from the towering column of black smoke. We were both gasping for air after hurrying the six blocks from the old warehouse. It was the first time I had tried to run on my new leg . . . not a good idea. Pope helped me along. I had one arm over his shoulder and he had his arm around my waist. People stared at us as we hopped and skipped along the sidewalks looking like participants in a three-legged sack race.

"I know, I know, but I have to call Ruthie to tell her I will probably be late for dinner with her parents." He looked frazzled from our day's experience. He'd lost his suit coat, and his tie was hanging loosely down his untucked dress shirt from which some buttons were missing.

I used my plaid sleeve to wipe the sweat from my forehead. "Jeeze, look at that smoke. We coulda stopped that if DeBower's goons would have let us go. We could've gotten to the police in time. Like I said, now the police will be too pissed to listen to our story. Better to talk to the FBI first."

We pushed through the Fed Building door and interrupted the plump security guard manning the front desk. He was listening to the Gopher pre-game show on WCCO. As we approached him the radio announcer was interrupted by a news bulletin about the downtown intersection blaze. "We need to talk to the FBI," I said to the guard with a nod toward the radio. "About that."

He looked us over and said reluctantly, "Well, there are only a few agents here on Saturday. I'll call to see if one is available."

After a few seconds he hung up. "Okay, elevator's to your left, fifth floor. Agent Williams will meet you." He turned his attention back to the radio.

"Thank you," Pope said. After we got on the elevator, Pope said, "If your involvement in this gets out, it will affect the sale of your company."

"Listen, my involvement *will* get out. Those bastards, DeBower and Redman, will make sure of that," I shook my head. "Gotta go on the offensive before they get caught. When they start talking they'll spin the story."

The elevator door opened. Facing us was a man with a gray crew cut and his hands on his hips. "I'm Agent Williams." It was not a friendly greeting. He didn't offer to shake our hands and he was checking out my beard and long hair. Phones were ringing in the background. "The guard said you wanted to see us about the demonstration and fire."

"Ya. I'm Bjorn Olson and this is my friend David Grimm. We have information about the organizers, and I'm afraid I inadvertently was involved in financing the march."

"What do you mean by that?" Williams asked.

"I sent the organizers a check a few weeks back to cover expenses for the pre-march rally, but I swear I didn't know until this morning exactly what they had planned. We tried to stop them, but they held us 'til it was too late."

"Follow me," he growled and led us down a hall to a bare interview room. "Sit." As we sat, he closed the door. "I don't know if this crap is even in our jurisdiction. Seems it's a local police matter. Why aren't you talking to them?"

"Well, I thought anti-war demonstrations were of interest to you guys, 'specially the organizers," I said. "Plus, I thought we should talk to someone less emotional about this stuff instead of a cop on the beat. We'd probably get the shit kicked out of us by the police. The news is full of stuff like that against demonstrators."

Williams shook his head. "Most of the time the police are provoked when that happens."

Pope said, "Could I use a phone please? I must call my fiancé."

Williams nodded and indicated a phone on the credenza. "Dial nine first."

While Pope was dialing Ruthie, I looked at Williams. "Maybe that demonstration isn't in your jurisdiction, but our being held against our will for two hours is kidnapping and that would be in your bailiwick, wouldn't it?"

"It's not kidnapping if a ransom wasn't demanded. If you were only held for two hours maybe it could be called false imprisonment. That would be a local police matter."

Pope held up his hand in an attempt to quiet us while he greeted Ruthie. "Hello Dear . . . I am fine, but I find myself in a bit of a situation."

There was a knock on the door. "Excuse me," Williams said. He opened the door and stepped out.

"I am extremely sorry, Ruthie, but I will not be able to join your parents for dinner this evening. I find myself detained for an undetermined length of time."

Williams returned and slammed the door. "The situation's taken a turn for the worse. There have been fatalities at the fire. We've called the police and they're on the way. We're holding you two for their arrival."

***

DETECTIVE PATRICK HADAWAY said, "What do you mean you didn't know what those guys were going to do with your money?" His red Irish mug was glistening with sweat. The armpits of his baby blue shirt were stained with wet rings. His nose was barn red.

Pope and I were in separate interrogation rooms at the downtown police station.

"Okay, I was naïve. I thought it would be a peaceful safe march. When I found out what they were up to I tried to stop 'em. I went to law enforcement as soon as I could. They held us—"

He pushed his mug closer to me. "Naïve is a code word for being stupid."

DAVID, A.K.A. POPE

I DID NOT KNOW WHAT was happening with Bjorn, but in the interview room where I was being questioned, Detective Frederick Cottrell was having his way with me. "You know, you might be charged as an accessory to several crimes, including unlawful assembly, property damage, and manslaughter, just to name a few. We'll just have to see what happens."

I was scared, but of course I knew all I had to do was tell the truth, and that's what I would have done regardless of the circumstances.

After an hour of interrogation, Sergeant Hadaway, Bjorn's interrogator came in, and he and Cottrell compared notes in the corner of the room. I was relieved when Cottrell said, "Well, at least their stories match up. Sounds like Olson is guilty of stupidity, and Grimm was just in the wrong place at the wrong time," Cottrell said. "Let's see if the guys have brought in those two slime-ball professors. If they have, we'll dance with them for a while and see what tune they sing."

Hadaway said, "Problem is, unlike these two, the profs will lawyer-up right away."

"So what? With what Olson and Grimm told us we've got enough on the profs to hang their asses anyway. Gonna be fun making them sweat."

"Okay, but let's hold these two until they can be picked-up by someone that can vouch for them. Have 'em call for a ride."

BJORN

OZZIE DROVE PA to the police station to pick me up. Ozzie said he was worried the whole trip 'cause he thought Pa would blow a gasket. He stared straight ahead with his jaw clenched and never said a word. Ozzie told me Ma was too scared of Dad's reaction to even come along.

Ruthie, alone, and Ozzie and Pa arrived at the police station within ten minutes of each other. They sat in the gray waiting room with several students from the march. Some of the students looked defiant, but most looked teary eyed and frightened. Pa was already pissed enough, now he had to sit in the same room as some of the demonstrators he loathed. His face was frozen in anger.

When Pope and I entered the waiting room, we each got a very different reception.

Ruthie ran to Pope, jumped up and gave him a passionate kiss through tears of joy about his release.

When I approached Pa, Ozzie grabbed Pa's arm just in time to stop him from delivering a hay-maker to my jaw.

***

OZZIE DROVE PA and me to where I had left my GMC before the rally. I was alone in the back seat. "Come on, Pa, won't you at least listen to my side of the story?"

"God damn it, Silverman is gonna find out about this. You've probably ruined your Ma's retirement. Those dead kid's folks and the Dayton family are gonna see you in court." Pa said without turning around. "We've been working our asses off helping to build the company. Now you gotta stick your anti-war, pinko nose in the wrong place even after you agreed not to. I guess your word ain't worth shit."

Ozzie kept his mouth shut, probably wondering what would happen next. I was sure he agreed with Pa.

I bit my tongue for several seconds, not wanting to escalate the argument, but I had to respond. I spoke softly. "First of all, being against the war doesn't make me a pinko. You of all people should know I'm a capitalist. Second, I'm the one who got the talks with Silverman started about buying part of our company. If that falls apart, I'll find someone else. Third, I tried to *stop* those assholes today. You can ask Pope."

We pulled up to my GMC, but I didn't get out . . . I needed to finish this. "And fourth, don't question whether my word is good or not. I consider it one of my most valuable possessions. I wanted to see what the organizers were doin' with my money. Contributing to the cause was okay in the Silverman agreement. I didn't go down there to help in any way. I went to the rally to see what they were doing with my money, and when I didn't agree with their tactics I tried to stop the bastards. If we could've gotten to the police in time, we would've stopped 'em."

Pa was tense like a coiled snake, ready to strike.

"If their goons hadn't held us captive we'd be heroes instead of goats." I took a deep breath. "But you know what, Dad, the greatest sadness in my life right now isn't all the stuff that happened today or even my broken body . . . it's our broken relationship."

Silence reigned for a long moment. Ozzie kept his hands on the steering wheel and sat as still as a sphinx. Finally Pa's body went from tense to a slump and he turned in his seat to look at me. Tears left his one eye before he spoke. "Son, don't worry. We'll work it out."

Chapter 40

Two weeks later, November 1966

DAVID, A.K.A. POPE

I was about to marry a divorced woman. The fact she divorced because her first husband slugged and beat her did not nullify the rules of my Church. I begrudgingly got over the fact we were not allowed to wed in a Catholic Church. I begged Father Distel to officiate, but his hands were tied by Church rules. He could only offer a prayer during the service as a friend.

Thanks to Shu and Trudy's support of the congregation, the wedding took place at Parley Lake Moravian Church with Reverend Susan Hill presiding. It was a small affair attended by our parents and close friends. My parents arrived looking much happier than they had at my first wedding.

Maple trees guarded the church and blazed with autumn colors of red, yellow, and orange. A November chill was in the air and reminded everyone the sky-blue lake would soon host ice skaters, hockey pucks, and ice fishing shacks instead of waves and sailboats.

When I entered the cozy church it triggered memories of Ursula's many melt-downs and how I had missed the opportunity to be Nick's godfather. I soon erased those bad memories with thoughts of Ruthie. A reception would follow at Danny's Island Escape. This would be the start of new, happier memories.

The few wedding guests sat in the front two padded pews on each side of the maroon carpeted aisle. It was a late Sunday afternoon and the shadows were growing long.

Ruthie's radiant face bore a semi-permanent smile that thrilled her lone attendant, a friend from her Northwest Airlines days. Ruthie was wearing a beautiful ivory suit, and I was in a black blazer with tan slacks instead of a suit. We wanted an informal feeling, serious but celebratory. I did make sure I had buttoned my collar this time, and Ruthie had worked over my unruly hair.

Reverend Hill began the ceremony with traditional comments, then introduced Father Distel who began his prayer. "Bless this union and—" He was interrupted by a commotion in the second row of pews where Ellie Schumacher was sitting with Trudy.

Danny Johnson, who had not seen the inside of a church often, was in the balcony surreptitiously throwing toilet paper spit balls at the back of Ellie's head. The first two missed their mark, but the third thwacked her right between her pigtails. Eight-year-old freckled Ellie, forgetting where she was, spun out of her pew and ran for the balcony stairs, yelling, "I'm gonna get you, you little brat!"

I think she had a crush on him, and vice-versa.

Groomsmen Shu and Ozzie stood frozen and helpless at the altar, but Trudy and Barb sprang into damage control and corralled their offspring. The snickers from the audience soon quieted down.

Bjorn was also in the wedding party, but he seemed uncomfortable in the blazer I had loaned him to wear over his plaid shirt. He had trimmed his beard and long hair for the occasion. However his partial ear and neck scars were still covered. I know he was happy for us, but I was worried he was feeling sorry for himself for not being likely ever to marry or have children of his own.

With a smile on his face, Father Distel finished his prayer. "And if this union is blessed with children, may they be spiritual and as spirited as those we have just witnessed. Amen."

When it came time to say our own vows, I asked Reverend Hill, "Would it be acceptable if I say my vows in my own words?"

"Of course," she answered. "This show belongs to you two."

Ruthie looked surprised, but also pleased. She knew I would speak from my heart.

"My dearest Ruthie, I feel I am the luckiest man in the world, standing here while you accept me as your husband." I held both of her hands and stared into her eyes. "We have both experienced pain and disappointment in the past. I swear on all that is holy, I will love, protect, honor and be faithful to you and do my part to help make our marriage all that it can be. I will do everything in my power to live up to your expectations."

Even though it was not in the sequence of the ceremony's plans I took her in my arms for a long, tender embrace. Reverend Hill was one of many witnesses to wipe away a tear.

The rest of the service went off as planned. I did not have the old urge to up-chuck in tense situations.

Instead of walking down the aisle together after we were pronounced man and wife, all the guests stormed up to the altar for hugs and high fives with Ruthie and me.

***

MY YELLOW-AND-GREEN EDSEL had been decorated with a few wedding phrases: *She Can't Cook. He Snores. Hot Sheets Tonight,* and *Just Hitched—No More Freedom.* My car also was towing nine empty, noisy, Folgers coffee cans as it pulled into Danny's parking lot for the reception. We were grinning from ear to ear.

Young Danny Johnson was the first to get to our car and opened the door for Ruthie. She got out of the car and Danny took her hand. With a quivering chin, he said, "I am very sorry I caused a ruckus at your wedding. Please forgive me." Obviously he had been coached by Barb.

Ruthie bent down and cupped her right hand under his chin. "Danny, don't feel bad. You are most certainly forgiven. And you know what? That's what memories are made of, you helped make it a memorable day." She then planted a quick kiss squarely on his lips.

Still blushing, Danny led us past the waving palm trees through the double doors of the Island Escape. As we entered the main room we were greeted by cheers from the assembled crowd. We were stunned by the décor. Ozzie and Barb had outdone themselves decorating the restaurant, and it looked fabulous. Cut flower arrangements adorned every table. Dozens of large, three-dimensional, white crepe paper wedding bells hung from the ceiling and white crepe paper ribbon crisscrossed the room.

A tuxedoed waiter approached carrying a tray with two tall champagne flutes with a white rose attached to each. He lowered the tray and served us. Ruthie and I then noticed everyone in the room was holding a full flute of champagne.

On cue, Shu, Bjorn, and Ozzie stepped forward together, each holding his glass high in a toasting position. In unison they said, "To Ruthie and Pope, we all wish you the best of everything. May all your dreams come true." The whole crowd cheered, "Here, here!" and downed their champagne.

We were surprised, thrilled and happy. Together we raised our glasses and I said, "Thank you. Thank you, great friends. Now let the party begin."

Starting the next day, it would be a working honeymoon. Ruthie and I would be heading for San Francisco to attempt to disengage from our obligations of the computer timeshare company.

BJORN

NO ONE NOTICED as I eased away from the wedding reception early. Alone, back at my room adjacent to my office at the plant, I draped Pope's blazer over my folding chair, splashed some cold water on my face, took off my flesh-colored plastic leg, and dove into my single bed. After a last look at the two Polaroid photos tacked to the wall above my bed, I reached for the chain to turn off the bare light bulb.

Pope's trip to the west coast worried me—that among many other things. I closed my eyes for what turned out to be a fitful attempt to fall asleep. My mind was racing with thoughts of everything from trying it with Vivian again to those poor kids burned with fuel oil to wondering whether Dayton's store and those kids' parents might sue me to hoping Pope wouldn't get screwed by his partners to Ma needing some time off to hoping the cops had nailed the hell out of DeBower and Redman to thoughts of May and hoping she was okay to cursing the *war* to telling myself for the millionth time if it hadn't happened MK would still be by my side to hoping she's all right and happy to wishing I could just sleep to the sudden awareness that damn it I needed to pee.

I reached for my crutch and hopped over to the crapper. On the way back to bed I stopped at the small fridge to see if Ma remembered to leave me some of her famous potato salad. It was there. I took it out, grabbed a tablespoon, sat at the card table in the dark and ate from the bowl. My mind was still cranking and my foot was cold on the bare cement floor.

Chapter 41

The same night

DAVID, A.K.A. POPE

S hrill referee whistles blew and pots and pans were turned into drums
outside our wedding night motel room. Shu, Trudy, Ozzie, and Barb
made the racket until we unlocked the door and let them into our room.
Stories and laughing kept us up all night. Then they drove us to the airport
early the next morning to see us off on our flight to San Francisco. There were
no hot sheets on our wedding night, but perhaps we did set a modern-day
record for laughter.

Ruthie slept soundly with her head on my left shoulder the entire smooth
flight, but I could not sleep. I was too intent on rehearsing what I was going
to discuss face to face with my West Coast partner, Herb, and my East Coast
partner, Sam, by speaker phone.

Our entire financial future was under a smothering threat. Somehow I
had to negotiate my way out of my joint and several personal guarantees of
the leases on the company's three computers. Bjorn had given me some ideas
on how to approach the subject, but I still had an uneasy feeling in the pit of
my stomach.

I had arranged with Computing Data to take over the Minnesota portion
of our company if my partners did not want it. However, that arrangement
would not release me from the personal guarantees. If the company failed,
those guarantees would haunt me financially, even to the point of having my
wages from Olson and Dad, Inc., garnisheed.

I stole a glance at my lovely, sleeping bride and thought, *I need to protect
you and provide for you.*

When the red tail of our Northwest Airlines plane broke through the
clouds I gently rubbed Ruthie's pink cheek with my fingertips. I wanted her
to see the Bay Bridge and the sparkling Pacific. The pilot circled the plane for

the approach to San Francisco airport. Ruthie ignored the view, she only looked at me. Her wedding day hairdo was suffering from sleepitis on the side she had buried against my shoulder, but through my tired and bloodshot eyes I could only see perfection in her.

When I had called Herb to arrange the meeting, I also asked if he could meet us at the airport. After some hesitation he said, "Rent a car and find your own way."

Ruthie did a wonderful job navigating us to Herb's office. When we arrived at the address in Santa Clara, he did not shake hands or offer us coffee. He looked at Ruthie, whom he had met at my office months back, then at me and then again at Ruthie with her arm through mine. Then he sneered. "Traveling with your secretary I see. You should never fish in the company pond. This must be another reason you didn't keep your eye on the ball . . . too busy boinking the hired help."

"Herb, you do not understand. Ruthie and I were married yesterday and even so, we have *never* been intimate, not even last night. Your comment was most insulting. We are moral people."

"Ha! A likely story. The hell with it, I guess I don't give a damn what you do anymore." He showed us to a cramped conference room and immediately dialed Sam's number in New York. With only perfunctory greetings, Sam said on the speaker phone, "Well, you called the meeting. What the hell's on your mind?"

I looked at Ruthie, who nodded slightly, and then at Herb, who was looking out the window at nothing but a parking lot. Herb and Sam knew exactly what was on my mind as I had told them my reason for wanting the meeting. I saw no reason for a long preamble. "I have come to the conclusion I do not have the talents to be the owner/operator of a business enterprise. You both have run profitable offices and mine has been a burden to you."

Herb said, "Really? You catch on quick."

After an hour and a half of tense discussion they agreed Computing Data could have the Minnesota portion of the company, provided Computing Data would take over all contractual, employee, customer, and office lease obligations.

As nonchalantly as possible, I said, "Of course, I would have to be released from the personal guarantee of the computer leases."

"Bullshit! No you wouldn't!" Sam yelled on the phone. "My old man and Herb's mother started that leasing company just for those computers. This was your bright idea, we won't let you wimp out on your obligation."

I said, "Would it be possible to get them on the phone so we could discuss this?"

During a fifteen minute break to get the two parents on the phone, Ruthie and I huddled together in the lobby so I could explain my plan. She had total faith in me and agreed to the plan after she gave me a comforting hug. We returned to the conference room, wary but hopeful.

***

SAM'S FATHER SOUNDED like the high-powered investment banker he was, "You, of course, understand your personal guarantee was part of the underwriting package we presented to the brokers to secure funds for the computers. It would not be in our best interest to let you out of that agreement."

"Yes, sir, I do know why you needed my guarantee, but, with all due respect, my assets at the time were very limited and my guarantee was not worth much. After a difficult time in my life, my assets are worth even less now."

Herb's mother, a vice-president at Wells Fargo, said, "That may be true, but we have a hook on your future earnings."

"Yes, however, I believe Minnesota law allows me to keep enough income to live reasonably. So the amount of my future earnings subject to my guarantee is unknown. Also, my wife is not a party to the guarantee so her income is not a factor."

Herb's dad said impatiently, "I'm late for an important meeting. Do you have a proposal or are you just hoping we'll let you off the hook? I'm here to tell you that is not going to happen."

I said, "I was an intern at Computing Data during my college years. Even though it was an unpaid position, they gave me an almost worthless share of stock for each day I worked. The company did well, as you know. Now, my shares in the company have a value of approximately thirty-eight thousand dollars. I propose you remove my personal guarantee in exchange for that equity position."

Herb slapped his forehead. "You have *got* to be kidding! You expect to trade your share of over half a million dollars of lease obligation for thirty-eight thousand dollars?"

"Yes, that is my proposal."

Sam's father said, "I have to get to another meeting. We'll get back to you about an hour."

Praise the Lord. An hour and a half later the two parents agreed to my proposal. I believe they thought the odds of having to enforce the guarantee were slim and taking the money now was the better gamble. In addition, even if they did have to try to enforce the guarantee at some unknown future date, I might not have enough assets to make it worthwhile.

Our parting with Herb and Sam was abrupt. They barely took the time to say good-bye. I had mixed feelings about the whole experience. I was proud of the business concept I had invented, but I felt guilty for not having made the Minnesota office a success. I was a bit uncomfortable about the borderline ethics of not disclosing the true reason I wanted to separate from the company. The phrase Bjorn had uttered, 'Let the buyer beware,' bothered my sense of fairness. I thought perhaps prior to signing the final documents of separation, I should disclose to Sam and Herb my real reason for removing myself from the company. I would have to get Ruthie's opinion prior to acting.

We stopped for a seafood lunch along the shore on the way back to the hotel. Ruthie did not take long to get my mind back to a positive state. What a gem.

Before she and I began the activities we had postponed on our wedding night, we took stock of our lives. I had just lost my business, therefore, her job, plus my thirty-eight thousand dollars in Computer Data equities. Our assets included an apartment full of old furniture and a used Edsel. We also had return airline tickets to Minneapolis and around five hundred dollars to our names. But we also had each other and for now that was enough.

Chapter 42

July 1968, one and a half years later

DAVID, A.K.A. POPE

I look like a blimp," Ruthie said in her eighth month of pregnancy. "Take it slow, give me some extra time to waddle to the elevator." She had her arm around my elbow. "I think this dress was made by Tillie the Tent Maker."

We were anxious to leave our apartment and be on our way to Schumacher's housewarming. I was not comfortable without a coat and tie, but after all, this was going to be a picnic so I had on casual clothes: khakis and a button down blue oxford with a t-shirt. The t-shirt was a gift from Ozzie. "Take your time, dear. We are leaving plenty early. You look wonderful. Your face is radiant. You are the cutest darn blimp I have ever seen."

She glanced over at me with a grin and gave me a playful elbow nudge to my ribs. "You won't think things are so cute if you have to deliver the baby in the Edsel. By the way, there can only be one Pope, so if we have a boy, he will have to be either Bishop or Cardinal."

"Just so he or she is healthy and takes after you," I said with the proud smile of a soon-to-be father.

"I wish they would have had the housewarming last month, my waddle was less waddley then."

"Well, they could not have it then. They wanted to make sure Bjorn could be there and his trial was scheduled for last month."

OZZIE

I CHECKED OUT the load in our Chevy station wagon with palm trees painted on the sides. We used it for smaller catering jobs. Our two catering panel vans were in use, one unloading food for a post-game Twins' party at Calvin Griffith's house at the other end of Lake Minnetonka and the other at a polo match in Hamel.

It was a busy Sunday, all three boats were fully booked for brunch cruises. The two-court ladies volley-ball tourney behind Danny's was in full swing. Noisy spectators were quenching their parched throats. "Is that the last of it? Barb and I gotta get going."

Sid Emmer, the daytime kitchen honcho who looked like he tested all the food that came off his stoves, said, "Yeah, boss, get the hell out of here. You two need a day off. Besides, all the help will be glad to get rid of you for a while. Enjoy the housewarming. Hope my fine cuisine doesn't kill off all of you."

I grinned. "If it does, Ma has instructions to force feed the leftovers to you."

"Behave yourself. Here comes the boss lady and Danny," Emmer said.

"Hi, Sid," Barb said. "Thanks for getting all of this done in time; see you tomorrow. Danny, hop in, we've got to get going. Ready, Oz?"

"Yup. Gonna be fun to see everyone together again. That is, if we don't have any more blow-ups about the war."

SHU

OUR NEW WALKOUT ranch rambler was perched on the gentle slope overlooking Lake Mattson, exactly where we had practiced bedroom activities a few years earlier. Maple, oak and elm trees, all fighting for the sky, shaded the house from the hot July sun. Trudy now admitted Dad and I had done the right thing when we'd agreed to buy this farm from the Kelzers, especially now that the debt was softened by platting and selling five other one-acre lakeshore lots. We called the little subdivision Reflections. Depending on the time of day or night, the lake reflected trees from the other shore, clouds, sunbeams or moonlight. Once in a while the reflection would be rippled up by the splashing of largemouth bass.

Ten years of living in the old, drafty farm house had been worth it to get this neat setting for Trudy's "almost dream house." "Can't get too fancy, gotta watch the costs," I reminded Trudy again and again.

Her comeback to that usually referred to the cost of my new pick-up with "the fancy air-conditioning." Most of the time we agreed on the house's specs and it resulted in a homey, solid and practical house. I left the decorating stuff to her good taste. Our strong relationship was only slightly tarnished from the stress of building the house.

"Here comes the food. Oh, ya, and Johnsons," I called out to Trudy and Nick as I spotted their station wagon rolling up the tree-branch-canopied driveway. "I'll help 'em unload. Nick, come along, you can help too."

When they came to a stop, I reached to open Barb's door. When she got out I gave her a squeeze. Then I went over to greet Ozzie and he said, "Hey there, Shu. Good to see you. Whoa, you're gettin' kinda broad in the beam, buddy."

I said, "Can't pound a spike with a tack hammer." Then I looked at Ozzie's rear and said, "'Course your skinny ass probably's big enough for your tack."

We laughed, patted each other on the back and went to unload the food cases and carry them into the kitchen. Trudy was by the oven and greeted them. She was making some kind of snack for the crew. Barb said, "Congratulations on the house, you guys. It looks wonderful. Love the avocado appliances."

"Well, the color went best with the shag carpet in the dining room," Trudy said proudly. "This food smells great. What's in the containers?"

Ozzie said, "Barb chose the menu. Of course I approved. We're gonna feed you guys some baby-back pork ribs rubbed with Hawaiian barbeque . . . got some crushed pineapple in the sauce. With the ribs you get Danny's famous potato salad kicked up with a little jerk seasoning and fruit salad with yogurt, brown sugar, and rum dressing. Then after we all take a mandatory nap, we'll have the key lime pie. Shu, that should keep your broad beam from shrinking."

Trudy said, "Wow, that sounds great. I can't wait to dig in, but that's for later. Let's go to the back yard. Shu has a cooler of Grain Belt impatiently waiting."

"Isn't that Bjorn's pick-up out front?" Ozzie asked. "Where's the tow head?"

"He's in the basement," I said. "He came out last night. We finished a room down there so he can stay here when he wants. Even has a drafting table and his exercise equipment down there. He's really got his upper body built up. Looks like he could take out Gorgeous George in the ring in a coupla seconds."

Ozzie said, "Really? Hey, how about makin' a room for me down there, too?"

"Well, a lot of bucks for this house came from Land Master through Olson and Dad," I said. "I don't think you'd want to contribute that much just for a spare room in the basement. Besides, it gets the Swede outta that room of his at the plant once in a while.

"He bought that pontoon boat down on the lake, too. Takes the kids fishing every time he's out here. They call 'im Uncle Bjorn."

"That's great, but I'm worried about him. Hey, here come Pope, Ruthie, and their almost kid," Ozzie said. When they entered the kitchen he continued, "Hi, Ruthie. You look beautiful. Dang-it Pope, you promised you'd wear that t-shirt I gave you."

"Hi, everyone," Pope said with a wave. "I have it on under this shirt."

"Shee-it, that don't count. Take that button down off."

"It might offend someone," Pope said.

"B.S. Take it off."

"Well, okay." Pope turned his back to us and took off his blue button down shirt. He slowly turned around with an embarassed look. The t-shirt read, from top to bottom:

POPE

POP

POOP

There was a drawing of a dirty diaper under the last word.

"Oh, my God!" Trudy said with a hand to her forehead. "Time for a Grain Belt. Great taste there, Oz."

"Hey, just my natural humorist talent coming through," Ozzie said with a shrug and a grin. "This is a great house, Trudy. Good job. Good thing you had your way in the design and decorating instead of your hubby. If he woulda been in charge, it'd look like a barn. Let's go get that Grain Belt."

"Ya, but it would have looked like a dang good barn," I said.

Everyone walked slowly to the back yard so Ruthie could keep up. We settled in the lawn chairs around the cooler and popped open barley pops for the adults and Squirts for the kids. Nick, Danny, and Ellie then escaped the adults and headed to the beach. Bjorn came out of the walk-out basement.

"Hi," Bjorn said with a wave. "Musta fallen asleep while listening to the radio. I guess my subconscious didn't want to hear any more bad news. Sorry, I didn't know you were all here." The ladies got up to give him a hug and the guys waved. I gave him a beer.

Ozzie said, "Now the tow head is up, turn that Elvis music up a little bit."

I said, "Ya, I guess there's been enough bad news what with the murders of Bobby Kennedy and Reverend King. Best to keep the dang radio off."

Trudy said, "Well, there's some good news with the Paris peace talks starting, and Bjorn, the fact you're trial was called off. How'd you manage that?"

"Ya, well, I hope the peace talks get the damn war stopped," Bjorn said.

Ozzie faced Bjorn, pointed to him and said, "The way to stop the war is to beat the bastards instead of the pansy-assed politicians runnin' the show from Washington and pussy footin' around. Let the generals turn the military loose."

Pope jumped to his feet. "We're here to celebrate our good friends' new house. Let us leave the Vietnam war talk for another time." He pointed at

Bjorn and Ozzie. "Okay?" Bjorn and Ozzie held up their arms in surrender and nodded.

"Okay," Ozzie said. "But I just wanna show you guys *my* t-shirt." He unbuttoned his shirt to expose an imprint on the chest area of an olive drab colored undershirt.

Ruthie said, "My God, Ozzie. A peace sign? You of all people? Have you turned into a *flower child?*"

"Not quite, Ruthie," Ozzie said. "Come closer and read the fine print."

She stepped over to him and read aloud, "PEACE - (Through Overwhelming Firepower)."

Even Bjorn had to chuckle.

Pope said, "Ozzie, thanks for the philosophy lesson. So, Bjorn, we are all anxious to hear why the trial was called off.".

Bjorn explained, "It turns out Dayton's insurance company, not the Dayton family, was the one pressing for the trial. Don Dayton and I met a couple'a times without the lawyers. He came out to look at our company. He saw how many people we employed and about the Brotherhood guys. In the end, he didn't want to ruin Olson and Dad. Also, he knew the D.A. wasn't going to press criminal charges 'cause I tried to stop the demonstration."

"How about the dead kid's folks? Why did they back off?" I asked.

"Dayton talked to them on my behalf and negotiated a deal. I will pay for those folks' other kids' education, or hire them if they don't wanna go to college. I'm okay with that. I feel like I should do something for them, 'specially since I'll have no kids of my own. Those damn professors are going to jail, so they can't do anything for those families."

"Why did the insurance company back off?" Ruthie asked.

"Well, you may have heard about Dayton's building those big indoor shopping malls. First in the world. They told the insurance company unless they back off of the lawsuit, Dayton's wouldn't insure those malls with 'em. And I asked Silverman Brothers to inform the insurance company if they didn't back off, Silverman would encourage other companies they are involved with not to do business with 'em either." Bjorn raised his arms to the sky, bowed his head and said, "Thank God. Now let's talk about something else, I've been living and breathing this lawsuit stuff long enough."

"Wow, what a deal. Your whole company was at stake."

"Ya. God, I was worried about the employees. What if they all woulda lost their livelihood 'cause of what I did?"

"Well, I've got something else to talk about," Ruthie said. "Pope, tell them about Coach Wagner."

Pope shrugged. "I believe everyone knows he passed away last month."

"Yes, maybe they do, but tell them about your part in the funeral," Ruthie said.

"Well . . . ah, I was a pall bearer."

Ruthie coaxed him. "And?"

Pope said, "Of the six pall bearers there were other coaches and nephews. I was the only one of his former players."

Ozzie asked, "How come?"

Pope looked skyward. "His wife told me Coach Wagner wanted it that way."

Chapter 43

February 1970, one year and seven months later

Bjorn

Richie was incorrigible. He giggled when he pinched Ma's behind as she passed his blinking switchboard. She knew all behinds were fair game to him, but she didn't go out of her way to avoid his reach. After all, given her age, any attention was probably appreciated. Sitting in his wheel chair offered Richie a good view of his targets.

He not only kept the ladies in the Victoria office on edge, but I think they secretly liked his form of teasing, which no other man in the office dared duplicate without getting slapped. Richie was my first Brotherhood recruit and had been manning the reception desk ever since his predecessor, Betty, had run away with Lars, a married drill press operator.

Richie was the gate keeper, especially for me. I didn't meet visitors without an appointment. No one got past his desk to see me unless they worked for the company or was expected . . . that is, until that day.

"I need to see Mr. Bjorn Olson, please," said the smallish man in the cheap, but well-pressed suit. His eyes were close together behind his wire-rim glasses, and his thin lips seemed to be set in a permanent pout. He was carrying a small, maroon leather folder.

"Do you have an appointment?" asked Richie. "I don't see anyone on his calendar for this morning." He made the mistake of looking toward my office door.

The visitor made a bee line for my door. "Just a damned minute! Where do you think you're going?" Richie spun his wheelchair and gave pursuit. Too late. The man burst through my door.

I looked up from my drafting table and said, "What the—who are you?" Large pictures of Land Master equipment, Polarcat snowmobiles, and Olson Hospital, Rehab and Exercise equipment lined the walls.

From behind the visitor, Richie said, "Sorry, boss, this guy just barged past me."

With a severe, accusing look, the visitor pointed at me. "If you are Mr. Bjorn Olson, I need to speak with you. I'm sorry to come unannounced, but if I try for appointments, people usually put me off."

"Well, ya, I'm Bjorn. Now that you're here, whaddya want?"

The visitor handed me a business card. It read *Reverend Jonathan Feltman, Lutheran Social Service of Minnesota.*

"Look, no wonder you have trouble getting appointments," I said. "Didn't you see the sign on the front door? It says 'No Soliciting.' Our Employee Council chooses which charities to give to. Leave a card with Richie, and we'll get back to you after our fiscal year starts."

"I'm not here for a donation. May we speak in private?" The minister said firmly with a nod to Richie.

"Well, okay, but please make it quick," I said. Richie spun his wheelchair to go, but left the door open a crack. I put down my drafting instruments and turned to my gray metal desk, which was littered with stacks of papers. "Have a seat."

Reverend Feltman sat with his knees together, his hands on the leather folder, which teetered on his thighs. Through pursed lips, he said, "My office has been trying to find you for some time. After we located you, we verified some information with the Department of Defense." He raised his eyebrows and looked at me like he wondered whether that got my attention.

"So? I still don't know what ya want," I said with a shrug.

"I believe you would be interested in reading this," the reverend said as he reached into his folder to pull out a document. "This is a copy of a note found in a spent rifle shell. The open end of the cartridge was sealed with wax. The other end was drilled, with a dog tag chain inserted through it." He slid the document around a pile of papers so I could read it.

I began to read the small print. My disbelief grew as I slowly absorbed every line of the message that was about to change my life. The note literally took my breath away. It read:

had boy 5/3/65 chu lai
father born olson
maybe died
from wher start misispi
had olson compny
vc come mai hue quy

I couldn't speak. My heart was racing, and my mind was frantically trying to cope. I read the note over and over. Reverend Feltman raised his chin and held me with a cool, accusing, steady gaze. Several moments slid by.

It was Feltman who finally broke the silence with a holier than thou pronouncement. "That note was found around the neck of an Amerasian boy who was wandering with a pack of other outcasts near Chu Lai. He was taken to our missionaries. They contacted Lutheran Immigration and Refugee Service, of which we are an affiliate. Very clever of a prostitute to hide the—"

"She was *not* a prostitute!"

"Then you acknowledge that this is your son?" Feltman said with a self-satisfied look as he slid a photo of the boy across my desk.

My hand trembled as I picked up the photo and locked on to it. My heart was pounding even harder than when I read the note. Someone had tried to clean the boy up, but missed the dirt on his forehead. He was still wearing the rags from his street life. The skinny kid had light hair framing a frightened look and an Olson chin. He had his mother's eyes and nose. After staring at the picture for several moments, I quietly asked, "Where is his mother?"

"Our best information is that she was taken by the VC and killed for consorting with a GI."

I put my head in my hands, my shoulders sagging under the weight of all the information. *God, how can I cope with more? May is dead because of me. The docs say I can't have kids, but I have a son thousands of miles away. I have a complicated life already. The hell with it.* I looked up. "Sir, this information is of no concern to me. All this was long ago and far away. Besides, you can't be sure I am the father. Please leave and do not contact me again. Good-bye."

To my surprise, Feltman left without much of a fuss, I was sure he was used to getting the heave-ho in these situations.

***

SLEEPLESS NIGHTS WERE common for me due to physical or business concerns. Now it was the boy in the picture that kept me awake. I would close my eyes and try to sleep, but his eyes—or should I say May's eyes—were looking back at me. I had no doubt I was the father. I came to the conclusion that only a shithead would abandon his own son.

I asked Ma and Pa to lunch outside the plant three days after Feltman's visit. This was big-decision time, and I wanted and needed their input. It took me a while to get the story out to them, because after all, I had to tell them their little boy had misbehaved while he was in 'Nam.

After I explained it all to them, Ma got up from the other side of the booth and came to put her arm around me, while the old man reached across to pat my hand. Not only did they agree that I had made the right decision, they couldn't believe I would do anything else.

They went back to my office with me to listen to the call I made to Feltman.

***

IN LESS THAN TWO WEEKS, Richie's gatekeeping was ignored again. This time it was a redhead with a behind he would have liked to target. "Where the hell do you think you're going?" Richie asked, in as friendly a way as possible under the circumstances.

"Where I darn well please," MK said as she headed for and opened my door.

I glanced up from my work, my face frozen in surprise except my jaw dropped open a bit. We had not spoken since I told her to leave Fort Sam. It had been almost five years since Ma had told me about MK's wedding and over three years since I had seen her across the room at a restaurant.

MK coolly said, "Hello."

Untying my tongue and recovering from shock, I said, "Hello."

In the past I thought she had lit up a room just by entering. Today was not a light-up day. Her arms were crossed and there was no smile or sparkle in her eyes. However, Father Time had taken her on a journey from cute to beautiful, but he had taken her eyes from sparkling to wary.

"Ah . . . this is a surprise. It's nice to see you," I said, not having a clue as to where this conversation was headed.

"Yes. I'm sorry. I just felt a need to stop by. Good to see you too. I like your long hair—not too sure about the beard. What's *that?*" MK said, pointing to something on my desk.

"A mayo jar."

"I can see that. What's *in* there?"

"Oh, that. It's a dog turd."

"That's what I thought. Why in the world do you have it on your desk?"

"I won it."

"You *won* it?"

"Ya. It's a traveling trophy. Our receptionist, Richie, doesn't like it when one of us doesn't return phone calls and then he catches hell from the person calling the second or third time. That's when he awards the trophy."

"Oh, you mean like when you didn't return my calls the past few days?"

"Ya, I guess," I mumbled and looked down at my desk.

"Dad tells me you live here at the plant."

"Well, we're pretty busy. I don't do much but work . . . handier that way."

"The folks at the hospital are thrilled with the new re-hab equipment you guys donated. It looks very inviting, not like the old stuff that looked like torture tools."

"Ya, the stuff turned out pretty good. We donated it, but we get to use the photos of it for our advertising. Oh—how's married life treating you?"

"It was challenging, I'll say that."

"Was?"

"I filed for divorce last month. He had a few problems."

"Such as?"

"W.L.E.S.—World's Largest Ego Syndrome. He'd take a crap and think it smelled like lilies of the valley."

I put my hand to my mouth to hide a smile. "What else?"

"P.A.C.—Penis Awareness Complex. He figured every female he came in contact with would want to be a hostess to his organ. A lot of them did. He's now charged with insurance fraud because a couple of ladies had monthly appointments with him at the clinic. He collected from their insurance companies for servicing them on his office couch. That makes the jerk a male whore . . . and me an idiot."

"Jeeze, MK, I'm sorry."

"Oh, well, made my own bed and all that. Where does that door go?"

"Never mind, nowhere."

She walked to the door and reached for the knob.

"No, don't go in. It's—"

She opened the door and walked into my small room. As she looked around, she must have realized it was my home.

"MK, please don't—"

She held up her hand toward me and continued to look around. An open shelf held Wheaties, a half-loaf of bread, a couple cans of tuna, Spam, and a few cans of soup. Under the shelf were a small refrigerator and a hot plate. To the left were a toilet stool, a sink, and a white metal shower stall. To the right was a single bed, a drafting table, and exercise equipment. A short closet pole held my plaid shirts and jeans. The cement floor was bare, and one small window looked out at a solid wall. A card table with one chair held salt and pepper shakers and a sugar bowl. Piled under the window were anti-war posters stapled to wood laths.

She turned to me with a pained, questioning look.

"Well, I don't spend *all* time here." I shrugged. "Usually go to Chicago two or three nights every quarter and—"

"Yes, Dad said you were on the Land Master Board of Directors. Congratulations."

"Ya, guess they wanted one of the members to be a supplier and member of the Brotherhood."

"Right. I don't suppose it had anything to do with that brain of yours. My God, Bjorn, you live like a hermit."

"Actually I stay with Shu and Trudy a few nights a month. They got a new lake place. And I eat at Ozzie's a coupla times a month. Then there're the times at the cabin after I go to Polarcat. Like I said, I'm not here all the time."

She noticed the two small, curling Polaroid pictures thumbtacked to the wall over my bed, the only pictures in the room. She walked over to take a closer look. One was a picture of May and me on a beach. The other was a picture of MK and me up at the Mantrap Lake cabin.

She turned to me with tears streaming down her cheeks.

"Did you—stop loving me—when you were with her?"

"No, I swear."

"Where is the boy going to sleep?"

Oh, shit, so that's it. That's why she's here. Mike musta told her. "Oh, MK . . . God, I'm sorry I wasn't faithful to you. I'm so ashamed. That's one of the reasons I asked you to leave Fort Sam."

She got herself under control and while wiping away tears, said, "You really hurt me when you sent me away. I couldn't understand. Now I do. It's not like we were married. My God, forgive yourself. You don't have to live the rest of your life on a guilt trip."

"I try to lose myself in work, but . . . I think about you every single day."

"Don't play me," MK said, showing her Irish temper. "You didn't answer me. Where is the boy going to sleep?"

"I . . . I haven't thought about that. It's gonna take a long time to get him here."

MK said, "I'm sorry I barged in on you. I just had to check out what Dad told me about you fathering a son with someone else. Seemed the timing of the conception was while you and I were an item." Her arms were crossed again, and the color of her face was getting dangerously close to the color of her hair. "I guess my choice of male partners needs some refining, that is, if I am *ever* to take the risk of being humiliated again. I feel like the whole state must be laughing at me."

"MK, please, I—"

She held up her hand to stop me from saying more, turned on her heel and stomped out of my office.

Chapter 44

March 1970, one month later

BJORN

I didn't fit in. Five of the other six Land Master board members were older, richer and wore expensive suits. They had MBAs and if ever in the military, were officers. The others arrived early to every board meeting to brag about their private golf clubs and latest heroic golf shots. They were clean shaven with well-coiffed razor cuts. Most were on their second or third wife and some were probably already sleeping with the next one.

I had no wife or sex life, wore a plaid shirt and jeans, was a high school drop-out, was wounded as a PFC and had never held a golf club, let alone belonged to one. My anti-war-looking beard and long hair grated on my fellow board members. At least my upper body was in better shape than any of theirs 'cause of my exercise regimen.

When I wasn't present, I was told they called me Paul Bunyan. Ben "Colt" Qualset was the seventh board member. He had called earlier to say he'd be late for the meeting 'cause his plane was forced to land due to the weather. He was the largest Land Master Equipment dealer. After he returned from World War II as a sergeant in the Army Rangers, he had inherited his dad's blacksmith shop in the small town of Milford, near Lincoln, Nebraska. From that start he developed the company and owned four Land Master dealerships—two in Nebraska and one each in Oklahoma and Iowa—and was a part owner of another one in Mankato, Minnesota.

Each of his dealerships covered the equivalent of several city blocks. He had turned each locations into a social, entertainment and education center for his current and future customers. Farmers and ranchers attended seminars at Colt's dealerships and winter coffee-klatches around his dealerships' pot belly stoves.

If you were trying to win a governor's race in Nebraska, you'd better have the endorsement of Colt. Our other board members were invited by the company to serve as directors. Colt had invited himself and no one had dared object.

The conference table at the Chicago headquarters of Land Master was made of polished black walnut and was large enough to accommodate the landing of a sizable helicopter. The window wall provided an expansive view of Lake Michigan's shoreline. I purposely arrived a few minutes late for the meeting to avoid the bragging and small talk. Willard Fox, the CEO, got up and shook my hand and clasped me on the shoulder. The others acknowledged my arrival with an obligatory nod.

I took a seat at the far end of the table.

Mr. James Wilson Condon, a retired CEO of a Fortune 500 company and chairman of our board opened the meeting at 10:05 a.m. "May I have a motion to approve the minutes of the last meeting?"

One of the other members launched into a rambling discourse, objecting to a small detail in the minutes. I rolled my eyes. After about ten minutes of debate over a non-issue, the minutes were approved as corrected.

"Financial report, please," Condon said.

"You all received the financials last week," Sam Haen, the CFO said. "Are there any questions?" He knew there would be. There always were even if none were needed. Haen was a member of the Brotherhood and having questions lobbed at him from board members for no other reason than to make the questioner feel important was his version of child's play.

A twenty-five-minute discussion followed, accomplishing nothing more than members showing off their prowess of reading financial statements. I remained silent and grew more and more impatient with the grandstanding.

"Mr. Fox, the CEO report, please," Condon said.

Just then Colt burst into the room with a huge, blazing cigar and wearing cowboy boots, a leather jacket with studs, and a turquoise bolo tie. He was carrying his Stetson hat. "Hey, boys, go ahead, keep going. Sorry I'm late. Goddamned Piper Cub didn't like the thunderheads," he bellowed. "Had'ta put 'er down in Dubuque 'til things blew over."

He sat down next to me and pounded me on the back as a greeting, darn near knocking me off my chair. "Hey, son, you need a damn haircut," Colt said with a chuckle. "Either that or get yourself some falsies and a dress and shave that beard. We need a lady's touch on this board." He roared at what he felt was a great joke and cuffed me on the shoulder. "Sorry, Fox, didn't mean to interrupt. Get on with your report."

I couldn't help but laugh. Colt was a refreshing change from the pin-stripes.

Fox held the power on the board and everyone knew it. He reported to and was employed by the board, but he was the one who led the company to new heights every year and had the backing of Silverman Brothers, the largest shareholder.

In spite of his report of significant progress company wide, the board members went into their nit-picking and micro-managing mode with suggestions and questions. I guess they felt they had to justify their board positions. The discussion was still in progress after fifty agonizing minutes.

I'd had it. I stood up and slapped my open palm on the table.

The others stopped and looked at me.

"Gentleman, I'm sure we all have more important things to do than travel all this way for a second-guessing party. I know I sure as hell do. I thought a board was to give the executives broad oversight and long-range visions of what the company goals should be. We've wasted over an hour and accomplished absolutely nothing of importance except taking up the valuable time of our CFO and CEO. So far this meeting has been mushy bullshit."

Colt looked up at me and said, "I second the mushy bullshit motion."

I said, "Thanks for the second, Colt. I'm outta here." I started gathering my papers.

"Mr. Olson, just a minute, do you have something in mind for discussion? We have appreciated your input in the past," Condon said. Other board members looked like guilty children seeking forgiveness for spilling red Kool-Aid on white carpeting.

"If you're finished with your other business, yeah, I have something I would like to discuss before I leave," I said.

"Go ahead. You have the floor," Condon said. He probably hoped I'd blundered by sounding off.

I went to the front of the room where there was a flip chart with blank paper and black and red markers. I drew two black circles in the upper left hand corner, one above the other. With the red marker I shaded in three-fourths of the lower circle and one half of the upper. I labeled the bottom one with a *U* and the top one with a *C*. Then I pointed to the circles. "The bottom circle is the U.S., the top is Canada. The shaded areas show our market penetration. In a few years, the way Mr. Fox is leading us, these circles will be pretty much totally shaded. Our growth then will be provided only by new products.

"Okay, so what?" Condon said impatiently.

"New products alone will not sustain Land Master's growth curve. So then what?" I drew a red circle in the upper right hand corner and in the lower left corner I drew two more circles alongside each other. The bottom ones I labeled A and B, and by the upper right circle I put an E.

Sam Fink, the oldest member, said, "What's the point?"

"Jesus, give the boy a chance," Colt said. "He's just gettin' warmed up."

"The *points* are these:" I pointed to the E circle. "Europe." I pointed to the A and B circles. "And down here Argentina and Brazil. This company needs to expand its manufacturing and marketing into those areas to keep up our growth curve. We should either buy someone out or start from scratch in those markets."

Most of the board members were stunned to silence.

Fox, Hean, and Colt were wearing broad smiles.

Colt said, "Boys, I think Paul Bunyan just axed one of our big problems."

***

THE SEATS IN THE UPPER DECK of Northwest's new 747 were plush and comfortable. Land Master always flew board members first class, except for Colt. I suppose they paid him to fly his own plane to the meetings. A very presentable brunette served me a second Manhattan and said, "Here you go, sir, and your Chicken Kiev will be served shortly."

I had just set a decade's long course for a major corporation to follow. My own company was prospering with three busy divisions. I think I was respected by my employees. I had several U.S. patents and money was certainly no longer an issue.

In the first-class section I was sitting in the lap of luxury.

I would soon have a son living with me.

I had learned how to live with my wounds, both physical and emotional.

I had closed a lot of doors to bad places and numbed a lot of bad memories.

Most of the time I lived like a hermit.

My life was empty and I was miserable.

***

IT WAS A TYPICAL COLD, windy March night when the 747 put down in Minneapolis long after dark. When I walked to my pickup in the parking lot my prosthetic leg twice slipped on frozen puddles.

There were a few snow flurries on the way home. I didn't stop at Victoria. I kept going the seven miles to Waconia even though it was almost midnight, and the roads had started to ice up. My mind was made up. I was going out to the peninsula on Lake Waconia.

I practiced my speech.

I pulled up to a large two-story home and went to the front door. No lights were on. I pressed the doorbell. Several times.

A light came on in the foyer as well as the outside light over my head. MK, with sleepy eyes and tousled red hair, peered out the door's side window. She opened the door.

I stayed on the stoop and started my rehearsed speech before she could say anything, "I can't stand being apart from you any longer. Many years ago I proposed marriage to you, and now I would most humbly appreciate an answer. I ask your forgiveness for any hurt or humiliation I've caused you. We were good together and we would be again." I stopped for a breath. "Your happiness would be my number one goal. I have never stopped loving you."

She hesitated briefly while holding her robe closed to keep out the chill. Then she said, "Why don't you come in instead of jabbering out there?"

Chapter 45

Afterword
June 1970, three months later

BJORN

"I thought you'd never say yes," I whispered in Mary Katherine's ear as our flight left LAX bound for Saigon. Los Angeles was the first stop after our quickie Las Vegas wedding.

"Well, we had a bunch of issues to work through first, didn't we?" MK said with a smile. "Want me to itemize them?"

"God, no. We don't have time, it's only a fourteen-hour flight. And you know we solved that serious peanut butter problem by deciding to have both chunky and creamy in the pantry."

As the California coast slipped away and grew smaller beneath us, the knot in my stomach grew larger.

I was going to the place where I saw death close up.

I was going to the place where I was responsible for the death of a woman I loved.

I was going to the place of the war I hated.

All that, I hoped, would be overcome by meeting my son.

And, of course, I now had someone at my side to help me face my past.

"It took me a while to put your pushing me away at Fort Sam up on the shelf with the peanut butter," MK said. "I guess humans don't take rejection very well, especially red-headed ones."

"Do you think we'll ever get back to the feelings we had before my stupid Fort Sam decision about you?"

She thought for a moment before answering "I think we have to be realistic about that. It won't be easy to totally erase some things, but we're on our way. We'll just have to make some new, good memories to override the bad ones. Just like we just did in Vegas."

"I'm just glad your forgiving me woke up my little soldier. That was a pretty damn big issue—forgive the pun—for me."

240

"I think it was a big issue—excuse the pun—for both of us. That was a win-win outcome." She leaned over to kiss me on my clean-shaven cheek.

My beard was a victim of our negotiating of issues. I lost that debate and the whiskers. Then I remembered another negotiating point I lost. I was wearing a black V-neck sweater-vest over a blue button-down shirt with khaki pants. They were gifts and a strong fashion hint from MK.

"And now you want to adopt my son—I don't think they make a pedestal high enough for me to put you on. You are a special person."

She reached for my hand. "Hey, babe, you are too. And your folks will be thrilled when they learn we're renaming *our* son, Karl."

***

LUTHERAN SOCIAL SERVICE headquarters in southern Saigon was housed in a two-story, whitewashed, French Colonial building surrounded by stately coconut palms. A low-slung, unpainted cement block orphanage for "the children of dust," as the locals derisively called the Amerasians, was located next door.

MK and I were led to the administration area of the orphanage, stepping over puddles on the gravel path. It was hot, muggy and pouring rain. She kept out-pacing me even though I was holding the umbrella. Her red hair was a mop of wet curls.

We were met by a matronly Mrs. McQuillen and her assistant, Lin Ho Wan, in the waiting room of the Adoption Liaison Office. Children's crayon art of stick people and animals adorned the bulletin board, the only décor in the sparse room. McQuillen said, "Mr. and Mrs. Olson, welcome. We are so pleased you are here. Lin has double checked all the paperwork and has assured me that everything is in order."

"It's very nice to meet you both. You are doing wonderful work here," Mk said as she glanced around the room.

I said, "That was a pile of stuff to check. It took me damn near forever to get all that red tape put together. You'd think everyone would want these adoptions to happen fast, especially for the children's sake." Then, embarrassed, I said, "Oh, jeeze, I'm sorry. I know the red tape wasn't your fault. I'm anxious to meet my boy."

"Certainly. I understand," Mrs. McQuillen said. "Have a seat," she nodded toward two straight-backed wooden chairs. "We didn't tell your son about your existence until this morning. I'm not sure it has sunk in yet. That's our policy because we need to make sure folks will honor their word, show up and see these things through.

"He speaks limited English. His mother taught him. He said his mother and grandfather told him you had been killed, so today's news was hard for him to comprehend. Because of that I would suggest you take things slowly with him." She stood and smoothed her skirt. "I'll be back with your son in just a moment."

MK and I clung to each other and tried to remain calm. I said, "Now I know how Pope feels when he's under stress. I feel like throwing up. They said our boy lived on the streets for months after May was killed. Must be a tough kid."

"Hang on, Bjorn. I'm with you all the way. I know coming back to 'Nam was hard for you, let alone the excitement of meeting your son." Her calm voice reassured me that we had made the right choice. She lit up the room even with her wet, bedraggled hair.

Mrs. McQuillen came through the arched doorway with her protective arm around the boy and her hand on his right shoulder. He had his left shoulder behind her leg and his cheek hard against her thigh. He was clutching the folds of her gray skirt with his other hand. When he finally did look up, his eyes darted back and forth between MK with her wet red hair and me with shoulder-length hair the color of his. Caucasian and Asian genes had reached a compromise on his face.

Questions filled the boy's eyes under his furrowed brow.

MK saw the square Olson chin and light hair. I saw May's dark eyes studying me.

We were stunned by how thin the boy was in his ill-fitting, hand-me-down clothes.

We both stood and I steadied myself, holding on to the back of a chair, awestruck at facing my son. I stammered for something reassuring to say to him, but couldn't come up with words worthy of the event.

MK slowly approached the boy. She knelt down, smiled and held out her hands, palms up, to him. After several moments of studying her face, he let go of the skirt with one hand and put that hand in hers.

Karl, with May's eyes, then looked up at me and said with a French and Vietnamese accent, "You . . . not die? You come . . .take me?"

***

Pearl S. Buck wrote in *East Wind, West Wind*, "He will have his own world to make. Being neither East or West purely, he will be rejected by each, for none will understand him. But I think, if he has the strength of both his parents, he will understand both worlds, and so overcome."

But, that's another story.

Watch for the author's next book, *Writer Man,* to be published in 2015. Follow or contact him at www.FredPlocher.com.